BLOOD RUNNER

Blood Runner – Book 1

SECOND EDITION

JD Stanley

JD STANLEY

Second paperback edition 2020 by JD Stanley DBA Roaming Druid
ISBN: 978-1-9994362-7-8

First paperback edition, 2017 by JD Stanley
ISBN: 978-0-9947899-5-2

Ebook edition 2016 by JD Stanley DBA Roaming Druid
ISBN: 978-0-9947899-0-7

This novel is a work of fiction. Names and characters are either a product of the author's imagination or used in fictitious circumstances. Any resemblance to actual living persons was completely on purpose and you know who you are. Vampires and the gods, of course, are real.

Roaming Druid
Toronto, ON Canada
Permissions@RoamingDruid.com

Front and back cover design by JD Stanley.
www.jdstanley.com

DEDICATION

For the Baby Bite I know

And for Michelangelo - "It's like meditating"

Here be pirates… sort of

OF THE AFFAIRS OF CREATION, THE FORGOTTEN PRIEST, AND NARAM-SIN

(Sumer)

She is the heart. She is forever. She is the Great Mother, Nammu. From that nebulous, primordial sea, with a single thought she gave birth to the mountain that was Heaven and Earth.

And so it began.

Great in their own rights for she could not conceive of less, they were magnificence held in thought without form. They were elementals. They were the first gods--*An*, her son, King of Heaven and her daughter, *Ki*, Mother Earth.

In turn, together they begot *Enlil*.

Brought into being out of all that was, Enlil was the Lord Air, the Great Mountain, the majestic lord of all. With a single breath, he separated the heavens from the earth and in this way became king of both Heaven and Earth.

Surpassing in beauty and sublime, *Enlil* could not resist *Ki* and carried off Mother Earth leaving father *An* with only Heaven for his own.

Each of their thoughts combined to become a god and so all the gods came to be born out of Lord Air and Mother Earth.

The great ones came first: *Enki*, Lord of Wisdom, keeper of the divine laws and who knew the heart of the gods; his twin sister *Ereshkigal* who became Queen of the Netherworld after she was stolen away by the fearsome monster *Kur*; *Inanna*, Queen of Heaven; her brother *Utu*, the sun god; the beautiful *Ninlil*, sister of the Lord Air, and all the rest until the entire pantheon was born.

The father of all then founded a city for himself, a great city where only gods did dwell. The mighty city of *Nippur*, it was from that sacred place he asserted his power and directed all the rest of creation. *Enlil* blessed them with the pickaxe and assigned the fashioners to assist in the making of all that was to be.

Charging each god with a task toward all their greater ease, they applied themselves thusly. Following *Enlil's* example, each god then pointed a finger and founded a city, one for each god. Much more than only places, each city was themselves and gave birth to all things beyond themselves--the plough, the sheepfold, the grape press--all those things necessary for the comfort of the gods.

And so the world came into being and was so organised.

The very image of their mother, *Ki*, the Lord Air then came to his sister. When *Ninlil* was not as willing as their mother had been, besotted and selfish in his greatness, *Enlil* took what he wanted.

The pantheon grew dismayed by his immoral deed for though he was their king and lord, they knew even the gods must be held to the divine laws. Secure in this, they seized him and banished him to the Netherworld for his crime.

Though heavy with his child, in her duty to the Lord Air, *Ninlil* followed. But this disturbed *Enlil*. It would mean his son, *Nanna*, the bright moon, would be forced to dwell in the gloom of the Netherworld and never fulfil his destiny to travel across the heavens in a reed *gufa* boat bringing light to the pitch-black lapis lazuli sky.

The Lord Air pondered and then the Lord Air schemed. Disguising himself as the man of the gate, the man of the river, and the man of the boat, *Ninlil* reached each in turn. Slick words and his own intent gave her three more children that left bright *Nanna* free to ascend to the heavens where he belonged. With *Ninlil* none the wiser, soon after, the Lord Air schemed further. Escaping his punishment, *Ninlil* followed him home to *Nippur* where he returned to rule with a tighter hand than ever before.

With the Great Mountain back at the head of the pantheon, the world came to be full of wonders--the sun and the moon in the heavens, the fashioners creating, and the animals grazing upon the land. But it was not enough.

In this land of only gods, though they were the great ones they could not labour and with nothing to affect, the land remained still and quiet. The gods lamented they could not procure their own bread and Mother *Ki* implored *Enki* in his infinite wisdom for a solution. Bringing the tears of the pantheon before him to lend weight to her request, she asked him to fashion servants of the gods.

Together with Great Mother *Nammu*, they rendered the heart of the clay over the Abyss into mortal beings until then unknown. *Enki* instructed Mother *Ki* to decree the newborns' fate and bind it upon the will of the gods for all time.

And so, by his decree and Mother *Ki's* words, the newborns' name was made Man.

When they came to dwell in each city, each in their reed houses and each belonging to their own god, the gods of the pantheon were satisfied.

While imperious and indifferent, the Lord Air turned his eye from their commonness.

Spurred on by their success and eager for more, the gods came together with Man and filled up the whole of the earth with these, these elemental children borne into flesh. They were quick and they were bright and curious and they became record keepers of all the godly wonders that surrounded them. They were called the *Sumerians*, the First People.

Craftsmen worked in sacred service in the temples of each city's patron divinity and they thrived, awash in the blessings of their gods for what their mortal hands could fashion. Overseen by the priests who healed the sick while keeping the tally for their gods, these were record keepers of another sort. While elsewhere in time other almost-men were simple, the First priests fashioned clay tablets. Scratching down the number of goats and wares their particular god did bless, they accounted for every activity under the watchful eye of each of their gods and remained obedient in the manner prescribed.

And the gods nodded their approval.

In the sacred centre, *Nippur*, even when the people came it remained a most sacred place. Here, on the river to the sea where humanity first learned to harness the wind for their boats as they had oxen for their ploughs in fields no others yet knew how to farm, there was an *aszipu*. This doctor-priest called *Kurshram* came to love the goddess he served and she took him as her consort.

The goddess was *Ninlil*, sister to the Lord Air.

The priest was faithful to her temple and kept her household in the manner in which she liked and she bestowed many blessings upon the people for his love.

And the people rejoiced for being so blessed.

While *Enlil* snarled and still coveted her for himself.

Blind and cruel in jealous desire, he levied a full portion of blame upon *Ninlil* for spurning him and enticing a lesser. In rage, he cast her to the Netherworld where she passed through the seven gates of the palace of *Ereshkigal* to face the sentence of the *Annuna*. Reluctant, the seven-who-decreed-fate passed judgement against her at the great god's command for, sadly, though they knew she was wronged, he was *Enlil*--exalted and brilliant and holding all their existence in his hands. He could not be denied. *Ereshkigal* took her life and hung sweet *Ninlil's* spirit on the wall with the rest of the guilty to pay her price.

No matter he was her downfall, even in condemnation *Ninlil* pined for her only love. A goddess and so elemental still, even from so far beyond the world, her heart cried out from the Netherworld to touch the earth-- unseen and unheard and yet somehow reaching the heart of her beloved.

Driven by their devotion, her *Kurshram* braved the world beyond the world where the living were not meant to tread. Unheard of and impossible, he heeded none of it and fought a hard, human way through the flaming palace to save her. A priest and so a man wise in the ways of the elements, he knew what to do--he offered up his own spirit in trade for his beautiful *Ninlil*. He knew it was allowed for the Lord of Wisdom would know the heart of the goddess and as long as a balance was struck, one for another, he could use this to save her. At his request and for a second time, *Ereshkigal* took a life not meant for that place and put his spirit in place of his love.

In the single moment they passed in exchange and he saw her freed, *Kurshram's* heart was satisfied. It strengthened him enough to endure her eternity of punishment while *Ninlil* was again free to walk the earth and dwell within the temple household he had kept for her.

The great *Enlil* oversaw all these events and considered.

Seeing this display of love for his sister, so unselfish, so pure, it gave him reason to pause. He then ordered *Kurshram's* spiritless body buried in his own temple, *Ekur*, the most holy of places.

Buried at his feet, where he might keep better watch over him for all time. Ensuring the soul and the body stayed apart.

From *Ninlil*.

And so, *Kurshram* slept in his tomb in the here.

While paying *Ninlil's* price in the Netherworld.

And balance was held in the old way.

A thousand years did pass in the faithful priest's slumber until there came a dark and terrible day. New men came to that sanctified place, men from *Akkad*, who in their arrogance sought to claim the land of the gods for themselves. When the king called *Naram-Sin* came, his lust was so great he sought to make himself a god and established a new capital city, *Agade*. One where he no longer answered to the will of *Enlil* and the pantheon.

And the gods grew angry.

Naram-Sin did worse. Docking his ships at sacred *Ekur*, temple of *Enlil*, he sought to carry off the treasure trove and in mindless avarice desecrated the sanctuary of the Lord Air. Sacred tradesmen fell, pious guards crumbled before the army, and within the most sacred inner reaches of the sanctuary, temple priests threw themselves before the horde only to be cut down and trampled into their own blood.

Death raced on a red river that swept this Water of Life into every corner of that sacred place. Staining the stone, it seeped into every crack and chink in such quantity it reached even into the crypt below the feet of the great god. Washing into *Kurshram's* grave, as if the very tears of the wronged and weeping gods, it called him to service.

And stirred his flesh from its lengthy slumber.

A priest he was still and in waking he might have lived to serve again, but it could never be. Only half a man with all his memories far away in *Ereshkigal's* palace dreaming on his beloved, the ruined temple left him no purpose beyond floundering in the darkness of the crypt in which he woke. In walking half-life, he recalled nothing of men for this is a failing of the flesh without spirit. And so within the temple ruin, like a slate wiped clean, darkness and the Water of Life became his only friends.

In his rage for the desecration of his temple, *Enlil* spat out a terrible retribution. The Lord Air called upon the Gutians as his divine avengers to smite the false city of *Agade* from the earth, leaving nothing but dust.

The punishment of *Naram-Sin* was harsher still.

Ereshkigal claimed his soul for the Netherworld while the Most High mocked his self-imposed godhood and decreed him *Namtar*, the demon responsible for death. The imperfect man who cannot eat or drink, he continued on in madness craving power he could never possess and was in this way emasculated by *Enlil* for seeking to wrest authority from the hands of the gods.

Thereafter, *Naram-Sin* walked the world in ignorance without spirit and bringing death, as was his portion. A thief still stealing, he pursued the Water of Life though for naught, because he cannot live. Nor can he rest, for how can death come to Death?

The ways of the elements and the gods decree that each curse must have its own undoing and so it is with even his. To achieve his rest, he must find a soul to take his place in trade to hang on the wall of *Ereshkigal's* palace with the damned. But as a demon fallen from the lips of the highest divinity, he might only be traded for by the divine.

None of the pantheon has yet offered.

The luckless, faithful priest, *Kurshram*, does also still wander. Stumbling through darkness in walking slumber, he dreams on she who he cannot recall while forever separated from his memories. Spirit still secure in the Netherworld and so long detached from the flesh, the world goes on around him while he remains forgotten by time and left without place or purpose…

1

(Canada – Present)

Wine I'm telling you, that's what it is. Fine wine poured out in copious, sinful amounts and yet there's never enough to go around.

Not for me.

It's everywhere, spilling out onto the ground. I hear talk of it every day on the radio. All wasted in a thousand corners of the world while I'm relegated to cat burglar stealth and all manner of duplicity to catch a single drop so I can live. What the hell is wrong with them? Humans... Don't they know? How can they not comprehend what it is they're squandering?

I'll never understand them, not if I live ten more millennia. Sitting right here in my wing chair ruminating on the world beyond the French doors to the garden, time and again I've put my mind to it. Tried for years to unravel that mystery. Decades. Centuries. I still haven't the foggiest. You'd think after all this time I'd have got myself a clue.

Why are you creeping into my secret place? Who the hell invited you? Yes, I know you're there, attempting to lurk in the shadows. Hoping. Perhaps, you're another blood runner looking for a clue, yes? Sorry to disappoint. I've no answers for you, mate. Only questions and loneliness and several lifetimes of persecution. No, let's not tell our sad stories, I can't take another. Just clear off.

Never mind my name.

Sorry? Shit… Gordianus Antonius? Ha! Now there's a blast from the first century past. How about Olaf of the Ten Oaks? Not on your list then? Long before your time, baby blood. And for the record, that nitwit Richard Perkins was a piss-take. Or perhaps a cautionary tale. Sometimes, I forget.

Or wish I could.

Would you believe they dubbed that stupid bastard Twitch the Witch? All his flapping about caught notice of the locals, you see. Bloody eejit. The land, though… Ah, the thought of it… There were hills there. Nicer garden than this one. Restful. Damn, but I loved that place. You ever have a home, little one? That was home. Certainly not the first, clearly not the last. Not anything special, mind, but home, nonetheless. For several lifetimes, as though the land called me back time and again. No matter now, I suppose. An ocean and a lifetime away.

Bah! Nothing is restful now. Times change. Digital imaging and computer records? The enemy. Getting so a bloke can't hide a bloody thing from anyone anymore. I do miss the old days. You have no idea, boy.

Take Twitch. One of those hill people, apothecary-types who the locals shunned and side-stepped round in the day-to-day. But whose company they'd brave when they had a need. You wouldn't know, but doctors were scarce then. More you'd find eccentrics, hermits. *Witches* they called them, who lived alone and knew things. Times were simpler. You could get away with it, of course, because who would know? Funny, the locals never caught on the only emergency outside the occasional broken bone or fever was caused by the same mad bastard they called on for help. Well, not until the end, anyway.

The way it always goes.

A blood runner's life is short in any locale. Guess I don't have to tell you that, eh? Or, perhaps, I do. Only the way it is, little one, so don't stand there giving me those big, sorrowful cow eyes. You'd best make your peace with it. That's my only advice. Learn it. Because it will never change.

What you need to do is get yourself a good, tight *modus operandi* and stick with it for as far as it'll take you. Less complicated that way. Right, I suppose that's another piece of advice, so while I'm waffling on, here's one more. Don't get greedy, little brother. Don't expect you should ever be allowed more than you're due. It will only catch you up in the end the way Twitch went. A monumental muck-up of his own making, that was. As I said, cautionary tale. Take a page.

You don't have to tell me it's hard. I live it, boy. Hunger makes you eager, bloodlust makes you blind. You grow lost on a single drop. Before you know, you've been careless and the next sound you hear is that bloody fat lady singing an epitaph over your temporary grave with several strands of garlic for a new necktie. Things that never change. Such shite. What's with the garlic, anyway? I mean truly. I thought everyone knew that only works for rubbing onto the tips of the silver bullets used to shoot werewolves. Or not. Never had the pleasure to test that one myself, actually, but I have it on good authority.

How was Twitch greedy? How's this instead? Bugger the fuck off. I told you, not trading. I'm giving you some sterling advice here, isn't that enough? Jeez, you've some balls on you for a pup. How the hell old are you, anyway? Can't be a day over fifty. Probably not even that. Come closer and let me smell you, Baby Bite. Damn, but you smell nearly alive.

Listen, you don't want to be sitting close to an old corpse like me smelling like that. Take a seat over there by the piano. Safer. Or leave. I don't have time for you, anyway. I've misery to stew in and that's going take me some time, so if you'll show yourself out the way you came in, I'd appreciate it. Really. Ta for the visit and all, but I can't spare the time.

Sorry? Who the hell told you *that* load of shite? The name, Baby Bite. Tell me the name of the walking blood clot spreading that tripe about. Last old boy... Bollocks! No one knows where I am. Answer the fucking question. Oh, *now* you want to leave? Sorry, but I can't let you do that. Not now. Now, we're going to have ourselves a little, ah, *discussion*.

What's wrong? Have I made you nervous in some way? You didn't think I got to be this old sitting on my arse, did you? Don't feel badly. No one ever sees me move. The hand is quicker than the eye, little one. Perhaps, once you've grown up you'll be half as fast. If you live that long. I suppose we'll find out then. So? Have you as many brains as balls or should I rid myself of my current problem?

Vampire justice? Oh lord... Someone's been reading Anne Rice before bedtime. Vampire justice... You're looking at it, mate. Judge, jury and executioner if you want to look at it that way. You shouldn't, though. That's a human concept and we're certainly not that. There's no justice for us. Justice is for the living and we've already been judged.

Welcome to eternity, Baby Bite. It's hell on earth.

Now give me the name before I'm forced to remove you from my social calendar. No, don't think, just speak and this will go a whole lot faster.

Ahhh... Right then. Well, that makes sense. We didn't exactly see, erm, eye-to-eye. Although I didn't think we'd cross paths again after I left him on that island, barking mad pirate bastard that he was. See? Bloody technology to the rescue again. Had to be. Damn, but I hate the modern world. If you can't ensure all the unstable, megalomaniac immortal trouble-makers you've gone to the trouble to remove from the world stay in a place where they can't get into your business again, what's left? Not like they're liable to die of old age.

Well, fuck.

All right, Baby Bite, I'm not going to eat you for lunch. Relax. I know why you're here. You hitched your horse to his wagon then? Brilliant. Scared the holy piss out of you, too, I'll wager. Yeah, well, let's say he needs some work on his social skills. If he didn't make you, then what are you after here, haven? Sanctuary? I don't know about any of that. None for me, so why should there be for the likes of you? Besides, I'm no team player, little one.

You can't stay here.

Look, I can't be your daddy, little man. I don't need the inexperienced likes of you shitting where I eat, so take yourself on out of here. Go on now, clear off. If he comes, I won't tell him you've been or that I know you. Which I don't, so makes it easy since I won't have to lie. I've got my own score to settle, so you go on now, little boy. Run. Far.

And don't come back.

Go!

And don't bang the screen on the way out.

Damn kids.

2

(England – Seventeen twenty-something)

"**Good gods, are you still here?** Did I not tell you to go last night? Why are you still creeping about my garden? I don't want you here, don't you understand? Bugger off. I can't protect you. No, don't start... If he comes looking for you over whatever it was you did, there's nothing I can do for you. Trust me, it would be far worse for him to find you here. I told you to run."

I don't quite recall how it began, but I find myself having this same conversation from time to time. Seems like it's always been this way. For reasons I've never been able to fathom, they always come to me. And I don't mean the baby bloods.

I mean humans.

That they've believed I could protect them from anything is mystery enough. But why on earth would they feel safe anywhere near me? Don't living creatures have some sixth sense or other about that sort of thing? I mean, really. Rather akin to a gazelle calling on her friendly neighbourhood lion for sanctuary, if you catch my drift.

This one, though? I have to admit, there was something about her right off. Something not quite human I suppose you could say. I didn't understand that bit, but damned if I wasn't drawn. I didn't want her to go even while I ordered her to and perhaps that was my first mistake. She wasn't listening to a word I said, anyway. Rather than stay outdoors where I found her lingering about my favourite garden on the other side of the Atlantic those years ago, when I turned my back on her in dismissal, she bloody well followed me inside.

Right into my house.

"I can't just run off, Richard. I won't make it. This is the only safe place. I'm telling you, he's afraid of you," her voice steady no matter she fell over my threshold the previous evening closer to undead than alive. Perhaps, that's what really caught my attention. That stubborn life. That, and it had been a great bloody while since anyone went to the trouble of calling me by name even if it was only the one from their generation.

When she arrived, she'd been bleeding. Like a bear to honey I was. I still don't know how I managed to patch her up without diving in. Although, to be honest? The little taste I had off my fingers was about enough to drive me barmy. Didn't even try to stop myself there. Naughty? Yes. Guilt? *Human* feelings of any kind? None.

"Look, you simply can't stay here and that's all there is to it. Trust me, you're better off taking your chances heading for the next village. Or the next county. Bugger and blast… Clear off, girl!"

"But he wouldn't come back *here*. He turned away, I told you. And from the speed he went at it he was scared. Just what I hoped for. Outside in the fields he might chance it, I suppose. But in here with you? You know he wouldn't even consider it. He's *afraid*."

"Him and everyone else, but that's besides the point." Him and everyone else but *her*. "You don't understand and I don't expect you to, but there's no place for you here. I live alone. I *need* to be alone. You don't know the first thing about me and it's just as well. Believe me, the faster you leave the better."

My lips were saying it, but feeling her heartbeat clear across the room I was hard put to keep my hands off her. The girl didn't know what she asked and one of us had to have the good sense to keep her from the wolf. But I didn't want to have good sense just then. She was right there, standing in my place of her own free will insisting she wouldn't leave. She wasn't even frightened, but I knew she would be soon enough and I didn't want to deal with it. So troublesome.

The phantom taste of her blood was still sweet on my tongue even while she stood there, stubborn, making me see her as a person. I liked that I could feel her. Savoured the feeling of her heart so alive just beyond my reach, considering the good meal to come. But then she was making me *see* her at the same time and I didn't like that part one bit. I didn't speak with anyone. I certainly didn't make conversation with anything I was inclined to hunt. It mucked up my brains. The sound of her heartbeat was filling up all the space in my head.

Well, if it had been as simple as that, I imagine I might have managed to hang onto my life there a few more years. I really can't say what happened to my thought process. It was more than the blood, you see. More than the life. I suppose that made me the stupidest bloodsucker on the planet.

Right in the middle of it, deeper and deeper into contemplating which way to strike while she continued to stand there making conversation, it struck me. I couldn't take that life. Couldn't consider making it end for my own gain. Somehow, she set off some crisis of conscience or something. It was ridiculous. Conscience... Never bothered me before.

But I can tell you, I was fairly bothered right about then. At least, I thought it might be conscience.

The girl needed to go.

"I don't need to stay forever. But for now? I promise not to get in your way," and as though that settled the matter, she turned her back on me and bent down to throw a log on the fire.

Why did she have to do that? She wasn't even listening to what I struggled to convey. And then of all things gave me her back in trust, never knowing I could be on her before she took her next breath. I stood there a moment, quivering, and then stomped out past her into the twilight, instead. She was confusing the hell out of me.

"Richard..."

I could hear her calling after me, but I didn't stop and made for the forest to hide in the gathering dark. I couldn't look at her any longer and she couldn't be allowed to see me for what I was.

"Richard, *wait*. Please, don't leave..."

It was evening and I was hungry and I had to stay away from her. No one had been this close to me for any extended time in longer than I could remember. And the girl had taken it upon herself to not only stay, but make herself at home in my space. *In my space*. I could feel her everywhere. Feel that life pulsing and vibrant and radiating out from her to seep into everything around her. It was torture. I could smell the copper from her bandaged cuts wafting on the evening breeze and it made me salivate.

I legged it.

I managed to put enough distance between us so she wouldn't see the human veneer give way to the hunting animal within as I vaulted a fieldstone fence on the next rise. I was still running when the moon was high.

It wasn't until three villages away that I got to eat. He was easy pickings stumbling out of a tavern the way he was and I was on him before he knew what happened. There was no enjoyment in it and it didn't satisfy me.

I should mention here that in the course of any given year, I almost never remember the particulars of a meal. Don't recall a face and to be honest, it's for no other reason than I have no reason. Do you ever recall the name of the chicken you've consumed at dinner? Lament the loss of his beady-eyed chicken consciousness to all poultrykind? Doubtful. Simply the way it is and I'm no different. I would need a reason to remember.

I had one that night, though.

I remember this single most unremarkable drunk. Not for the savoury sweet of it nor the monumental slaking of a thirst larger than the world. Or even for finding the bloody fulfilment that eased the fire in my brain for an instant. It was the contrast to what I ran away from, you see. That tiny taste of her. Even at that distance, I could still feel her heart beating, calling to me, enticing me, and that poor, drunk bastard was a pitiful substitute.

I was so sick with it, crazed with the feel of it, I didn't even bother dragging him off into the brush at the side of the roadway and had him right there in the moonlight. He was so liquored up no beguiling would take, but there was no need to make him docile. He didn't struggle.

To be honest, most of them don't and I've never puzzled out why. I can phantom walk among them, converse and interact and then shrink back to study them and the mystery of it will always remain. I mean, in how they never recognise they should be terrified of me--the dispenser of their mortal end--until the last clenching moment. Cheek-to-cheek, with a lolling head cradled in the crook of my arm. Right then while I pull back to watch a last ruby rivulet swell and run free, propelled by that same plundered, luxuriant life, that pearl of great price they never know they possess. It's there in that instant, in the afterglow of the clench, when they always know. Perhaps, it's the feel of their blood running off their own skin that tells them it's real, life draining when it should be coursing. I suppose I'll never know. Regardless, they always do and this one was no different.

I saw it in his eyes just as he saw it in mine while I wiped his blood off my chin.

And so I remember him, because he wasn't anything I wanted just then. I remember his life, because I used it. I remember his death, because I caused it. I remember his face, because I stared at it a long while there in the bright of the moon without benefit of cover. All of it became significant and at the same time none of it was important, not a whit. Because it wasn't what I wanted. I knew she was still there waiting for me, just waiting, because she had nowhere else to go and felt safe.

No accounting for taste.

I dropped him at the first gunshot crack. The deafening millisecond change that occurs in any sound or vibration that I perceive far above the human norm propelled me back home at a run. It was her. Out of the blue, her heart hammered jackrabbit fast and frantic. My grasp on it was murky and I couldn't make it focus. I could only surmise the one she escaped from had overcome his apparent fear and found her. I didn't even know why I was running.

But I ran faster, anyway.

Everything was burning when I burst out of the stubborn clumps of forest clinging to the edges of my garden. I don't know what I was thinking leaving her alone there to poke into my business and knew what this was about. I'd been found out and now my business was afire. Again. The brand new porch swing I knocked together during the winter and that I'd been so impressed with myself for having hung in time to enjoy the fine weather went up like a Roman candle right before my eyes.

"Bloody hell!"

It made no sense, though. The girl was nowhere to be seen. But I knew she'd not run away. I felt her there, panicky and wild and surrounded by the flaming jumble that had been my house.

"Hey! You in there… Hey, *girl*!"

"Richard? *Richard*! I can't get out. Help me!"

"*What*?" I wasn't going in there. No way. "Are you having a laugh?

You've already destroyed everything I own and this is my last shirt for heaven's sake. Get out of there yourself. And I'd get a wiggle on while you're about it. That roof's coming down right quick, girl."

Already bits of burning timber were falling in on her and I could smell the singe of her hair pushed ahead of the draft. She didn't squeal, though, and I'll give her that. She didn't even sound particularly afraid.

"The name is Maggie Chapman, not girl, you disrespectful bastard. Are you dead from the neck up? I don't care a toss about your sodding shirt. You *will* get me the hell out of here!"

I have to say, this particular scenario had never come up before. Most people simply ran away. Sometimes, they'd ask a small medicinal favour and then leave me some bit of baking in return before they scuttled off. But in between emergencies? Pretty much everyone stayed out of my way. And for certain no one ever spoke to me in this manner. The girl was yelling at, commanding me. As though I were some average cuss she was in the habit of ordering about. What was I supposed do with that?

"Ho! Don't get shirty with me, little lady…"

"Argh! Fine then. I'm sorry, all right? Now, for pity's sake, help me!"

"…destroy my house…"

"*Please*, Richard, I'm *stuck*."

"What am I supposed to sit on now? I only just put up that swing."

She stopped calling then and no matter it couldn't be heard over the roar of the flame, I knew she was choking. Could feel the breath wheezing in and out of her, stubborn and determined. Felt her heart tattoo in double time. She was moving around some, thrashing, but she wasn't coming out. She said she was stuck and it wasn't a lie.

Unfeeling in the face of her plight, the flames captured all my attention and I lost time. So animate with their consuming, serpentine life. I have a healthy respect for that power. Then again, as much as I can appreciate the beauty of it, as much as I envy its indiscriminate indifference in applying itself to snuffing out one life over another, to be honest, fire scares the holy shite out of me. It's hypnotic and deceiving and in the end brutal and perhaps a bit too much like myself to look at in the face with any comfort. I knew it wouldn't hesitate to get its caustic arms around me, either, because what am I, after all, but the illusion of fuel? Except in my case, some burnt flesh wouldn't kill me and I'm not much into horrible, unspeakable agony for all eternity. Okay, maybe not for *all* eternity. But it wouldn't be very fucking pleasant for a while.

The pounding of her heart through the flame got to me and drew me back to reality. I couldn't help it. I am what I am, after all, and no matter I'd eaten I was far from satisfied. It reached out and touched me in that gnawing place inside, lighting my own fire hotter than any burning building. Nothing but dark instinct. I wanted it for myself to consume, that life, and wouldn't allow it be wasted like that.

It became difficult to think straight.

The rain barrel off the corner of the porch was full and between one beat of her heart and the next, I already dunked myself into it to the waist and was through the flaming remains of the front wall. Far worse inside than out, it swirled with scorching confusion, dark and thick with smoke, but a blood's sight isn't dependent on light, so she was easy to find.

She would have screamed, I'm sure, if she wasn't choking so hard. I must have been quite the sight appearing out of the nothing as I had with rainwater billowing off me into steam in the heat. Fire creating surreal, amber cat's eyes in reflection that gleamed through the smoke. A demon winking in with the flames of hell behind for a backdrop.

Perhaps, not so far wrong.

The partition wall between the main room with the fireplace and the back room I kept my medicines in had fallen onto her, trapping her where she stood. No matter how she struggled, she would never escape on her own.

All my herbs were burning up fast adding an odd flavour to the smoke, an entire season's work and I didn't think to save any of it. My whole world was the beat of her heart. Her eyes were wide for only an instant before she convulsed into another fit of choking and she wouldn't have lasted much longer. Flicking the broken wall off her, I grabbed her up out of the mess on the floor and dashed out to the cool of the garden before she could understand what happened.

The rain barrel wasn't heavy so I dragged it over between the rows of parsley and feverfew where she was curled into a tight ball choking up smoke. I splashed water out onto her clothes and skin to cool whatever burns she might have. She didn't notice much of anything until I knelt down with some cupped between my palms.

"Here, girl. Drink this. It'll clear your--"

The toe of her hobnailed boot hit the back of my palms hard, throwing the water up into my face. "Don't..," she was still choking and gasping for air, but wagged an accusing finger at me, "...play nice. Took... you... *long* enough."

"Apparently, I was right. A real charmer, you are."

Her eyes glared out of the soot on her face and she didn't say another word.

"I got you out, didn't I? Wasn't that what you wanted?"

Instead of answering, her boot came up again and hit me in the shin.

"Ow! Well, there's a fine howdoyoudo. What the devil was that for? Nice way to thank someone for saving your life. Ungrateful trollop."

I stalked off a ways, because I couldn't stay that close to her and discuss anything. Besides, I was lying my arse off and couldn't look her in the face while I did it.

I stared off into the pines, considering. I left her alone in my house for hours. Unsupervised. Gods knew what she'd been up to. Shows you how messed up my head was when I ran off. I didn't reach this age allowing people to poke into my personal effects. That's a dangerous gamble I've never been willing to take. I hadn't even put in a larder when I built that house and it wasn't set up for illusion to any company. For all I knew, she could have been hungry and went searching for something to eat. And found nothing.

Wonder what she made of my sleeping arrangements?

I stalked back to the rain barrel, "Batty, high-handed vagabond... What did you think you were doing? Being some sort of martyr? I told you not to stay here. I *warned* you. Or did you know the truth before you started all that nonsense and that was simply a ploy to gain access? Sonofabitch... *Answer me.*"

She wouldn't and looked away. I tried to get into her head and force her to look at me and it seemed to have no effect on her. Unbelievable. See what I meant about there being something about her? Something not quite human. I didn't understand why nothing I did seemed to affect her the way it did everyone else and I must have snarled in irritation, because her heartbeat quickened. On top of my anger, it only raised my bloodlust. I think she attempted to say something right about there, but with all that inhaled smoke, she lapsed into more choking.

I was old even then. I'd been made so long before I couldn't remember how to feel badly for her while she struggled for breath. It didn't have anything to do with me or was anything important to me. It was nothing more than an inconvenience, because it prevented her from communicating with me when I wanted her to.

Whatever crisis of conscience I had was over.

Faster than she could react, I buried my hand in her hair good and hard for grip and hauled her up to dunk her head into the rain barrel. Water flew everywhere as she thrashed, but it didn't bother me. I held her down there a good long while, but not too long. If she gasped and got a lung full, she'd spit up what she was choking on. Speedier than waiting weeks for her to finish coughing.

I'm often impatient.

When I hauled her back out, she clawed at my arms and hissed at me like a viper when I threw her down into the rosemary, but it only made me laugh. Doubtful she would have taken any medicinal advice right about then, but rosemary is cleansing, so good for her to breathe in. I was only being practical.

"Damn, girl," that stubborn life was something else. "Guess that means you'll mend, yeah?" Even while she gagged up water, she never exuded any hint of fragility. It was a definite attraction. I wanted it for myself. How could I not?

I was thinking how fabulous she was and then not applying much thought to what it did to me, because I liked the feel of it on me. Until she did a very curious thing. Right in front of me, she changed. Grew still and calm and turned into someone else. She dried her face on her skirts and slicked her hair back and twisted it into a neat little knot at the base of her skull with casual deftness. She didn't even look upset and though I was out of practice at it, if I had to choose an emotion, I would have said she appeared relieved by the casual cruelty, the violence. As though she understood it and it appeared to settle her. So odd. She was confusing the blazes out of me again, making me think.

I didn't like it.

She smelled of wood smoke and damp ashes. She smelled of life. Her heartbeat was steady and strong again and she breathed in rosemary-scented night air with relish. It looked to be helping her, so had been the right thing, good for her. I think I was glad.

"Erm-- Girl?" I was struggling. "How do you feel? Better now?" I kept my voice gentle. It occurred to me I didn't like this change that had come over her. I wanted that other girl back, the one who ordered me about as though she were my keeper. While I hadn't hurt her, it seemed I killed her anyway with my naturally unthinking indifference, my inhumanity. I was no longer equipped for this type of interaction, conversation even. I couldn't remember the first thing about being a regular person, but in that moment, I gave it my all and didn't know why.

She didn't look at me and when she spoke her voice was raspy,

"Yes," but at least she answered. I breathed in some rosemary myself, but it couldn't do anything for me. I'd been dead too long for that.

I leaned against the rain barrel watching the house continue to burn. I'd build another. Wouldn't be the first time. I had a few extras out in the barn, my tools, but more importantly, a spare place to sleep separate from the house. I always did that for just such an emergency. As I had a few times before, I congratulated my forethought, because night was almost over.

I didn't know what to do with the girl, though. No question she knew all and I couldn't leave her running about during the day to tell half the nation what I was. She still hadn't made an attempt to leave, though. I didn't know what to make of it. Perhaps, I'd been harsh in my assessment of her planning the fire ahead of time. She might have only panicked. I tended the injuries she had, after all, the ones from whomever she'd run from, and she'd been grateful. Perhaps, my reality she discovered was too much in addition to her own troubles. Maybe. Didn't change the outcome, though. Another potential problem then. I had to think of something.

Unlike before, she no longer seemed interested in conversation with me and it forced me to look at the change that had overtaken her. My doing. Odd, but it made me unsettled to acknowledge it and it shouldn't have. I didn't like that, either.

Time too short for a puzzle that large, with precision learned from too many ending nights, I felt the approach of dawn. Knew right to the moment while in the back of my mind the countdown ticked off the seconds left before I needed to run. The sun was my enemy and so during the day I could stay in the root cellar under the barn. I never had a need to keep many vegetables, only enough to trade, so it was a good emergency home. The barn was far enough back from the house for the fire to leave it alone, so I wasn't worried.

In reality, I don't need to sleep at all and can carry on indefinitely as long as I can hunt, but that's difficult in the daytime when the world is awake. In the light, there are so many who might witness the demon who lives among them, which is why I generally rest then. And the sun burns far worse than any fire. About the only thing that can kill a vampire, it's always to be avoided. Right, well, I'd never had occasion to try to disprove that theory, either, but in anything even approaching fire-related, let's just say I was never much of a risk-taker. I didn't plan on being caught outside in it, girl or no girl.

I studied her another moment. I wanted to ask if she needed anything, but didn't know how without making my inhumanity more obvious. I scratched my head, unable to work out why she was even still there. She sat in my garden, quiet and still, a little bird at my feet. I had no social skills and little time for beating around the bush and while I'm sure there's probably a more tactful way I might have approached that conversation, I didn't know how.

"Why aren't you running off, girl?" I kept my distance and stayed leaning on the rain barrel. I thought the space might make me appear less threatening.

All she did was look down into her singed skirts.

"Look," it came out rather harshly, so I took a breath and tried again. "Listen, I told you I lived alone, that I needed to be alone. I never lied to you. You know why." She looked up then, her face blank. "I left you in my house half the night and now it's burning to the ground. It's not my first time at the dance, you know. The only part I can't work out is why you're still here. You should be running screaming through the county by now. Gathering up neighbours with pitchforks to oust the demon from their midst."

She cleared her throat, "I told you I want to stay. I've nowhere else I could go." Her voice was small, mirroring the way she behaved. The life wafting off her continued muddling up my head.

I grunted, "So that's it then? You have nowhere else to go, so you'd rather stay with a--" I couldn't say the word to her face. Damn, that girl.

"You're being serious," I tried to laugh at her, but it just came out in a bark and then trailed off.

"Yes." She sounded serious.

I looked back at the fire and then the dark horizon line. The flames from the house cast undulating shadows across her dirty face giving her the appearance of a shade, mysterious and otherworldly, and making us appear related. An illusion. What she was, was getting under my skin. I was having a difficult time facing her and didn't want to admit it to myself, so spoke to the tree line, instead. "They'll say I've cast a spell on you or some other tripe." Why was I behaving as though she had a say?

"I don't care." I felt her behind me, leaning forward in earnest. "I could help you. You'll see. Pay my way--"

"Codswallop!" Okay, that time I did laugh. What else could I do? She was obviously crazy. I turned from the trees to see her expression and it only fuelled my laughter.

"What's funny?" she looked up from the rosemary in stubborn confusion.

"What's funny? What's *ludicrous*, you mean. What's never going to happen no matter how hard you pretend it can?" I was incredulous and she was a blank. I laughed harder. "Do you think I can be what I am, but somehow manage to accommodate you solely because you ask? That wall must have knocked the sense right out of you if you believe it can be done, little girl." Before she blinked, I was kneeling down beside her with a hand hard on her jaw making her look me in the eye.

My laughter was gone and my voice low and heavy with sarcasm, "Should I treat you as my pet, then? Build a little pen for you in my yard? Keep you on a leash? Because we cannot exist as equals no matter what magical fairyland you've created in your imagination." I leaned close and whispered in her ear. "This is not a game. This is all that I am." I felt her shiver as I put my cold cheek up next to her warm one so she could feel it and continued to whisper into her ear, so she could hear it for the dark truth it was. "I'm everything they speak about in whispers. I'm the evil that travels through the mist at night. I'm the bringer of death the whole world fears, because they never see it until it's already upon them."

The chill of my lips grazed at her ear and she caught a tiny breath, but that was all. I let her heartbeat get inside me and make me stupid, so I wouldn't have to think anymore or worry about any crises of conscience or ponder silly, little girls who believed they could be roommates with a vampire.

And that's when she reached up to lay a hand on the back of my head. She tipped her chin up in my palm. Her heart was pounding in my ears and her breath a butterfly at my chest and I was all but blind in the lust except for the length of her throat below my chin. But I froze.

This was no hunt.

It seemed she was asking and that was something altogether different. There's no way she could know what she asked not to mention the heavy responsibility that came with being a maker--one I was not prepared to take. I was no father. It must have been the payment she spoke of or an offering or permission or I don't know what she might have been thinking then. But *I* was thinking there was no way. Not like this. I couldn't kill her and I refused to make her. How could I consign someone like her to hell? I knew that hell and had been judged for my own sins long before. I didn't know hers.

It was difficult to speak, "Don't. You don't want that." I released her jaw, but she grabbed my hand back up and set it against the warm skin of her cheek, holding it there with her hand.

"Yes, I do," she even looked me in the eye when she said it, tipping her chin up more to see me, breathing fast, little feather breaths between her parted lips only an inch away from mine.

I stared back into her eyes, full in the lust and heightened outside of the physical and saw her inside there. It didn't touch me, because it couldn't, but she seemed quite serious about what she wanted. "*No.*" I was whispering, but the words were hard, "Tell me what you're asking from me. You've asked me for sanctuary. You've asked me for protection. What are you asking from me now? Tell me, girl, what is it *exactly* you think you're asking from me?" I continued to stare into her eyes to make her face me while she thought it through and while she answered.

"I--" She snapped her mouth shut. After a strained moment, she sighed and took her hand away from mine. She let it fall from her face, her expression perplexed. "I don't know. I thought that maybe..." She searched my face and then frowned, pressing her lips into a hard line. "I don't know."

The moment passed and I stayed close while the lust leached out of me. "Say it again," I whispered.

Lowering her gaze, she repeated herself in a small voice, "I said, I don't know."

She stopped calling me by my name. I didn't like that and realised I missed it already. A condition of my reality, one moment to the next it was a different world for me, flitting from thought to thought, existing in each moment separate from any others. I was already onto the next thing. "I don't know, *Richard*."

"Pardon?" in confusion, she pulled back farther from the frost of me.

"Everyone else calls me Twitch. You called me Richard since you came and now you've stopped. 'I don't know, *Richard*,' you meant to say."

A sad ghost of a smile touched her mouth. She spoke in a whisper, "I don't know, *Richard*."

She was still close enough for the warmth of her breath to break up against my dead skin. I closed my eyes and savoured every dancing molecule. I didn't know how I was going to survive, but knew she would. She would, because I would let her. And everyone else would stay the hell away or die.

The herald of dawn tapped at my unconscious.

My eyes flew open, "Daybreak." I'd lost track of time. "*Blast*. I have to get inside. You're with me now, yeah? Quick, girl."

She didn't even question. She looked around, "What can I do?"

"Nothing here." I was up and pulling her along with me. "I have a place in the barn. Not much time." She couldn't move as fast as me, but did a passable job keeping up. The house continued to burn and the roof caved in with a shower of sparks and a belch of smoke to hurry us along.

"Here," I hauled on the trapdoor in the barn floor. "Root cellar." We were down inside only a moment before the heavy door fell to block out the kiss of the sun on the horizon.

Her heartbeat was still inside me, fluttering and lively, and it made the dark, little space more inviting. I watched her standing stiff in the black, fingers stretched out and searching and I knew she was blind here. But I wasn't. In that confined space, her breathing was amplified a thousand times to my inhuman ears. Singing a song I'd forgotten how to sing, but that I loved. She couldn't hear me and I watched her swivel her head back and forth while her fingers continued to sweep empty air.

"Richard?"

I walked around her in a circle on my cat feet taking her in, admiring the treasure she was. I couldn't help myself. She was a mystery I couldn't solve, but somehow mine to keep. At close range, I indulged myself in her vigour. A sweet hors d'oeuvre to savour, I hoped it wouldn't pique my hunger or she might not be as safe as she believed. I inhaled the scent of her, her fresh, raw skin scraped in multiple places allowing me to relish the lifeblood within. I let it twist through my brain the way that I loved until I was stupid with it.

"You smell like a dream," I spoke softly out of the dark at her ear and watched her stiffen in surprise.

"This *is* a dream, Richard," her voice was hollow and tired and she reached a hand up to the place she heard my voice come from to lay a palm against my cold cheek. If I could have died again, it would have been then. "Only a dream. And I'm in it with you."

I continued to let her have the soft voice in the dark. It was the only soft thing about me and all I could offer. "You're not afraid of me."

"No, Richard." Her hand moved to splay her fingers over my lips, to feel the voice she couldn't see.

"Like a wolf with a sheep, girl. You should be."

"You should be, *Maggie*." She pressed her warm fingers against my mouth when I tried to speak. "I told you, it's not *girl*, it's Maggie. You meant to say, 'You should be, *Maggie*'."

"Touché." I chuckled into her hand, "You should be, *Maggie*."

"That's better."

"Which part? You here in my root cellar all to myself? Or you telling me what to do again?" I snarled, but it was only half-hearted, "Are you certain you're not frightened?" Somehow, she took all the starch out of me without doing anything at all. "Not even alone in the dark with a disreputable man, but with the likes of me. What's to become of you in the dark, trapped down here under the earth with a hungry wolf, Maggie Chapman?" The hand at my mouth shook and she wasn't smiling. "What's wrong?"

I stepped away and examined her more closely with my otherworldly sight. I couldn't see anything wrong with her, but she must have been exhausted from fighting the smoke. It made sense. If I wasn't going to hunt then I would rest, too. There was nothing else to occupy ourselves with until nightfall, anyway. She refused to answer and I saw that blankness come over her again that she no doubt thought I couldn't see. While I surmised some of it was likely brought on by exhaustion, there was more underneath, but didn't know what it meant. When it appeared she wasn't going to volunteer anything, I changed the subject.

"Right, well, it's been a long night." Maggie's head whipped around to the sound of my voice. "I'm sure that wood falling on your head didn't do you much good. You need rest. There's a cot to your left there. It's yours. Can you find your way?" She turned and then hesitated in futility, so I took her arm to guide her. "Here," and led her until she bumped it with her shins. "I'll be close by. When it's safe to go out again, I'll know." I left her there to stretch out on a pile of sacking in the opposite corner.

Maggie got herself lowered onto the cot and struggled out of those boots of hers in the dark. She didn't lie down, though, and continued to sit on the edge. I propped myself up on my elbow to watch her. She sat there unmoving and I didn't know what to make of it. I didn't know if she slept the previous day and she must have been worn out from her adventures with the fire, but she didn't budge. When it didn't appear any answers were forthcoming, I stopped worrying about it. Rolling over to rest, I left her to her own devices.

A few minutes later, Maggie's voice whispered out of the dark, "*Richard*? Richard, where are you?"

"Here," I rolled back over. Her eyes searched through the darkness to place my voice. "Over here, Maggie-girl." She appeared relieved to hear me.

"Richard?"

"Yes."

"Are you going to stay over there?"

"That was the plan."

"Is your cot comfortable?"

"You've the cot, but I'm fine. Get some rest."

She sighed, "I can't."

"What's the problem?"

She made a face and paused in consideration before she confessed. "I can't breathe."

"Shit." I sat up, concerned. I should have pulled her out of the fire sooner. "Does your chest hurt? Are you in pain? You don't feel dizzy, do you?" The perceived need made the healer in me eclipse the blood runner lurking in the darkness.

"It's not serious," she was shaking her head. "Not in that way. From the fire or anything. It's just--" She threw her arms up into the air in defeat, "It's the cellar, all right? Being boxed in. I can't see and I feel trapped. I can't relax. So stupid..."

"Are you having a laugh?"

"I'm sorry."

"There's lots of air, Maggie."

"Of course, I know that. But I feel frantic, anyway. I can't help myself."

"Good lord. Maggie, I don't go out in the daytime."

"I know, but I could. You could stay down here and I was thinking I could sleep up in the barn. Keep an eye on the house--"

"*No!*" I hadn't meant it to come out with so much vehemence and it shocked her into silence. She hung her head. There was that thing again, that timid bird in answer to my wolf snarl. I hated my graceless nature just then without wanting to.

I tried to coax her back with the soft voice in the dark, "I'm not angry with you. But I can't go out and neither can you. Maggie, you can't open the door. Not in the daytime. I thought you understood." It wasn't only that, though. In the span of a few hours, I now considered her mine. Right or wrong and however unnatural it was or more warped it could become, she was *mine*. The thought of her being out of arm's reach was threatening and I didn't like it.

She continued to sit with her head hanging, saying nothing.

I couldn't stand it. Her not talking was worse than her making me have conversations I was too out of practice to have. I was in front of her with a finger under her chin before she could react, "Maggie-girl... Look at me."

Her chin came up, but I knew she couldn't see me through the black. "Hey, now," I was compelled anyway, "I didn't mean to bark. I'm not good with people. Obviously. Doesn't seem to be anything I can do about it. I'm, uh, sorry about that."

Her gaze searched out my face, but she couldn't find it in the pitch. She felt up with her fingers again to find my mouth, instead. I fought back the ache the contact with her warm skin caused. She didn't say anything for a long while and in truth, I wasn't capable with her touching me like that. It was such a dangerous game, but one I never wanted to end.

"Richard?"

"Yes, girl?"

"Stay with me."

The three-word whisper belted out like gunfire and far from what I expected. I shook my head even though she couldn't see it, "Maggie," but she could feel it. "You don't want that."

"Please," her fingers traced the line of my lip until I couldn't think.

"I... I really don't think that's a good idea..."

"Why? I think my honour will be safe. I trust you."

"Trust me... *I* don't trust me."

The warmth of her fingers travelled down my chin and found my shoulder and then slid down my arm to find my hand. She moved over and tugged on my fingers to pull me closer. "There's room. Please, Richard." Her voice was sincere and without pretence, "Don't make me be alone in the dark. I really can't stand it."

There was no arguing with her. I was lost. For the first time in forever, I climbed into bed with a live, human woman by invitation. It was a benchmark day. I wriggled myself all the way over to one side which turned out to be a pointless exercise, because Maggie still had a hold of my hand. She hopped right in after me and threw my arm over her.

"Harlot."

"Don't flatter yourself. Tell me something. Anything, really. Please."

I was afraid to move. It was like lying next to the hearth, but so much more, because she got inside me. "Right, well--" I cleared my throat, "I don't know what to say now."

"Honestly, anything at all, Richard. Just talk to me."

I huffed, "All right. Since you're asking. There *is* something. Considering this moment. Considering…" I lost my voice when her fingers came back up onto my mouth. Why did she have to keep doing that? I cleared my throat again. "I mean, considering how wonderfully close we are here, I suppose I'd like to ask why you burned down my house. We could be sleeping in comfort right now instead of this. You wanted to stay, you said. Why did you do it, Maggie?"

The warm, restless fingers stopped. "I never said I burned the house down, Richard."

"What now?"

"I was only in it at the time."

That gave me pause. Catching her warm fingers in my cold ones so I could keep a thought in my head, I stopped their restless fluttering around that was driving me half-mad. "Then..?"

"I don't know what happened exactly. I was sat on the floor against the back wall so I could watch the hearth and keep an eye on the door for when you returned. I must have nodded off. When I woke, there was so much fire already there was no way out. And then the wall caved-in over top me."

This was a new development. Here I thought she'd been the villain and turns out she was only a fellow victim, "Lucky you woke." I felt her shiver against me and cursed my lack of tact. "Sorry. Please, forgive my perennial inelegance." But she *was* lucky. "If you hadn't woken, you couldn't have called for me and then, well…"

She took a breath and I saw her grimace. Felt her wince though she tried not to.

I considered, "If it wasn't you, then..?"

She shrugged, "He came back. Must have. It would be like him, so over the bloody top. Who else would it be?" She flinched with every word and I knew the heat must have seared her lungs. No matter I'd got her to cough up most of the smoke they were clearly tender. I thought about the way I treated her and it made me uncomfortable for no real reason. No reason I was still capable of recognising, anyway.

"Well, you're not the only one with a past to outrun. I'm not exactly the most popular man in the county. Might have been one of the locals. Though I believe I would have known if that were the case." When she called for my help, I left her longer while I went on about my usual selfish way. It was my own bloody fault she'd been alone to begin with.

No wonder I'd known. I had a taste of her, after all. Enough to put her inside me. And she trusted me enough to reach out for me. It had to be what called me back, though I'd never heard the like before.

I vowed to behave better. If I could still remember how.

Her pain felt as sharp as her heartbeat to me. "Blast, girl. You're hurting more than you're letting on." Not seriously damaged, she would heal in time, but knowing it was my fault made me squirm. My promise to behave better grew concrete. "This is no way to start off, you know. Lying right to my face. I *am* a doctor. You'll be found out every time."

Her eyebrows raised in surprise.

It made me chuckle, "And I can see those eyebrows in the dark, girl."

She had already made me laugh more in one evening than I had in decades. I didn't understand what it meant, but in my way, I was glad for it. It reminded me of something a long while ago that was too difficult to remember with a dead mind. Though still in uncertainty, she was quite relaxed with me and I liked that, too. Even now, up against the frost of me, she hadn't taken her fingers back from my hand and it only intrigued me more. I wanted her to know me. I hid from the world, but didn't want to from her. It seemed the wrong thing. She'd been straight with me, so I would be straight with her. "Ask me something, Maggie. You must have a question or two. It's all right. Ask them."

I watched her struggle in the dark, watched emotion flitter across her features and drank in every animate detail. The words were hesitant, but she spoke them, "You're so cold, Richard." She left her fingers in mine and walked her other hand up to my mouth again to trace my lip. "Even your breath. I feel it now still, so know I wasn't wrong," she was speaking to herself. "I thought I was delirious or raving when I was stuck under the wall. You weren't there and I was wishing you were and then you suddenly *were*."

The harder questions were the ones I always avoided thinking about myself. But there could be no avoiding with her there in the dark. She made me feel obligated, answerable to her. I did my best. "Here," I took the fingers I'd caught in my hand and pressed them against my dead heart so she could feel. "This is why."

She sucked in a breath in wonder. "No beat." She shifted as she considered, "It didn't seem real. All that heat and steam, but all chill when you carried me out. It frightened me a bit. How did you do it? Was it so you could walk through the fire? How long before it wears off? I thought there was something wrong with me," she said with a smile I couldn't share.

I inhaled the warmth of her, "No, Maggie-girl, there's definitely nothing wrong with you. Only me."

She shook her head at me in the dark, "Don't be silly. There's nothing wrong with you, Richard. I've known worse men with beating hearts and sunshine smiles and hot blood that turned them mad. Men... not really men... all of them the same. Why, my--" she caught the rest of the words. "You're nothing like any of them. Put it out of your head."

"Easier said than done. Unlike them, I'm dead."

She didn't speak again for a long moment and I didn't mind while we stayed frozen there that way with her hand over my unbeating heart.

"You're far too melodramatic for a doctor, you know. Such allegorical embellishment."

She was going to make me say it outloud. Well, I had encouraged her. I sighed and sucked it up. "That wasn't meant to be allegorical."

"Not allegorically dead?"

"No."

"*Actually* dead, you're saying."

"Yes."

She paused. "You understand how that sounds, don't you?"

"Yes."

"This is your big life hurdle? Death?"

She really didn't seem to be taking this seriously at all. "*Yes*, dead. How many times will you make me say it?"

The warmth on my skin over my heart was wine and the restless fingers across my lip, opium. I was drunk on her and getting drunker by the moment and didn't care not to be again. Then Maggie was shaking and it roused me. Eyes crinkled up in pain, she struggled for breath, but she was laughing quietly in the dark and I had no idea why. Confusion, I discovered, would be an ongoing condition.

"How is that funny?"

All that came out was wheezing while she tried to answer.

"Maggie?"

"*Dead*? I..," she choked, but worked to get it out, "… they told me… you… supposed to be… a *witch*," and let her forehead rest against me in the aftermath of too much exertion.

I had to think about that one for a minute. "A witch?" Her head bobbed against me. "No, I'm not a witch, Maggie. It's only what the townies call me. Twitch the Witch." I was still thinking.

Blast.

"You were in my house. Didn't you notice the lack of, ah, food?" The breaths she took were more even and I knew she could answer me now, but she left her forehead resting against me. Even in revelation, she stayed close. As though she belonged there.

"No. I told you, I nodded off resting against the wall watching the hearth waiting for you. I'm not uncivilised, you know. It's not polite to poke around someone's house uninvited. Next thing I knew it was on fire. Well, that and you came when I wished you back to help me. I thought you could hear my thoughts."

"Well, yes, but-- No, not your actual thoughts. Okay, in a way." I sighed, "It's complicated."

"Obviously." She paused there with her forehead against me. I was getting in pretty deeply and knew it couldn't last. "You truly understand yourself to be dead? You certainly don't appear so." Her brow furrowed up against my singed shirt as she struggled to understand. I thought everyone knew of the existence of my kind. "No heartbeat. You heard me across a distance, see me in the dark. You say you're dead, then how did you come to be here? Are you spirit then? Perhaps, this truly is a dream." The warm fingers fluttered over my mouth, testing my reality. "If you tell me so I'll believe you. And I'll stay in it with you."

"No, not a spirit, Maggie."

"A man can't walk without a heart. Man or beast then?"

"I used to be. A great while ago there was a man. Now, not much more than beast."

"How did this happen?" She spoke to herself again, "Not a witch. Not a spirit. Not a spell. Definitely solid, flesh and bone. You think, you laugh. You snarl like a cantankerous ferret when you don't get your way, though don't seem to re--" She sucked in a quick breath and shook her head against me. "No, this is not a dead man. Man or beast, dead is still dead. This is something else."

I wanted to tell her everything, but it was serious. And thorny. All the things I thought she knew she didn't and I'd have to say. I knew how it sounded. Even I didn't like the sound of it in my own ears. I didn't want her to be afraid of me, not after this closeness, and I knew she would be. I brushed the back of my hand down her hair in gentleness to steady her.

I let the soft voice in the darkness cushion it, "I can feel you in a way you can't understand, Maggie. Can feel your heart beating, but it's more than that. I can feel the energy that drives you, the life. I might not be alive, but can feel it from everything that is. You especially now. More completely, because of something I did." I didn't want to admit to that indiscretion, that crime, but I had to.

"When I dressed your wounds when you first came? Your blood drove me mad in the way all blood does. I tasted it off my fingers and put you inside me the way I was craving in that moment. I couldn't help myself, Maggie. I *am* dead and blood is life and I need it, plain and simple. I need it to 'walk without a heart', as you put it. I ache for it, hunt for it. When I ran away from you? It was because I was hungry and you were so stubborn standing there in my house after I told you to leave. I was afraid I would attack you for what I'd already had a taste of." She grew very still against me and I could only imagine what she felt in that moment. I had a difficult time getting it out, "I didn't want to kill you." It was something I could no longer feel and so she was alone in it.

Compelled to tell her everything, I was somehow unable to keep it to myself. "I've been dead for longer than I have memory. Can't recall my life. Can't remember who I was or where I was. It's quite lost to me. I don't even have a memory of who made me this way, but it no longer matters. What's the year now? Seventeen twenty-something? It's not even important to me. I remember fifteen-twenty... Twelve-twenty... Eight-hundred-odd. It's one in the same for me. I don't even know my real name, but it's of no consequence. I'm Richard now and I like when you call me that. I didn't even know I could miss something like that.

"You've made me think of things I haven't thought of in lifetimes. And I want to be the thing you're asking of me, but I truly don't know if I can. I am the *undead*, Maggie. The stuff of fables and nightmares and children's night terrors and I'm *real*. When you put my hand back on you in the yard? That might have been your last moment alive. I know you don't understand, but--" I was babbling, trapped into justifying my existence and every action and somehow couldn't stop.

"I swear to you, I will protect you from everything and everyone, because-- Well-- How to explain..?" I danced around the artless words, because they were all I had. "You belong to me now. You're tied to me. I don't know how else to describe it. And it can't be undone. Not while you live and I carry your blood within me. That's my fault really. And because of it, you can't belong to anyone else. I won't let you. I feel it in me, rage at the thought of anyone else near you. At the same time? I might well be your undoing, girl. I feel you and smell you and it's everything I crave and I want to tear your throat out and eat you alive. I truly don't know if those two states can co-exist, if one can hold the other at bay." Any other words caught fast, unpalatable and jagged and too harsh to say to her. I might have lost the ability to empathise with what she felt, but in sudden revelation understood what had been making me squirm. It was shame. And I didn't like that.

But I couldn't lie to her.

Maggie wasn't talking and I hated it more every time it happened, because I kept causing it. I loathed what I was. Maggie was stiller than death and it was hard to witness. I took my hand from the back of her head, so she wouldn't feel trapped by it. I didn't want to frighten her any more than I already had. I stayed very still while she absorbed what I told her. Her warm, little hand was still over my silent heart and it made me ache in a way I'd never known before, because I understood then she would take it away. I swallowed hard and waited for her verdict or tears or screams.

We stayed that way a long while, she and I, and didn't sleep. I know she didn't. Caught in a frozen moment--cold and warmth, death and life, stillness and heartbeat--neither of us moved. I didn't want her to go away and knew she would. I tried to prepare myself for it, but found I didn't want to. Instead, I revelled in her life. Let it wash over me and inside me, so I would always remember before she left me forever. Where I would always feel her at a distance while never allowing myself to possess her.

A lifetime later, the small, warm fingers sandwiched between my cold, dead heart and cold, dead palm fluttered. Her forehead still rested against me and she didn't move it. I made to take my hand away so she could leave without threat.

"No."

I froze.

She twined the fingers of her hand into mine and settled her face into my chest, "Good night, Richard."

3

(Canada – Present)

"**If you want to sneak up on me,** you'll need to be a mite quieter, Baby Bite."

My duffel bag wasn't quite as full as I wanted yet, but I was working on it. I felt the pressure of time for no real reason. Okay, except that since I learned that mad, inhuman bastard was off the island where I stowed him it meant all bets were off.

He was mine.

Almost three-hundred years ago, I went out of my way for the good of the world and now he was throwing it in my face. I even left him with a potential shot at life. Well, it wasn't life, but it wasn't death, either. Though death was what I intended, in the end, I wasn't capable. Couldn't be the same animal he was and chose to rise above that for whatever it was worth at the time.

The value of those scruples I wasn't even supposed to possess seemed bloody pointless now. He was out and causing his special and horrific brand of havoc again. More though, he escaped his punishment and it was egging me on. I wasn't feeling particularly merciful in my old age and, as a matter of fact, I was ready to even the score. He caught me in a weak moment that last time and I had none of that left in me now.

I wasn't quite certain how I would go about it yet, but it would get done. The little bloodsucker had given me a clue. It was ages since I'd been down to the Caribbean so at least it wouldn't be a wasted trip. The information was a bit stale, a couple years or so, but it was a place to begin. It was difficult to decide what to bring. I didn't want to go unarmed.

"How'd you know I was here?"

"Please, Baby Bite, don't insult yourself." Kids... What can you do with them? I should have done myself a favour and made a heart shish kabob before I whacked the little shit's head off, but I couldn't be bothered to waste the energy. What would be the point? It only would make a mess and then I'd have to clean it up and that would be a waste of time I didn't have.

"I really make that much noise?"

He sounded hurt, as though I said he smelled and needed a bath. Which he also did, but I'd be gone soon, so what the hell did I care if he wanted to stink up half the nation? Not my business. He was an irritant, though. And in my space. Again.

"Like a heard of elephant." I tossed another shirt into the bag and rummaged through the room looking for makeshift weapons that wouldn't set off the metal detector at the airport. "If I'm not mistaken, didn't I boot you out yesterday or was that a figment of my imagination?"

"Well, yeah, but I didn't think you were serious," he sauntered in, but side-stepped round the room, so he wouldn't have to turn his back on me. Perhaps, not quite so thick.

There had to be *something* useful in my house. I pulled out drawers with methodical application. "Did I sound serious? I thought I made myself quite clear there, Baby Bite. Perhaps, what we've got here is a failure to communicate." I yanked a cabinet drawer out too quickly and it came off the runners, crashing to the floor. "Shit!"

"Want some help?"

"Please, do fuck off."

"Jeez, I was just tryna--"

"*Don't*," I bent down and threw everything back in. "Not interested. I have things to do and you're not one of them. Stay the hell out of my way, Baby Bite."

"Alan."

"How's that?"

"*Alan*. My name's Alan. You keep calling me Baby Bite, so--"

"I don't care what the hell your name is." What was with this idiot? "I care even less you're here, except for you making a better door than a window. I don't care you *exist*. Good lord, take a bloody hint. *Move*," I brushed past him dragging my duffel along to try the back porch for possibilities. I stomped down the stairs with my new shadow in tow. I glared over my shoulder at him, but he wasn't running. I snarled and ignored him. "Alan. That's certainly fear-inspiring. Alan..? What the hell's an Alan? People have no imagination anymore."

I was cranky and wound-up thinking about getting my hands on that parasitical pirate twat. Still working out how I would do it, I wasn't in the mood for conversation. I didn't know why this little one was there or why he came back after I threw him out, but I stopped analysing why things happen a long while ago. How he found me was anyone's guess, but, perhaps, he was only the messenger of the information I needed to achieve the peace I had so far been denied. If that were the case, then he'd served his purpose and beyond that? I couldn't be arsed. I wished he would vacate my space, though. He was distracting me and I needed to think with a clear head and knew I wasn't. Right, well, it wasn't his fault my thought process was miles from logical, but I wasn't looking too closely just then. Revenge isn't a business built on logic.

Baby Bite ran to keep up with me, "Listen, I wanted to ask you--"

"Do you have an off switch?"

"There's more than just me--"

"In the world? Yes, I'm aware."

"Ha-ha, funny. Anyway, there's about five or six of us. Well, a few more--"

"Is that all?" He was after something, but I didn't want to hear it.

"Okay a few more than that, but--"

"Didn't I used to have a mirror around here somewhere?"

"I wanted to ask if it was okay if they came, too." He was panting to stay with me while I ran around the house.

The video game and computer generation--pathetic. It even spread to the 'runners. I imagined they had their dinners delivered by the blood bank and didn't know the first thing about hunting. No wonder Billy scared the shite right out of them. They must have thought they signed on for a room service Caribbean holiday there with that one. Until reality set in.

They didn't even know what we were. It was a whole new world and even among our own kind we were antiques. Hell, I was fairly certain William Blackthorn wasn't even as old as me so maybe the baby blood was right. Billy only spread the word I existed to flush me out and kill any cover I had in payback. It might be I truly was the last old boy. For all I knew, it was the truth. I may not remember my maker, but could feel the distance from everyone else. Felt the weight of all those years piling up on top of my existence. Felt the difference. I'd never met any others quite like us and last of my particular kind next to him didn't seem outside the realm of possibility. Long before Christianity was a distant thought, I was skulking about searching for my supper. My world? Try a thousand years before that and you'll be closer. Go two millennia and you'll be in the neighbourhood.

I wasn't like these ones here, not like this Baby Bite. Though cursed with a similar affliction, I was a different animal. For a long while, I suspected I might have been born out of the bowels of the earth and not created in the same way they were. I remembered the first Roman Empire. I remembered Egypt and Babylon. I remembered when men believed only the gods in all their forms lived among the heavens and never dreamt of flying there. No, my birth was out of something no one remembered. Almost certainly. Somewhere in the vicinity of blood sacrifice and the rhythm of dark and mysterious things that hadn't been seen since and now only existed in legend. Perhaps. Mesopotamia had been a dangerous place after some mucking about with the sorts of things that opened cracks in the fabric of the Now that had no business being opened. Trust me, not everything in legend is imagination though most of the real names are now lost.

I had told Maggie I didn't remember my life with any specificity. Not my real life. But I'm quite certain that happens to us all once we're turned, no matter the avenue that gets us there. There's most certainly a reason, though never took the time to analyse it. What did it matter? Not as though we could go back.

I knew about herbs and healing and had always continued to use that in one capacity or other so must have worked at that in life. I had no recollection of studying it except in my travels around the world that added to what I already knew. And again, what did it matter? It brought them to me, all of them--the bloods and the humans. And you know that had to be for a reason, because I never took out an advert. It was as though I was gifted the opportunity to pay back for what I hunted. To atone for existing on the wrong side of the scales. A balance struck.

And so there would be one again, a life for a life--judge, jury and executioner.

Soon as I could puzzle out how to kill the bastard.

No, we weren't like this Baby Bite here. The Christian symbols they shunned didn't work on us, we were too old. Which cut off several avenues of eradication. I imagined sunlight would fry him up, but that would be tricky for me to manoeuvre, because it would do the same to me. Right, well again, even by this time I hadn't taken the opportunity to experiment, but a vampire is a vampire is a vampire, right? Not as though I had anyone to ask.

Simple would be the best way to go. A stake through the heart wouldn't kill him, but would slow him down some if I hammered him to his bed. Anyone else and I'd have gone with straight-up decapitation without a second thought, despite the parts wouldn't die. Except I already tried that and it wasn't the right choice the first time given the outcome. Clearly. Even if I put the pieces at opposite ends of the world, he was a crafty bastard and had disciples. Nothing would prevent them from digging the parts back up and bringing him back again. It needed to be permanent. I was quick, but I suppose I would find out exactly how quick I really was. I'd need to strike fast. Before he yanked out the stake that would hopefully buy me enough time to do what needed to be done, *Maybe a crematorium…*

There were advantages to being so old, but disadvantages, as well. We were so old, Billy and me, the language that might have brought us to life, that called up the demon needed to make and unmake things like us, was long dead. Part of the life I no longer recalled. Back then? For all I knew, I might have made myself. Cursed myself in my own stupidity stumbling over a spell for immortality or some other misadventure. What I *did* know? The problem with things from back then is that they *always* come back, because they're primal, prototypical and monstrous. The only way to keep them in check is to know a counterspell. Or how to break the particular curse. Or to lock them up in specific bindings so they can't do any damage.

Except I didn't have that information. No one would.

While my memory was long, I had no recollection of any banishing spells for proto-vampires. A black magic secret society might have some bits and scraps. Or possibly some Mithraic followers of the god of light and truth, the opponent of darkness and evil, would be helpful. But they didn't crop up in Persia until too long after to have used the same language that might have created us. Too bad. That might have solved my problem.

Besides, even if by some fluke, some crazy coincidence, I happened upon the right counter *and* knew how to speak it in the correct language with the proper pronunciation out of my own mouth, I could bloody well unmake myself before I finished speaking. Then I'd never be certain I got the arsehole. Short of confirmation the curse that made him was spat back down into the pit it came from, there was no way to ensure he stayed gone and I knew it. If it even *was* a curse. Which was also only a stab in the dark.

I had to get a plan together in a hurry.

With Baby Bite still in tow, I blew through the parlour. I wanted to sit in my wing chair and contemplate my garden, but didn't feel I had time. Billy the Black Death was getting away from me again and escaping his just deserts and I couldn't rest until it was over.

"Why do you have a sundial in your garden?"

Noise interrupted my introspection. "Good lord, are you *still* talking?"

"A sundial? What's that about? Is that an old man joke or something? I don't get it. Seems kinda stupid don't you--"

"Shut your hole."

"Hey, old man, what's your problem? I was just asking a--"

"Shut it. Don't think, just do it. You'll be better off."

He was laughing, "But it's a *sun*dial, man! You're a vampire..? Seriously, that's fucked up."

I was at his throat with a snarl before the last word left his mouth. "Still amused, Baby Bite?"

"Whoa! Take it easy, man. I was just messing a--"

"Well then, me, too. Just taking the piss, yeah? Isn't this fun? I'm having a hellova time here."

"Jeez, you're crazier than Billy."

I stared him down hard with my hand on his throat. "I didn't invite you here, little man, you invited yourself. I don't owe you a bloody thing. You invade my home, babble on about moving a crowd in here, and then have the nerve to insult me? Who do you think you are?" He was shaking under my hand. "It's not a *sundial*, you ignorant bastard. It's a memorial to the ashes buried under it. That's all you need to know. Never, *never* speak to me of it again." I dropped him then and he fell to the floor in a panting heap. I hadn't even realised I was forcing him up the wall. I turned on my heel and leaned my forehead against my arms on the fireplace mantle across the room until I got myself back in control.

It still got to me, was still so very raw. Three hundred years and it was still the thing driving me to find Billy now that I had the scent of him again. The sundial had seemed the only appropriate memorial to her. She was the sun in my night, the light in my darkness. The light and shadow chasing each other around in a circle reminded me of us. It was for the light. I didn't put her in a box, because she was afraid of the dark. I put her in the garden, in the sunshine, where she could see the sun and not have to hide inside with me anymore. It seemed right at the time. It still was.

"Sorry." Baby Bite was contrite on the floor. For once, good sense prevailed and he held his place. Perhaps, he could be taught. I don't know why I even considered it, but it was already in my head. I knew he would stay. And I wouldn't return. Maybe it was only a primal need to be remembered.

I waved it away, but I couldn't turn around. Not yet.

He was quiet for a long minute while I gathered myself together. "He killed her. Billy. That's why you're so fucked-up about finding him. He killed her and you're going after him."

I spoke into my crossed arms, "I didn't say it was a woman."

"You didn't have to."

I sighed. "I thought I told you not to speak to me about it again," but I wasn't angry anymore. Mostly tired and all the steam had gone out of me.

"You only said about the sundial."

I appreciated the effort, but I hadn't had much occasion for joviality since the seventeen-hundreds. Still, he was trying to make up for being an arse and I let him have that one. "Yeah, I suppose I did, Baby Bite."

He got up and sat on the piano bench where he sat the night before. "So, what's it like?"

"Huh?"

"You've been carrying that grudge a long time, dude. Trust me, it shows. She must have been something."

The corners of my mouth turned up without meaning to, though my voice was thin and the words barely made it past my lips, "Yes, she was definitely that." I straightened and spoke to the wall. Uncomfortable in conversation at the best of times, I wasn't looking at him and talking about this.

"Cute?"

"I suppose if you prefer that in a snack food. I spent most of my time working to keep myself to myself, if you catch my drift." Why lie? It was still the truth no matter what else there was.

"You must have loved her a lot to stop yourself like that."

"Love?" I snorted disdain to cover my discomfort, "We don't *love*, Baby Bite. We're not capable. Didn't your maker teach you anything? It would be pointless, wouldn't it. To love a human being... How could that amount to anything beyond an even worse nightmare than the one we already live?"

I felt his gaze on me as he seemed to consider. "Okay, then what? Why the vendetta act?"

I stewed in it a minute before I could force myself to speak of it. "You were right. He killed her. Took her before her time. You know he was a pirate and she'd been a prisoner on his ship. She escaped when they came into port. I helped her for a time. Eventually, he caught up and made her pay for running away and I couldn't stop him." I took a breath and tightened up my resolve, allowing the harder, more bestial parts of me to remain the only parts that mattered. "Not complicated. A life for a life. This is payback."

He tinkled the piano keys in distraction, "Payback, eh?"

I turned around and grabbed up my bag again, "Yes, payback. It's an old concept, but I'm an old man, remember, so don't worry yourself over it. Now, pass me that hand mirror over there, so I can get out of here."

"A mirror? Come on, man. You're the freakiest vampire I've ever met. What are you gonna do with a mirror? Or is it only the rest of us who don't have a reflection?"

I growled. "A switchblade would be confiscated by airport security, don't you think, smartyarse? I can break the mirror at the other end and a sock roll makes a comfy handle."

"Hey, that's pretty good."

"I *have* been around a while, y'know." I took another look around the room. As I pushed the mirror into the interior of the bag, I knew a broken bit of glass wasn't going to do it, not even close. I sighed and pulled it back out again. I handed it back to Alan, "It's not enough. Blast." I rubbed my temples and then in sudden decision, yanked the drawstrings on my duffel and tied it up. "Fuck it. I'll figure something out at the other end."

"Is there anything I can do?"

I looked him hard in the eyes a long moment. "No." He'd already served his purpose, given me the impetus I needed. There was nothing more he could do and now it was my turn to pay back to keep the balance. I swallowed down my distaste. "All right, I'm off. Not certain when I'll be back exactly, but shouldn't be long." Of course, that was a lie, since I didn't expect to return at all. But he was only a kid and I didn't think he needed to worry himself over it.

I slung the bag over my shoulder and headed for the front door. "Right, so you can bring your little mates. Just don't break anything. Most of this lot is older than all of you put together. And don't forget to water my garden. I've my mobile. Ring if anything happens. It's Dr. Death. Easy to remember. Satellite phone dialling instructions are on the bureau in my room."

"Doctor? I thought you were an apothecary."

I stopped in the open doorway, "No, you eejit, my *number*. d-r-d-e-a-t-h. Spell it out on the fucking keypad."

I slammed the door on Baby Bite trying to use his brain and walked out into the night.

4

(England – Seventeen twenty-something)

The change in atmosphere at sundown woke me as it always did. Together on the cot down in the root cellar, Maggie's hand was still twined in mine.

I nearly thought it had been a dream, but the heat of her seeping through my chest told me otherwise. I let her heart get inside me and fill me up and sighed my contentment into the dark only I could see in its entirety. Maggie nestled closer in sleep. Peace surrounded her.

Fantastical to me, but I knew she believed she was safe and I suppose it allowed her to rest the way she needed. The last couple days might have been a regular occurrence in my abnormal life, but I understood it must have been stressful for her. No matter how strong she appeared, the smoke inhalation hadn't done her any good. She needed to recoup some energy if she was going to spend the rest of her time racing to keep up with me. I let her have it. I swore to myself I would do everything in my power to ensure I never broke that mysterious trust she had in me. Even if it meant fighting the greatest demon of all--myself.

At rest and when she should have appeared the most vulnerable, Maggie still exuded a strength that had nothing to do with physicality. So odd. While I couldn't be caught at it, I examined her in detail. She seemed no different from any other human I had ever encountered and yet at the same time, she was like no other. Perhaps, it was only my ability to see beyond the human spectrum that made me aware of it. There was something else, as well, something more, even while in reality there appeared nothing more at all.

Every life gives off energy and I was accustomed to seeing it, so that part didn't surprise me at all, but this was not the same thing. This was something else. It annoyed me. New things were not in the habit of crossing my path and anything outside my experience and understanding became tough to assimilate. Soulless and so long out of touch with humanity, I was unable to apply empathy to temper my curiosity so clinical curiosity was the usual outcome. This was just plain peculiar. And then made me wonder if my eyes had been in use so long they were starting to fail me. I didn't even know if that could happen.

After I couldn't hit upon the answer, annoyed, I distracted myself with the design of the new house I would build. For myself, I would have been content to stay in the cellar, but to keep up my human disguise I needed another to satisfy the neighbours. I looked back down at Maggie and my plan changed shape without my meaning to.

I caught myself and frowned. Seems it didn't take much of her to make me change my mind and I didn't understand that, either. Well, she was a bit of a bossyboots, but I think I liked it, so with contrarious self-distraction refused to expend more energy on it and went back to calculating lengths of lumber.

And left her with her peace while I kept silent, busy watch over another night.

"Where is it coming from, Richard?"

The first stack of fresh-hewn lumber appeared between one night and the next. More came at sporadic intervals between cellar rests along with other sundry items. Tonight, a brand new spindle-backed rocking chair was set out at the end of the road. Maggie took an instant shine to it and adopted it for her own--it now had a permanent home on the porch I finished building the night before.

"I've been here a long while, Maggie. You heard the legend of Twitch the Witch. It's what brought you to me. That fire showed up for miles. Everyone knows what I might have lost without asking. They may not want to speak with me in passing, but they appreciate my worth to them and don't want me to leave. They would do the same for each other. Seems it's what they do."

With my house plan sorted, I did something I hadn't had a need to in a great while and sacked some potatoes and carrots and dipped into my store of pelts to take to town during the night. I left them at the back of the mercantile as payment with a list and we woke to find a delivery left near the ashes of the old house under some tarp.

In the past, I'd gone to town more. But as time marched on and more people established themselves between my hill and the nearest town, I went less often. Now it was only once a year or so for a keg of nails or glass jars or tobacco. My reclusive behaviour fuelled the legend of the fearsome witch in the hills, of course. There were still one or two who were infants when I'd come who might recall differently, but the rest considered me the demon they feared, yet the healer they had counted on since they were born. That single trip to town would fuel chin-wagging for months, I knew. As would the list of provisions be picked apart and speculated upon many an evening more. But I didn't mind.

To be honest, it amused me to think of the speculation. From the things I requested, they'd probably assume I'd got myself a woman up there. I liked the thought of it for no reason I could explain. I had always been alone, lived alone, and here she was right in the middle of my life as though she was always in it. It gave me an odd feeling. At least, I thought it was a feeling although I couldn't quite remember the distinction.

The plan I worked out for the house was quite a bit more ambitious than the last one, but I made several adjustments to accommodate my new addition. I never needed a kitchen or larder before. Or a real bedroom. This house had a high peak roof from whose rafters I could easily dry my herbs. It took more wood, but I thought it would serve me later. I put in a loft to work from that left the rest of the house for the creature comforts and territory I thought a woman would want. I didn't ask, I just did it and Maggie appeared happy about it, so assumed it had been the right thing.

Cautious and used to planning ahead, I created myself a secondary escape route in case of emergency. Adding a hatch in the roof above my loft, it sat between timbers with the edges disguised by thatch and wouldn't be obvious to anyone who looked. You never knew when a mob armed with pitchforks would come to call.

Something new I hadn't ever considered before were windows. What did I need with them? The old house had had none, but in deference to her obvious problem with enclosed spaces, I put two in the front and one in Maggie's room, but that was all. Even still, I constructed heavy shutters to block out the light as a precaution for myself. I didn't like feeling exposed with them open and she didn't like feeling smothered when they were closed, but we might find a happy medium.

Since that confession day in the cellar, we didn't speak much, but that was mostly my doing. Honestly? I wasn't good at it. Horrid, really. Even while I did things in the course of seeing to her welfare, I didn't get close. I had this panicked feeling the wolf would escape and savage her and I didn't want that, so kept deliberate distance between us.

All that stubborn, rampant humanity was a bit much for me at the beginning, muddling up my head and leaving me in a drunken stupor from which I never wanted to wake. As we settled-in, the safety buffer of space made it easier. I still craved it, though. I can't lie. That first day had been beyond what should have ever been allowed between my kind and hers. I knew it in my head, but everything inside me wanted it back the way it was before. The new house was full of her. Steeped into every wall and floorboard, even the earth of the garden seemed to pulse with the lifeblood inside her.

In truth, I think it drove what was left of my mind not already rotted by time quite mad.

A living hell far worse than the one I already existed in, I never wanted it to end. I wanted her there forever. I wanted her life, but that wouldn't bring me what I wanted, so it became a paradox of epic proportion that had no solution and never could.

She was there and alive. I was there and dead. That was all.

So many nights I fled into the forest to disguise I went out hunting more than something for her dinner. And knew she watched me go from one of the front windows. She knew what I did every time I left.

And I didn't like it.

Her eyes on my retreating back were always hard on me. I can't say she judged me, because she never did, but I began to judge myself by the human yardstick I thought she should be using on me. It was something I'd never done before, because, quite frankly, I'm not human so need a different form of measure. I could never meet her eyes whenever I returned, though. Couldn't. It always felt wrong and the guilt ate me up. It didn't take long for it to affect me in a way nothing ever had before.

Until I stopped hunting altogether.

Nothing. Not a drop. I don't understand what compelled me. I suppose I wanted to please her, but to do that I had to become something I could never be. At least, I believed so in my own madness.

I held out for a very long while refusing my own nature. I made myself stay away from the house the longer it went on and the barn became my world. Always busying myself with building something. Always some pretext that occupied me until it was daybreak again. As the weeks wore on, I stopped venturing into the house while Maggie slept and took to the root cellar again where I wouldn't be tempted by her near me. That wolf was always so ravenous and she was such a tender lamb. I managed to avoid much contact with her for four entire months until she came looking for me.

"Richard? *Richard…*"

It was evening and I was awake, but I couldn't go out. Not any longer. I hadn't been in the house for even a moment in several days. It had been easy to disguise for quite a long while, but in that week, it finally caught up with a vengeance and my body was breaking down. Hard. Four months without blood and I was close to a hibernating bear, lethargic and wanting nothing more than to loll about in my den until spring. I didn't even have the energy to stand.

The sad part of it was I knew it wouldn't kill me. I'd simply slip away to the Land of Nod, lying still and cold until a particle of blood happened my way. Some droplet on the end of an animal whisker brushing by me. A spider grazing me with the scent of its dinner trailing behind. It would wake me again and I would catch the first thing that came to hand--a beetle, a mouse, a fly--and be reborn. I wasn't even concerned. It had happened before during some of those garlic necktie interludes, buried in a nice warm place beneath the earth. I have to say, during those times it happened not by my doing I almost found it restful. This wasn't. This was with purpose, twisted as it was with no fruitful outcome to be had.

Maggie pulled up the trapdoor in the barn with a grunt and shined a lantern down looking for me, "Richard? *There* you are. Didn't you hear me calling? I've been looking for you everywhere. What are you doing down there?"

The lantern was blinding, "Ugh," I threw an arm up too late to keep it from dazzling my eyes. "Maggie... light..." The supernova moved away from the square of the opening. She rested it on the floor behind her, setting her in quivering, yellow backlight.

She was the most beautiful thing I'd ever seen. An angel hovering above to my demon lurking below. And she was far too close.

I'd been right that first night when I told her she smelled like a dream. All those things I had worked to avoid she delivered right to the wolf's den. And worse, was in the process of climbing down the ladder bringing them closer.

"No, Maggie," I flopped over on the cot, but there was no stopping her.

"You can't stay in here like this. It's not good for you. You need fresh air," she hopped down the last rung with a warm, fall cloak billowing out around her. I had an odd vision of an angel descending the ladder into hell and shook it away, angry with myself.

"You shouldn't be here." I rolled away and curled up against the wall, so she couldn't see me. "Go. Please." The smell of the blood inside her filled up the small space and her heartbeat resonated against my back from where she stood by the ladder in indecision. Her breath in my ears was deafening and I knew something bad would happen if she didn't get out. "*Fast*, Maggie-girl." I didn't have the energy or the willpower to argue with her. "Clear off!" Breathing hard, I urged her out as much as I urged her closer so I could get my hands on her.

It was madness. How did I get myself into this situation?

There hadn't been a single instance when she ever listened to anything I told her, so I don't know why I believed she would then. Before I knew it, she was right behind me commanding me to face her. Demanding.

"What's wrong with you, Richard? Look at me. Why are you doing this to yourself?"

"Go, girl."

"No, I will *not*. Stuff your stupid pride or whatever the hell this is that's making you act this way. I won't leave you down here like this. It's not right. Why are you keeping yourself in here every night? Why won't you come out anymore? You said you would protect me and you've left me alone out there and I don't even know why. You owe me an explanation if nothing else. Won't you even look at me? What are you hiding from? *Look at me.*"

There wasn't much she would see with the lantern left up top on the barn floor, but a little light broke the dead black. In the shadow of the earthen wall where I huddled there was nothing to see. I wasn't alive anyway and in the condition I was in there wouldn't have been much left to look at even if I had been. It would scare the hell out of her and even in that moment, I couldn't bring myself to do that.

It was hard to speak and the words came out in whispers against her grit, "Please, step back."

"Why?"

"Maggie, won't you listen… just this once?" It was a good cellar, dry and tight, but it was getting on in the year and frost had already made an appearance several weeks before. With chilled air swirling down into the space through the open trapdoor, her every breath and word was an icy plume that hung suspended over me in time. I wanted to inhale them all and take them inside me so I could live.

Maggie stepped back for no reason at all and I thought she was going to listen to me for once, but I should have known better. I found out why when she lit the tallow candle so her curiosity could be satisfied. So she could see what she wanted to see and what I never had any intention of ever showing anyone, least of all her.

The light from the tiny flame lit up the withered rack of my back and Maggie gasped, "What have you done to yourself?"

I growled, "Put it out."

"You'd better tell me what's going on. Tell me *now*."

"Leave, Maggie. Before it's too late."

"And what's that supposed to mean?"

It was a very long moment while I fought the wolf, so I could speak. I never lied to her before and couldn't start then, "Before I kill you. Go, girl. Before I tear your throat out."

"*No.*"

The snarl was inhuman and involuntary. It squeezed out of my own frustration as I spun and looked her head-on and somehow made myself hold my place. The candle wavered in her hand, but damned if the girl didn't stand there and face me.

Doubtful I even looked like the same person anymore and the thin veneer of humanity that hid me was long gone. I saw the reflection in her eyes against the candlelight and knew I was the monster that had hidden inside. It was alive and snarling in all its darkened glory. I wanted blood, any blood, *her* blood, and watched her take a step back while I judged the distance and the effort it would take with my lifetimes of practice. I was weak, but it wouldn't take me much. I only needed one and she was right in front of me.

All I could hear was heartbeat and all I could think was how good it would feel and I was already drunk on it without a taste, sailing away to that place I love right before the clench. It was too easy. She wasn't even trying to run.

Her eyes were wide as she beheld the real me for the first time and her ragged breath only urged me on. Her heartbeat was everywhere and everything, the cadence of the life I craved. A siren song, the song of the living that the undead can no longer sing, but that captures every moment of our waking attention. I wanted it, needed it.

No question I would steal it from her.

The expression on her face changed then, "Oh, Richard..," and she raised the candle higher. Not to defend herself with the flame when she might have burned me with it and in my weakened state bought herself the moment of my surprise to flee up the ladder and lock me in. No, my Maggie-girl never thought to hurt me to save herself. She brought the candle up to examine me in concern. Her brow furrowed and she grew quite sad, "Poor Richard, what have you done?" She was only whispering, but the words seemed very loud in that tiny, dark room.

The beast couldn't understand her and yet, somehow, it got to me and I paused right at the moment I would strike. I'll never know why, but it allowed me to keep my promise and fight the demon for her a little longer.

Maggie took a step closer again, the breath puffing out of her to hang between us. A ghost of life floating in the centre of a surreal and evil drama of the damned and soon-to-be-damned. A tentative hand drifted out through the ghost and touched the frost of my cheek and she grew even more concerned. *She* grew concerned for *me*, for the beast that wanted to take her life. It was an even bigger paradox than my own. I snarled in frustration and confusion and she stepped even closer.

"No!" I growled at her to make her leave, but she wouldn't have it. The room was suddenly freezing and I was colder, but there was sweat on my brow. The little bird that used to answer my wolf snarl was not making an appearance that evening.

"You don't frighten me, Richard. You never have," her voice was strong and sure and she let the warmth of her hand seep into my skin.

I couldn't hear her and felt truly mad in that moment. Felt stepped out of reality, because there was no way, earthly or otherwise, I could have kept myself off her in that starved condition. Somehow, she was still there in one piece and untouched with her very live hand against my face.

"Richard, look at me." She was using that tone again, the one she used when she was being in charge and making me do what she wanted and that I could somehow never ignore. I didn't want to hear her, but she wouldn't leave it. "*See* me. See me here with you and know I'm not afraid of you. You said you would protect me and you are. Right in this moment you are, no matter what you might believe. You've shown me what you are and I'm telling you I'm not afraid."

I barked a laugh without mirth, "...s-s-should b-be..." I was shivering and it wasn't with cold.

"I know you would never hurt me."

"...want t-t-to..."

"No, you don't. You'd have already done it. I wouldn't have even seen you move."

"...s-step back-ck..."

"*Listen* to me. It's not in you to do me harm. I know what's in you better than you ever could. You're not capable. Just because something compels you, doesn't mean you would ever let yourself. *Look at you*. Still thinking of me, warning me off. I'm telling you it's not in you. Trust me and trust yourself as I do. Please, come out of here."

I knew what I had to do. "Yesss..," I stopped shivering and knew I didn't have long. The stillness was almost upon me.

"You'll come out and stop this nonsense then?"

"Step back... let... me out," it was so difficult to make words.

An odd quiet settled over her and she didn't get out of the way. She stared hard into my gaunt features in the candle flicker, considering. "You're going to run away, aren't you?" She tried to catch my gaze to see the truth, but I wouldn't look at her. "If you come out of this hole you're going to run away and not come back."

"Maggie--"

"Don't lie to me, Richard. Not now. Besides, I see it, feel it in you. Don't waste your breath," she moved her hand to my mouth without a pause the way she had that first day we were in the cellar. Right to the very instrument that would consume her. I almost cried. "You can't run away from it. You think you're running away to keep me safe and don't think I don't understand what a noble act that might be, but Richard... You can't run away from what you are. This may be what you are, but not *who* you are. If you run away now, it doesn't matter. Don't you see? This thing will follow you wherever you go. It can't be separated out of the man right now, because it *is* the man. But it doesn't define him. Are you listening to me?"

"I--" I couldn't speak with her hand on me anymore and shook my head in futility. The smell of her life was all over me, the beat of her heart thrumming up against me and inside me and all I could do was shake my head. I was too weak for anything more and fell over from where I crouched.

"Richard!"

I didn't feel well at all. I was very tired.

And then I started to laugh there on the floor and I'm pretty certain it was all inside my head.

That feeling. That sleepy, not-quite-in-the-body feeling I worked so hard against myself to reach. Finally. I was going away to the Land of Nod. Maggie would be safe now and I was relieved in my success that kept her from the wolf. I hoped it made up for the day I dunked her in the rain barrel. With any luck, a decade or two would pass. Or if the universe rewarded me for my good deed, it would be a century before the bloody kiss I craved woke me again and she would be long gone, having lived a life in safety. I hoped it was a century, because I would always hear her while she lived and didn't know if I could be strong enough to stay away.

The dirt floor was soft and I didn't mind. It wasn't the best place I'd ever checked-out, but it wasn't the worst. At least, there was no garlic. Half-disconnected, it took me a while to understand Maggie was beside me on the floor tugging at me, working to get my attention.

"Richard... *Richard*. Damn you, answer me."

"...already damned..."

"Knock off that tripe and tell me what you need. What can I do?"

Funny how warm it was in the Land of Nod, something I didn't have the pleasure of experiencing walking about out in the world. It was lovely and warm and a vacation from the reality of the hell I lived. I didn't mind being in it for as long as it would last. I hoped the next bloody spider kiss wouldn't come for a very long while this time. I was in no hurry. I had eternity to battle the demon wolf and I wanted to be warm and dream of my Maggie-girl in a way I could enjoy without guilt.

There was no analysing it, I didn't need to. It was what I wanted and this was the only place I could get it. Because I was a monster who would seek to destroy her during every moment I existed in the same place at the same time. I would wait for another day until she was no more and keep her in memory. It was safer for her. She said what I was couldn't be separated from the man, because it was the man. She was right. I'd always known.

"You'd better stay here with me until this is sorted. This cannot be all," Maggie was muttering to herself and rolled me over from where I fell. Starved the way I was, she didn't have a difficult time moving me. There wasn't much to move. Without finesse, she flopped me over onto my back and I felt her over top of me. Then she grew angry and yelled at the wrinkled, old demon I had become, "Damn your stubbornness. Don't you leave me now when I've only just found you. Don't you *dare*. I didn't know, I tell you. Not *this*. Please, stay," she dropped her head down and pressed her face against my chest, muffling her words. I heard her begin to cry, "I need you... and it's almost winter... don't leave me alone in the dark..."

I heard the words, but was already too far away to answer. If I had had a heart, though, she'd have torn it out with that. I knew how she hated the dark. At least, she had windows in the new house I built her, so she wouldn't feel smothered any longer. I was glad I put them in.

It was dark where I was, too, but I loved the darkness, so wasn't afraid. Relief allowed me to relax. This needed to happen. Because the only other thing I truly wanted was to make her and have her be in it with me and she would have been terrified for an eternity forced to live in the night like the animal I was. It was only logical. This was better.

It was the right thing.

*****

I've no idea what happened then, because the Land of Nod is very far away from the root cellar. I don't know how long it was before I could think again. Time has no meaning there. My first thought was Maggie and if she was still alive. I wondered how much time had passed.

I wasn't in the root cellar anymore. I feel the electrical tension of the earth as a living thing so knew I was buried in it, but not as far down as the cellar. I'd been moved. I wondered if Maggie did it. The earth was all around me. No wooden box, just the smell of the world under the world where the living walked and dwelt. It had always been my place--in the darkness, in the decomposing ground, rotting right along with the vegetation and snuggled up with death.

I felt warmth and the beat of my dead heart in rhythm with whatever small life had happened by for me to steal. I felt alive. An eternity passed while I revelled in drunken wonder at the almost-life that mimicked the life of my little, stolen pearl. It was always glorious, that rebirth. I never wanted it to end.

Curious, though.

I couldn't remember it ever feeling like this before. No stray droplet on a whisker was responsible. I knew the difference. Nothing but a kill felt even close. It must have been something larger, a dead wolf, or even a felled deer. It had to be big, struck and fallen somewhere close by or hoisted up into a tree to finish off with a killing cut to bleed before butchering. I stewed in it, my brains steeping with the electricity of a life in sacrifice. The familiar rhythm of it carried me away. That song. I wanted to sing and could almost remember the words.

It got down inside me and spread out through every cursed molecule I possessed.

I wasn't packed in tight and when I moved my hands soon discovered I was laid in a grave of stone. Shallow, I hoped. A burial like that took time and forethought and care to construct and knew then it must have been Maggie's doing. No one else would have taken the time. Anyone else in the county would have thrown a lit match on me like as not.

Poor Maggie. I hated leaving her, but it was better this way. I saved her from the wolf. There was even a certain symmetry in the grave of stones she'd made to keep the wolves from digging *me* up. I wished I could have told her I wasn't dying. I don't think she ever quite understood there wasn't much that could cause that for me. I hoped she hadn't been too afraid alone in the winter dark, but I'd left her the house with the windows and her spindle-backed rocker and everything else of mine at her disposal to keep herself safe. She had lots of food, I'd seen to that with several additional deliveries from the mercantile and months of hunting and preserving.

I could almost admit there in the dark that I planned it from the first. It had been an unnatural association from the first day. It shouldn't have been allowed to go on even as long as it had, but I'd had to see to her welfare first. Perhaps, not a conscious decision, but in the end, appropriate.

There was enough room over my face to squint my eyes open and make the coins slide off. I saw the flat headstone in luminescent relief the way I saw all things in the cold black. Laid with an even gentler hand than the others, it perched on stones set by my ears, so it wouldn't rest against my face. A lump came up in my throat to think of her worrying over that. And worse for knowing how she must have had to force her hands to put it there and walk away. It wasn't a good feeling.

The more aware I became, the more all the things she did after I drifted off registered. My jaw was tied shut with one of her own kerchiefs and I fancied the scent of her still lingered on it. Dried flower petals and lavender and lemon balm was under my hands. My clothes were gone. When I moved around some in the confines of my stone prison, I felt the shroud she wrapped me in and knew she had even gone to the trouble to wash me down in scented water. It was almost more than I could take.

All that time I kept myself away from her and in the end? To have left her with a monster she still put her hands on with so much care and concern was more than any wound she might have thought to inflict upon me. I loathed myself more with every moment and turned my thoughts away before I could think about any tears she might have shed while she did it. I was truly every bit the monster I knew for having put her through all that. I hoped centuries passed, so I wouldn't be forced to face her children's children and have to confess.

My face was wet and prayed rainwater dripped off the headstone over me. If I was crying, I didn't want to know about it.

I breathed in more life until I felt powerful. Let it come over me hard, so I would stop thinking and feeling. So it wouldn't hurt. Rebirth, any rebirth, always brings us so much closer to the very first and so, if only for an instant, we become so much more human again. And I didn't want to be that way anymore if I had to feel shitty about it. That copper-scented tonic washed away all my weakness and made me whole again and I took it for the little I knew it would last, because it's what I craved. What I always craved. What I always would crave.

My heart beat stronger by the second and I grew drunker on that wine of stolen life. The copper tonic was heaven to my hell. Could taste it on my lips and knew it wasn't rainwater dripping off the headstone. Blood seeped through the earth and down into my narrow prison. I couldn't get enough and lapped it up the way I loved and the way that I needed to survive. It was warm and alive and thrumming with something I could never achieve on my own. Life coursed through me and my heart beat steady and hard while my head sang the song of the living. Sang with life.

Human life.

And then knew why it was so familiar.

The cursed demon I was snarled down there in the earth while

Maggie's blood continued to seep through the ground to feed me until I was whole. The stones had settled, but as I struggled they loosened around me. Our hearts in cadence was the most beautiful song I'd ever known, but while mine was strong and powerful, hers was thready and weakening. It urged me in frantic escape. Blood continued to trickle down no matter how I turned my head. I didn't want it anymore. Not this one. I spat it out, but it continued to dribble across my lips and run down my chin.

Maggie was up there, right on top of me. And she was dying.

More thrashing and I broke through the cairn pile she built and in a fit of rage exploded out of my prison of death. Stone tumbled every which way as I reached for the night air. Maggie moaned near my head, sprawled by the marker she still clutched with one hand from where she tried to catch herself as she fell.

"Maggie-girl," I shook my feet loose and threw myself at her in trepidation. The moon was high, lighting up the scene in garish relief. Spattered blood, *Maggie's* blood, was everywhere, staining the marker and the stones and seeping out of her into the ground at an alarming rate. The smell of it was everywhere. The taste of it on my lips and the feel of her inside me was exquisite, brilliant agony.

I spotted the wound on her upper arm and stemmed it with the first thing that came to hand--her kerchief from off my jaw. I cinched it tight. It looked bad, deep and into the meat, but I had to stop the lifeblood leaking out of her first or no further examination would matter. There was already a mahogany puddle under her reflecting moonshine. Other wounds, various punctures, cuts, and scrapes I tallied could never be responsible for that quantity and I had to find the source. Then I saw the killing cut--a clean and surgical slice in the side of her neck matching the one on her arm.

That came from the blade of an axe.

In a frenzy, I tore at the shrouding around me and wadded it up against the wound hard while I swivelled my head around in frantic search.

All that had saved her was that she'd not turned her head. The artery was struck, but she fell in an awkward heap with her head pressed against her shoulder buying her precious time. I could tell to the beat how long she had. Could tell to the moment and I urged her beyond it and through to the next while I thought. If she moved, if the night was colder and she shivered, the tentative wet seal holding the edges of the gash would break and it would be over in a few beats of her heart. I couldn't move her to help her but I needed to stop it. I didn't even know if I could.

Desperate, I resorted to using her own blood to mix a mud poultice as a temporary seal over the wound and tied more shrouding around her throat to slow the flow. It was tight enough to choke her, but she was far away from knowing and gave me enough time to whisk her into the house.

The sinister evidence of the death chase was too noticeable to ignore. Broken glass jars she must have flung in self-defence littered the ground. Crockery and cut wood were strewn everywhere. One of the front windows was smashed from the outside-in while her spindle-backed rocker lay discarded half off the porch. It didn't take much brain power to see the drama. Or the blood. It was all over. In sprays and droplets, smears and bloody fingerprints from everything she put her hands to as she ran from one place of apparent safety to another. Then I saw the axe a ways down the path to the road. Hurled into the ground, the handle pointed up to the sky that lit up one bloody hand print, evidence of the one who wielded it.

The red print was large and male.

I wanted to kill the whole, entire world in retribution. I would have settled for the would-be assassin had Maggie not been dying in my arms. I would have found him. I could run like the wolf I was and I would have caught him and made him pay a thousand times over until he begged me to let him die. Instead, I took her inside the little house I built for her and hoped she would live through the night.

It must have been him. *Him.* The one she never told me of, but who terrified her enough to brave my questionable company. It appeared he overcame his fear of me. Likely, after having made a silent visit at some point and discovered my burial.

Everything I had ever learned about wounds became important that night while I coaxed her blood into staying with her and her heart to keep its beat. The next night, too. Somewhere in there it crossed my mind I could make it all go away for her. It would be so easy. There would be no suffering, nothing like she already endured. I had never done it myself, couldn't bring myself to do it even on the day of the fire when she seemed to be asking for it. But this wasn't the same circumstance and so it was in my head.

If my few past peers were correct, draining her to the point of the death she was already so close to and then feeding her my own dead blood would make her mine for eternity. Alone, I could admit I craved it, but I beat back that particular demon with renewed purpose. Maggie's words rang through my head, that I would always protect her from myself no matter I might be compelled otherwise. She was more right than she knew. Determined to provide proof, she would wake to learn her faith had not been misplaced. She believed I wasn't capable of doing her harm and her belief alone gave me the strength. I had saved her once before only so I could kill her myself.

This time, I saved her so she could live.

It was a long week before I allowed her to wake for even a moment. Already feeble, it didn't take much to coax her body to stay in slumber. It would serve her better. The few stitches I braved in her neck needed time to knit or the bleeding would start all over again and she couldn't afford to lose any more blood. I hadn't been keen on sewing her up like a garment, but I had to do something. Muscle was cut along with the artery and she'd have a spectacular scar if she survived. I couldn't vouch for her ever being able to turn her head again, though. Every poultice I knew, every herb, healing balm and wound bath were employed to help her. Her arm fared better even deep as that one was, with the stitching taking with greater speed. The rest of her smaller injuries were healing on their own. I fed her strong broth and trickled blood-strengthening tonics into her mouth.

Once the crisis passed, on examination, it was easy to see how she'd thrown up her arm to protect her head from the axe as it swung for her. Her upper arm had taken the brunt of the force. The blade had been sharp and cut deep in a diagonal line up close to the shoulder where the same line continued under her ear. I shuddered to think what might have happened if she hadn't put her arm in the way.

The axe-wielder had been weak, though. Another reason she still breathed. The honed edge of the blade made it a devilish weapon, slicing through tissue with little effort, but without some power, the bone would stop it as it had. She might have lost her arm. As it was, it would always be stiff, but as days passed, I believed she would do more than only survive.

*****

(Caribbean - Present)

It was dark when I reached for my mobile to make it stop buzzing around on vibrate. The satellite hotspot I stuck on the wall outside the window didn't disappoint. I despised such things, but the old days were long gone and they were now a necessary evil.

The hotel room had a bed, but there was that problematic window in the main room. I dragged the pillow and a blanket into the tub and slept there where the bright, Caribbean daylight wouldn't reach behind the closed door. Seemed a waste of time when I might have put the hours to use in search, but I allowed myself time to get my bearings and clear my head. After this, I would devote the whole of myself for however long it took to catch up to him. I wouldn't be satisfied until Billy was looking me in the eye up close and personal.

And I let myself tear him apart.

I fished around for the satphone still jiggling against the floor next to me without looking and clamped a hand on it. The lit screen displayed my home number. I groaned.

"What happened?"

"Uh, nothing. You um… Hello? Jeez, you even answer the phone weird. How did you know it was me?"

"Who the fuck else would call me from my own bloody line, arsewipe." I sighed, "Caller ID? Ever hear of it? It's a modern invention, but I find it handy."

"Sure-sure. Well, that makes sense." Baby Bite stopped talking. I heard noise in the background.

"What the hell is going on in my house? How many people have you got in there?"

"Oh, just a few. Chillax, man. I told them you were all scary and evil and would probably rip their heads off if they messed it up. Don't stress. I'm keepin' em in line."

"Scary and evil, eh? Didn't work on you, Baby Bite."

He laughed, "Well, I'm just that kinda guy."

I took a strengthening breath. "So?"

"So, what?"

He really was an irritant. "The reason? Why are you ringing me already? I just bloody got here. How much could you have destroyed in three days?"

"We didn't destroy anything. I know that's an old man thing or something, but quit wigging-out already. Jeez, I just wanted tell you--"

"Tell me *what*?"

"I was gonna tell you before you left, but didn't get a chance. You just ran out the door, y'know--"

"Yes-yes--"

"The hurricanes. I didn't get to tell you about the hurricanes."

"Oh for--" I suddenly regretted my quick exit and snap decision to tell him about the sat phone. How was I supposed to focus with this nonsense able to reach me at a distance? "I know about the hurricanes, Baby Bite. All of them. *And* the tropical storms. *And* the earthquakes. *And* the wars. *And* whatever else is going on. I hear the news, mate. The whole bloody world knows about them. *And* I'll be going now--"

"*Listen.* That's why we left. We left Billy like I told you, but stayed down there a while. Until we heard about the others."

"Eh? What others?" I closed my eyes and willed him to make his point, so I could get on with my life.

"There was nothing left down there after the bad hurricanes, okay? Nada. Everyone's good hiding places on all the islands were gone. Destroyed. We were booking it from place to place. Hiding in fucking holes and shit. We didn't have anywhere to go, anyway, so we followed them."

I growled, "Them *who*?"

"*Us.* Vampires. All of us are moving north. From everywhere. You don't know? Been going on for a while now. It's like a... whaddayacallit? Migration or something."

"What the bloody hell are you babbling about? Migration... That's the most ridiculous thing I've ever heard. Stupid git. Call me for that--"

"*Wait.*" He sounded serious, so I took a breath and let him talk. "This might help you, okay? Everyone left. As far as I heard and from what everyone else here is saying, they *all* left. At least, as far as the Caribbean. Creatures of the night from the south are moving north is the 411. Vamps from Europe are moving overseas, too, but not quite as many. Guess they still have places to crash. Bunch from Asia."

I looked up through the dark and watched the vapoury evidence of the living energy of the other hotel guests around me undulate misty courses against the ceiling. "Where did you get this information?"

"Asked everyone here. They all say the same. I kid you not, old dude.

84

Canada is the new home away from home for displaced vampires everywhere."

I had to think about that a minute. We've been hunted a long while, pushed into darkened corners of the earth now being uncovered too quickly for the way we need to live. Upheaval, war, and violent weather would destroy long-term retreats and there had been a hell of lot of all that in recent years. I could see it.

Most of Canada is still unpopulated and has more night than anywhere except Russia, I suppose. We don't feel cold. What the hell do blood runners care? I could see the attraction. I came for the same reason, the anonymity and places to disappear into and it served me well for a couple centuries already. It was quite easy to hide. There was so much space back when I'd come and there still was. Almost no one had ever seen me and I liked it that way.

"All right, Baby Bite." *Damn.* "So, what is it you're meaning to say exactly then? That I could have avoided this lovely little excursion?"

"Correct-o-rama. Basically. Homeboys say no one's left. And Billy probably left, too. Nobody's seen him. Good bet he followed the rest of us."

"Can anyone confirm this? About Billy."

"Couldn't say, but chances are good."

I ground my teeth in irritation, "You couldn't have mentioned this *before* I boarded a bloody plane? I detest flying, you know." Twit, a total moron.

"Hey, just tryna do you a favour here. Take a chill pill, old man."

"All right, all right. Fine… Nobody can verify he left?"

"So far."

Being denied didn't make me happy. "I'll do some investigation myself. To be certain. And then I suppose I'll be back." It pained me to think about going back at all never mind without achieving satisfaction, but what else could I do?

"Copy that." Something crashed in the background.

"What the fuck was that?"

"Hey, well, it was good talking to you again."

"Baby Bite--"

Someone was banging the hell out of my piano like Jerry Lee Lewis, "Glad I got a hold of you--"

"What the bloody hell is going on in my house--"

"Wasn't sure that Dr. Death thing was gonna work. Thought you were yankin' my chain--"

"Any one of your little cohorts lights that concert grand on fire and I'll take it out of their hides--"

"Hah! Good one. Naw, they wouldn't do that. It's cool, old man. No worries. Seriously. See you when you get back." He was talking way too fast.

"Baby Bite. Dammit *Alan*--"

"Gotta motor. Audi!" the connection cut out in my ear before I could protest further. I hoped the house was still standing when I returned.

"*Buggery bollocks!*" I tossed the satphone back on the floor in irritation. "Obnoxious little prat." It took me a moment to shake off the thought of anyone touching my things. It sounded as though an army was in my house and Baby Bite was fast becoming the bane of my existence. My perspective had been a bit skewed when I left, I suppose, since I had zero intention of making it a round trip. Forced to return, now I would have to deal with him and whatever else had dragged itself over my threshold along with him. I scrubbed a tired hand over my face, "Gods give me strength…"

I sat up in the bathtub in the dark for a time and focussed, working to verify if what he said was true. I felt around for everything that had life, felt the earth, and hoped for a clue. Baby Bite was right about one thing, there wasn't much life left. It was easy to sense. Even the earth felt different, filled with death. Wouldn't be much to hunt even this many years after the first big storms. I had a fair notion Billy the Black Death would have left looking for greener pastures. He wasn't one to go long without a good meal.

Captain William Blackthorn had earned his title by stealth after he stole his first ship and ate the poor bugger who'd been her captain. And his reputation with a voracious appetite that earned him his nickname.

A sudden and mysterious rash of unexplained deaths and kidnappings struck every port his ship had come to call. The deaths for his celebratory feasts of his most recent conquests and the kidnappings as provisions for the next leg of his journeys. There had been pirates better with a sword, more profitable in their expeditions, but none more feared than Billy the Black Death.

Women had always been his favourite. He would stoop to feeding on a misbehaving member of his crew when the need arose, but Billy liked them sweet. He'd had a flunky named Günter who gathered new crew members for him when others ran off in terror and who organised hunting parties to steal the girls away. After a trip to port, they stashed them in a locked box in the cargo hold for whenever the need came upon him.

And it was in that place that Maggie had grown afraid of the dark.

Night had fallen and it was time to go out to do some hunting of my own. I would suss out if Billy was still down south and if not, I would hunt him down. Billy might be a maleficent, poisonous cock, but I was a wolf.

I would find him.

5A

(England – Seventeen twenty-something)

"Captain William Blackthorn at your service, *Mademoiselle*." He swept the wide-brimmed plume from his head with a grand gesture and bowed low from the waist, "*Très enchanté*."

"Oh, my," the young woman tittered with her fingertips and her attention held by the master of the largest three-masted square-rigger at berth, the Pandora.

An impressive vessel on par with the navy frigate man o' wars patrolling for pirates, the ship was a substantial acquisition for any pirate captain. Two decks, twenty pieces of cannon, twice the cargo space of the pirates' favoured sloops and holding a crew of two hundred, it was much more than a trophy. Fast and practical, it gave them a fighting chance against the navy frigates hunting them out in open water. With the attraction of being sturdy enough to cross and recross the Atlantic or range east all the way to Australia at the captain's whim, it allowed them access to the whole, wide world. And limitless opportunities for plunder.

The scaled-down, less elaborate twin of a mammoth Spanish galleon, for Billy, it was all about the status--the dazzle of the first impression and the expense needed for its upkeep that alluded to his vast wealth. He now fancied himself a wealthy and well-bred merchant mariner and that's how he preferred to portray himself. Pandora was his card of introduction. Like every other true seaman, he spent the bulk of his infinite life on the water and couldn't help he loved her above all. He'd had other vessels over the years, but this one was his lady.

He looked up then from under his eyebrows and skewered the young woman on lightning wit learned through centuries of practice enticing the fairer sex. "If I may be indiscreet, *mademoiselle*," he glanced left and right over the back of her hand and whispered for her ears alone. "Of all the fair ladies in all the ports I've ever had occasion to call, none could have had me in fetters for only the line of their dress yet, *maintenant*? Here am I, *chéri*, not only your prisoner, but your servant," he let his lips graze her skin and then stepped back to a more socially acceptable distance.

The woman's hand was at her mouth in coy, but her eyes sparkled and Billy knew his work was already done. He would see her again after they put out.

In the box in his hold.

The smile reached his eyes, because it was real. But it was far from warm and something she could no longer recognise under the spell of his whispered beguile.

They chatted about nothing while he gave the appearance of wetting his lips with expensive claret and then drifted away from the small cocktail ball sooner rather than later. The chase over too soon and the momentary thrill gone, he already craved the next.

The night was wild though warm. The harbour was in chop and white froth and the seas would be worse until the storm passed. A day or two at most. Just enough time to reprovision and be on their way. Some of the crew had run off as they always did whenever they put in somewhere, but they'd already been replaced.

Billy smiled into the night, "Fresh meat," and laughed down deep in his throat in animal appetite.

The hotel balcony opened onto an unobstructed view of the approaching storm and Billy stood in it head into the wind, eyes closed in savour.

"Come glorious madness. *Venez mon frère*, come my only brother and let us make merry havoc together as we have for so long." His laughter was hearty and carried far on the wings of the storm, wafting inland, the shadow of a darker angel who had come to call.

The texture of the air changed then. Someone was on the way to disturb him. Pathetic, all of them. Even Günter stumped about in human blunder, but at least he knew enough not to disturb the master's introspection. He almost missed the little toad, now that he thought about him.

If he did his job right the last time, there would have been no need to be without him again. There were always some unavoidable errands that needed attention during daylight and Günter away was limiting no matter his dubious gifts.

And he hated being inconvenienced.

It was all that bitch's fault. She was an unholy demon in her own right. The beguile talk had never worked on her, not from the first moment, and something he'd never known to happen. A mystery that only encouraged him more. The chase had gone on a great while and it had been glorious. And then later frustrating when he couldn't get what he wanted. Angry and smarting from her rejection, he had her abducted and thrown into the hold with the other women. But she wasn't like them.

"*Garce*. Not like them at all, were you? *Cunt...*"

There, she continued to resist him. Caused trouble, stirred up her fellow captives and wound up the men. Through the months as they sailed their usual route, she grew so vexing, even scheming and calculating her conquest no longer amused him. Just clear of the Bahamas and nosing into the Atlantic on their way out of Montego Bay back to Europe, he threw her to the crew to use. It should have burned the spunk right out of her, but it hadn't, haughty, little twat that she was. And isolating her in her own box alone in the dark only changed her attitude in that she became withdrawn. It was obvious afterward she withdrew to contemplate the plan of her later escape.

Billy ground his teeth. The smallest thought of her drove him mad. He still didn't quite know how she accomplished it, but he would never forget. Five months later at the next port they put into where they stayed longer than buying supplies, as dawn pulled up out of the horizon and he was secured in a hotel room for the daylight hours, his beloved Pandora was set afire. And Maggie ran. She was a hellcat and a liability and he hoped Günter had had his head out of his arse this time and got the job done. The last time would have been poetic justice, but Günter, bloody simpleton that he was, didn't even have the presence of mind to wait and confirm she died in that fucking house fire.

That first night while the ship burned, Billy went after her himself. There were dark dealings and blood work and piracy and all manner of wickedness going on under his charge--he wouldn't chance word reaching the British navy. While no one would believe the stories of the captain's appetites, they would be quite interested in the ill-gained profits on board. Not to mention more than half the crew were wanted men, the kind who fit right in with his line of thinking. None of them was keen to have their descriptions or location spread about. Adding piracy to their crimes only ensured they would all swing. He could have sent a party out after her, but she had *burned his ship*. It was personal.

It took him two days to work out her direction and catch her up. She must have asked for help or information, cried and wheedled her way onto the back of a carriage, to get so far. He knew her. She was intelligent and resourceful. Capable enough to escape and he gave her credit for it, but he had to kill her. An eye for an eye. She hurt his lady, his Pandora, and so she would pay and that was all. Truth be told, her stubborn resistance still galled him. He could have taken her, but to break her and make her want, *ask*, to stand by his side in darkness would have been bliss.

At least, until he grew bored with her and looked to something new.

The girl travelled in daylight and knew she was safe. She never knew what he was, never understood, but with him long enough to learn his habits. A stranger, filthy and penniless, whoever she spoke with turned her away or directed her to the only one who might bother with her without silver or something to trade--the reclusive witch in the hills. Hard on her heels, Billy almost had her, too. So close.

The human presence in errand drifted into his introspection and distracted him.

"*Qu'est-ce qu'il y a?*" he spat over his shoulder at the man who waited by the balcony curtains.

"Captain?"

"What the hell is the *matter?* Yes, I know you're there. Five entire minutes I've known you were on the way. Out with it! Can you not see I'm occupied out here?" Billy gave him his back and leaned on his hands on the balcony rail looking out in the night. Bloody human beings and their ridiculous ways. Why couldn't everyone be a vampire and understand his needs?

"Boatswain's Mate with a message from the Quartermaster, sir." As apprentice to the Boatswain, the officer in charge of the deck crew and maintenance of the all-important sails and rigging among other things, lost among their large crew, he'd never had a direct conversation with their infamous captain. He didn't relish one now, but there were few the Quartermaster considered brave enough to face a direct address. He should have taken it as a compliment only it didn't feel that way at the moment. "Mr. Norris says to tell you that woman is aboard, sir. The one from earlier?"

"Fine-fine. Thank you for the update although I'm quite certain I would have deduced it upon my return. But thank you for disturbing me, nonetheless."

"Apologies, sir, but I thought--"

"*Oui*? Well, there was the first of your mistakes then."

"But--"

"Get out. And don't ever speak to me again."

"But, Captain, you said--"

"*Arrêtes*! And get *out*. Or are you hard of hearing, as well?"

"Aye-aye, Cap'n."

"I shall return before sunrise. Alert the Quartermaster I want Pandora ready to cast off then."

"Sir?"

"The Sailing Master will need the time to get his charts in order."

"But the storm, sir."

"*Excusez-moi*? Did I ask your opinion? That was an order. Away! I did not intrude upon your shore leave. Quit hounding me during mine. Get off with you, you godforsaken bilge rat." Why did everyone surrounding him need to be so infernally stupid? It was a curse. Another curse. He spoke to the night and sighed, "Always room for one more, eh?"

"Captain?"

"*Chut*! No more. Leave me in peace. I wasn't speaking to *you*. Can you not see my friend here? My only friend... *Avec plaisir, mon ami*, let us partake of this night and dance with joyous abandon..."

The Boatswain's Mate tamped-down a shudder and pasted an impassive expression over his face. Their captain was beyond odd even for a pirate of questionable repute. Dusky and exotic-looking as a Persian, he was certainly no Frenchman. That disguise came and went, as did the moments of lucid thought and all the long-time crew knew it, the few of them there were. Better not to anger him--crewmen had a tendency to disappear in numbers proportionate to the height of his temper. The mate backed away into the night and left their master to his own devices. Whatever they might be, he didn't want to know about them.

Billy jammed his fists into the stone railing in frustration. Thinking about that bitch hopped him up and ruined his night. Günter better have finished his fucking job or there'd be hell to pay.

How did no one know that witch they sent her to was a vampire? How could they not know? He'd been so close that day, had his hands right on her. Vengeance at hand, she screamed while he allowed her get away from him only to catch her up again for his amusement. He let her get up the road one more time.

"Don't you know who lives here? A *witch*. He's a real and true witch, so stay back or he'll put a curse on you. I don't even care. I'll brave it. Can't be half as bad as your stinking maggot arse."

"A witch?" Billy's laugh had been hearty. There were no witches in the world. He'd been in it long enough to know. "Yes, let us see this witch. Go on then, *qu'il vienne*! Call him out and let him come. And then throw yourself at him in offer and see if he fails to turn you away or follows the rest of the world." He tried the beguile even though it couldn't work. He kept trying, "Come back to the ship, Marguerite. *Viens, mon cœur*... At least, you have use there."

"Bastard."

"That may well be, but we shall never know. *Pauvre petite*... I'll ask you once more. Be mine."

"Let me be!" she threw rocks at him off the road. "Why can't you just *die*?"

He laughed harder then, "Hellion." He couldn't help it. She was simply too alive to resist, too delicious. She drove him mad and he toyed with her for his own pleasure.

Panting, she backed herself up the road, almost at the path and inching closer to the witch's hill. "Stay where you are. I'm warning you. Everyone's told me he's utterly mad. Madder than you, sick whoremaster that you are. I'd rather brave that than have anything more to do with your festering sore of a crew or that rotten, floating corpse mill again."

Billy didn't like his ship insulted and then remembered he was mad at her for the fire, "Shut your fucking hole," he snapped. "Don't think I don't know who started that fire, *ma chérie*. Who else? Who is it *always* causing me trouble? Tell me, did you alert *all* His Majesty's Navy or only run thither and yon screaming bloody blue murder, *ma bichette*?"

She held out a useless warning hand to keep him at bay, "Stay back, I tell you. The witch is watching you," she hissed. "Can't you tell? Don't you feel it? They say he's everywhere and nowhere and feasts on human blood and flies like the wind. He conjures spells and mixes potions and howls in the night. He's mad I tell you and I doubt he'd think twice about gathering your entrails for sauce and doing the rest of us a favour. That's what he does, you see. Why everyone knows. Favours for a price. And I don't care how much it bloody costs me or what I have to…"

Billy had stopped listening. Maggie didn't know what she was talking about, but Billy was surprised to find he did. Shocked by the sudden discovery, he raked her with a final look before melting away into the night. Half-dead and frantic, Maggie ran like the devil up the hill path, convinced Billy was afraid of the witch the same as everyone else she spoke with.

For the most part, vampires are solitary and territorial and one didn't wander into another's proximity without something happening. He wasn't about to get into that over a little piece of flesh. Günter went out with strict orders soon after Billy's return. He should wait until her new protector left her alone. And then burn the bitch up.

An eye for an eye.

He didn't wait for him and pulled the smouldering ship out. They got lost at sea in the event the navy had been informed while the Master Carpenter and his crew made repairs on the fly. Günter didn't catch up to them until a month later.

Billy seethed. Another vampire having at her after she resisted him for so long? And she had run to him. *Run.* There was nothing he could do about it then. But he would ensure she got her just reward.

"Günter." Billy snarled, "Fucking *idiot...*" Billy wanted her dead with no possibility the other vampire had made her. Where would be the justice in that? Günter never waited to see, couldn't confirm, had no proof to offer. It wasn't good enough.

Billy wanted evidence.

Sure enough, when Günter returned to check, she was still alive. The distinction of her being turned was lost on him, so all he could report was that she still lived and had taken up residence with the witch in a new house. Of course, she must have been made then. No human being would be a willing guest in that way. And no vampire would keep one unless it was for sport and there was no evidence of that.

He ordered him back yet again with different orders. When she was alone, to catch her as she slept, stab her with wood and cut off her head. No way she could survive that and there would be nothing the vampire-witch could do if he found her. Günter could move in daylight, after all, so had that advantage over creatures of the night.

"He'd better bring me her fucking head this time."

The wind came up and snapped the draperies behind him, but he didn't hear them. Almost three years he waited for her death and still no word from Günter. They had a good resting spot in their standing rendezvous location in the Caribbean where a note would be left. But nothing yet. They would soon be on the way back and he willed it to be there now.

A word, at least, about the only thing he wanted to know.

5B

The end of the second week of my rebirth came and went and the weather was fine and warm. The night air was soft and I left Maggie's window open, so she could feel it. It was good for her. I was relieved to see signs of healing, but she remained so very weak. Her face pallid, the effect of so much blood loss was obvious and I applied all my energy to making her strong again. Her own blood had given me my new life so I paid her back with my skill.

Most of the time she remained asleep, but it was for the best. I didn't want her moving about with her neck the way it was. In her weakened delirium, she didn't even realise it was me caring for her. I thought that was better for the moment, since the shock of seeing me alive would likely do her harm. If she wasn't aware until she was stronger, it was just as well.

Whenever she stirred, I mixed her a thin millet gruel and fed it to her a few drops at a time like the fragile, baby bird she'd been reduced to. The millet was better for her blood than corn flour. It seemed she was in pain as she often moaned in her oblivion, so I also gave her white peony root tea. One of the blood tonics I knew that would make her strong, it was better than willow bark for her aches and kept her comfortable while it did its work. She was quieter once I added it to her healing regime, so kept it up at regular intervals.

I despised seeing her in pain and the long hours watching over her got to me. If I'd been with her instead of hiding in pretend death, I could have saved her from attack. It was my fault and something she shouldn't have had to endure. She couldn't hear me yet, but I whispered to her, anyway. Promising to do better, I hoped she would hear my willingness to atone and come back to me.

There was no way I could leave her in her current the condition, so ignored my own need to feed. I felt it, though--the hunger, the ache. No matter how strong I was, that unholy thirst crept over me as it always had. I sat in her spindle-backed rocker out on the porch feeling the world, feeling the life that pulsed around me and thought about things she said. About not being able to separate what I was out of the man. It was the truth and I knew it now.

I wasn't a man though I had the appearance of one. That particular animal was something I hadn't been for a very long while. I wished I still were. Wished I could be that again for her. I wasn't even human and wished on only that much, but that wasn't meant to be, either. I was cursed. I was the undead.

I was a vampire and that was all.

There were things to fix and things to clean and in between caring for her I busied myself making things right again. All evidence of the attack was now gone. There were already enough reminders she would have to carry with her for the rest of her life and I didn't want her waking to see anything more troubling. For the moment, I boarded over the broken window in the front room. I knew it would displease her, but wouldn't risk an order at the mercantile for more glass until I knew how much time had passed. I still wasn't certain. It was summer again and it seemed I slept the winter away. But Maggie's hair had grown out since I last saw her and I really had no idea how fast a woman's hair could grow. It might have been ten years for all I knew, though thought less from the size of the trees up against the perimeter of the garden.

That was also changed. Maggie's doing, of course. Part of the garden she'd left to its own devices, most of it herbs and plants she wouldn't have had a use for or known. It was comforting to me to see she hadn't pulled it out to make room for other things. As though I were still there keeping watch over her. Perhaps, why she left it. If it had kept her company, I was glad. It was windblown and weedy, had reseeded itself in nature's random way, but everything was still there and I could use it again. I'd already been at it to find what I needed to help her. I would bring it back to life as she had for me and as I now did for her.

The rest of the garden she turned over for vegetables I never bothered with. Beyond carrots and potatoes to trade, I needed no others. There were peas and celery now, and corn stalks waving in the night breeze and cabbage hunkered down near the dirt next to bright green leeks and a riot of flowers around and through. It was full of colour and life. A reflection of Maggie. I loved the look of it and could even see the trace of life she left with every touch through my vampire eyes that I hated, but that I was glad I had to see it. I loved the changes she made, because it had been her hands that made them. The same hands that had taken such care with the monster I left there for her. She hated the dark, the night, and even after the sun was down it was now cheery as day. It would be how I would always remember her, making the night as though it was bathed in warm summer sun I could never see.

I rocked an hour away out on the porch until I heard her moan. Time for more peony. Even after I got it into her, she seemed more restless than usual. I was restless, hungry, and it gave me pause. For better or worse, we were truly tied together now with so much of her blood inside me. I wondered if she could feel my edginess the way I could feel her heart beating.

If it were true, then the longer I went in hunger, the more frantic she would become through no fault of her own. The madness was settling into me already and though I had the discipline to deny it while it grew, that didn't make it go away. I felt the night, felt all the life out beyond our little house and ached. I was the wolf and I needed to be nourished. Maggie needed rest and whatever my needs, it couldn't be allowed to interfere with her healing. I wasn't sure what to do.

An awful thought occurred that she might now know when I took a life, might touch that sin along with me. The rapture of the clench was something I was happy to share with her, but it was more the killing that worried me. That she would feel the bloodlust and the death and it would frighten her if she realised. Or sicken her if she understood. While it would quiet the unnatural feeling that may now be forced upon her, I could never make her a party to murder. That wasn't part of what she was.

That part was all me.

Of course, I couldn't be certain that's the way it was, but I had my suspicions and wouldn't take any chances. After much internal debate, I decided to go out. That murder was my solution made me uncomfortable, because, deep down, I knew though she would never judge me for it, it would sadden her. But it would buy me a few more weeks. She would soon be awake and I could evaluate how tied we were then. There might be some hard decisions in my future, but putting them off until then would save me from that pain until we reached it.

Rooting through the jars and sprays of dry herbs up in my loft, I found them all too old to have much potency. Potent was what I needed. There was more out in the garden, so I gathered up fresh lavender and mint to make her a tea that would quiet her and keep her asleep. I got as much of it into her as I could, checked the dressing on her neck for the millionth time and tucked her in again. I bolted the windows with the heavy shutters, so no one could see in or *get* in. After some deliberation, I nailed the door shut from the inside, as well. I could get in and out without the door, but no one else would be able to and that made me feel safer to leave her for a short time. I looked in on her once more and then left her in her room.

And let the night take me over.

Always careful around her, I wouldn't allow myself to revel in all I was and it often felt limiting. Only a human approximation, my own interpretation of human behaviour was about the best I could manage on a good day. But there were some things about me, my own quirky, unnatural behaviours, that I kept tamped down and so they remained unshared. But I revelled in them now while I had the rare opportunity.

I stood before the cold fireplace and wallowed in them.

It was so good to simply be. Shrugging off the uncomfortable human suit, I threw my arms wide in relief. I breathed in the night and became it. Growing somehow insubstantial in reflection of the inhuman demon I really was, I became more myself and coalesced into something substantive. Perhaps, only my own perspective, that it was a true transformation, but since I'd never had a witness to it, I never heard a report. It still felt like heaven not to mind my Ps and Qs. I swung myself up to the loft without bothering with the ladder and kicked open the hidden roof hatch with a bang. I was laughing when I hoisted myself outside.

Since Maggie came and more so since my rebirth by her blood, I could admit I had become saddled with an unnerving and very human guilt. It made me feel the need to atone for every life I ever stole. I'd grown a conscience, it seemed. And I knew I couldn't have one of those and survive. But in being my blood-stealing natural self? I could still admit that nothing, *nothing*, dulled the singular bliss of being what I was.

To throw off the human veneer and allow myself permission to delight in all those things inside me, nothing human could compare--no sight, no sound, no experience. Sight beyond the spectrum of the human eye, sense of the earth all about. Of life as an entity that embraces and, if I'm being honest, as much as I wished to have it back I enjoyed a certain freedom in disconnection from humanity. Even an appreciation of simple pleasures for the beauty of their simplicity. And limitless appreciation for the greater ones in ways a mortal man couldn't unravel with his human mind during the entire course of his life. It is indeed a curse to be given all this along with immortality juxtaposed against a need to steal blood, to entice and beguile to get it. To take life. It was a curse, is a curse. The one I lived. For that moment, though, I was lost in all of it, only in being.

I was hunting.

I flew through the forest with the other shadows, a dark wind winding through the trees on silent cat feet. The world at a distance from me, the pulse of every life, every single life everywhere, broke over me in delicious, electric waves that drowned me in bliss and I crowed into the night in ecstasy. Racoons and my brother wolves scattered into the thicket ahead of the approaching death they sensed and I left them to their lives. They weren't what I craved. With the demon running free, a cold pulse beat through me, urging me forward toward the blood, always the blood, to take the life that would give it to me.

Despite growing more lost by the moment, I still felt Maggie from a distance right through her drugged sleep. Felt her heart beating and knew it beat in time with the cold pulse of my own excitement. Or, perhaps, mine beat in time with hers. Because that was what I truly wished and what I actually wanted underneath and couldn't help myself. More than any effect of ingesting her blood, in truth, it was my own desire that pulled us closer together in that way, because I would never let her go.

In the heat of that moment, I daydreamed over the wound in her neck and the wash of blood that had come out of her in a way I refused to allow myself while I looked after her. It had been on my hands, on my clothes, all over the house for so many days in a row and I could deny myself only because I was already satisfied. Maggie had fed me and I was sated for a time. But it could never last and no amount could ever be enough. If she bled a thousand times and fed me a thousand more it would never be enough. My hunger for her was insatiable, my need unquenchable and in that moment I lived it.

It was dark and wrong and wonderful in monstrous wickedness and I craved it so hard. It was in me and I allowed it while so far away from her simply to get it out of my system. So I could go back to her and continue to be strong and protect her. It lived in effigy for a few stolen moments in the forest, all that could never be touched in the flesh.

In thought, I let myself creep into her room to watch her as she slept. Saw her throat in moonlight and the pulse that beat there that I had felt without touching her since the day I licked a single drop of her life off my fingers. I let myself watch in exquisite torture and knew she had the ability to take my every thought with one single beat of her heart.

She held a power over me I could never hope to possess.

Thinking about her throat made me swallow hard in anticipation. Long and slender, pale skin showing the veins beneath, and so enticing. For the likes of me, it was hard to resist. I knew she wouldn't deny me, either. If I struck fast, she would never be afraid, never realise. But I didn't want it to be quick. No, I wanted it to last forever. To savour it, to spin it out until I was barmy with it. And more, I wanted her to want it. So much sweeter. In the need shared, mine to take and hers to give, the pleasure would be doubled and a heady thought.

That she cared for me could make her want me. At least, I dreamt it could be true. She knew my need and in my dreams I watched her not only not deny me, but beckon me closer. Put her hand on my mouth in that way she did, unafraid of the implement of her impending death. She was so brave and bold, my Maggie-girl. The thought of it raised gooseflesh on my dead skin.

I dreamed of her hands in my hair guiding me closer, watching the desire in my eyes without fear. I would kiss her mouth and whisper secret melodies until she was drowsy to keep her from the smallest pain and hold her close to keep her from the smallest anxiety, because she trusted me. The phantom feel of that velvet skin beneath her ear on my cold lips made me shudder. To pierce the skin, to break through it so gently, was a pleasure I would dream on for countless thousands of years and to set the blood inside free for my taking, my eternal rapture. My lips would embrace that loving wound and she would feed me then with her hands in my hair, holding me to her throat until I could drink no more. And that moment would never come, because I would never be satisfied and it would go on and on for as long as the Netherworld allowed me shadow life.

The whole forest ran from me then. A dark shadow full in bloodlust, I ran and ran in search of the blood that I craved before I went home and made my dreams into reality.

I never know which direction I'll be pulled when I hunt and I never understand the reason. I don't lie in wait, don't plot and plan, but something does guide me to a particular point at a particular time and then I'm fed. Not greedy, my needs were always met in this curious way for as long as I can recall. I never questioned it, only something that was, and I didn't question it now. I felt the pull, felt a call, and followed without conscious thought. All dark instinct and unholy sense and hell-bent need, it led me to the window of a cottage very far from ours.

The night was warm and the window open to take in the air as I'd done for Maggie. A man rested on his bed and when he spied the dark shadow of death I was passing by, he waved me inside.

"I would not pass through without an invitation, sir." While I swayed in bloodlust, the beguiling words crept out that would forever signal the beginning of the danse macabre.

"A friendly wave is no longer considered good manners among the spirit world then?"

"I meant no offence. Only the way of things in the night," I gave him a slight bow in mock respect and waited on his decision.

"Then come, friend. Bring yourself inside and speak with me a mite."

I stood by his bed, almost a vapour in the darkness, my voice hoarse and shaking, tuned to beguile, "And what should we speak of?"

"What should we speak of? By heav'n, I thought you'd forgotten all about me is what."

When I took in the look of him and then glanced about the room, I pulled back a fraction from the edge of reason. "I haven't known your name, sir."

"A trifling matter now, I s'ppose. So, do my old eyes see true? Finally, after all this time, are you Death come to take me?"

I considered him another moment, perplexed even in need. I needed no beguiling melodies here. Wonder softened my voice and my manner, "I could be, if you're quite ready to go."

"Gor Blimey, I've waited too long already, my friend," he said in expansive explanation. "Every day was I a-waitin' and never you came. After these old legs grew wobbly, even the porch after supper was beyond me. Can you imagine? Had to give up my pipe then. I ask you, when a man's pipe is taken from him, when he's too old for wifely comfort, too toothless for a crust of hard bread, what's left to stay for?"

I had to laugh. What a most curious person he was. I was intrigued. "Your needs are simple and it sounds as though you've had them all met. Was it a good life then? Did you savour it for the treasure it was?" As I had done for Maggie, I gave him the better part of me and offered him the soft voice in the dark.

The toothless grin was answer enough, "Did you see me missus?" He laughed and winked, saucy, old bugger that he still was, "My beauty was always a warm comfort on a cold night. Well, that and she makes a right hare stew. Fit to make angels fall straight down from heav'n. Always had a bit of an affinity for hasenpfeffer, y'see."

"She sounds like quite a woman. Are you quite certain you're ready to leave her so soon?"

"Soon? Ha! Don't spare it another thought, friend. I am *eight and ninety* year old. My pipe was my only comfort left, y'see. Now, I've not e'en that. I tell the missus anon at each sundown in case you happened by. I'm quite ready. At your leisure then. Let us away, friend."

I was in a whole other place, vaporous and only half in touch with the world and as real a reaper as any other. I was pleased to take him at his request, honoured even, by his honest dignity. Full in bloodlust still, it was different, not quite so black.

I had somehow become useful and turned the curse against itself for an instant.

Before I brought him the rest he craved, I set him in his chair on the porch with his pipe and let him have some smoke and he was the most contented man I'd ever known. We chatted about fishing and the New World that beckoned so many at that time and the now-disgraceful price of tobacco until he said he was ready and laid his pipe by. He regarded it a moment and then changed his mind, offering it to me, instead.

"I've nary a use for it now, my friend." I didn't want to take it. It didn't feel right, stealing from the soon-to-be dead. But he wouldn't have it.

With reverence, I accepted the gift at his insistence. "On my honour, know you will be remembered." It was a vow I would always keep.

I told him I would take him in his chair so he wouldn't fall and his wife wouldn't be obliged to lift him and he thanked me for my concern. *Thanked* me. When I pulled back from that gentle embrace, he was still smiling as he faded away.

He looked so peaceful there. As I drifted off into the night with his pipe tucked into my belt, I felt peaceful, too. As though taking his blood had given me something I was missing. I'd been so hopped-up on Maggie, on taking, and the fates had given me this curious, old man in substitute who came to me of his own accord.

And it was okay.

Not the object of my craving, it was satisfying in a way I'd never known before. Than I'd *ever* known in all my time. Balancing and peaceful, it felt as though it put the world to rights with myself as the instrument of that balance. The total opposite of what my curse normally produced. I wanted to sing.

I wanted to tell Maggie what happened, that I did a good thing with this unholy curse, but she didn't even know I was alive yet. And then I worried, because I left her locked in the house so long alone while I celebrated my darkness. Night was almost over and I raced back on the wind and the animals didn't run this time. Everything was peaceful, just like me.

Much to my relief, Maggie had slept through the night and no one tried to break in, so I pulled the nails out of the door and opened the shutters again for some air before sunrise. For once deeply calm, I wished I could share the experience with her. Humming to myself, I mixed her up some more millet gruel while my mind wandered over the evening's events. When I heard her stir, I ran to keep her from thrashing and pulling the dressing off her neck.

Her clear, bright eyes pinned me in the doorway.

All the while I tended to her, I thought of about a thousand things I might say when she first woke clear-headed, but none of them came to me. Mostly, I hoped the shock wouldn't make her pass back out.

She put a shaky hand up to her poor throat and tried to swallow. The colour drained from her face as she grimaced. It must have hurt like hell.

"Wait now. Let me just--" Swivelling my head around the room searching for a cup or bowl I could bring to her, there was nothing. I'd left it all in the kitchen. I pointed a warning finger while I thought what to do first, "Water. Some water. Don't move, girl. Keep yourself right there. Won't be a moment," and ran out to the well.

On my knee beside her bed, her eyes were wide as she searched my face in concern and wonder while I dribbled cool well water across her lips. She was looking for the demon she buried, but that shrunken idiot who forgot to tell her he couldn't die was gone.

My smile was hopeful and encouraging. Chagrined by my previous stupidity, my voice was soft for her, "Hello, Maggie-girl."

Sudden tears poured out the corners of her eyes as she sniffled and struggled to speak.

"Hey, there... Maggie..," I tried to soothe her, but the waterworks continued, so I got off the floor and perched on the side of the bed. Winding my arms around her, I held her while she sobbed. Between seeing me and then the axe handler as a last memory, she had good reason and I didn't mind. It was heavenly being close with her while I was already sated and not beating back anything sinister for a change.

It took her a while, but she wound down and rested her head against my chest and put her hand over my heart. So familiar. This time, though, I was warm and my heart was beating and for a little while I could be real to her and I was glad. She couldn't manage more than a whisper, but as always, she had to know everything.

"How?"

"How which? How am I alive or how are *you* alive?" She swatted me and sniffled some more. "Still feisty? Good to know some things never change."

"...horrid man..."

"All right, all right," awake five minutes, she was already making me laugh. "You're here, both because I'm a very good practitioner and because you, young lady, are stubborn as an ox. And *I'm* here, because--" That one was more difficult. I didn't know how to tell her. It was no laughing matter and I grew serious, "I'm here, Maggie, because of you." She tilted her head a little to look up at me and flinched. "No-no, easy," I tucked her head back against me, so she wouldn't strain. "You shouldn't move about just yet. Please. Over a fortnight I've been in mortal terror of you ripping those dressings off and buggering up all my work. You've had quite a time, so be a good girl, all right? You've got some stitching there and while I'm definitely no tailor it's a right proper job, if I do say so myself. Not quite all scabbed yet, though. Since I really don't want to have to start all over again, no wiggling for you."

"'Kay." She thumped my chest, insistent, "How?"

Not so easy not to be lecturing, "Maggie," but at least I could be honest with her, "there was something I didn't tell you. Seems stupid to bother now since the proof is obviously right here, but--" I sighed. "You know I'm not like regular people. Not at all and I know you've never quite understood. Not all of it, I don't think. Not a spirit, not a man, but here I am right here again. You see that. You remember about the sunshine, don't you? That *that* might do me harm. And if my head came away from my body? It would likely be over. But when I stopped hunting…" Why was it so hard to get out? "I can't die that way, Maggie. More like a bear hibernating through winter. You understand what that's like. I reach a certain point, become weak, and then fade off to sleep and that's what happened. I fell asleep and waited."

When I didn't say anything more, she prompted me. "For what?"

Of course, she would make me say it. I could never give her only a little bit of truth. Still a most exasperating person, I was glad to have her back. "Right, well, I can stay in that state for a long while. Quite a long while really, and time doesn't pass for me. Like sleeping. A century could come and go and I would be none the wiser. So I stay that way until whatever happenstance or accident brings me what I need to live again. Until it--" yeah, it was certainly difficult getting out. "Well, until it brings me blood, Maggie."

The room was quiet, but the birds outside were chirping their predawn song and it flittered between us for a long minute. And then Maggie pressed her face into me and sniffled some more.

"Don't cry, girl. No… Hush, Maggie… I would never have wished for that to happen to you. Not ever. But in the end? It was you who brought me back. When you fell. Where you fell to be exact. And a good thing it was, too. You brought me back just then when you needed me most. So I could be there to save you. And so I'm glad for it. For that I'm glad for it. When you needed me, Maggie, you called me back. Again. This is getting to be a habit, you know." She chuckled and sniffled and I laughed into her hair, "Not that I'm complaining. Certainly not this time." She seemed so small there in my arms as I held her, "And so here we are, again. Together." She was so fragile still and not at all how I was used to seeing her. I didn't like it. It would take her a long while to recover from this, but I would continue to give her everything I knew.

Her tears dried up as her head started to bob and she shook from being up too long too soon. "Too much for a first day, girl. That's enough. You need rest and I don't want to hear any of your high-handed, back talk. You best make your peace with being ordered about. Back down you go."

Her eyelids drooped, but she was smiling and it was lovely to see after her being so still for so long. I brought her the millet gruel and she stayed awake long enough to take some of it with a hand resting on my wrist as though she were afraid I'd disappear if she didn't keep hold of me.

"I'm not going anywhere, girl," I laughed.

"Making sure."

"Still trying to be in charge?"

"Always."

"Right then, that's enough talk. No straining. I want you well again or I won't have anyone to argue with."

"Richard?"

A shiver ran up my spine. Good lord, how I loved when she said my name, "Yes, Maggie-girl?" It stopped me dead every time and would never change.

"Stay with me."

Daytime was coming. It was so close, but found I couldn't refuse her. "Maggie, it's almost morning. I--" It was futile. "In here?"

"Please."

There was no denying her. Ever. "I need dark." There were a lot of things I needed that I could never say, but that one I managed.

"'Kay."

"I'll have to shutter the window. Block the sun out of the cracks, too. You understand?"

"Yes."

When I tried to leave to close the window, she wouldn't let go of my wrist. It tore at my inhuman heart. "Maggie," I loosened her fingers and set her hand on the quilt, "I won't be long. I promise." I shut up my home for daytime as I had for four thousand years and put out all the lanterns but one. When the window was sealed, I set the lantern on the blanket box next to her bed. "See? Here I am. That wasn't so long, was it?"

"Yes."

"Silly arse."

"Yes…" She was close to dozing already and so much more peaceful than when I left her earlier. I felt at peace. Perhaps that helped her, too.

I was as afraid to be near her as away from her just then. Her heartbeat was everywhere--in my brain, resonating inside me in cadence with my heart while it still beat--calling me, compelling me to be close to her. So many times she told me she wasn't afraid and it was still true. I stood over her, taking in the feel of her the way I had in mind earlier and it left me breathless.

She stirred and looked for me through lowered lashes she almost didn't have the strength to raise. When she caught sight of me shuffling from one foot to the other in indecision, she smiled in sleepy patience. "I don't bite, Richard."

I laughed right outloud and scrubbed a hard hand over the back of my neck, "Good lord, girl."

"Come," she yawned, "be close with me in the dark."

"Yes, Maggie." I perched on the edge of her bed and pulled off my boots and turned the lamp down low.

"No. Put it out."

"Are you certain? Not too dark for you?"

"Not anymore."

For a second time, I climbed into bed with a live, human woman by invitation and knew it was because she was mine. I liked the thought of it more as time went on. It was the oddest sensation.

However unholy or inconceivable our association, when I got in there with her and settled her against me, it felt like the most natural, most right thing in the entire world. I savoured every nuance against it never being allowed to come about again.

She sighed in contentment and nestled close and a curious ache filled my almost dead heart. It was painful and wonderful at the same time and something I was sure I couldn't remember even as far back as when I still lived. I wasn't certain, didn't want to be sure, and could only think that no matter, it could never be allowed. But I pulled her closer and held her safe in protective arms and knew I would fight the whole world for her.

"Mmmm... you're warm, Richard..."

There it was again, that twist in my brain whenever she spoke my name and I couldn't turn away from it. It shouldn't have happened. Shouldn't have been possible. I wasn't even human never mind alive. It was insane and I was mad for knowing it for what it was. I rested my still-warm lips against her forehead and died a thousand deaths for acknowledging it by name. It might be different from what the rest of the world knew, but in my own way, I knew then I was lost in love with her.

I couldn't tell her, of course. When it was safe and she was well, I would let her go. Send her on her way, so she could have a life. She only had one and I hadn't saved it so she could waste it up in the hills with the likes of me. I lived alone, needed to be alone. In the greater scheme of things, it wouldn't matter anyway, because I would always feel her wherever she went for as long as she lived. It would be so brief compared with the endless span of decades and centuries in my own future. It hurt more then, because I would also know to the beat and to the breath her last day on earth no matter how far she might venture from me. I already mourned it.

It wasn't right for someone to know another's time, but then I had lots of practice. Even in the rapture of the clench, I had enough sense to pull back. Sensed when to pull back before the end or be taken down with them. It was one of the realities of my existence. I could get out of it, of course, but I had to want to, had to want to come back. I always had before.

Lying there with her, I could be the most honest with myself. If there was ever a way I could have everything I wanted and be satisfied? It would be to finally let myself have at her and then let her take me down with her as she died. To be touching the last beat of her heart as it stilled and stopped my own with the taste of her blood still sweet on my tongue sounded like heaven to me no matter how gruesome a concept.

It was hard to admit, but that was only because it was the truth. And if I left the human yardstick behind while I thought it, it made so much more sense.

Hurting her wasn't something I wanted and it wasn't about that at all. I would sooner destroy myself as allow anything to happen to her. Especially if it meant protecting her from myself, though I was happier now knowing I could deny the wolf even when it was difficult. My nature simply forced me to crave her in a different way. The fantasy I dreamed on was simple. I'd been in the world so long, I was tired of existence. Perhaps, I could visit her when she was very old, after she had the opportunity to enjoy her life, and bring her release the way I had the old man.

And beg her to take me with her.

Something else I could never tell her about, that ache to leave the world. It would only worry her over me more than she already did and I didn't want to do that to her. I knew then I couldn't share what had happened with the old man, because she could never understand. I knew how he felt, exactly how he felt, and could appreciate his decision with singular clarity. She could never fathom all the years I'd spent in conscious thought. So rarely to rest, so fruitlessly to live. A great distance between existence and life, the latter was something I could no longer recall how to have even if given the opportunity as a gift. If I was to steal away right then and there, slip my arms from around her and walk out the door into the light, it would likely vaporise me. I could follow the old man into rest, although it wouldn't be half as peaceful a passing.

But it wasn't only about me anymore. There was Maggie to consider. However foreign a concept to me after so long alone, I understood my departure would hurt her and I couldn't do that. She already cried over me once and I wouldn't cause that again. No matter how bad I'd been at it so far, I also promised to protect her and wouldn't mind the opportunity of making that up to her.

So, I didn't walk out the door right then and stayed there with the live, human woman who was somehow mine and who I also somehow loved and pretended I was an almost-man, almost alive, just for a little while. It was a nice dream while it could last. I breathed in the scent of her and held her hard.

"Why..?" Maggie was talking in her sleep and fidgeted in agitation, "...*won't*... I *won't* ... No!"

I let my hand trail over her hair and down to stroke her cheek to settle her again. There would be some hard days ahead for her. Without a sleeping draught or something to relax her, no longer unconscious, her memory would devil her until she finished fighting it out inside herself to her satisfaction. It was difficult to watch. My poor Maggie. Her heart raced and her dream terror was obvious. It was painful and I suffered along with her. Dragged along by her blood inside me, I was now a party to the battle that had taken place on the ground under which I'd slept.

"...stick me back in that stinking box... ...will *not* go... *and* his fucking death ship..."

In the time since she came to me, she never gave me a clue about this man who scared the life out of her and this sleepy fragment was already more than I knew. A ship? We were far from the harbour there in the hills with several villages in between. My mistake to believe she came from one of them nearby, run away in the night from what I had assumed was a husband or father who kept a ready switch and followed the old code.

There was more to Maggie and if she never said another word, I already knew it. There had always been something about her, something different. It explained her behaviour better to me even without further information. That she had never been afraid of me even after I had to confess was the least of it. It was the air about her. I never understood it, though catching up fast. A ship? That could mean anything, though the context spoke of something darker than a simple ocean crossing to the New World. I didn't like the sound of it.

To me, a death ship could mean a bringer of plague, but common sense told me this sounded more like a scourge that killed. And that could only mean one thing--they had been around as long as ships were built. Death didn't frighten her and she would have seen much in the company of sea-faring marauders. And a box? I didn't like the sound of that at *all*. The slave trade was brisk at that time and that would explain much, even all. If she escaped before sale, they would certainly try to find her, recapture her, and attempt to recoup the loss or kill her to keep her from exposing them. It seemed to explain everything.

One of the advantages of being in the world so long was I knew the ways of men. Knew first-hand they never changed. Continued to pursue the same pleasures and past times, perpetrated the same vile acts, followed the same urges as they had since the world was born. I saw the same story enough times from the deck of ships I'd maintained and others at a distance to know it for what it was. I swore vengeance on the axe-wielder again and on everyone else who was a party to it. My little bird deserved better and the crime would be paid for.

His Majesty's Navy might not be able to find them. But I would. No matter how long it took.

6

dozed off in there somewhere and woke to Maggie's eyes on
me in the dim. She'd already been up and lit the lantern so she could
watch me. I hadn't noticed a thing and it didn't wake me. There had
been nothing for me until sundown. Unusual I slept, but more that I
wasn't disturbed by her moving about. Maybe it was only that I trusted
her. Maybe I was exhausted from looking after her. Maybe I was visiting
death.

Maybe I was a coward and afraid to speak with her.

"Is that you?"

"No, I'm a figment of your imagination," her smile lit up the
shadows.

"Ah, I thought so. I think I had this dream before."

"Me, too."

"It didn't end well, as I recall. Let's wake now before we reach the
end." I made to get up, but she stopped me with a hand on my arm.

"Don't go. Not yet."

"You shouldn't be talking so much," I warned her with a frown, but she waved it off, intent.

"You didn't answer my question."

"Which one, little lamb?"

"You were warm last night. You still are."

"You didn't ask." Another thing about that dream--it was always over far too soon. Therein the reason I was afraid to speak with her. "You must have dreamt it."

"Okay, then I'm asking now. How?"

"Maggie," I didn't want to have this conversation. Not now. Everything was so nice. As I said, that particular dream never ended well and I was right in wanting to leave it lay. But of course, we never could. I sighed.

Maggie put her hand up to catch my breath against her palm, "See? Right there. Warm." I gritted my teeth and jerked my face away without meaning it to be harsh. "Richard," there was wonder in her voice.

I hadn't let myself be this close to her for this long since that first night in the cellar and I'd been cold then. That night, any warmth I gained from feeding burned right off in my frantic race back to the house in answer to her plea. Like an adrenaline rush and over all too soon, I was already cold to the touch again by the time I reached her.

In the course of things, her not touching me had become a habit. It never dawned on me before, but it seemed the odd times she *had* touched me were between times I fed. When the faint humanity I stole had already faded away leaving the cold, dead flesh and unbeating heart she knew. This was a whole new me for her and one she was eager to discover. But I didn't want her to. It was part of the dream that couldn't last. Then she walked her fingers up to my mouth in the gloom to feel me breathe.

I don't know whatever possessed her to do that the first time, but she was still doing it and no matter my previous resolve, I couldn't help I still wanted to make her so badly. I wanted her to never leave me, so she could be brave and do that forever. I knew I did. Any time she was near me I couldn't be anything less than honest with myself and here it was again. And people thought *I* was the witch. I shook off the spell before I cast my own. I grabbed her fingers and moved them, "Yes. I know."

She put them right back, because she wanted to and already had far too much practice getting what she wanted from me. "Are you alive now? Is that what this is? Is that how you've come back to me? Has this made you a man again?"

There were many things done and said by her that got to me over the time we were together, but I have to say, that one felt the most cruel. It jerked me out of bed, "No," my answer brusque. Uncomfortable, I walked right out the door of her room to light the lanterns in the rest of the house for the night.

"Richard, wait."

I didn't need them, of course, but I needed to be busy just then. Building up a fire in the little kitchen stove to make her what she needed to eat wasted more time. And for certain she needed more peony tea. I hadn't given her any before she went to sleep and she must have been aching. All I could do was look after her and not think about any other stupid things anymore, because when that job was done she had to leave. Just go. I didn't know where I would send her, but she had to go and that was all.

"*Ri*-chard."

I lived alone. Needed to be alone. She was going to have to find somewhere else to be.

"Damn it, Richard, *answer* me."

I hollered over my shoulder, "Stop straining your throat, I told you! I'll be right there. Have some patience, girl." All manner of ruckus was going on in the kitchen for only some tea and porridge. But I was annoyed at myself and slamming things left and right, because I couldn't do anything else with it.

"What on earth are you doing out there?"

"Did you hear me tell you to stop talking or was I speaking to myself? Just stop. Do you ever listen to anything I tell you, girl? Ever? I'll be there in a tick. *Stop talking* or you'll hurt yourself. Or at least tear through that scab and then I'll have to paddle your backside. Just behave yourself until I get back in there." I rattled more cookware for no reason. Stomped about in my sock feet waiting on the water to boil. Slammed the cupboard door in the bottom of the sideboard for no other reason than the satisfying crack when the hinge tore off the wood. I pulled a bowl off the shelf with an annoyed jerk and sent the pile under it crashing to the floorboards in a hundred pieces.

"Bloody hell." Snarling like a wounded bear, I sent the bowl in my hand sailing across the length of the room with inhuman speed to shatter against the wall in a spectacular explosion. "Fuck me!"

A throat cleared behind me. I hung my head to hide while I composed myself, leaning on one hand against the dry sink until the storm passed.

"Problem?"

I've no idea how she got out of bed and across half the house, but she was the most stubborn person I'd ever known. Likely, she ordered the furniture out of the way to accommodate her.

My tone was saccharine, "Oh, no, no problem at all. Everything's bloody fabulous in here." I crunched through broken crockery without noticing and stopped in the middle of the room, "And who told you, you could get out of bed? Hmm? I'm quite certain I told you to stay put."

"Richard--"

"How the blazes did you even walk that far?" I saw her there, but didn't *see* her, because I didn't want to. "Have you any idea how many nights I was sat up over you trying to make you well again? Do you? Blast it... I didn't even know if I could save you--"

"But Richard--"

"...been awake not even half a fucking day, damn stubborn girl. Won't stay put five sodding minutes when you're too weak to be walking about yet and liable to do yourself more damage. I can't fix anything if you won't have some common sense--"

"*Richard.*"

"What?"

"Your feet," she pointed a still-shaky finger.

The kettle started to boil behind me while blood soaked through and stained my socks.

"Shit."

Maggie pushed herself off the wall from where she leaned for support and started into the room. "No, girl," I held out a hand to keep her away. "Don't move. Don't come in here."

There was a moment's hesitation, but she caught the tone in my voice and kept her place. I reached back and pulled the kettle off the stove and then opened the fire door.

"But wha--?"

"Don't," I leaned over with care, "move," and picked up the larger pieces of crockery I stepped on that were marked with my blood and threw them into the fire. Maggie's eyes widened when I pulled off my socks and threw them in, too. There was no evidence of the cuts that had bled aside from some drying smears. They were already healed. I avoided her eyes.

All my anger was gone. "Best you set yourself in the other room while I look after this." When she hesitated, while I couldn't look her in the eye, I tried hard to give her the softer part of me, "Please, Maggie." I kept my eyes pinned on the dancing flames in the stove watching my socks burn up while she hung in the doorway. Then I heard her move off into the other room.

With care, I cleaned up the rest of the mess with the broom, making sure to get every piece. When I was certain I got them all, I hoisted myself up to the loft to slip outside the fast way. So I wouldn't touch the floor where she might walk.

There had always been some things I didn't want her to see and this was one of them. The bleeding had stopped the same instant it began, but there was still some dried blood on me I needed to be rid of. I didn't want it anywhere near her. With all those half-open wounds she still had, I was liable to make her by accident if she touched any and I didn't want that.

Grabbing a bucket, I filled it from the rain barrel and went a ways into the trees so she wouldn't see. I washed the blood off there and watched the grass whither and die as the rose-tinted water trickled off my dead skin and cursed it by association. Nothing would grow there again.

I refilled the bucket and brought it inside to wipe over the floor with a bit of rag and threw that into the fire, too. It wasn't good enough, though. Maggie might walk over the boards in her bare feet one night and while I doubted there might be enough residue to do her any harm, I wouldn't allow a single particle anywhere near her. It was my job to protect her and more often than not from myself and I was only doing my job. I grabbed another scrap of old cloth and wound it around some kindling and lit it off the stove. Playing with fire is far from my favourite past time, but I ran the flame across every inch of the floor to burn up anything that might be left behind. That rag went into the fire, too.

When I was done, I put the kettle back on the cast iron top and boiled it up for her tea and made a little thin porridge. By the time I could allow myself to face her, I'd convinced myself I wasn't avoiding her, but being careful for her benefit not to mention getting her food, because she needed it. The porridge was in a saucer since there were no bowls left and I balanced it on a hand and the tea in the other to bring in to her. Maggie had drifted off in front of the cold hearth.

Sometimes? I really was a big, giant arse.

"Maggie-girl," I tried to rouse her with a gentle voice, but she was faded away from overexertion.

"*Shit*," I set the food down on the mantle. All I could do was scoop her up and put her back to bed where she belonged, fix her dressings, and leave her be. The way I should have the first day.

While she slept, I rattled around doing nothing constructive, poking at things up in my loft that were now useless. It matched my mood. I didn't even bother putting my boots on and stalked about in my bare feet. After a couple of hours, I went outside and rebuilt the cairn pile she buried me under and straightened up the marker while thunder rolled around the dark trying to decide if it had the energy to turn into something. I felt dead and it seemed a suitable activity just then.

After I placed the last stone, I ran out of impetus and only made it halfway back to the house, dropping into the dirt of the garden Maggie had made her own. She was all over the thing, in every stalk and leaf and made it all very alive. She was asleep inside, but it was nearly like being with her. Almost. I couldn't hurt it, though, the way that I could hurt her with my cursed inhumanity. It surrounded me in safety and let part of her be near me. I could look at it and touch it and appreciate it for what it was without doing it harm in only being myself. I hung my head and caught a look at my feet and my gaze slid off through the trees to the grass I killed. And knew I was lying to myself.

I snarled and the noise flushed a hare out of the vegetables. Without contemplating it, my hand flashed out and caught it. I sucked the lifeblood out of it before I broke its neck. Animals were something I almost never dined on, because they never truly satisfy me, but I did that night. In that moment, it seemed appropriately inhuman. I snarled again and in disgust, hurled the carcass far away from me to leave for my brother wolves.

In self-loathing, I threw myself backwards into the plants and stayed there unmoving, staring up at the thickening cloud. Mingled herb scents washed over me on the night air, but no combination of them could wash the curse away. Or the incongruous sudden and very human longing inside me.

I stayed there a long while.

I felt crazed. My universe had been so predicable for so long, my courses few, and barring any extraordinary circumstance nothing changed for me. Not ever. The deeper parts of myself were what they were. I knew who I was, what I was, and that had never changed.

Only that was no longer true.

Something was happening to me. It was obvious. And to be honest, it was starting to scare me silly. Though I appreciated the little sideways step I took toward humanity with the old man, at the same time, it made things more difficult. And it wasn't only that single experience. It was so much more and had been since my rebirth.

On the inside, down deep where I lived and where no one could see into, I was beginning to feel a split. The dark and violent soulless entity tearing away from another distinct entity--a singular human compulsion, a manic obligation to shield from danger and harm. The division was clearer by the day and it turned my universe upside-down.

A war brewed there between the two of us without my having chosen a side. And Maggie in the middle of my world became a mirror reflecting the raw and roiling clash at the front line. The animal and the man were both awake somehow and knowing each other for what we were. With each working to gain a permanent toehold. And more, seeking means to destroy the other. I was tearing myself apart in a very real way, at the root of my own existence. I ran my fingers up under my hair and tugged at it in distraction, struggling to gain a grip on my mind.

When it started to rain, I didn't even notice. It was nearly morning before I hauled myself out of the mud and filthy and waterlogged, slogged back into the house. I felt like shite.

"I wondered when you would decide to come back in. I nearly thought I'd have to go out there and carry you in myself." Maggie had dragged her rocker into the house and was rocking a little with a blanket on her lap and her head resting with care against a cushion from her bed.

A puddle formed around my feet. A pathetic picture I was.

Her expression was mock-sorrowful, "Honestly Richard, don't you have enough sense to come in out of the rain?"

All I could see was Maggie. It seemed she'd been up for some time, because she looked settled in her chair and had washed and changed clothes. Even that new long hair of hers was rearranged somehow so it was up without anything appearing to hold it there. I think my jaw was hanging.

"Are you all right?"

I blinked, "I--" There was a woman in my house I'd never seen before. An almost-man again, it struck me a lot harder than it might have on another night. "It--" the filthy, bleeding girl who fell over my threshold was gone. At least, I thought she was. Though I was certain she couldn't be, because she was doing a first-rate job still muddling up my old brains. I struggled to form words. "Ummm..." My heart beat strong again from the rabbit, almost alive, and it picked up the rhythm of hers until it was all I could feel. "I mean, sweet mercy."

She laughed at me, but it wasn't unkind, "That's a new one. Is it as bad as all that? I was mostly aiming for human, actually. No one should go that long without washing. Speaking of, have you looked at yourself?" She was playing with me and treating me like a regular person and simply being herself and it was everything I craved and everything I wanted.

Well, not quite.

"No-no. It's only-- You look so--" I was helpless and wished I knew something intelligent and complimentary that was meant to be spoken in one of those sorts of moments. I didn't have a clue and could only shrug, "*Different.*"

"Flatterer," she teased me, but it was obvious my reaction pleased her. I wished there was more I did that could.

I couldn't seem to tear my gaze off her, "What are you doing out of bed again?" I was going for gruff, but it wasn't coming out that way at all. More like a caress, "Didn't I tell you, you're liable to hurt yourself again." My voice was giving out, "...or... you know... wear yourself... out..." That heartbeat that I loved so much was all over the room and pressing hard up against me. And while I'm sure even to a human she might have been quite lovely, to me, with my cursed, but so sensitive vampire sight that could take in the smallest, subtle detail in its entirety, she was breathtaking.

"I'm all right. You needn't worry about me so hard *all* the time," she was smiling, though, appearing touched by my concern. "See? I'm resting. That's why I brought in the chair."

"You--" Being near her made me blurt out the hardest truths and I couldn't stop it from happening. "Maggie-girl, you make me ache so hard for things I can never have." The words fell soft toward her across the room. "I," I swallowed hard. "Maggie, I..."

The smile slid off her face and her expression grew stricken, "Don't say it, Richard. Not that." She tried to be gentle about it, "Not aloud just now. Let's not. It can't change anything here."

I took a shaky breath, "No, I don't suppose it can." Cloudy water and clumps of mud continued to drop off my clothes and soak the boards under my feet--a corpse pulled out of his grave. And maybe that was a bit more truth than even we needed between us just then.

Her eyelids drooped and she let her head settle back onto the cushion, already tired. "I know it, though," she said with her eyes closed, so she didn't have to see me while the words were in the air. "I know."

If there had ever been anything I wanted another person to know, it was that one single truth. I didn't have to ask how she knew. Never mattered if I did or said the exact opposite of whatever it was, she always knew. More than this, though, we were so connected I had a notion she knew a lot more about what went on inside me than she let on. I had a feeling, several of them now, in fact. And truth be told, I couldn't seem to make myself mind.

Then the invisible herald made its appearance in my unconscious as it always did. But so much more often since I'd known her, always when it was the wrong time. "Dawn, little bird. Almost time."

"Yes," she was still speaking with her eyes closed, growing sleepy. "I can hear it coming up over the edge of the world."

So, it was true. I wondered how many other things she knew. And then again, maybe I didn't want to know.

I was filthy and there wasn't much I could do about it with so little time. Only one day out of her bed, I found I didn't have to spend time closing up the house for daytime. She'd already fallen into our familiar routine and done it herself. There were only two lanterns to put out. Of course, I'd have to give her hell for all the work she did to cover the windows. She pulled out the special draperies she had packed away in my absence. They were simple but effective--heavy felting dyed black sewn onto several layers of quilted hemp sacking to block out the light. It made her feel better than having to see the wooden shutters locking her in. It made me feel better to see them back again, another of her little touches that made all things right.

Without the extra jobs, it left me time to wash the mud off. While the rain still poured down, dawn would only ease in behind the cloud. The type of morning I didn't mind so much, it let me steal an extra few minutes of day for night. A little gift I was given every so often that allowed me to live in almost-light for a moment. I couldn't relish it long, but standing in the rain dumping more buckets of water over my head out of the barrel, it did let me wash. In the end, I pulled my shirt off, wiped down the rest of me with it until I was passably unsoiled, and then ran for cover.

*****

"Whatcha doin'?"

Out of the clear, quiet night, an unfamiliar childish voice scared the holy hell out of me. I missed the chisel head, slamming the hammer into my thumb, *Bloody blue mother of--*"

It didn't hurt me much, not much could, of course, but the surprise about put me away. No one ever snuck up on me like that. My mind must have been farther away than I thought.

For reasons I was pretending not to look at with much specificity, after not getting any use but charcoal out of the last one, I decided to build myself a new porch swing. It would be nice to sit out and swing and watch the night. I knew how the old man felt in that way, about the simple pleasure of the evening porch sit and how much he missed it. It reminded me not to let that one get away from me. Unlike other people, the day to give that up would never come for me, so I should enjoy it more for the ones who had. Well, that's what I told myself, but really it was for Maggie. There was no reason for the carving and ginger breading that took me over a week of sneaking out to the barn to work on other than I thought she'd like it. I was deep in denial.

A pair of blue eyes twinkled in the lamplight out of a dirty face crinkled up in laughter. "Are you all right, sir?"

I set the hammer down and glowered at him from under my eyebrows, "Am I all-- Clearly you're unaware it's impolite to creep into a stranger's barn." I set my arms akimbo and tried to appear an authority figure to scare him away, "And what are you doing out at this time of night, little man?" He must have been about eight or nine, a curious little interruption and one I had no idea what to do with.

"Oh, aye, sir." He shrugged, "Felt like a bit of air is all." He wandered about, half in and half out of focus in typical childish fashion, trailing a hand over the newly planed wood. "Whatcha makin' there?"

"What's it look like?" I eyed him with suspicion. I had no experience with children other than the occasional patient with parents present or young bloods which is hardly the same thing. I had no idea what he was about or what he wanted. Or why he wasn't running away from the witch.

The tip of his tongue appeared in the corner of his mouth, "Well... Looks a bit like one of them fancy benches outside the millinery. Near to." He picked up a nail and put it down. He picked up the hammer, examined it for a moment, and put it down in a different spot. He picked up a chisel, turned it one way and the other to let the blade catch the light, and then put it down in a different spot, as well.

I huffed annoyance, "It's a porch swing, if you must know." He was still wandering around, trailing his little boy hands all over my things and I didn't know how to make it stop, "Hey, *heyyy*, would you put that *down*?" I took the saw out of his little fingers. "Quit. Quit *touching*, would you, please?"

His gaze darted everywhere, looking at everything, but he made a valiant effort to keep his hands at his sides where his fingers wiggled in anticipation against his legs. "You're a different sort, aren't you now, sir?"

"I beg your pardon?"

He squinted up at me as though I were some daft twat, "*Different*, y'know? Not quite like e'eryone else."

Who did this kid think he was? "Do you have any manners at all? What sort of question is that meant to be?" I took up the chisel and went back to carving out flower shapes to match some of the ones Maggie had planted in the garden. No-no, definitely not in denial.

He squinted in perversity, "Well, you are. Only sayin'." He didn't appear to have any intention of vacating my space and leaned his chin on my workbench to watch.

The big chisel was too thick to make the leaves, so I switched to a smaller one. "Right," I don't even know why I was speaking to him, "so it was an observation. What makes you think so?" Maybe because he wasn't running away.

His toe banged against the floorboards with rhythmic precision, *tap-tap-tap*, "'Cause you're not like e'eryone else, 'course."

"I see," I concentrated on the little curls of wood that spiralled up ahead of the blade. "And in what way do you mean, if you don't mind me asking?"

He cocked a head to one side, considering. "Well," he looked me up and down while choosing his words, "you don't want nothin' and ev'rybody else does. You just *are* is all." *Tap-tap-tap…*

A spiral stopped mid-curl and I looked down my elbow at him, "Just are, eh?"

"That's right." *Tap-tap-tap…*

"Humph."

"Lot o' folks want… Well, just want is all. Makes a body tired. Not you." *Tap-tap-tap…*

"Hm," I chiselled out another leaf. "Well, I suppose that's as good an answer as any." I was beginning to like this boy. He used plain talk and he was honest. I had no idea someone so young could be like that.

"Why?"

I worked a stem into the leaves, "Why which?"

"Why you're the only one like that. It's better, y'know?" He stuffed a fist into his cheek to lean on.

I had to think about that one. "I used to be like everyone else. Long ago." I watched him out of the corner of my eye, "Supposing I only wanted a change."

"Is that very hard?" he pointed at the carving. "Looks tricky," his gaze glued to the little curls coming off the corner of the chisel as I worked them out of the wood.

"Not overly." I worked it a bit more. He watched my every motion, every tip of the blade, every turn. It should have bothered me having someone at my elbow while I worked, but it surprised me to discover it didn't. He seemed to belong there. I let him watch. "You just have to see it in your head really. How you want it to look at the end. And then you make it come out of the wood. Like a drawing only backwards. You take out the bits you don't want in it, you see. What doesn't belong. What's left is the picture."

His concentration was total, the fingers of his free hand wiggling down by his leg, *tap-tap-tap…* I made another set of leaves and a stem appear. "That's a keen bit o' work. Like magic really. No wonder folks say you're a witch. Could you teach me how to do that, y'think?"

Disconcerted, I looked back down my elbow at him, wondering how his brain could switch from one subject to another with such ease and without any pretence at all. "Sorry, no. I don't think so."

His forehead puckered and he worked to hide his disappointment. "Oh," he said in a small voice.

Damn my inhumanity. Even with all Maggie's talking at me, making me talk *with* her, I was still bad at it. Especially with this little person. It was a bit too far outside the realm of my experience.

I cleared my throat and set the edge of the blade back into the wood, "It's the sort of thing you can't teach someone, is what I meant. You need to, well, you need to have the touch, as they say. Something you're born with." I hoped I sounded encouraging to an eight or nine year old.

His disappointment deepened, "Oh," he said again in an even smaller voice. "Guess that leaves me out then." *Tap-tap-tap…*

"How do you mean?" I didn't understand his reaction. "Have you tried it before?"

The tapping stopped. "No, sir. I weren't born with that." He pressed his fist further into his cheek, but continued to watch me work. "See, Papa says, when I were born? All I brought with me was misery."

The chisel skipped a little and I coughed to cover my surprise, "Really?" I didn't think humans acted this way with their offspring. I didn't know.

"Always told me so."

My hands kept at the detail, "So..?"

"How's that?"

"Is it true then?"

"Dunno."

"Of course, you do. Anyone would know something like that about themselves if it were true." I put down the hammer and chisel and switched to the awl to pick out some of the leavings, "So, is it?" But didn't set to it right off and leaned backwards against the edge of the workbench.

A toe scuffed through the shavings on the floor, "Guess'o."

"You guess it's true or you guess you know? Because if you want *my* opinion and not that it matters a lick, anyway," I turned the awl over in my hands and picked dirt out from under my fingernails with the tip, "but I didn't see you bring any misery in here myself. So naturally, I'm forced to ask what all that's about." I regarded him over the tip of my nail for a second. "Sorry, simply not seeing it."

"Truly?" The fist left his cheek and he turned around backwards to lean on the bench beside me, "Y'think differently?"

"Not a question of what I think," I concentrated on my nails while I continued to speak to him with feigned indifference. For reasons I couldn't explain, I was compelled to change his opinion. "Only what I see is all. Hell, people say the same thing about me all the time."

"But it's not true. You're just different."

"That's right. Look at the things they say about me, for instance. Fly on a broom? Snakes growing out my bloody head? Turn you into a newt? Ridiculous."

"Aye," the answer was slow while he considered. The serious look left him and he pulled a splinter out of the shavings on the floor and picked at his own nails. "Ridiculous."

"Right, well," I bit back a laugh, "there you go then."

"Bad luck about the broom, though. That'd be *smashing*."

"Well, yes," I coughed the laughter away and covered it up by turning back to my job for the evening. "Indeed." I pointed to the finishing file, "Right, as long as you're standing there, you know how to use that?"

"Aye, sir."

"Make yourself useful then."

The grin was ear to ear.

I set the tip of the awl into the scrollwork to clean it up, "Of course, I have to warn you."

His tongue was back out in concentration as he slid the file back and forth, "Sir?"

"You know my secrets now. I'll need your promise you won't tell anyone there's no snakes and I don't boil children in a cauldron. Would ruin the mystery, don't you think? Next thing you know, everyone would be running up here, knocking on my door, disturbing my peace and quiet. I'd never have a free moment to sit on my new swing here. I'm sure you can understand."

"Oh, I'd not breathe a word. Not one single word about that. You can count on me, sir. I won't tell, not a soul. I *promise*."

"As long as I have your word."

"Let's shake on it then." He spat on his palm and leaned over with his hand out, "Go on."

I looked at him blank for a beat. He was so young, barely born, and very much alive to be near. I wasn't hungry, but I could still feel it from him. Feel the intensity of it. It was just habit to avoid touching anyone for that reason. Easier. It's difficult to interact with anything that makes you salivate, if you know what I mean. However, he was a curious little man, honest and forthright, and so for him I went to the trouble. "All right, here's mine on it then." We clapped hands while he beamed.

The ratty sleeve of his shirt pulled up when he put his hand into mine and I saw the bruises up his arm while I still had a hold of his palm. I took another unconscious step toward humanity while a few things occurred to me right then. More than a few. Before I let go of his hand, I caught his gaze and then looked down to his arm, "I have something you could put on those."

He jerked his hand back and smoothed his sleeve back down in a hurry while he looked away. "That's nuthin'." Abandoning the file, he retreated back around the edge of the workbench, putting space between us.

"Looks like a pretty big collection of nothing to me. I'm rather an expert."

Tap-tap-tap.

"A bit known for it around these parts, actually. My vocation." I eyed him closely, looking for a reaction, "Apothecary… healer…"

Tap-tap-tap.

I considered him another moment as he withdrew farther without moving an inch. Maybe I should have let him. But I didn't. "Nothing to add? Nothing to say for yourself?"

Tap-tap-tap, "Nope, nuthin' to say about it," he shrugged.

"I see." Funny, he reminded me of Maggie just then. Her little bird to my snarly wolf. But I hadn't done this. Someone else was responsible this time. It seemed I wasn't the only one in the area with an inhumanity problem. Not my business, though. What could I do about it? I winced on the inside as something I couldn't describe to anyone tore itself by another inch in reaction to my potential thoughtlessness.

Eyeing him with hard decision, I spoke from a place of greater conscience, "Right, then I will. Go take yourself on up to the porch at the house there. Go and set yourself down and if Maggie comes out, tell her I said to give you a biscuit until I get there."

"How's that?" he seemed dazed.

"Porch. You. Go. Biscuit. It's a simple set of instructions. Off you go." He hesitated. "Hullo? Get yourself on up there, boy. I'll be right there to patch you up. *Shoo.*" One more look into my eyes and he hightailed it out of the barn. I figured I'd give him a minute to see if he ran off or did as he was told.

Taking my time putting my chisels away and pulling a tarp over the unfinished swing, a few minutes later I wandered out swinging the lantern. He was still there. Maggie was all over him and I knew she would be. By the time I got there, he already had a plate of biscuits and honey on his lap and she was setting a glass of iced tea next to him where he sat on the step.

136

Something struck me very hard as I watched her fussing over him. Another reason she had to go--so she could have a life, a regular life where she could do that with her own. There were so many things she deserved and this was one more in a long list I could never provide. It was hard to see, even in only an intellectual way, and gave the knife another twist.

"Found Maggie, I see."

"Yes, he did!" Maggie was exuberant. "And how did you expect him to choke down a dry biscuit? You know nothing about children, Richard."

"Humph," I dumped myself down beside him on the step. "Well, *he* doesn't know anything about witches if he thinks I'm not just feeding him so he gets fat enough to stick in my cauldron for my dinner," and gave him an exaggerated wink. The little man snickered through a mouthful of biscuit.

"*Richard,*" Maggie about had a coronary. "What sort of a thing is that to say to a little boy? Shame on you."

"Yes, yes, yes, let's not *frighten* the delicate little pain in my arse, shall we? Not like I don't owe him one or anything."

Now he was laughing. "Got you good, too."

"*You* scared *him*? I don't believe it."

"Truly, mum. Jumped 'bout a mile, he did."

"What?" now Maggie was laughing. "I can't believe you let this sweet, little thing catch you off-guard. You're slipping."

"Apparently. And it wasn't a *mile* for your information. I was only, you know... Momentarily taken aback."

They were both having a good laugh at my expense and I liked the scene, that little vignette in time. I would remember it as a happy moment. I tucked it away into the vault of my memory with the too-few others.

"All right, all right, have your laugh then," I moved off the step. "Wait right here." I went up to my loft and threw some cabbage leaves into my mortar to mash them down for a poultice and after a moment's hesitation grabbed the witch hazel, too. It couldn't hurt. From what I saw on his arms, the bruising looked fairly extensive. He wasn't cut, that I would have known, but I was sure there were more injuries that needed attention. If he skittered away like a frightened rabbit and I never saw him again, at least I could send him away on the mend. I hadn't even asked his name, but it didn't matter, because beyond these few medical services I could offer him, there was nothing else I could do.

Out on the porch, I rubbed witch hazel into what he would let me see to disperse the blood while Maggie distracted him and then to promote healing, spread the macerated cabbage on his arms and let it sit while he ate some berries and sugar.

"That stuff stinks," he wrinkled his nose.

"You'll live," I stretched out my legs beside him on the step again. "Be happy I didn't make you eat it. The smell's the best part."

"Yuck."

"Those berries any good? Maggie grows those out in the garden there, y'know."

"Oh yes, they're good 'n sweet. Will you have some?"

Maggie caught my eye over the top of his head, "Maybe later. Only wondered if they're worth the trouble yet."

A rider was coming up the road fast and Maggie and our little guest strained through the dark to see while I watched his approach from where I lounged. I had a fair idea who it was. Ours was the only place with any lamps lit in the night, but that didn't encourage people up to my hill. Tonight though, the little boy had come and whatever strange draw had turned him my way was liable to, in turn, draw the parent who would be looking for him. It was another of those things I had been in the world too long to bother puzzling out.

The horse ran straight up the path and pulled up short outside the glow cast by the lanterns hanging on either side of the front door. I rose to meet them. The plate of berries tumbled to the ground next to me and I could feel the little guy's heart wind up. The man didn't bother to dismount.

"You got my boy there," bleary-eyed, he spoke to the air around me rather than to me. Threadbare, ill-fitting clothes in the same condition as the boy's spoke a loud commentary on the state of their household.

"Depends. He have a name?"

His face twisted into a sneer, "Myles."

I turned and addressed my little guest directly, "Your name Myles, little man?"

"'Course, his name's Myles, y'conjuring fuck. Don't play thick with me." He pulled a beat-up pistol from his belt with difficulty and levelled it at my head. "Hand 'im over!"

I was slow turning back. His face wore a mask of rage disproportionate to the situation while the barrel of the weapon jittered about without regard for the direction. What had occurred to me in the barn appeared to match reality. I was feeling something but couldn't remember what it was called and wasn't sure what I was supposed to do. "Best you watch your tongue while you're stood on my land, friend."

"Oh, excuse the fuck outta me," the sarcasm was thick, but the alcohol was thicker. I knew he hadn't come for me. He wasn't even interested. "Get yer sorry arse up here, boy. *Move.*" He motioned the boy over with a couple of floppy flicks of the pistol that he didn't seem concerned about aiming in his own child's direction.

Myles stayed rooted to the spot.

"Quit yer fannying about or I'll teach y'a lesson you'll ne'er forget!"

He took two hesitant steps forward and then faltered, shaking hard in the thin light.

"Just wait 'til I get you ho-- Gor Blimey! What the bloody hell is *that*?" Two steps closer and the poultice was obvious. "What the blazes y'done to 'im? You causin' trouble, boy?"

"*No*," Interjecting, I took a step closer to deflect his anger from Myles, "he was certainly no trouble. He became turned about it seems.

Lucky for him he wandered this way, too. There's wolves up in these hills." I tried the beguile on his father, but he was beyond drunk and it didn't work well in that situation. "He's a bruise or two from where he must have taken a tumble, but he's right as rain now." I weighted my words anyway. A light touch here and there in Myles's defence until the man's arm dropped and the handgun fell into his lap unnoticed. "I simply put something on the bruises to speed their healing. The poultice needed to sit a mite, so we gave him some berries. We were set to take him back down ourselves when you happened by." I kept it conversational and informational and that was all.

He eyed me with suspicion, but the blind rage was tamped down some. "I've no coin for any of yer hocus pocus, witch."

"I didn't ask for any."

He stared down at me hard for a long moment, unmoving. "Aye," and looked past me to Myles again. "Away wi'ya, boy."

Myles did a very dangerous thing then and stepped behind me. Maggie was no help. Forever brave and foolish as she was, she came down the steps to stand behind him and put a hand on his shoulder in sympathy. Myles vibrated between us.

Myles's father snarled, anger leaping back into his eyes, "Gimme what's mine, witch!"

The boy's fear radiated out in every direction. I reached out again and gave his father another push, harder this time, twining the beguile around his soggy mind to bind up his emotions. It calmed him some, at least enough I thought Myles would be safe to leave with him. I didn't want anything to happen to him. I had no understanding of what this person was capable of, but it had been an eye-opening night for me in the ways of human interaction. It might have been the wrong thing to send the boy away, but I didn't know what was allowed. All I could do was the things I was good at, throw them in, and hope it helped.

Leather creaked as the man teetered in the saddle, "Come, Myles," but he held his place and stayed bound.

I turned my attention away and gave the boy's shoulder a squeeze. I wiped off the cabbage for him and when he looked me in the eye, I swear he could see right inside me. And I could see right inside him. He knew what would happen and then I saw it, too, and there was nothing either of us could do about it. I gave him my hand again the way I had back in the barn and made an unspoken promise of my own. Without my understanding how, he knew and nodded and then turned his back on me.

"Aye, Papa," Myles went to him then, head hanging and dragging his feet and his father snatched him up by the scruffy collar of his shirt. He no sooner threw the boy across his horse than he whipped the poor animal about and took off into the night without another word.

I watched them go down the hill a long while. Almost all the way to their house. I suppose, I wanted assurance he reached it in one piece. Maggie put an arm around my back and leaned into my shoulder, watching along with me at what I knew she couldn't see. She was very upset.

"You know this won't end well."

I watched the dust trail on the road pluming out behind the horse for a time before I spoke. "You don't know that."

"I wish there was something we could do."

"We already did, Maggie. He's someone's child. That's all."

"Richard," she chided me softly, "you *like* him. You only get gruff and short like that over things you actually care about."

I cleared my throat, "I'm sure I don't know what you mean."

"Yes you do, you great, sappy sod."

"Maggie--"

"Deny all you want. Already caught," she tipped up and kissed my cheek and then left me there contemplating while she took the dishes back into the house.

By the next week, I had the new swing done and hung it without telling Maggie what I was up to. The scrollwork and carving impressed her, of course, but when I told her Myles had come back three more times in the night and helped me with it, she liked that more. Especially when she saw we'd carved in our names side-by-side under the seat. And so we sat on it and swung and sometime during that night, I felt a curious ripple in the air. I didn't understand it until the next day.

When I woke hard on the heels of sundown, even from up in the loft inside the house I could smell it on the wind. The blood. I thought it was Maggie and it scared the shite out of me, because I had allowed myself to doze off instead of keeping watch over her.

I ran right out of the house, but she was sitting on the porch shelling peas. It was everywhere, but wasn't fresh. It was cold and still and dead. And not of the animal variety. A sinking feeling in the pit of my stomach spurred me on in frantic search as I tracked it. Maggie looked on with concern etched across her features.

Then I found Myles's body.

Lying face down by the side of the road near the end of the path to the hill, he was beaten almost unrecognisable. I thought he might have crawled there trying to get to us and we didn't hear. But when I turned him over to examine him, it became obvious he couldn't have made it with the injuries he had. He was dumped there some time during the day.

In death, he was even smaller and more fragile-looking than he'd been in life. I didn't know him, he was nothing to me really. But seeing him discarded in the mud and high grass like that churned up something in me. With care, I gathered him up into my arms and held the cold shell of him against the cold shell of myself. Gaze pulled down the hill in the direction of his home, my lip curled in anger.

I looked back down at his face in wonder and confusion. His eyelashes were feathered against his cheeks still plumped with the remnants of baby fat he would have lost in another year or so. He looked like a cherub, another angel who came to the devil I was. So different from everything I knew while he lived, in cold death we were more alike. It bound him closer to me in a way that made sense to me even while it wouldn't to anyone else. Because this wasn't about simple murder. Like Maggie, he had become mine.

Maggie made her way down the path to where I stood holding him. She pulled up short and then ran at me as I turned around.

"No!"

As she tugged his small body from my arms, I looked over the top of her head back down the hill in the direction of his home. I kept the snarl from passing my lips as I gathered her and the boy against me and worked to comfort her.

We buried him in stones to keep him safer than we had in life and set up another marker beside my own. Maggie cried for hours.

That night, I stayed in the barn alone.

The next, I let the night take me over and kept my unspoken promise to Myles.

*****

(Canada - Present)

"Who told you to come here?"

A rather large young person yanked the door open at the rattle of my keys in the lock blocking my way. "And who the fuck might *you* be?"

"No way, man. Don't play games. Nobody gets in that's not supposed to."

"How about this then? If you don't answer my bloody question, you'll all be out of *my* house," I showed him the keys, "without cover in time for sunrise. How would you like that, little blood?"

"Oh, shit. Sorry, man. Alan said you were on the way back."

"I'm sure he did. Well, we can all certainly rest easier knowing *Alan* is on the job." He got out of my way in a hurry and went running off yelling for Baby Bite. I put my duffel down in the front hall and surveyed my sanctuary.

I'd been invaded.

Mountain bikes leaned against my Louis XVI armoire. Various genres of music blasted from different directions. Coats lay discarded across the top my grandfather clock. Voices yelled and called from every compass point. The house felt very, *very* full. Not only full, though. Like Baby Bite, their radiating energy broadcast the same curious condition-- late adolescence or early adulthood. Nearly alive. I never knew anything like it, so many little vampires all collected together. Perhaps, Alan was right about the migration, though I doubted the storms were the only impelling factor. More like the old boys were gone, the makers and the leaders, and this was what remained.

"Good lord," I raked my fingers through my hair and worked to calm the storm brewing inside me. The next moment, someone zipped by on a skateboard and dashed any hope I had of achieving internal peace. I snatched him off by the collar before he could blink. "Excuse me, would you please not do that in the house? That's Italian marble on that bloody floor, boy."

His eyes were wide with surprise, "Whoa, man."

"Take it outside, little blood," my gaze drilled into him in beguile and he shook his head, fighting it. It worked on bloods, too, the younger ones who hadn't learned to harden themselves to it. Though not for the same purpose, of course. More like the big dog in the yard throwing the little one down and exposing his throat. There could be only one alpha. "Clear?"

"Yeah-yeah, message received." I released him and he grabbed his board from where it rolled into the wall. "Peace, man," holding up one hand in surrender, he walked backwards all the way to the door. And then legged it.

I grumbled in annoyance, "Destructive little pecker." I wasn't about to go running all over the house looking for Baby Bite, so I pulled out my satphone and rang my home number. I ground my teeth through the delay while it connected, each click fuelling my annoyance.

"Hel--"

"Where the fuck are you, Baby Bite?"

"Wha..? Hello? Oh, it's you. Jeez, do you even know how to say hello?"

"Stuff it. Where are you?"

"I'm right where you left me. In the house, remember? How else could I answer the phone?" He was laughing, "Are you juiced or something, old man?"

"Juiced?" I waved it away and massaged my forehead with my fingertips. "Never mind. Look, mate, I'm standing in my front hall and see about eighty-five baby bloods running riot over my house causing mass destruction as we speak. Care to explain or should I just de-craniate you right now?"

"Huh? What the hell's de-craniate?"

"Tear your head off your shoulders, little man."

"Shit--"

"Start talking and it better be good."

"Okay-okay, don't get your panties in a bunch. You're in the hall? I'll be there in a sec. Just chillax, dude."

It didn't take long for Baby Bite to come skidding into the entryway, satellite phone still in hand. I couldn't help but feel self-satisfied. They should all be afraid of me. It would make it easier.

I lit into him before he even got close, "I thought you said five or six, maybe a couple more. This is not five or six or even ten. What the fuck is going on and how the hell did they all get here so fast? I was only gone *twelve days*. Are you completely mad?" I sidled up on him and he held his hands out to keep the prowling tiger at bay.

"Just wait, okay, before you freak-out," his hands stayed out as we fell into a little side-stepping circle dance around each other. "I can explain. Lemme explain--"

"Speak!"

"Look, it's like this. I called the rest of the crew. Like I told you--five, six bodies. Ten tops. That's *it*. But word gets around, y'know? Everybody's got a phone."

"Everyone's got a bloody phone? That's the best you've got?" I had to raise my voice to be heard over a sudden blast of Tupac that rang through the house. "Who are all these people then? Where the fuck did they come from?"

My poor house. In two hundred years, it never had its foundation shaken by the kind of abuse it was taking now. Boots stomped across floors. Doors slammed left and right. Lights were on everywhere, video games screeched and roared, music blasted, laptop and tablet screens glowed in every corner. I was far enough out to be off grid and self-sufficient for power, so I wasn't worried about it. It just pissed me right off, plain and simple.

"Some of 'em are Billy's, for sure, but I really don't know where the rest came from. I swear. Some of them don't even speak English, man. They just showed up. I couldn't turn them away. Seriously, none of them have anywhere else to go."

This was not conducive to my happy life. "What utter shite."

A football sailed into the front hall with two baby bloods running hard behind it. I reached out and snagged it out of the air and they pulled up short. "Yours?"

"Yes, sir," they both looked contrite and I liked it that way. Better behaved than Baby Bite.

"I have a job for you two." They gave each other a look and then waited. "Do you know who I am?" They shook their heads. I shot Alan a scowl. "I'm the reason you're here, apparently. Master of this house. And for your further edification, you can start thinking of me in those terms. It may keep you out of trouble. Understood?" They nodded. "Right. Now that we've been introduced, I want you to tell every single one of your little cohorts I'm home. And to get busy picking up the fucking mess they made. *Now*. Move it out boys. Double time." They ran for it.

I watched them scurry away. "They can't stay here, Alan. Not all of them. There's too fucking many to house. Where are they sleeping? Like bats from the rafters? I mean... *bollocks...*" My mind raced. "This isn't a city. In case you hadn't noticed, there's not a lot to divert attention out here. Provide cover. Or have you missed the decided lack of anonymous crowds? It's dangerous, little man, don't you know that? Might as well put up a bloody billboard out by the highway pointing the way to vampire central."

"I guess," dejected, Alan hung his head.

"You guess? This is the reality here, Baby Bite. Do you really expect them to all fit comfortably in this space for more than a few days at most? After that, everyone will start getting on everyone else's nerves. Mainly mine. I live alone. I need to be *alone*. I didn't even want *you* here and now look at this chaos!"

"I know," his distress seemed genuine, "Sorry, man. It wasn't supposed to be like this. I swear."

"What a pile of wank," I sighed. My gaze wandered off him to stare into the intricacy of the large tapestry hanging on the wall while I calculated. "Do you truly comprehend why so many of us cannot exist in the same space? It's not practical. The hard truth of it is there's not enough to eat, Baby Bite. Humans are few and far between here. We could wipe out an entire town in no time flat. It wouldn't be right. And it would bring attention to us. We couldn't even explain this many--" I threw up my hands in frustration and turned back to him, "This many *young people* living together. How could we, unless I suddenly established a charter college out in the middle of nowhere here or something equally ludicrous? Just the effort to keep up that type of pretence," I made a disgusted noise. "Most of the ones I've seen look too young to vote. I don't know what identities they're working with, but I hope to hell they can all at least sign for themselves." Then the penny dropped. "Wait a minute. Wait one minute--" I gave him a hard look.

"That's why you hooked up with Billy, wasn't it? Because you can't. You need an appearing adult to survive. Bloody fucking hell!" I kicked my duffel, "Fuck, fuck, *fuck*. I can't play nursemaid to a sordid nest of baby bloods. I told you I can't be your daddy, little man, I can't do it. It's insanity! That sort of thing takes planning and space and back-up plans. And, hell, it takes a whopping great gob of technology, goddammit, and I fucking hate technology."

Alan sat right down on the floor and rested his face in his hands and said nothing. He looked as though I signed his death warrant and perhaps I had. "We didn't have anywhere else to go." His voice was small and a long way from the brash young blood who crept into my sanctuary without invitation.

"Aw, fuck." Anything else wouldn't have bothered me one bit. But not this. That resignation. It always got to me and there wasn't anything I could do about it. Couldn't even help myself. It was the little bird to my snarly wolf and I had no defence. "Sonofa*bitch*," I stomped about waving my hands, but knew it was useless. Somehow I'd inherited a huge family of Baby Bite clones. This wasn't my world and I wasn't prepared for this sort of thing. Everyone was stepping on everyone already. In *my* space, touching *my* things.

And I couldn't turn them out.

"Arrrgh!" all my counter arguments scattered. "Look," I squatted down on my haunches in front of him, but he was lost in space. I snapped my fingers, "Hey, Baby Bite. *Alan*," he looked up, blank. "You know I have my own business with Billy, right? You understand this?"

"Yeah, I know you have your own life to live. I get it."

"Okay. And you know why it's important to me I go after him?" my voice softened without meaning to.

Baby Bite nodded in sympathy, "Yeah, I heard ya. He's a crazy ass and you're the only one of us who could take him out. You'll be doing all of us a favour. That psycho really scares me, y'know? We'll be better off with him gone. I don't wanna hold you back, old man. Don't worry about us. We'll figure it out."

"No offence, but I really have no interest in how he might affect any of you. Really. That part is about me. Something I need to do. Of course, I have to find him first. And since I have nothing but time to do that in, I suppose," I took a deep breath, "I suppose I'll be doing some travelling." I looked off across the hall so I didn't have to look him in the eye. "So you may as well stay here while I'm gone. Someone needs to water my garden while I'm away, anyway. Make yourself useful. Your little friends, too. At least temporarily until they figure out some other arrangement."

"Seriously?" Life came back into Baby Bite's face, "We can stay?"

I still wouldn't look at him, but it didn't matter. They were all now mine. "Yes, you stupid twit. Don't you understand English? Shit. Don't make me say it again or I'll change my mind."

"Schweet!"

"I must be right out my fucking head. Guess that puts me and Billy on equal ground then." I stood back up and was mostly talking to myself, "Could help me find him. One nutter to another."

"Hey, wait a minute," Alan was very alert. "Why don't you let us help you?"

"Eejit. Why would you even want to? It my beef, little blood. You get involved and it'll get messy. For *you*. De-craniate, remember? Not only in my repertoire."

"Not like that, old man," he was laughing as though I had missed the joke. "You hate technology, right?"

"Bloody right. It's the scourge of the modern age."

"Yeah, like I didn't already know. You haven't even figured out how to say hello on the phone yet. *Anyway*, not *all* of us are technophobes. You could have your own team of research assistants. Track his movements once he left the islands. Credit card transactions, deeds, car rentals, anything. We've got enough computer power here to launch the space shuttle. We could find him easy if we tried. Whaddaya say? Would that help you out? Pay our way some?"

Considering the task, alone, it could take me another hundred years to find him again. Not that I didn't have that much time, but maybe Baby Bite was right. There were a lot of them and it could be a point in my favour. Give me an edge. I didn't want the help, but at the same time it was a whole new world full of things in which I was woefully under-schooled. But they knew. And they were right here. I didn't want to take the help, but I'd be foolish not to. It was hard to make myself say yes.

"Well?"

"Don't rush me. I'm thinking it over."

"Okay-okay." He knew he had me, too. I think I hated that the most.

"So let me get this straight. You're saying you could find him through his receipts? Things he buys, rents, or whatnot? From here without going anywhere. That can be done?"

"Most definitely," Baby Bite got up off the floor then and grabbed my duffel bag for me, motioning me up the stairs.

Who was I to blow off a personal assistant? I walked up. "If you can really do it, then yes, it would help me out. Of course. Even still, it can't be that easily done. He's old school, like me. Prefers cash. Been around long enough to know not to leave a paper trail."

"Yeah-yeah, I get that part. But see, here's where we can be even more useful."

We reached my room and I was glad to discover no one had taken it over. At least, he kept them out of something. "How do you mean?"

Baby Bite grinned, "Because some of us were with him. He needed us to help him set up some of his electronic accounting. Not all of it, but enough. Even if he changed things in the past couple years, we still understand how he operates. His patterns. What he's comfortable with, y'know?"

I had a balcony with French doors matching the ones downstairs that opened onto an overhead view of the garden from my room. I threw the doors open onto a nice night and almost didn't notice the multi-layered music fighting for airspace. I leaned on the railing and inhaled the night, "Hm."

I threw my head back and felt the earth, felt the life, and for the first time in a very long while, felt I had a reason. I would have my revenge. It was Billy's doing, too, so I didn't even need to feel responsible for starting anything. The day Baby Bite showed up, I knew I was being called out. There was no other reason for Billy pointing them in my direction, exposing me. He wanted it. Perhaps, he wanted to die.

And maybe I would give him what he wanted, because it suited my purpose.

I spoke with my eyes closed, "Tell them to get busy. All of them. Find him." He started out of the room, but I stopped him, "Alan?"

"Yeah?"

Considering all the information they might have available, an old haunt made a sudden appearance. I shook it off the next moment without turning around, "Never mind. It's a pipedream. Mesopotamia's long gone. Just find him. Do that much for me? And I'll do the rest."

Alan paused before answering. When he spoke again, his voice was tempered with something I didn't understand, "I'll get them on it right away. You won't be disappointed. I promise."

7

(England – Seventeen twenty-something)

t wasn't until we put the marker up over Myles's grave that I finally learned how much time passed in my own burial. A little under three years. Thirty-one months by Maggie's count. Nine-hundred-forty-three nights I hadn't woken. That was all. Not as long as I thought and yet infinitely less than would pass in Myles's rest.

Thirty-one months in or out of the world was a hiccup to me, a forgotten moment, an idle thought staring at stars. I couldn't believe it was so brief. It was meant to be longer, a lot longer, but that call back wouldn't let me rest. I was destined to exist, it seemed, in unexplainable harmony with lives beyond my own.

The inscription over my cairn was simple, only one word--*Beloved*. It never occurred to me Maggie would have no idea what to add beyond that. It made little difference to me, of course. I'd had a thousand lives, so marking time on the last one meant nothing.

But Myles only had the one, so it was important to record.

It was important to *me*. To remember the brevity of it. The emptiness created when it was gone. The hole that couldn't be filled by any other person. The singularity and significance of each human life weighed heavily on me as I walked back to the house that night. And dumped more ammunition into the middle of my internal war.

My courses had changed. I no longer flitted from one thing to the next without connection or conscience. That was obvious. No matter how short her own life would be, Maggie had already impacted me more than anyone else in history except, perhaps, the one who made me. That other person took something away from me, though, while Maggie only gave. With nothing more than being herself, she drove me to be more than I was. Even to invoking some need within me to strive for more.

In giving up her lifeblood to my resurrection, with every day that went by, I was more and more convinced it was this that changed me on a fundamental level. Clung to it. Can admit I even blamed it sometimes when the whole thing got away from me and scared me silly with its raw and savage fury. And I *was* frightened by it. Terrified, in fact. The world changed around me and I went along with that, but my changing self? No. I didn't even know what I was anymore and lived in a perpetual state of uncertainty. The more unsettled I became, however, the more it seemed to make her happy.

Who can understand the mind of a woman?

Two months after Myles's death, Maggie was more or less herself again except for some weakness and, of course, the scars. And those I dedicated myself to healing and fading as far as possible for her. I was quite compelled. There were deeper injuries beyond my skill to heal away, though. She would always have difficulty turning her head to one side no matter how much I wished I could fix it. Her arm fared the best with the joint spared and while stiff, she had the full use of it again. I filled her with blood meat to build her up, venison dinners she complained about, because it wasn't her favourite, but which she ate, because I told her to. Vegetables from the garden and continued blood tonics along with it all served the same purpose. As the days went on I was glad to see the pallor leave her face.

"What do you think, Maggie-girl, grouse tonight? Duck? Hare, perhaps." A live, human woman needed food, needed meat to eat, and in the midst of meeting her needs, I set upon a new course of eating for myself. A necessity. The by-product of my internal war, within a short time of my rebirth I soon found it too difficult to sneak away to hunt.

It wasn't even that I still tried to judge myself by the human yardstick I believed she should. Now in possession of whatever slim humanity I'd gained, when the blind hunger fell over me in all its intensity, no guilt-soothing, conscienceless blanket descended with it. A constant battle fought by conflicting emotions I was not equipped to navigate, the war between the darkness and the healer raged on.

"Duck, I think." She smiled down at me from the new porch swing where she snapped beans, "Yes, I would like that." She still tired if she did too much, but sitting and swinging she could do some of the chores she was compelled to do while conserving her strength.

When I hunted for her dinner, now it was also for mine. I made a very conscious choice to turn from human blood and let the same animals that gave their lives for Maggie do double duty. They all needed to be bled before she could eat them, anyway, so it became a rather accommodating situation. No matter what I craved was the human essence to fuel me, I could live off the lesser, shadow lives of animals. I'd done it before a time or two, though never with such focussed purpose.

"Back in a tick. I best not see you moved from there, woman." I scowled in warning, but she was never afraid of me.

"Or what? You'll turn me into a newt?" A bean sailed across the porch at me while her eyes twinkled with mischief. How did I survive all the centuries before she came?

"Behave."

"Never."

"Incorrigible."

"Hurry back."

"Yes, lamb. *Rest*."

I continued to survive, though. At least, now I could look her in the eye without cringing, because I was no longer the demon killing off her brothers and sisters in humanity. I swore to myself I would maintain this focussed way of life until she was old. And then make the scenario that haunted my dreams into reality and beg her to let me die with her.

Weeks passed while I pursued this new course and unspoken though it was, in time, Maggie noticed. We never discussed this part of my life, not in plain words, and I always steered away from it. There were no words I knew to explain it to her in some manner that didn't paint me as anything other than a perversion. Despite that, she was attentive enough for the change to make an impact.

"You've been drinking animal blood, haven't you?" in her usual way, there was no dancing about and she got right to the point. "You stopped running off in the night for yourself. You only hunt for my dinner. Don't lie to me, Richard. I know you must be then."

It was always a bit unnerving to me when she came out with something that way, but she asked, so I was compelled to answer. "Yes."

"Why? I can tell it's not as good for you. Your colour's been off and you look thin."

That she would notice something like that would forever perturb me. I choked on it and worked out a few words of explanation, "It's not so easy, you know." I had a creaky, old chair that fit me just right that had survived the fire. A little singed now, but broken-in through lots of use, the addition of some old quilts made it comfortable--my favourite spot. I settled in and stretched my legs out in front of the fire. "This. Us. What I am. It's not the same anymore." I stalled and cleared my throat. The words fell without inflection, "There's a war in me about it, girl. Feeling I'm doing wrong to follow my own nature. Trying to live, yeah? Takes some of the war out of it is all." I watched the flames dance and could say no more.

"You never talk to me about this," Maggie was in her rocker sewing together a new shirt for me. "You hold it so hard and never share it. Not since you first told me. Why?"

"Why?" I laughed without humour. "If there's a," I gestured in futility, "a *good* way to discuss it, I don't know it. Never had to before. With anyone. Leaves me rather speechless."

She raised her head from her stitching and shot me a brief look I couldn't read, "Speech-making was never your forté," before she dropped her head back to her work. "But this…" She concentrated on her stitches, "I know what you do no matter you've kept me from it. I know how you're compelled to hunt… people. I know they die when you take their blood. That you crave it."

Why did it sound so much worse to hear any part of it from her? It made me cringe and took my voice. All I could do was hunch my shoulders against it and get lost in the fire.

More stitches took up time. "Do you crave their deaths, Richard? Is that part of it? Or only the result?"

"No! I mean--" I scrubbed a hand across the back of my neck, uncomfortable. Damn, but she got right to the heart of anything she wanted to know. "No, I don't crave their deaths, lamb."

The very loud crackling of the fire worked to fill up a very long pause. "Do you wish to make them suffer? Crave that also?" her voice small against such a large question.

A cold chill ran up my spine. "No, Maggie. I don't seek to make them suffer," I was whispering, because discussion of the nitty-gritty of my hidden existence stole my voice. "I don't ever want to do that," I wriggled the question off my shoulders, uncomfortable. "Not any part of my need."

She looked up then and examined the stricken look on my face. "I knew you couldn't," she said after a long moment, her tone tender. "It's not in you to do me harm. It couldn't be that way only toward me despite all you believe." She gave me a penetrating look. "You're not that sort of man."

I gave the fire my attention again, "I'm no sort of man at all," because it was too hard to look at her and talk about this. "Not for a great while." Maggie was very quiet in her chair nearby, studying me. I squirmed under the intensity of her gaze. "This was no choice. Especially, not what goes with it. Outside my belief about what it might be, there's a reality here. Thought disappears. It's like--" The words fell in ones and twos, hard fought words that leaked out the truth. We might never go there again and I owed her my honesty, because she had a right to know on what sort of animal she'd misplaced her affections. I tried hard. "There's a... trance? It overtakes me. Dream uncontrolled. But if I work at it, fight it?" The words worked their way out from between my teeth that had clenched with the effort to describe that hopeless fight to someone who could never know. "Then I won't fall in, you see? So hard to fight off, but... If I keep... thinking... Touching the world, perhaps? The thoughts hold me somehow. And don't let it take me over. Then I won't... don't... kill anyone." I didn't feel well. Confession is supposed to be good for the soul, but then I had none so all it brought me was disquiet.

The creaking of her rocker was all the noise in the house as she listened, attentive as she always was to my seldom words. She seemed to let them sink in and weigh them for a time before she spoke again. "Yes, I saw you fight it. That day in the cellar. I remember."

"Except--" I dragged the heal of my palm across my forehead a couple times to rub out the headache building from making myself speak about what I didn't want to. "It's constant, Maggie. Not so obvious. Not so, you know, dramatic as that day I was starving. But that's the feeling in me. It's very big." I snuck a guilty look over at her and found her eyes still on me, hard and direct. I couldn't hold them. I looked away and shifted around in my chair. "To fall in, is to know nothing. Bliss. It's everything. But what I am, that existence? Now it eats me alive. A war, like I said. It feels wrong now. Afterwards."

"You like it, though," she was nodding to herself. "That feeling. That place you get to without going anywhere."

There could be no lying about it and that confession was more difficult. "Yes," I barked a laugh at the perversity of it all. "I suppose I should I deny it. That would be the right thing to do. The human thing, yeah? But then I'm not human, am I. I know what it means and crave it anyway. Can't help myself. It's not about them right then. It's about me. It's--" I savoured the guilty memory of it and lost my voice. Maggie said nothing, but I felt her gaze on me until I found it again.

I cleared my throat, "Over the years, I've met others before. Not many. A few. Same black curse, walking death. I'm not alone in it, it seems. I don't know if that makes it better or worse. They have a name for that place, that feeling. They call it The Rapture." I spoke to the fire, "And that's exactly how it feels, Maggie. Being in rapture. Awash in warmth. Celebration. Being reborn again and again. That moment is the most perfect instant captured in history. Better than every other before or after and you know no others. Every good thing is in you then. Your heart speeds up and it stirs your brains dizzy and you want to throw your head back and howl in ecstasy until the end of time."

Maggie abandoned her sewing and listened, intent. "How could such a thing ever make you suffer so? It seems a gift," her words came out with breathless curiosity.

"Gift?" a grim smile stretched my mouth while I continued to talk to the fire. "Right. One that can't last and never does. Nothing more than a stolen moment to savour. And then it's gone," I gestured, casting that dandelion fluff moment away on the breeze. "Always too soon. And then all that's left is still, cold death."

"But--"

I didn't hear her. I was somewhere else and still talking. For one brief moment able to articulate the thing that had no words. "It's quick to disappear, but never quite quick enough, you know?" A disparaging laugh escaped between the words. "Drains away just slowly enough to cause its portion of agony. To really let you feel the life fade, yeah? Feel the cold creep in. Heart slowing again. Torturous... Dying again like the first time, but made so much worse, because you know it's coming. Who would have thought an eternity of death could be made more shite than it already could be, eh? But it is. It is, because you *know*. You *will* die every time you steal that tiny, delicious morsel of life. And regardless, are still driven to steal it. Even in The Rapture there's no real joy, because it's an illusion. A cheat. A shadow of what life is. But, of course, even that's made more shite. Because the shadow is also a lie. It's death in craven disguise. Death and dying and yet I'm still compelled to steal the life that can't last. And doing that brings more death. Brings death to someone who lived a real life and not a shadow life like mine." Wood crackled on the arms of my chair where my hands had clenched over the ends without meaning to. I forced them open again.

"Richard," her voice was soft with empathy, "it's so awful and desolate. I could never imagine," there was a shudder in her voice. "How could this be put upon a man? It's not right you suffer so."

I laughed again without humour, "And rightly so I should suffer. It's been a thousand lifetimes of death and dying broken up by seconds of bliss. Bliss... Not even my own. I have to take them from some other poor bastard just to live again for a heartbeat or two. And the price of my longing is death on my hands." I grimaced, "You know what the worst part of it is? I take the life to live, but it's not even life I'm given. It's a shadowy half-life that means nothing. Feels nothing. Accomplishes nothing. It's been so long, to touch The Rapture is to remember and then in the same instant know I was denied. Only it doesn't matter, because I want it for myself, anyway. Can't even help myself--"

"Don't--"

"You can't know, can't understand that need. That longing. It's everything. It fills up the whole world. The only thing that makes it stop is to let the stupor come over me and not think so I can take what I need. Nothing else makes it stop. Believe me, I've tried. There's no substitute. And I'm weak, Maggie. Weak and pitiful. Tried to go without so many times, but in the end? I go on and on being a thief. A *murderer*--"

I didn't hear her sewing slide to the floor and refused to hear her words when she tried to comfort me, "Richard, you're not responsible and it doesn't define who you are. It never could. It never has. There's nothing to gain by torturing yourself with it now. Please, don't do this--"

"And now it's so much worse. You can't imagine. You made me live, girl. Gave up your blood to the ground where I lay in wait like the thief I am and you fed me. *You* fed me. Without meaning to, I know, but you did. And through that, in some way I don't understand... Perhaps, that you're still alive? Or your wild, magical belief in your own safety here? Or that I'm--" I barely caught myself and it went unsaid. I took a shaky breath. "I feel again. Some. Enough. Too much for what I am. Now it's war. Now I *feel* the killer I am. *Feel* the conscience prick to even think about it while at the same time it's what I crave to have five moments of peace inside myself--"

Her hand was on my shoulder and I don't know when she moved or how long she'd been standing there. I was lost. All my words used up, there was nothing more to say. Without seeming to have moved again, I found her perched on the arm of my chair with her hands in my hair and her warm lips against my mouth. Since the first day, she'd been the master of muddling up my old brains and she always would be. Her heart was so loud inside me it blocked out everything and I drowned in the scent of her so close to me. Even in weakness, she was the most alive person I'd ever come across. But now almost healed again, the spark of her dazzled me with its perfect brilliance until I couldn't keep a single, coherent thought in my head.

Without stopping to consider the consequence, I pulled her down into my lap. I held the warmth of her against me hard and kissed her harder, because I loved her so much and had never been able to show her the way she wanted me to. But that's not all there was and not all there ever could be. The thunder of heartbeat and the lightning of electric need would always overtake and sour everything good I could ever know. Even the love. In unthinking, it called me and I dragged my lips from hers to draw them down to the soft spot under her ear in anticipation.

Goose flesh rose on her skin and I heard her moan, but it was far away from me. I nipped at her throat and she laid her head back and didn't even try to stop me. I think I was laughing, but I might have been sobbing in contemplation, because I hadn't let myself in so long and ached for it. Ached for the blood and here she was, laid right across my lap in offer. I was breathing hard and so was Maggie, but she was in a different place. A safe place, far away from the monster I would always be. She didn't know and never could.

Until I caught up her head in the clench.

Head caught fast in the crook of my elbow and bent back hard to expose the artery for my greater ease, she shook up against me. It was harsh and unexpected and had to be uncomfortable.

"Richard…"

And I couldn't let go.

I pulled her chin back another inch and licked my lips.

"Richard, too much… hurting me…"

Something wasn't right. The beguile ensured no one ever struggled to ruin my feast, to intrude on my single moment of peace, and yet here was no calm. The heartbeat ricocheted around my brain at the speed of light and warmth rose up under my hands and something about it was wrong for that moment, but I didn't care.

I snarled.

Maggie continued to shake under my hands, her words whispers, "…my neck… be easy, Richard…" The hands braced against my chest could never hold me back. Nothing could do that. She started to cry, but it was far from me and I had lost the ability to understand what that was, so it made no impact. Her fingers clutched at the fabric of my shirt. I was in that other place of sudden blindness that protected me from seeing what was in front of me while I did it.

I bit into her neck.

Not hard, not in malice, because in achieving my stolen pearls it was always with the greatest of reverence. With ravenous precision, I pierced that soft, new, pink skin where she had healed while she shook and the tears ran.

"Richard... hear me... I know you can..."

It was wine. The only wine I ever wanted. The only wine I ever needed and it was so warm, warm and alive and perfect. And familiar. The tears running down her face wetted my arm and when there should have been silence and peace, her voice reached me inside. The fingers now splayed out against my chest were shaking and the weight of her in my lap registered. All these things came to me a-piece and then took a moment more to make sense.

I tasted her blood on my tongue and knew what I did.

Full in Rapture, I ripped my mouth from her neck and softened the hard hand leveraging her head back. My other arm slipped behind her, instead of in need, then to cradle her with care against me in my own horror. She shook harder.

"Maggie, my Maggie-girl... Are you all right? Speak to me, girl. What have I done to you? Say something. *Anything*."

I wanted to push her off me and run away, so I wouldn't have to face her. But I couldn't leave her, because she was mine and I was responsible for her. I hurt her and had to fix it. There could be no forgiveness for what I did and she would never trust me again, but I wanted to fix it anyway. I told her I didn't trust myself despite she did and this was the reason. I tried so hard not to be that *thing* and be what she wanted. But here was the proof it wasn't possible no matter how much humanity I might now feel in my possession. I simply wasn't human. I wanted to die.

And knew I'd have ample opportunity for that over time eternal.

"Richard?" her voice was muffled.

"Yes, lamb," I leaned over and spoke softly into her ear.

She wiggled around some and though I didn't want to, I eased her back a little to see her face. She'd stopped crying and I wiped away the tear tracks with my thumb. "Richard," she was smiling, a tentative little upturn at the corners of her mouth, "do you know how deeply I'm in love with you?" Her eyes were heavy-lidded and her voice full of emotion.

That was about the furthest from what I expected her to say. Damn, but she did keep me in a constant state of confusion.

It didn't make any sense. She was delirious. I must have drained her more than I realised. I frowned in concern, "Can you ever forgive me? Did I hurt you badly? Let me see. Here, let me make it better. Please, Maggie. I have no right to ask you to trust me again, but--"

Her fingers on my mouth silenced me.

The look in her eye was self-assured, "I always have."

I tried to protest, but she wouldn't let me. "No. No more talk out of you. You've done more than enough for one night already, I think. Now, *you* listen. Understood?"

When I tried to answer, she shook her head. Little blue twinkle lights zapped in and around the edges of my vision while her pulse broke up against me hard enough to hypnotise me and make me lose it. I fought it and stayed found. Swallowing hard, I nodded without verve.

A finger traced the outline of my top lip. I knew there was blood in the corner of my mouth and wished I wiped it away before I was forced to sit in silence with her examining me in detail. It was the guilty evidence of what I did, but I faced her, anyway. I owed her that and she would do whatever she needed to do.

Gaze focussed, she raked my face. I watched her gaze drift over the blood and then back again. The tip of her finger came back across my lip and wiped it away. My heart beat so hard in tandem with hers they must have been able to hear it for miles. Ripped away mid-Rapture, I was not all of myself even while I was more so. I was still half-flying and not quite in the world even while she was all of the world sitting there in my lap. It was most disconcerting.

But not as confusing as when she wiped the blood on her finger across my bottom lip.

There was no judgement in her eyes, no mistrust or anger. I was afraid to move, though. I didn't believe what was happening and thought it must be only my skewed perception.

"Isn't that what you wanted?" her voice was soft and encouraging and I knew then I must have been dreaming or gone mad. I wanted to say something, anything, but my voice was gone, swept away by that tiny motion and her words. The blood on my lip was scented with her essence and I wanted to lick it off. Determined, I refused and worked to stuff my brains back into my head.

"I see you fighting it, but you don't need to. I put it there. It's all right, Richard." There was no way she could be serious, but I knew she was. "You have my permission."

There was no way I could look at her just then and half-crazed, but somehow in control, I closed my eyes in savour and sucked the blood off my lip. It was cold, but I didn't care. It was still better than any live animal blood. To me, better than any human, too. It was a marvel how she never feared any part of me and now, even in this, she was so self-assured that it was far beyond my ability to comprehend.

"Look at me," her voice was strong and expected my attention.

I gave it to her. "Yes, Maggie." I was breathing hard, but she grew calmer, surrounded by an aura of serenity.

The next moment would be etched into my memory in brilliant clarity for every second of every year I continued to exist. With her eyes locked on mine, she reached up and scratched at the already clotting blood at the side of her neck.

"For you, my love," and when she pulled her fingers away they were covered in fresh blood that she put to my lips.

From her throat to my mouth it was still warm and I licked it off her fingers with her eyes on me, the only living thing ever seeing me as I was and not afraid. The only human being who had allowed me to feed with permission I'd not forced from them with stealth or singsong words that became spells of enchantment. The only living thing that had ever fed me and lived for me to continue to love, because I loved them all who kept me alive. But this was so much more. It was not a simple love of the humanity I craved, but of the heart. I knew it was where I drew the strength to tear myself away when I might have killed her like the rest. The way she loved me, the depth of it was clear and saw past the curse to the man and unacknowledged human needs and to the memory of the soul I had once possessed. It was a wondrous thing that wasn't possible yet it existed there in that moment even if in no other.

It was hard to breathe, but in a good way. She looked so happy. There was no explanation that made sense to me and it was only something that was. I wanted to ask her, but didn't know how with any grace. I didn't want to be so tactless in that moment of perfection.

She turned her head to the side, but her eyes were on me, inviting me to her throat, *inviting* me. It was ecstasy. But, of course, it couldn't be allowed. The offer without fear was an experience in itself, though. So close to my own secret daydreams and very real. It did something to me, deep inside. Unlocked some frozen part of me. It made me smile, because I knew I was completely happy with her and for a real and true reason that I gained for myself even as I was. It was real and she was real and in turn, she had somehow made me real again for an instant.

I kept my eyes on her as I dipped my head to the fresh wound in her neck and licked it clean with sparing, gentle concern. She couldn't afford to lose any more blood than she had and I would never ask that of her. What she'd already given me was everything I longed for and satisfied me like nothing ever had before.

And she was still alive.

I straightened and brushed my knuckles up and down her cheek in caress, "You are a wonder, girl." Her eyes were shining. The fire burned low and the room had darkened around us without our notice and it was cosy and close and dim. I still had little to offer her, but I gave her the soft voice in the dark, because she deserved the best I had in any moment. "If I never have another day to speak these words, I want you to hear them now. I don't understand how or why, but you see me as I am and tell me you love me. More even, because of it. I'm not quite the same anymore. Your doing. I'll tell you this, girl, the man you've made me *does* love you. Even against the demon that possesses you. Well, that makes it into something else, I suppose. Or nothing. Or more. I know that doesn't even make any bloody sense. And you know what? It doesn't change a single, sodding thing and yet, it changes everything."

As she had since the first, that hand came up and her fingers fluttered over my mouth. It was something that compelled her that I never understood. Although right about then, it seemed her continued defiance of my curse and I liked it very much, even when it muddled up my old brains.

"Your colour's better now. *That's* changed."

I had to laugh, "I imagine so." I kissed her fingers at my lips, and then my brow furrowed with concern again. "Did I hurt you much? I didn't mean to make you cry. Can you forgive me for that?"

She put her hands up on either side of my face to look straight into my eyes, "I wanted you to do it, Richard."

I sucked in a hard breath.

"I have known you and watched you and learned you long enough to know what would happen. You ached for it. And you just proved my trust in you was never misplaced. I knew it, but you didn't. Not until this moment."

She really did pay attention to everything I was about. Seems she knew me better than I knew myself. I swallowed down the protest. "You're right. Not until this instant. I've been running away from you every day since the first. But this is what I've wanted and what I've been fighting. I didn't think it was possible. I thought I would kill you, Maggie."

She held my gaze so I would know she wasn't hiding anything, either, "I know. But you can't. And no, you didn't hurt me. Not with what you wanted. Only when you pulled my head back, because of my neck. You know. But that's all. Other than that?" She smiled, "You were quite gentle, actually. I cried, because you were yourself with me for the very first time. *All* of yourself and it was a beautiful thing. I *saw* you in there, in that moment. Unhidden and real and no longer lost to me, but found. I saw it all."

Her hands were still on my face and she ran them back into my hair, "I'm sure no one's had the opportunity to report on it before, but it's actually quite intimate. Very. The closest and most honest we've been together here. Now I know my finding you was no accident. After all this time. My love..." She settled her mouth on mine again and I let her do it.

She continued to babble sweet words of nonsense I couldn't hear. That wonderful song I had tried to remember for so long rang through my head and my heart and I knew it was because she taught it to me again. Odd how I chased the world, nature scattering at my step, commanding the darkness and the night and the magic of the beguile that bent the human mind to my will, and yet here with her? She was the one in charge. Larger than life without being so, I would always let myself be led by her. It was my rest and my rebirth in every moment and it was very, very right.

Here, I was the man she sought, no longer the thing and only because she had given me of herself and made it happen. She had her own magic, it seemed, that I would carry inside me every day afterward. There was no thinking involved in that perfect moment that would soon pass and we took it while it breathed. I picked her up, dragged the old quilts off my chair and laid her on the floor in front of the hearth in the almost dark.

And lived.

*****

(Canada - Present)

In the weeks since Baby Bite and company came, the house was in complete upheaval. So much for my sanctuary--they were everywhere. I loved my house, but, of course, the visible building wasn't all there was and it took me several weeks to decide to give up her secrets to the horde. I suppose I hoped they'd all tire of the chaos and leave on their own. No sense spilling the beans for nothing, after all. But so far, while a few had moved on, that was slow in coming.

In the years since I left Britain, I improved the construction and expanded. Only practical, over many decades, a second, in-case-of-emergency habitat grew a distance from where I settled. I was off in the bush still even in the modern world, so had ample space for anything I might take into my head. In spending so much time alone though, in truth, some of the renovation arose from sheer boredom.

Every vampire needs a hobby.

The result was a sprawling labyrinth under the forest floor that allowed me to wander where the sun could never find me. Two-hundred years earlier, I ran into an artesian well pocket that I made a cave and the hub of the labyrinth once I directed the water with purpose. I even had a swimming pool. The rest I dug out a section at a time when the mood struck me and it ended up rather something akin to a network of mine shafts and caves on more than one level.

I kept candles and lanterns and all the old things I started the household with there. You just never knew when you might need to make a quick exit from the modern world without packing, after all. More important, it was secure and hidden and had everything I could need and over the years even brought it forward with the times. Off-grid along with the house, fixed to where that immoveable Canadian Shield highland came to a point on a ridge, small and efficient windmills and some solar panels brought the whole works to life. It was a good system. No towers, wires buried and disappearing into the earth--even from the air there was nothing to see.

"I thought you didn't like technology, old man," in awe, Alan tripped around behind me.

I skewered him with a withering look, "I don't, so don't go getting all sentimental on me. It serves a need. And since when is a windmill considered modern? I haven't stayed below the radar this long being an idiot, you know. You could take a lesson or two, little blood."

"Whatev." Ignoring me, he took it all in, "A pool? Trippendicular!" and cackled like a kid at Christmas. "No wonder you never go anywhere. I can't believe you were holding out on us all this time."

"I can't believe I let you in here," I grumbled, but it was too late for that. Now, it was all about being in the revenge business. "Right, so is this enough space for your twisted little purposes?"

"Cheeuh!"

"Brilliant. The lot of them should be able to spread out now, but remind them not to get too comfortable. The important message here is *temporary*. There's some old furniture in that room over there you can pull out. There's more than enough power for whatever you might need. Work out the rest yourselves. Exits out through the cellar behind the shelves, yeah? There's only two more. But those won't get you very far unless you fancy meeting a bear in a cave on the other side of the ridge or have a hankering for taking in some white spruce miles from civilisation. You want to run wire for whatever, aerials, transmitters? Follow the power cables and hide them. I'm quite serious about that. No one's seen a fucking thing here in all this time and I aim to keep it that way. You have nowhere else to go, remember? Don't fuck it up. For any of us."

"Message received."

"Right then. Now, I see all those little satellite dish things upstairs. Please, tell me there's no service contracts on those and you and the mosquitoes own them." I scowled.

Baby Bite made a face, "We're not *that* stupid. No service contracts, no names. No snail mail to the town postal station addressed to anyone. But snail mail?" he made a sour face. "*So* 1987." He gestured overhead, "We'll set them up next to the windmills. That'll be nice and high. Between us, we own enough servers networked together to bounce IP's. Proxy servers and VPNs, dig? Untraceable. Encrypted. Don't sweat it. Everyone's got sophisticated routers, lots of hardware firewalls between us and the nosey. All good."

I stopped walking. "Beg pardon?" It sounded like a different language.

His laughter echoed around the pool room, "Man, have I got things to teach you."

There was no getting away from it. The world was creeping up on me and now it was in my secret place and there was nothing I could do about it. "We'll see about that, Baby Bite."

"Yeah, we will. Hey, if you're so paranoid, what's up with the phone? I know you have a cell, speaking of service contracts. You can't tell me--"

"Burner phones, mosquito. And the house phone is a secure satellite uplink, right? Or did you wipe that from your memory, Mr. Technology? I own the company. The whole smash. Smartest business move I made in years. Satellite was launched by a name linked to a corporation that links to a business number that loops back through several foreign investments owed by nationals of other countries. Any transactions are more than six degrees of separation from me through all that. Again, not thick, just didn't know what you were talking about."

"Fair. So, can I get a sat phone?"

"Don't push your luck."

"Okay-okay. Jeez you're a pissy old man."

"Don't forget that, either. Now get those little shits out of my sanctuary and give me back my peace and quiet."

"Yes, Dad."

"Fuck right off."

He ran ahead to the dry cellar with more energy than I could remember having in several lifetimes. Alan seemed excited about the whole thing. All I could muster was calculation while I tried to work out how I would accomplish my goal.

*****

They were young, optimistic still. Prone to excitement. They couldn't yet appreciate the value and luxury of a nice, secure place to hide for any length of time. They'd learn. It was better once they were out of the house proper and underground. Easier on my nerves.

I worried about them, though, and couldn't help myself. They were still new. They were brash and inexperienced, lost and without direction. I didn't know what to do with them, but hoped my influence might rub off on them some. We weren't alike in breed, but there might be something I could give them.

In my time since Maggie was gone, I continued to turn from what I was with deliberation and stuck to animal blood. It changed me somewhat, I suppose. I missed it, of course, craved it in a peripheral way, but after Maggie nothing could compare. I was a wolf so hunted what I needed from among the weak of the animal kingdom and left humanity to its own devices. Unless called upon.

In that curious way I'd always followed, sometimes still I would run off to the forest, compelled by fate in one direction or another without understanding why. And I would be useful again. I carried a bag with my herbs and first aide supplies and listened to the call of the earth and the pulse of life surrounding me. Sometimes, I healed--a hiker, a plane crash once or twice, accidents on the Trans-Canada Highway. Sometimes, I answered a plea and was satisfied. I never used the beguile on another human being again since Maggie's time and so it was always with clear-headed permission.

I simply couldn't be that other thing anymore. Couldn't be that savage. Again, probably the stupidest blood-sucker on the planet, but I was what I had become. The internal war continued and pushed me through some sort of vampire evolution until I became something else again. Not quite vampire, not quite human.

Not quite all in my head.

Could have been simple insanity from existing for so long, but I wasn't about to look at it too closely. Perhaps, Billy wasn't the only one soft in the head. My only desire to be left alone, now I had a huge family--sixty-three of them in total had somehow found their way. Funny the things fate chose to throw in my path. If I wasn't raving mad before this, sixty-three little bloods were bound to push me in that direction.

At the same time, they'd come to me for a reason beyond a place to hide. They would help me exact my revenge and then Maggie could be at rest. Finally, after all this time, she could have her ease. It couldn't clear my conscience, but it would be better than having done nothing at all.

I kept the carved porch swing Myles helped me make for her and brought it with me to the New World all those years ago. It was a stupid thing to do, I suppose, since it took up space on the ship I might have used for other things, but I couldn't bear to leave it behind.

After she was gone, I kept my house in the hills back in Britain for a short time, but it couldn't be the same again and didn't last. Part of the reason I sought out the New World along with others at that time.

It was difficult to be there with the family burials all side-by-side. Myles's little marker between ours where we should have kept him in life and not let him go that night. Maggie's in reminder of her pointless, empty death right up near the appearance of my own that could never be permanent. If it was possible to die of a broken heart, I should have the night I laid her in it. But, of course, I couldn't die, so I suffered.

Ol' Twitch had got greedy right about then, too. Greedy with hate and anger and revenge and ruined the whole thing going after Captain William Blackthorn. Word got around. In the aftermath of her death, I wasn't thinking straight to be honest. People put two and two together with rumours circulating up from the docks and further motivated me to vacate.

When I went over to North America the first time, it was more a scouting expedition than anything spurred on by the need for distance between myself and what had happened. Trapping was the game of the times and something I knew, so I gravitated toward what they called Upper Canada then. Space was vast. Space and freedom and new beginnings to be made, the likes of which I'd not seen since the world was newer. It attracted me. Finding it a satisfactory retreat, I staked a claim. The weather was nearly familiar, though the winter harsher, but I didn't mind--it kept people away and ensured my lack of discovery. I went back again and pushed farther north to satisfy my need for solitude.

In the old days, I kept dogs to sled in supplies, half-breed wolves that tolerated my existence near theirs. Sadly, the modern world was no place for creatures that wild, so I no longer had the luxury of their company, but I had everything I needed. With the highway close now--a couple days' hike, a quick-ish snowmobile or four-wheeler jaunt--my little baby bloods could reach the world they were born to if they had a need. I could stay put and never go there unless one of my tools or a window broke. I was fond of radio, though. Connecting me to conversations with people while remaining anonymous, I had several that wore out from time to time and forced me to buy new ones. I enjoyed the music, too, and had taught myself to play by ear on the concert grand I brought in a century before. Other than that? My needs were still few--tobacco, music, tools, and I fancied some new clothes from time to time. That was about all.

Early evenings still found me in an altered version of my porch sit. I hung the swing not from the porch, but from a stand that sat right in the earth in my garden next to the sundial where I could be surrounded by the life. And Maggie. The last time I came over, I didn't leave my Maggie behind. Giving her a second memorial in the old way, I burned her body to ash that I took with me so she would never be alone in the dark. I left the graves looking undisturbed, torched the house and barn, and walked away into the night to disappear off the face of the earth. To anyone who came later, it appeared our little family had perished in the horrible fire that wiped out the buildings and someone had given us a burial. While Twitch the Witch became consigned to local legend that was later forgotten.

I was glad it looked that way.

There were nights I still spoke to her sitting there on our swing. I couldn't help myself. More than only humanity, she taught me the art of conversation and I missed that. Sometimes, I heard her answer. Sometimes, it was only the wind. Sometimes, I wished I could join her, but her death was still not avenged, so there could be no rest until that was accomplished. And I would keep that promise, as I had the one to Myles.

"Hello, Maggie-girl. Have you missed me? I've been run off my feet and had no time for visiting. Can you forgive me?"

Trees sighed in the breeze. It was the warmth of her breath on my cold skin all over again and I knew she was there in some way. It always made me smile to know she was close by in whatever way she could be. Nearly like her being there. As she was at the old house, here she was also part of the garden. She brought it to life and it let me be closer to her than I might have otherwise--a miracle I would always celebrate.

"Have you seen these young ones? What do you make of that? Funny, after all this time. They *are* hopeless. Unschooled, undisciplined. Nearly alive, they are. I've a fair notion you would understand them better than I. Help me with them, would you, lamb? Definitely need another perspective here," and couldn't help but laugh to think of them and me in the same place. We were chalk and cheese and my only parenting experience a handful of visits from a little boy three hundred years in the past.

"Have you seen that little one? You know the one I mean. Reminds me of Myles some. Walked right in and didn't think anything of it. He's, uh, *something*," I laughed again. "Keep an eye on that one. He's come for a reason."

For my own amusement, I hung bat boxes all around the garden and the bats kept the garden pests at bay. Clouds of them swirled across the night sky, twisting ribbon pennants overhead. Dark butterflies that made the night more alive. It could never be alive enough after Maggie wasn't in it no matter how many things I filled it with, but I continued to try.

"Ah, Maggie-girl, they make me miss you more. The house is full and still it's empty." I pulled out my tobacco pouch and held it between my hands in my lap, contemplating. "If there's a place for old blood runners there, I'll come to you soon, I think." I swung in silence for a beat and then continued to speak to her on the wind where I knew she was free to watch me and witness my accomplishments. "Have no doubt, they'll find him for us and then? It'll be done. I swore it and you know I can't lie to you. You only need to hang on a little longer. Just a little more, lamb." My gaze slid off into the night to watch the bats without interest, lost in thoughts of revenge and Maggie and death.

I filled a pipe with some shockingly expensive pipe tobacco. A ritual of many years, I took my time packing the same pipe bequeathed me by the old man who invited me to take him. Still remembered in my prayerful contemplation as I promised him I would, from time to time I took smoke in his memory. I took smoke for myself, of course, but the expensive one was always for him. An offering to the first bend in the road to my future so to speak. I still heard him laughing whenever I did it.

Alan cleared his throat behind me.

"Honestly, Baby Bite. You'll need to be considerably lighter on your feet if you want to sneak up on me."

He materialised out of the shadows, but stayed on the back porch. "You were, uh, busy. I didn't want to interrupt."

I blew smoke at the moon, "I wasn't, 'uh, busy'. I was ignoring you and talking some things out. I do that. Ever heard of a private conversation, little blood? Manners. Always room for those." I puffed some more and sent more smoke up in offer and memorial.

Alan wasn't talking which forced me to ask if only to get it over with and my evening back to myself, "So? What do you need now? Something else destroyed? More money? What is it *now*?" It was a private moment and I had had so few with her to begin with I was selfish with the few I got in the present. There wouldn't be time for many more and I wasn't about to squander them.

Footsteps creaked the back stairs and he braved coming down into the garden.

"Watch where you step, little man."

"I know." The dirt path was close enough and he hunkered down on his haunches near the mint. "Nice night."

"Hm." I puffed on in silence, but he didn't say anything. "Good lord, did you come out for a chat? Shall I put the kettle on then?" I ignored him and watched bats swirling and sweeping overhead. I told myself we weren't friends, but he was mine now. I allowed him to overhear me talking to Maggie. It was all right. He'd grown on me. I suppose it was because he did remind me of Myles. It was the lack of pretence, I think. He was what he was and I had to respect someone like that, even annoying as they could be. Of course, it was Baby Bite times sixty-three with the house full of them. At least, they all spoke in plain words and concepts I could understand. I had to admit, if I was going to have houseguests, unlike humans, these ones made sense to me. Okay, except when they were discussing computers, but beyond that, it seemed to be working out.

"Did I tell you how we found you?"

The tone of his voice caught me. "You said Billy told you I was up here."

"He did," his head bobbed. "By accident. It slipped out one day. That there was one old boy left and hiding out somewhere in Ontario. We found you ourselves, though. *We* did. Me and the little bloods."

Smoke spiralled up while I thought, "Right. You and the mosquitoes. Brilliant."

He was making matching spirals in the dirt with his finger, "Wanna know how?"

I sighed in discontent, "Do I have a choice?" The scowling was how we connected, so it never fazed him.

"Hey, if you don't wanna know, I'm down with that, old man. Just thought you might be interested in the status of your own celebrity." Gazing off in the distance watching the bats swoop and twirl in the darkness, his attention was in my direction.

"Wha..?" Okay, that got me. "Please, tell me that's some form of teenage sarcasm."

"Hate to be the one to break it to you, but there's a local legend in this area. Story goes back about three hundred years, give or take."

"Oh, please. Quit shining me on," I looked him in the eye to see if he was messing with me, but I knew he wasn't. Like I said, the boy had no pretence. He could only tell it how it was. He shook his head. "Fuck me."

Baby Bite laughed, "You're a mythological character in native lore, Dad."

I pointed a warning finger in his direction, "I told you, I'm not your daddy, little blood."

He ignored me, "Um, Six Nations to be exact. Sometimes Watcher-of-the-Dark or The Red Shaman. The one that comes up most often, though?" He continued to draw in the dirt, so he didn't have to look at me,

"The Blood Runner."

I stopped swinging and choked on my smoke, "*What*?"

"Yeah, it's across the tribes."

"Now you're just making that up. Bollocks."

His mouth opened to say something more, but then snapped shut.

"What is it? What else aren't you telling me?"

"Look, it's nothing, okay? Nothing you have to worry about or anything like that. Not in that way. It's just, well, word's out, is all. A little. Like I told you. Everyone's connected. Text, social…"

He wouldn't have come out for nothing. "Get over here and speak to me." He looked up from where he hunched on the ground. "Yes, over here. Park your arse *here* and tell me what's going on. There's more, obviously. Elaborate." With reluctance, he shuffled over to sit with me. At the far end of the swing, he tucked his feet up like a boy and rested his elbows on his knees. Good lord, he was young. "Well?"

The bats flittered past the yard again and he watched them while he chose his words. "It's not just here, okay? It's other places. Blood Runner. Kind of a rumour, but more than that, too. A vamp myth. Everyone knows it. All of us. The coincidence with the name was too huge to ignore, if you get what I mean."

I couldn't say anything for a long moment while I absorbed that one. "Sorry, 'all of us' who? A vamp *myth*?" I didn't want to understand, because I was afraid to know. I couldn't meet his eyes.

He knew it, too. "Yeah, just what you're thinking. The last old boy. The oldest of us all and still kickin' it in the modern world. So old, he was around before bloods and crosses. Not even one of us, but the same. The Blood Runner." I raised my eyebrows in surprise. "I knew before I got here. Everyone's heard the story. I can't believe you never heard this anywhere you went." He shrugged, "You always lived the way you lived, keeping to yourself, so maybe why. Didn't matter. You affected the lives of people, *living* people, wherever you were. Helped sometimes. Healed.

Rumours start, people talk. It's what you call us, how you think of yourself. You even said it to me the first night I came here, that we're blood runners. Part of why I came back the next day. You met a few of us over the years, right? Must have said it to someone somewhere along the way. Used those words. It only takes one to get something like that started."

I scowled, "Well, someone's village is missing their idiot. Load of tripe. Even more ridiculous than your migration theory," but it was only half-hearted, because it wasn't ridiculous. That was *my* term, blood runners. For making the blood run, running away from the blood, to the blood, because of the blood. It was a catch-all phrase for the whole situation to me. I'd never heard anyone else use it before, but he was right. I must have said it to someone in the past. Very long in the past. "*Shit!*" I got up and stomped around the yard some.

Alan stayed on the swing. He already knew enough to let me get it out of my system. He didn't speak again until I stopped stomping. "There's more."

"Hell's bloody bells! Of course, there's more. Naturally, there's bound to be more. Well, out with it then. My picture's in circulation on a vampire most wanted poster? Or has it gone all modern now and GPS tracking co-ordinates lead you right to my bloody door?" He started to say something, but I wasn't in the mood, "Yes, I know what GPS is. You think you and the blood bank crew are the only ones who know things?" I stabbed my finger in his direction and couldn't get out anything else more coherent than profanity.

"Look..." Had to give the kid "A" for effort. He was still working to get out the rest while I went right off my nut. "Besides looking for Billy, there was something more you wanted us to find. The thing you said to forget about." I skewered him with a look, but it shut me up fast. "You didn't think we could, right? That's why you waved me off. I gotta come clean... Some of it I did before you even mentioned. Because I already knew. Did it when you took off to the Caribbean. And then there's the stuff I looked up before I came back the second day. Names. Old names of yours you said the first day I showed up. Did some big time searching, linking. Okay hacking. Cross-referenced with legends in other places I knew about. Verified enough. Also, why I came back. I knew it was you, dude. Me and my crew? Not the rest of them down there, but you know which ones I mean. It's been a hobby. Looking for Blood Runner. Like looking for the Holy Grail, you know? Just bullshit to pass time, chasing down pieces of old stories. We never expected to find anything real, man. It was a story, a rumour. A *myth* for fuck's sake."

"A motherfucking *myth*? Holy Grail, my arse. Do I look like a blessed relic to you? *Shit--*"

"A few years ago, Billy told us about an old boy. Marooned him on an island. Hated his guts. D'uh. Said if we weren't happy with him, we could be stuck with a bastard like that. Knew Skippy's twenty. Canada. Ontario, like I told you. Probably found out you went over to Upper Canada back in the day, but wouldn't know where to look. I got the impression, if he knew? He woulda already come, guns blazing. He really didn't seem to like you much. Far as I know, though? No one else anywhere knows anything closer than that--"

"Oh, well, thank goodness for that. Gods forbid there's anyone *else* who doesn't know yet." I was pissed off. So much for the appearance of my anonymity.

"*Anyway,*" he was still trying hard, so with great effort I backed myself down a few notches. I threw myself back into the swing. "We found you through those local legends. We were doin' what we always do, just poking around. We have a lot of info between us, looked into a lot of shit all over the world. The local legends matched the stuff we actually verified from Europe and Asia. It was just too close to ignore. The name for one. C'mon... And man, you're not like us, y'know. You help people. Left witnesses to you popping up out of the night like a ghost and disappearing again. For years. And the Trans-Canada Highway? Not sure what you've been thinking there. But there's some urban legends floating around now fuelled by history buffs linking them to native lore. No one cares but us. No one could do the amount of work we have, linked stories to Europe or ancient Asia or Africa. We just have more time on our hands than regular people. The only reason we knew more was going on."

"Brilliant," I grumbled and scrubbed my hands over my face. Damn, but I was tired all of a sudden.

"Sorry, man." In all honesty, he sounded contrite and concerned for the mess the same as he had when everyone had shown up.

I couldn't even muster enough energy to be angry with him. I let out a heavy breath, "Don't worry yourself over it. Not your fault, Baby Bite. Apparently, it's mine." I laughed in futility, "Been around so long my own fucking reputation is catching up with me. That's how you know you've been in the world too bloody long, eh? Fuck me."

He dropped his head a little and turned shy on me, "If I could just tell you, though, when I knew it was you? You have no idea, man. Yeah, I was kind of a pain in the ass, making jokes and shit. But underneath? I was really nervous. You're like the first vampire."

"First vampire?" I snorted and tried to laugh it off, "Doubtful. Not even the last of my kind, I'm sure. The rest just have enough sense to hide better. My failing that. Never cared enough to work at it. I simply wanted to stay beyond notice. The reason I was never a leader. Takes too much planning and work."

I looked off at the sundial and wondered what Maggie would make of this situation and then had to laugh some more. She would tell me it was good for me and she was glad I was speaking with people. And that she knew I cared about the little bloods. Damn that girl.

"If it helps any, for your peace of mind maybe? Me 'n my posse know you're the old guy Billy told us about *and* that same old guy is also Blood Runner. But not the other guys. They know *about* Blood Runner, because everyone does, but not that it's you. Don't think it's a real person. Get me? Kept that part to ourselves. They just know this is a safe place to hole up. That you're old enough to look after us. Smart enough to keep us safe. Have enough resources to help us out. And you put Billy in his place, so you must be an okay guy. But that's all. I swear. They just didn't have anywhere to go." He looked guilty, "Me, too. I really didn't. I mega appreciate you taking us all in. Most sincerely. I can't tell you how screwed we'd be otherwise. You being who you are, though? Just the cherry on top."

"Stop it."

"Seriously. I can't believe you don't know how people view Blood Runner. I'm telling you, it's like… like if there was a real Indiana Jones finding the Ark or the actual Holy Grail, man. Dude, *I* found the Blood Runner!"

"All right, Junior, enough already. Give it a rest." He quieted down, but was still smirking at me off the side of his shoulder. "And wipe that stupid grin off your face, will you? Don't force me to de-craniate you now that we're so wonderfully close and all. Although I could probably use the space on my social calendar with so many of your little friends come to kiss my friggin' ring."

That broke the tension and he laughed and seemed to gather some of his regular self together again. "All right. Have it your way, old man."

"Toss me that tobacco pouch." I knocked out the pipe bowl and reamed it before I repacked it. "I need to think." I puffed in quiet contemplation with Baby Bite swinging along at my side, happy to keep me company. At least, now I understood his rabid attention.

All I did to keep myself separate from the world turned out to be a good thing. People were *searching* for me. I couldn't believe it. Being left alone was the only thing I ever wanted and beyond being hunted by humans, come to find out I had next to my own kind looking for me, as well. If Alan and his mates had figured it out, it stood to reason someone somewhere else could do it again. And I didn't like that. It was obvious I stayed in one place too long. The price of old age--I'd grown stubborn and complacent about my home. I believed I was invisible.

What I was, was a wanted man.

If Billy got himself a crew of these new breeds, computer-savvy young bloods who were into the legends, too, I'd lose the element of surprise. Alan's migration theory might not be a load of bollocks, after all. Everyone was moving in the same direction already, possibly driven by the lore when the modern world encroached on them. If Billy knew where I was or put two and two together, no doubt he would have already gone after me. Perhaps, he was already. I resolved to be faster, because it was all I could do.

I needed information. And a plan. The forest swayed in the nighttime breeze with metronome precision, keeping time with my thoughts zipping from plotting righteous vengeance to worrying about my own hide to thinking ahead to the needs of the young bloods to Maggie and back to revenge. I might even twist the Blood Runner nonsense to my advantage somehow. Whatever it took. If it got me Billy, I'd use it. I didn't care anymore. When it was over, I'd be off to join Maggie in some way again and find my peace. Finally, after so long.

Baby Bite wouldn't be happy, I knew. I hated to rain on his legend parade, but I was tired and couldn't think about that. What could I do for them, anyway? I was an old vampire in a modern world I could no longer hide in. If I got Billy, at least it would be safe for the little bloods. My contribution to the cause. I shook my head. Maggie would have given me that knowing *look*.

Because I did care.

I stayed sat on the swing and concentrated, casting my mind back as far as I could make it go. Trying to remember anything useful. Or half-remember anything the little bloods could research for me since they were clearly so good at it. Either way, this would be a complicated undertaking.

Billy wouldn't go down easy, but neither would I. We would be well matched. But no way he was getting the drop on me.

"You said you found out some things before I ever asked you. After you knew my names. Was any of it about Mesopotamia? It's the oldest location I recall. If Billy is as old as I think he is, then he likely comes from the same area." I sent up some more smoke.

"Funny you should ask that, old man," Baby Bite smiled. "Ask me why."

His expression was mischievous, so I played along, "Oh? Why, Alan? Why funny I should ask that at this particular juncture?"

"Because there's things in the world that humans have never understood. And it just happens a lot of them came right out of Mesopotamia."

"Okay, that much I already knew, little man. Try again."

He waggled a finger at me, "Oh, don't dismiss it all so soon. Some of those ancient, misunderstood things only defy explanation to human beings, if you get where I'm coming from. A lot of it makes perfect sense from your perspective. And yes, is also specific," he looked pleased with himself.

"Oh?"

"Yeah."

"Interesting?" Now, I was intrigued.

"Absofuckinglutely."

"Really?"

"Yes, sir."

"Hmm…" I listened to the night another minute, lost in thought. "Okay, let's go see the kiddies and show me what you've got."

He was grinning. "Excellent."

"I'll be the judge of that."

"You'll see."

I stopped with a hand on the sundial for a long moment and said goodnight to Maggie while Alan waited a respectful distance away. For once, without sarcastic comment on one of my habits.

Then I went in to be reminded of things in my four-thousand year past from a bunch of bloods so young they'd known television their whole lives.

8

(A.D. 1729)

"**N***igaud stupide!* **Simpleton... Idiot!** *Putain de bordel de merde!*" Günter's letter was, indeed, waiting for him when they arrived in the Bahamas. The crunch of it in his hand wasn't near satisfying enough. He ground his teeth, "*Et puis quoi encore...* What's next? Am I forced to do everything myself? *Always?*"

The crash of the captain's substantial oak desk overturning across his cabin preceded his stomping above decks. Confetti drifted in his wake as he shredded the parchment in his hands. The new dishonourable rat crew scattered, but a slow swab caught the full brunt of his fury. Captain William Blackthorn snatched him by the throat and crushed his windpipe before he had time to scream. He tossed him overboard with a flick of his wrist.

"Ahoy, ye bilge-logged water rats. Get your malodorous, Christ-cursed arses in gear and raise those fucking sails. We're putting out. *Vite!*"

"Cap'n..."

Whirling on his heel, Billy snarled at the unspoken question, "Who spoke? Which one of you stinking pile of entrails dare question me? Get on those goddamn ropes and get us moving. *Mon Dieu*, I'm surrounded by bloody morons. Every sodding one of you. Sailing Master, plot our course. Quartermaster, *move… this… ship!*"

"But Captain--"

Vibrating with fury, his eyes narrowed as he located the still-speaking offender from the cowering crew. The Boatswain's Mate took a tentative step forward to face him. "*You..*," Billy hissed, gliding up to him on the night to stand too close for comfort. "You *again*, back-talking an order. Why are you still attached to this crew, you gangrenous piece of bitch-humping chum salmon? I should have you keelhauled. These *petite* dainties could use an added lesson in respect. Did I not warn you never to speak to me again? *Didn't I?*" Spittle flew from his mouth and hit the man's face, but he didn't dare move a hand to wipe it away.

The Boatswain's Mate swallowed hard. Rage so complete, Billy's inhuman cat's eyes gleamed murder while the rest of his true face bled through his usual careful mask of humanity. It had been over two years since his last direct meeting with the captain. While he didn't relish one now, the new crew who knew nothing of him or his ways forced him to speak. He squared up his shoulders before the demon master of the Pandora and wouldn't back down. The crew took another step back. Men who hadn't seen the inside of a church since they wore short pants crossed themselves in dismay. Whispered exclamations of terror drifted through the night air.

Every man flinched while he raked them with sizzling disdain. "Shut your mewling yaps y'bunch of fucking pussies and cry for your whoremothers later. I'll be your deaths. I *am* death, so get over it!" Still toe-to-toe with the irritating mate, he spoke to him alone, "We're putting out."

"Of course, what the Captain means--"

"*What*?!" Billy's eyes bulged with the further defiance. "Did I give you permission to--"

"--is to secure the ship and be ready to put out in three hours' time. When the tide is no longer *out*, of course, *sir*. Certain the Captain means to put us through our paces this evening. Practice for an untimely emergency with His Majesty's frigates? With the home port so inconveniently shallow after some of the larger ports we've only left, this rabble lot could use the practice in that precision, as well." The man's knees knocked, but he stood his ground while the deck crew hid behind him.

There was confusion in the stunned silence, "The ti--?" Rage drained away until he only radiated anger measurable by human standards. "Yes, of *course*, that was my meaning," he snapped. "How else could we expect to pull out of the harbour? I would have thought that was obvious."

The man gave him a guarded commiserating look, "Unfortunately, sir, on the whole? What they lack in intellect they make up for with only their stench. The larger concepts do elude them and one-word commands are, sadly, more their speed. If I might be so bold as to offer my assistance translating your wishes, sir? There's no need for you to trouble yourself with trivialities."

Billy appraised the man at close range and reassessed his earlier opinion. He already appeared more intelligent than Günter and could be of use. He took a step back and calculated his value, "Your name escapes me this moment, crewman."

He snapped to, "Shakespeare, sir. Nigel Shakespeare, Boatswain's Mate." The rest of the crew continued to pray behind him, thankful the captain singled out anyone but them.

His eyebrows raised of their own accord, "Shakespeare? Like the playwright?"

"Only in name, Captain."

"Mate, hmm?" Intrigued, his belief in the illusion of his own good breeding made them social equals if the man came from good family. "Do you fancy yourself an educated man, Shakespeare?"

"I *have* education, if that's the question, sir." Nigel had no idea where their infamous captain was going with this line of questioning, but it made him more nervous. "University of Oxford at Oxfordshire. Then His Majesty's Navy, 'twenty-one to 'twenty-five. Boatswain's Mate and later Sailing Master's Mate."

Billy chuckled, "Ho! Seems we've a gentleman among us. Well, what do you make of that, y'festering gobs? A rose among the thorns in my side. *Très bien, monsieur*, good show." Billy slapped his knee and then considered him, "His Majesty's Navy, hm? Somewhat of a conflict in interests there, wouldn't you agree, Mr. Shakespeare?" Billy shined the brass buttons on his overcoat with the edge of his sleeve in disinterest that was anything but. "Are you a spy planted among us to curry my favour and find the means to hang me a thousand times?"

"*No, sir.*" He even managed not to flinch.

"Not a spy then? Hmmm… Well, then, tell me, Mr. Shakespeare. How does so obvious a career man get from His Majesty's Navy to a ship with the reputation of my Pandora? If I might be so bold as to inquire?"

Nigel cleared his throat, "Permission to speak freely, Captain?"

Billy waved his assent and crossed his arms in anticipation. The evening had become infinitely more enjoyable than before he emerged from his cabin, "Oh, of course. *Always*. Do tell." There was no pretence in the man, but he couldn't help but be suspicious.

"There was an, erm, *incident*. I escaped from an unfairly dealt charge not long after I was blackballed." He shrugged, "No one would take me on, sir, and I'm a sailor by blood. I belong at sea."

Head cocked to one side, Billy continued to examine him, checking for lies and found none. "Blackballed, hm? Escaped? My-my, that's quite a feat to elude the entire British Navy, as I well know. Interesting."

"Actually? Not so much interesting as creating further *incidents* that left the fleet short several, erm, officers. If not before, they'd dearly love to find me lollygagging about somewhere now, I'm sure."

"I can well imagine," Billy was forced to laugh. "And this incident, this intrigues me. Of what nature was this crucial and life-altering happening, Mr. Shakespeare? One so horrid as to cause an incarceration from which you were compelled to escape? I like to know the soul of a man who might share space with me on my lady. Tell me then, what was the charge?"

Nigel shuffled his feet, "Murder, sir."

"*Que oui*! Better and better still. Well then, of..? Whose..?" The captain regarded him with expectation, his mood continuing to improve as suspicion fell away. "Smartly now. Don't be shy, boy. Speak!"

"Ship's cook."

"And the reason?"

"Caught him trying to poison the captain, actually. Things became heated. Officers and crew intervened, so there were ample witnesses. He was quite a disreputable sort and no loss to the world other than to his very prominent and eminently powerful family. No one believed my defence. Wouldn't even consider it. It was the end of my career."

"I see, I see. Well, trying to poison the captain. Now, that's a serious business. Caught him red-handed, did you?"

"Yes, sir. I knew he was up to no good. I'd been watching him, you see. Didn't have long to wait. He wasn't even overly cautious about it, the simpleton."

Billy clapped his hands in glee, "Ah! And so, you lost your career *and* your reputation protecting the captain who later ordered you to the brig. Oh, *mon Dieu*, what delicious irony. A pity to be sure, but what I believe has now become my gain, *sans doute*!"

"Mine, as well, sir. Sadly, I've found more honour among the thieves, if I'm being honest. Their motivations are clear, purely mercenary, and never waver. Refreshing after the convoluted and slippery minds of noblemen I've known," he quirked a hesitant eyebrow.

Billy nodded, "There's truth there in that. Indeed. Well then, Mr. Shakespeare, tell me, how long have you been with us now?"

Nigel straightened and came to attention, "Five years, sir."

"Five years? Five? How is it possible I've not run into you before? Especially as it's painfully obvious you are the only other person aboard this vessel capable of speaking in complete sentences." Billy appeared dumbfounded.

Shakespeare shrugged, "I've taken my orders through the chain of command the way it's meant to be done, sir. Boatswain's Mate in a crew as large as ours? Other than that night Mr. Norris sent me out with a message for you, you would have had no need to speak with me directly."

"Indeed, indeed. Well, naturally not then. And what, if I might ask, turn of stars has brought me to the rare pleasure of your conversation *this* evening after all this time?"

He looked contrite, "I regret to inform the Captain that the First Mate's run off. Mr. Norris, the Quartermaster, as well. Who, I also regret to report, took it upon himself to set fire to the account books sometime after he put that note on your desk, sir."

"*What?*" Billy looked about, wild, only now aware the ship was almost empty. "Holy Mother of blessed Christ!" Billy took a couple of charged steps in one direction and then another, surveying fast and tallying the situation. He snapped a look back over his shoulder at Shakespeare, "Speak of it. What the blazes has been going on here? All of it."

Nigel took a breath, "I didn't realise what he was up to until it was too late or I might have saved them, sir. I only just found them burned to ash in the open safe before you woke."

"Curse that fucking bastard son for the devil dog he is. Wait until I see that thieving *sac à merde* again. He'll wish he were never born."

"Erm, there's more, sir." He swallowed, not wanting to be the bringer of more bad news, "The Boatswain, Sailing Master *and* the Master Gunner are gone, as well. Although, on a positive note, Sweeney, the Master

Carpenter, has decided to stay on with us for another turn as have a handful of crewmen." He cleared his throat and lowered his voice, "All the officer's mates buggered off with the officers, I'm afraid, sir. I'm the last. The rest are fresh off the land and all I could induce to join in the last few hours."

"Yellow *bastards*," Billy spit rancour. "*Bordel de merde!* May vultures pick their sorry coward gizzards clean while they all dance a burning jig in *hell*!" Billy stomped off a ways, cursing with every step, "Bunch of thieving, Christ-cursed, common-bitch-fucking-brothel-sons-of-half-breed-sea-devils." He came to rest at the starboard bow and grew lost staring off into the sea, arms akimbo.

It was difficult enough to run the ship in an efficient manner when he couldn't appear in the daytime and he relied on his officers to keep order. No trained mates meant starting from scratch. He sighed and ran his hands up into his hair working to calm himself. It wasn't the first time he found himself in this position. He spoke over his shoulder, "Shakespeare, you are hereby promoted to First Mate and whatever dubious honour that carries with it. In addition, you shall assume the greater portion of Quartermaster's duties. And oversee the crew for the immediate future."

"Thank you, sir."

"*Phah!* Hesitate in your thanks. I'm a fickle and intolerant taskmaster. Be forewarned." He eyed the gaggle of crewmen behind him and motioned to his new first mate. "*Viens ici.* Walk with me." They moved to the stern and up to the poop deck out of earshot. The captain leaned on the rail while he surveyed the men, "Tell me, Shakespeare. Out of that lot cowering down there, have we any officers in the making? Anyone astute enough to make an independent decision? Who could be trusted with the weapons?"

"Doubtful. None of them appear savvy enough not to stand at the muzzle end of a cannon, sir."

"*Merde,*" Billy made a disgusted noise.

"The tall one at the back there with his finger up his nose? That one broke out of the poke where he'd been incarcerated for buggery with the neighbour's bitch. And I don't mean the wife," he face reflected his disgust. "That one there has an addiction to opium, I believe. I know the look. This is the first time I've seen him standing, actually. Banking on a free ride to China more than like. Those four there together?" he motioned to several men more dishevelled than the rest. "A pack of rummies with bad aim and worse work ethic. Not a single mother one of the lot can read or write more than making their mark. Oh, and that sullen behemoth there glowering at the others?"

Following the line of Nigel's finger, Billy found the man circled by a ring of crewmen all a healthy distance away. "He is a beast, isn't he now."

"Indeed. Rumour has it he tore the heads off seven men with his bare hands after one of them asked him to give up his seat in a tavern. He ran off as the local constabulary arrived. When they finally found him, it took nine men to bring him in, but the gaol couldn't hold him. He broke out, literally, through the wall by the next day." Nigel eyed them all with trepidation.

"Nine men? Well, now that *is* something. A wild bear among men." If his exploits were only half-true this person would have definite use. "There is our new Boatswain, Mr. Shakespeare. That reputation should keep the rest in line and assist you with the men. The title should make him feel superior to the rest. Easier for you to guide as a comrade, *vous comprenez*? You shall be responsible for teaching him the rest once we're under way."

"Aye-aye, sir."

"Enough officers for the moment. Unless one of them shows sudden promise, we'll leave it at that until we take on fresh crew. You and I will share the Quartermaster's duties. You were the Sailing Master's mate at one time?"

"Aye, sir, although, to be honest, out of practice now."

Billy nodded. "*Entendu.* And yet better than none, hm? If you're still capable of reading a chart and might reacquaint yourself with plotting course, that will suffice. That, we'll share between us, as well. Until a better opportunity arises, of course," and chuckled without humour. They would be on the lookout for a Royal Navy vessel to kidnap one from, the only way to acquire a new one. The education required made it a position difficult to fill. His gaze swept the paltry crew below and he sobered, "How many are we?"

"Sixty-seven, sir."

"*Sixty-seven? Nom de dieu de merde!*" Billy slammed his palm down on the rail with a scowl. "We'll not get over the fucking reef with that number. *Fils de pute!*"

"Forgive me, sir. It was an eventful day and I didn't have much time."

Billy hung his head, "And the rest? Out with it. The account books are gone. Did they leave us reason to need them?" his voice tired.

"No, sir. Not as far as plunder. They took the lot. When the officers left, I mean. We've some stray gold coin, a few casks of rum, larder provisions, and sundry. They tipped out all the water barrels for sport. Raided the weapons, as well. Though there's a substantial amount of ammunition left in the magazine. I tallied all the leavings here for you, sir," he handed Billy a list.

Billy skimmed the meagre notations without enthusiasm and handed it back to his new first officer. He snorted disdain, "Fabulous that. Shot and powder and nothing to fire it from." He slapped his palm down hard again in frustration, "Every mother one of those fucking miscreants better hope to God they never cross my path again. They'll pay in blood, *mon ami*," he pronounced with dark intent.

Shakespeare took a steadying breath, "It was bad blood they made here today, sir. You'd be within your rights."

"Rights, hunh?" Billy shook his head in distraction. "Fuck them all, Shakespeare." Considering, he stared off over top the new crew. "Well, first order of business will be to re-outfit before we consider a departure. *Merde*, such a waste of time. Well, that's it then." Billy looked him hard in the eyes, "Make them perform."

"Aye, Captain. I've kept the deck five years. That will continue."

"*Très bien*. Pandora is yours for the next two hours' time. I must run to town and see an old acquaintance. That should set us to rights again or on the way of it, at least. I'll have supplies sent aboard straight away. See to the rest in the morning. Press-gang as you can to raise our numbers until we put out after sundown overmorrow. Phah!" Billy threw up his hands in annoyance, "This does displease me, Shakespeare," but there was no rage in it. He calculated rations and the time to their next destination. "Well, let us see what you can do with her before my return."

"Aye-aye, Captain."

Billy stepped back to the rail and addressed the paltry crew, "Listen up you cock-sucking gobs. *Écouter*! This here is our Mr. Shakespeare. He is your Quartermaster and *my* First Officer. You *will* address him with respect or I've a cat-o-nine-tails that will teach you how. In two hours' time, I expect this vessel ship-shape and standing ready. Mr. Shakespeare will give you your orders." He waved Nigel forward. "Your command, Mr. Shakespeare."

*****

Three-and-a-half months later, Pandora held position off the coast of England clear of the shipping lanes to avoid the navy. Günter and the captain were in loud conference in the captain's quarters. The crew flinched with every crash. When Billy flew up the stairs dragging Günter along by the scruff of his neck, Nigel winced but didn't intervene.

"Shakespeare!"

"Aye, Captain."

"We're going ashore," he growled. "It appears we've some *unfinished* business." He gave Günter a yank that sent him sprawling into the side rails. "Wait one day, a full twenty-four hours, then follow us in. Do *not* come into port. Twenty miles up the coast to the east, you'll find a bay with a pebble beach backed by birch wood. Drop anchor and bring a boat in to shore for us. I expect you to be waiting when we arrive."

"Aye," Nigel nodded. "We'll be there, sir."

"*Günter,* you louse-infested jackal son!"

Arms raised in self-defence, Günter continued to cower on the deck, mewling. Billy was beside him with a boot in the ribs before anyone saw him move.

"The reek of you makes me ill. *Lâche,*" Billy spit on him in contempt. "Get your spineless, mishandling arse off my ship. *Move!*"

With great care, Günter picked himself up and climbed down to the rowboat. Billy vaulted over the rails and jumped straight down the side before Günter was halfway down the rope ladder. The tiny boat didn't even rock when he landed.

Murmurs ran through the crew who saw before Shakespeare silenced them with a dark look, "Avast, you scurvy sea dogs, what the fuck are you gawking at? Back to work! You there! Get those lines faked down before we need them again."

"*Shakespeare!*" Billy barked up from the rowboat as they pushed away toward the ship Günter took to meet them.

Nigel hung over the rail to answer, "Aye, sir?"

"Anything happens to my Pandora while I'm away? I'll tear your balls off and roast them for chestnuts before I rip out your fingernails for a necklace and feed what's left of you to the sharks." His death's head smile flashed in the moonlight.

Nigel swallowed hard. "Very good, sir."

Günter and Billy reached the single-masted cutter resting at anchor in short order. It wasn't long before she caught two full headsails of night wind and streaked inland, disappearing from view.

They docked at the harbour and became lost among the rest of the docked vessels. During the day, Günter hired horses and when evening fell, they left for Twitch's house in the hills as fast as the animals could be compelled to run. It didn't take long--Billy and horses had never got along. The poor animals were compelled to run when they were anywhere near him. Riding? It was a flat-out race to leave him behind they couldn't win.

Coming up on the edge of where he knew he would feel the presence of the other vampire, he felt nothing.

"*Oh, quelle merveilleuse journée*. He is not about."

Günter scratched his head, "Who, Cap'n? We come for the lass, aye?"

"Do not speak to me, idiot," he snapped.

"But witch, he's dead, sir. I told you I saws his grave."

He glared at Günter at his side, "No thanks to you and that vacuous space above your neck." Nudging them forward, they walked the horses the rest of the way. With a sharp eye, Billy prepared for battle and made himself familiar with the layout of the buildings and any cover in relation to the path. And then grew distracted.

"Oh, *mon petite*," he breathed. "She's not been made…" He savoured the air. "Still mine to be had. Oh, this *is* a good day!" He urged his horse ahead in anticipation and then pulled up at the end of the path. He threw the reins at Günter. "Remain here, *imbécile*. She is only one small, human woman. I will show you how it is done."

"Swears I hit her. With the *axe*, Cap'n. Like as you said. Swung at her neck so hard, forced me to yank the blade out with a foot braced 'gainst her backsides."

"Not hard enough, obviously."

"I saw the blood, Cap'n. Swear it on my mother's eyes. '*xactly* as you told me. Jabbed her a couple or three times with a length o' wood as she slept. Feisty li'l wench she was, too, like as before. Led me a merry chase. Wouldn't go down even leaking her portion. Staggered up'n the burying ground when I was after her with the axe. Laid in a puddle she was. Arse over elbow right o'er grave there, blood ever' which way." Günter's lip was out in stubborn determination, "I calls that poetic justice, I does. Died atop witch's grave like." He pointed, "Up the back there. Sees it? In the burying place. 'Nother gravestone there now t'weren't before. She felled right o'er bigger one. Don't think she was drawin' breath, Cap'n. I swe--"

Billy help up his hand, "No, don't swear. Just shut *up* your babbling." Billy considered. "You say she fell over that grave while she bled?" He snorted, "And you wonder why I would be looking for him. You really are a waste of skin, Günter. I have no idea what value I believed you ever had." He dismissed him with a flick of his wrist. Reprisal was no longer on his mind, "Remain here. *Don't move.* I shall return with her presently."

"But, Cap'n, I--"

"*Chut!* Hold my fucking horse, *bon à rien.* Good-for-nothing whoreson."

Billy slid from the saddle and raised his arms to the moon that ruled what he was, the only god in his universe of eternal plundering. He let the darkness invade him. Swirling up from inside, it remade him even while it did nothing more than tear away the thin veil of humanity he sometimes bothered to sport in public. He wouldn't need it for her.

Stalking up the path on his cat feet, her heartbeat drew him. The beguile couldn't touch her and that otherworldly presence of hers would allow her to resist him. But he would never take what he wanted by force, not from her, and he calculated as he approached. It needed to be with permission. It needed to be voluntary. It needed to be the way it needed to be without his understanding why even when everything else he did was about stealth and thievery and plotting to overtake. There were always vaporous, unspoken rules whenever it came to her.

When the porch was in view, he caught sight of her through the open windows and a rictal grin stretched his mouth.

"Ah… there is my girl. Waiting for me are you, *mon ange? C'est ça.*" He crept up to the porch without a sound and ate her with his eyes. She was even more beautiful than when he last saw her. Away from him, she'd become a woman of regal bearing and uncommon loveliness. The dark queen he craved standing at his side. Didn't matter if he might tire of her in a week, because it was all about the chase.

And this one was still on.

Billy drooled in anticipation.

She hummed to herself as she walked about the front room, straightening up. The sound carried outside on the night air and drifted across the garden. Fascinated, he watched her, unable to tear his gaze away. Without the beguile, he would have to wait until she came out on her own or induce her out. Not something he was ever reduced to, tonight, he willed her outside, so he wouldn't be forced to wait. Worried her protector would return before he had his time, he resorted to trickery. Allowing himself to become more substantial, he stomped his boots around on the porch and then sat on the swing.

"Back so soon? That was quick. You only just left." She was laughing and waiting for an answer.

Billy made a noncommittal noise.

"Well, that's disappointing. What happened to your good mood, you crabby old thing?"

"Humph."

"Oh, Richard, what am I going to do with you? Well, you can sit and sulk on the swing, but--" Her voice failed on the other side of the wall and then she caught it again. "Well, I have some news. I was going to tell you later, but I can't wait any longer. It's very exciting. Guaranteed it'll make you smile. At least, I hope it will. I think. Well... I had it all worked out in my head, how to tell you..." Her voice drifted off again inside the house while Billy heard her moving about. Then her voice came to him through the open window closest to the swing, "Richard..?"

Leaning backwards on the inside wall right behind him, her hand rested on the open window ledge. Back-to-back with a layer of wood between them, it was the closest he'd been to her in a very long while and her heartbeat made his brains dance. He closed his eyes in savour. Her tone said it all, though, and it was then that he knew--she had stayed by choice.

"Uh-huh?" It turned his mood darker and twisted through his brain. Doubtless, her protector was in agreement from the careful house he built for her. He nodded to himself. Revenge was what he came for and that's what he would achieve. She was dangerous and would pay for setting fire to Pandora. That and more. For running away. For making him appear a fool before the men. For continued resistance. For making him waste so much time thinking about her. For distracting him from his courses. The revenge would be sweet. No Günter to worry about bodging it up, either. He would look after it himself.

"Richard, you know I don't know much about this really. Us. You. I've been trying to learn all this time, because... Well..." She sighed in distraction and started again. "I didn't realise for a long while. It seemed one of those things that shouldn't have been possible, all things considered. I didn't know *what* was going on to be honest," she laughed, a nervous little titter that tinkled outdoors and wrapped itself around his already twisted mind. Her fingers drummed idly on the window ledge, "Took me a bit to catch on. I didn't want to say anything until I was sure, my love. Because of the way things are, I thought it couldn't be real," her voice was breathless and wispy with emotion.

Billy's mood grew darker, party to a private conversation between the object of his obsession and his so-far-unseen nemesis. His lip curled and it was with great effort he kept the snarl from passing his throat. Her protector had kept her from him and revenge for too long and he needed her outside. She was so close. He gave her another noncommittal noise to encourage her.

"Well, I certainly don't have to tell you about things that can and can't be, of course. You know. But Richard, I guarantee you haven't had experience with *this*. It'll be new for both of us." There was a smile in her voice, "We can learn it together."

Billy's mood turned darker still, tainted by the obvious joy that existed between them. He moved his hand out to rest on the outside of the window ledge, the tips of his fingers grazing hers. If she moved farther out by his encouragement, she would be his for the taking.

So close.

"Oh, Richard," Maggie sighed contentment and brushed her fingers lightly over the back of his hand in tenderness, "it's wonderful. A miracle," she walked her fingers backwards up his arm around the edge of the window, reaching out to touch Richard's mouth in affection as she always did. Her voice was full of happiness, "Let me be close with you."

Her hand hovered in the air between them and Billy took the opportunity. Reaching his own hand up, he twined his fingers into hers. Chuckling in satisfaction, she was now caught and there was nothing she could do about it.

"Wha..?" Maggie whipped around the edge of the window as Billy yanked her arm. When the full horror hit her a second later, she screamed. Billy dragged her out the rest of the way and she fell onto the porch with a thump. "*You*," she breathed. "Why can't you just die and leave me alone?" He slapped her hard across the mouth to silence her.

Maggie didn't say another word, but glared up at him from where she rested. If she kept him there long enough, Richard would come. He always knew. He came to her before when she needed him and he would come to her again.

"What a lovely little *maison à la campagne* you've made for yourself here in the country hills, *mon petit oiseau*. Bit of a change from the lock box in the hold, I'll wager. Pity to be leaving it now. Ah, well, but you cannot outrun the past. There is simply no leaving me behind. *Allons-y!*"

Maggie forced herself to speak to detain him, "You won't get away with it. Richard will be back any minute. Don't you remember? He's a witch. He knows things. No doubt he's already on his--"

"A witch?" Billy's laugh was cruel. "*Je pense que non*. No, I really don't think so, *Mademoiselle*. I know what he is," Billy clicked his teeth together and licked his lips. "And I know how to dispatch him, as well. Don't waste your breath, pretty," his voice was dark and low and ominous.

Maggie's eyes widened, "Oh…" Aboard the ship, there had been the evidence without explanation. With Richard, explanation without allowing her to see the evidence. To her, they were so different, night and day. But here in the world, it struck her they were somehow the same. The same and more. There *was* more and it frightened her to acknowledge it. Billy would always return and there was no escaping him despite she would remain forever unaffected by his beguile. And Richard, poor beastly Richard, despite his apparent shortcomings was incapable of ignoring her when she needed him. Even from miles away.

In some way, they were all connected together. Connected by forces the human mind failed to perceive and only evident when pulled above to pay witness with a god's eye view.

Under the spell of the moonlight, she struggled to comprehend beyond the human haze limiting her there and it parted for an instant. Her hand strayed to the flat of her stomach and felt the still-tiny child Richard had given her. Her heart beat hard and fast in fear and she knew Richard would know. Had to. This one single opportunity after so long could not end this way. Billy could only answer to his instincts, but Richard was strong enough to protect her from him and would never fail her. Even backing up across the porch and not quite in possession of all the facts, she was sure of that much.

Even half-life couldn't dull his service to her.

A hearty laugh answered her seeming revelation, "Oh, *ma chérie*, you have always been so naive. Do you mean to tell me you had no clue? All this time, you did not know your witch and I were the same predacious breed?" He cackled in glee, "Ah, *mon Dieu*! This is too perfect," his cruel laugh continued at her expense.

"Shut up, master butcher," her eyes burned holes into him. "How dare you come here. What did you think, that I would simply return without a word? That I would go along willingly? Why? So you could stick me back in the bloody hold or amuse the crew some more once you tired of me? *Never*, do you hear me? Never!" Maggie scrambled up to run off the porch, but there was no escape from the inhuman master of Pandora. He was already down the steps ahead of her and she ran straight into his arms. Maggie screamed again, this time with fearful purpose.

"Shriek all you wish, pretty. No escape for you. *Viens, mon amour*, time to come home and answer for your crimes." Digging a hand into her hair, he planted a ruthless, possessive kiss on her mouth while she struggled in futility. When he pulled back, she missed biting him by a fraction and it only made him laugh at her all the more. "Oh-ho! All that life. Such waste. Ah well, nothing to be done for it now, I suppose. Come along then." Without effort, he threw her over his shoulder and ran down the path to his waiting horse while she continued to struggle.

Leaving Günter behind with a message for Richard, Billy rode hard for the coast, determined to make it back before sunrise with time to spare. When the vampire-witch returned to find Günter, that lingering bother would vanish. Sure to misspeak and let slip he wielded the axe, vengeance would be quick and brutal. And the half-wit would never mishandle his instructions again. He had the entire rest of eternity to settle his score with Maggie's protector.

It had been a productive night.

Without doubt, Shakespeare would be waiting on the shore, as the man's attention to his duties was without compare. When Billy pounded over the last rise, he wasn't disappointed. Nigel kicked out the fire as the captain came into view and hurried to struggle the rowboat back into the water, so he wouldn't be obliged to wait. He didn't need to be told--a sense of urgency surrounded everything their captain did.

When he saw Günter no longer accompanied him and he had acquired a passenger, Nigel raised his eyebrows, but knew better than to comment. Maggie squirmed and spit in desperation, but remained secure in the arms of her captor. Billy slid from his horse and leapt into the rowboat with Maggie still over his shoulder, an iron arm barred across her legs. She pounded his back in futility.

Billy paid no attention and looked off to his ship, "Soon, my lady. We'll exact our retribution."

"Retribution? Potty swine… You have no idea what you've done. Let me go, let me go, let me *go*!"

"Soon enough, *ma chérie*." He shifted her weight with casual indifference, almost unaware of it. "Can you not go any faster?" he snapped at his First Mate.

"Aye-aye, Captain," Nigel put his back into it and rowed to outrun the devil. Unfortunately for him, he was already aboard.

"Put… me… *down*..," Maggie panted with effort and got nowhere. Almost always queasy the last few weeks, upside-down and swaying with the waves, she felt ill. "For the love of God, put me down. *Please*… I'm going to be sick," she continued to pound his back with a useless fist. "Please, Billy," she couldn't even be insistent and only sounded tired and ill.

"Good effort, pretty, but you forget I have witnessed all your play acting before. Try again," his face stone, he wouldn't give her an inch.

Nigel braved a sideways look around the edge of his captain and caught a look at Maggie's green face. He cleared his throat to get Billy's attention. He motioned in her direction and nodded she was actually ill. Billy clenched his jaw and growled.

"Please, Billy," Maggie sounded pitiful. "Keep your hand on me, so I don't jump overboard. Anything… Just turn me right-ways-up. Please. I don't think I can… oh…" Maggie started to retch still slung over his back.

"*Mon Dieu!*" Billy threw her down without ceremony in time for

Maggie to hang her head over the side. He wrinkled his nose in disgust. "You never were much of a lady, were you?"

Maggie spoke with her head still hanging over the side, "Why don't you slice out your own tongue?"

All that got was a laugh, "Ah, there is my girl. Still full of pluck, after all. So much life that might be mine."

She splashed salt water over her mouth, "Keep dreaming."

"I have never stopped, *ma cocotte*." They reached the ship and distracted, left the taunting until they were aboard.

"Ahoy, Captain!"

"Ahoy, y'pack of peppered rat droppings! It's good to be home! Did you behave yourselves while your captain was away?" In an uncommonly good mood, it spread to the rest of the crew and they broke out in laughter. Grabbing Maggie up again, he flitted upward more than climbed the rope ladder, missing most of the rungs. When he reached the deck, the men mumbled in appreciation. "All right, all right, yes, it's a woman here. Put your eyes back in, boys."

"To the hold with the rest, Cap'n?" The new giant of a Boatswain, Harris, was already well-versed in their captain's appetites and took an uncommon interest in providing for them.

"No-no, not this one. This one? *Elle est très spécial.* Been with us before and now she's come home for a visit. Is that not sweet of her?" He laughed without reserve, the meaning clear. "Lash her to the mainmast where we can all have a good look at her." Hands took her from the captain and secured her against the mast in the centre of the ship.

Nigel swung himself up onto the deck as men hauled the rowboat up behind him. Maggie saw him clearly for the first time. She attempted to catch his eye, but he avoided her in front of the captain. It was almost dawn and if she wasn't dead in a moment, she would have the reprieve of day with him. Billy never discovered it was with Nigel's help that she escaped and she didn't break that trust now. She turned her gaze away.

From the corner of his eye, Nigel saw her straining to look across the bay to shore with longing and he ached for her. And then cursed himself. This was not what was meant to happen and his mind already worked. It wouldn't be easy, not by a longshot. Time was short and getting anything past Billy was treacherous. He had put himself at risk to help her before and he'd be damned before he failed her again.

Pre-dawn changed the colour of the horizon. Maggie and Nigel prayed thanks to the light, knowing Billy would have to make a quick exit.

"Shakespeare!"

"Aye, sir."

"I am retiring below. While we remain, fill up on clean water and wood. Some game while they're about it. Whatever can be hunted before end of day. Save us a trip later."

"Aye-aye, Captain."

"We shall attend to *her* this evening," he flicked a disinterested thumb in Maggie's direction. "Ignore her for the day. If she screams, leave her to it. No one to hear her out here and she'll grow hoarse soon enough. And keep the crew off her. She's mine." He looked out over the crew, "*Écoutez?* Hands off. No exceptions. Anyone touches the *lady* earns a ride on the bowsprit."

"Aye, sir!" everyone quite clear on the brutal consequences. Even savage men without conscience as many were, they would never chance it.

"*Bien!* Until this evening. Good day, Mr. Shakespeare. The ship is yours."

"Rest well, sir. See you at sundown." Nigel moved to take his station on the poop deck while Billy went to his cabin below him to escape the sun kissing the horizon.

He stopped on the way down, "Shakespeare?"

"Aye, sir?"

"On second thought, bring our guest to my cabin."

"Sir?"

"Un*tie* her and *bring* her to me."

Nigel's heart sank. "Aye-aye, Captain."

Some of the common crewmen went down to their quarters before the mast, forward of the foremast. Billy liked to see the ship alive at night while he was up and ran with a split crew who took turns on the night shift. It had been the same way when Maggie was last there and the routine was familiar.

The smaller day crew got busy as the First Mate rhymed off a list of duties and then pulled a dagger from his boot to slice the ropes off Maggie's wrists. He spoke under his breath, so the men wouldn't hear, "I'm sorry, Maggie. Are you all right?"

"Better now, thank you, Nigel. Nice to see a friend."

His brow furrowed, "Out here there are things I could do, but in his cabin?" He took his time getting the ropes off her, "I don't want to take you in there, woman. You know I don't."

She put a soft hand on his arm, "I appreciate the concern, but he'll be asleep. I'll just sit in the cage for the day. Nothing else has changed, I see. All more of the same."

"Still mad as a bag of ferrets and vicious as the dogs of Hell. I cannot believe this was his blasted errand." Nigel looked stricken, "This is *my* fault, Maggie. All for revenge. There's no apology great enough. I failed you. I can't even begin to ask for forgiveness."

She swallowed hard, "You weren't to know. Neither of us could." She held him no malice and gave him a weak smile. He had risked so much for her in the past and she would never forget.

When he looked into her eyes, he knew this time it wouldn't go easy, but he put it out of his head. Nigel's mind ran through exit scenarios. "I swear to you I'll think of something," he had a hand under her elbow as her guided her to the stairs without enthusiasm.

"Can you do something for me?"

"Anything I'm able."

"Someone will be looking for me. Someone..," she lost her voice and tried again. "Someone important to me, Nigel. Very important." She put a hand against her stomach and implored him with a look. "He'll come for us."

"Good God."

She put on a brave smile, "Would you keep an eye out for him? Wave him in the right direction if you can?"

"Done," he gave her a tight nod and then his brow furrowed. He spoke fast, "How will he know where you've gone?"

"He'll know," she was whispering as they reached the stairs.

"Then you have my word. Wait. His *name*, Maggie? *Quickly*," they were already at the cabin door and out of time.

"Twitch," she hissed. "Twitch the Witch, they call him. Richard Per--" and snapped her mouth shut when the door opened onto a candle held out in the darkness by an unseen hand.

"In the cage, Mr. Shakespeare."

"Aye, Captain."

Back above decks, Nigel squared his shoulders and decided to do something proactive and dangerous.

Some might have considered it noble or brave, but he didn't think so considering it was the least likely to get him killed in the process. He sent most of the deck crew inland to gather wood and water, giving them a rare reprieve--one they appreciated and part of the way he'd earned their respect. The rest he sent hunting and they all ran to it with relish. The other half of the crew slept and with the sails tied down and riding at anchor there wasn't much to do, anyway. He went in to shore with the men. Gesturing at the horse still wandering around on the beach, he announced he would return it to where it was hired. They never batted an eye. He caught it up and rode like hell for the closest village.

Everyone knew about Twitch the Witch and directed him to the hill far inland. When he reached the neat and cared-for home with the porch swing, he found it deserted except for Günter's inert body outdoors. It made his heart ache for them, although he couldn't say the same for Günter. While he considered the body, it dawned on him all the months he was missing from the ship he'd been searching for Maggie. To even the score for the fire. Nigel hung his head in regret, because it had been his suggestion. Billy hated fire and he knew. And all pointless now since he managed to catch her up again, anyway.

"Bollocks," feeling a coward for running off and leaving her there, he made a decision.

Leaving directions and a description of the ship in the event Maggie was mistaken about her man, he hurried back to the beach before the crew grew suspicious. And could still deny they knew about where he went.

Slapping the horse free on the road, he returned on foot to find Cook roasting rabbits for midday while the men chattered in fellowship. Away from the death ship, it was easier to breathe. Even hardened criminals as most of them were, it got to them and made them appreciate the small respite all the more. The couple of mouthfuls Nigel got down were tasteless and he couldn't enjoy the lightened atmosphere. His mind ran ahead with things more important. Returning to the ship with the next boatload of supplies, he gathered his wits.

Yet to find someone they could trust as a new Master Gunner, it was still Nigel's job along with everything else he did. Like the captain, he wore a key to the armoury around his neck. Before the crew returned, he took a musket and two braces of pistols and loaded them before hiding his small arsenal above decks within easy reach. A second dagger now rode his other boot and he buckled on his cutlass. He'd been ashore and within his rights to wear it, so no one would question it. Unless they remembered he hadn't worn it earlier, though he thought not. They weren't very astute.

The afternoon wore on while he dozed behind the wheel to keep an eye out for Maggie's man, but he never came. With trepidation, he watched the sun sink into the sea. Without help, there wasn't enough time for the clandestine set up of another escape around their always-suspicious captain. Of course, he was prepared to fight, but he was also under no illusions. Billy would kill him and then he wouldn't be any help to Maggie. All but the Boatswain preferred to take their orders from him rather than their uneven-tempered captain, but the crew didn't know Maggie. Even knowing the captain's unwavering brutality, coming to the aid of a woman with child might still be beyond them in fear for their own lives. He couldn't count on them.

When night fell, the captain surfaced from the darkness below decks dragging Maggie behind him. Nigel jumped up, alert.

"Mr. Shakespeare?"

"Aye, sir."

"Escort our guest amidships and reacquaint her with the mainmast, *s'il vous plaît*." He released the hard hand he had clamped around her upper arm and threw her in Nigel's direction.

"Aye-aye, Captain." Catching her so she wouldn't fall, he leaned into her ear on the way to the mast, "I've been to your cottage, luv. And left a note with enough detail for your man to find us," he spoke fast and low while his back was to the captain. "Günter, the rotter, was dead. That's at least one bother we've no further need to worry over. There was no one else, I'm afraid. I've some weapons from the armoury hidden on deck, but beyond that?" Nigel's expression was momentarily pained and then hardened in determination. He nodded to her, "We'll make it up as we go along then. Look for our opportunity, yeah? Chin up, lass. Not our first time."

The Boatswain made his report to the captain while Nigel was busy at the mast and it gave them an extra moment steeping in uncertainty. Maggie closed her eyes and took a calming breath. "That's right. We've done it before. My dear, dear friend at my side," she gave him a tight, sincere smile, but it was difficult to keep up the brave face. This time was different. She felt it. "Seems Richard's gone the wrong direction although

I don't understand how." And then pulled a face, "Günter. Pointed him to the harbour more than likely. The long way around." She sighed in resignation. "Thank you, Nigel. That was a great risk to take going inland. You truly are a good friend."

He held her eyes a long moment as he lashed her arms around the mast behind her and she smiled her thanks for what he tried to do. But it was futile. Whatever he might attempt, Billy would kill him before they blinked and then kill her, anyway. They both knew it.

With reluctance, Nigel stepped back and took up his position near the captain.

"Well, pretty, what do you say? Miss your old home?" He glared at her, "Or surprised to see it still all of a piece?" his voice dark.

She smiled sweetly, "What a shame it didn't sink. Obviously, I didn't put enough effort into the last time. Luckily, there's always the next." She had nothing to lose in antagonizing him.

Billy snarled, but didn't take the bait. He was in the revenge business this evening and that was all. "You created an enormous amount of work for our Mr. Sweeney and his mates, *mon cher*, that's true. But he got it repaired all right. Good effort, though."

She tossed her hair over her shoulders with a flick of her head, "All right, I'm done speaking with you now, *Captain*. We both know why I'm here. Get on with it. I really have no desire to speak with you ever again. Go on, whoremaster, kill me and let this business be done," her voice was strong and assured and resigned. Standing just behind the captain, Nigel visibly struggled to keep the sorrow from showing on his face.

"You are not in charge here, *Mademoiselle*. All in due time. We have some other unfinished business to attend to first that I'm pleased you're here to witness." He snapped his fingers and motioned to Mr. Harris, the giant Boatswain.

"What the bloody blue blazes are you doing?" Harris caught Nigel up by his elbows and held them hard behind his back. The man's hands were enormous and there was no getting out of it. "Have you lost your mind, you ignorant sod? Unhand me before I have you flogged!" feigning indignation, his stomach sank and Nigel already knew. Harris relieved him of his cutlass and both daggers with a snicker and then tore the key to the armoury off his neck by the chain.

He'd been found out.

"On to men now, Captain Blackthorn? Why, I thought women were your preferred flavour. My mistake," Maggie taunted him from the mast and he glowered at her.

"If there was only a way you could distract me, *chéri*. No, this evening is about vengeance and now, here is all the more reason. It appears our Mr. Shakespeare has been a naughty boy. Terribly naughty, indeed." He shifted to regard him head on. "What were you planning to do with the weapons, Shakespeare? Help my prize escape. *Again*. Or a mutiny, perchance? Ah *oui*, or both?"

Nigel winced on the inside and with a look beseeched Maggie to say nothing. "I had no plan, actually," his tone conversational. "Mutiny's not in my blood. Although that's a capital idea now that you mention. All things considered, I'd just as soon kill you myself and save the trouble. You know I'm not above murder. All those officers from His Majesty's Navy who got themselves in the way of my escape, if you'll remember. *Sir*."

They were both going to die.

Billy laughed, "See? That's why I like you Shakespeare. Honest to a fault. Well then, I assume from your lack of offering any further explanation you were planning to assist our guest this evening, *oui*?"

Nigel was a statue and said nothing, but it didn't matter. It was too late for any protest. He could see the wheels turning in the captain's mind while he decided the best way to dispatch them. No matter how much he might wish it otherwise, Maggie would take the brunt of it for both of them. He hated himself for not taking his own suggestion to kill Billy. In the years he served on his ship, he witnessed a great deal of mysterious behaviour from their captain. Not the least of which was his walking away from a pistol shot to the gut. All things considered, he held little hope anything he attempted could, in fact, bring about his end. Still, he regretted lacking the fortitude to find out.

Billy strolled the deck with his hands tucked behind his back, appearing lost in thought. Without warning, he streaked over to Maggie and hit her hard across the face with a closed fist. Stubborn, she didn't cry out.

"No!"

Teeth barred, he drew back another fist to hit her again, lower this time, but was distracted by Nigel kicking up a ruckus behind him.

Nigel struggled in the hands of his watchdog with manic determination, but couldn't get loose. "Leave her be, Captain! Let me take her beating. I volunteer. Willingly. *Please*, Captain."

Head thrown back in laughter, Billy sneered at him, "Oh, how very noble, Mr. Shakespeare. Such a gentlemanly offer, *n'est pas*? But let the punishment fit the crime. She damaged my lady and so she receives the same in kind. An eye for an eye, Mr. Shakespeare."

"Aye, sir, but--" Harris yanked his arms back in savage control and Nigel doubled over as his left shoulder dislocated.

Tears ran down Maggie's face as she watched Nigel take attention from her, "Oh, Nigel..."

Sweating in pain, he refused to be dissuaded and struggled more. He panted with the effort, "I know the code. She's not the one responsible. I'm the one. It was my doing, Captain. All mine. *I* thought up the plan, *I* let her loose, *I*--" he grunted as Harris gave his arms another yank. It didn't silence him, "*I* set fire to Pandora. It was me, sir. By the code, you must put me in her place. Even if she was wholly responsible? There's certainly no provision in the code for a woman with child." This time he screamed when Harris tore out his other shoulder. He sagged to his knees, but the larger man held him upright by his now useless limbs.

Billy's head whipped about to examine Maggie closely, working to get a beguiling grip on her, to get inside her where he could find answers. It couldn't work, of course, but he got all the answer he needed when he looked into her eyes. "*Salope*. Whose is it? Some drifter come to call?" He laughed in scorn, "Didn't your beloved witch become upset about that, *mon cher*?"

Maggie shook her head and fixed her eyes on the captain's, drilling him with the truth that would hurt him more.

Billy snarled, "*C'est une impossibilité*! Not in this world is it possible."

A slow smile lit Maggie's face, "Didn't you hear anything while you were lurking out on the porch, Billy? It's a miracle."

"No..," he breathed, refusing to comprehend. "How was this accomplished? What witchcraft is this?" he snapped at her. "*You will tell me!*"

She looked out over the water toward the shore. Maggie's voice grew distant, "He's no witch. You told me so yourself. And it did happen." Gathering herself, she turned her head back to look him in the eye again, "Know this, *Captain* Blackthorn. He *will* come for me. It might be too late to save me, but come he will. Whatever you do, whatever you hope to accomplish here, whatever revenge you seek all for the love of a *ship*? Will be nothing compared with the vengeance he'll swear upon you. *That* I guarantee."

"Shut *up*. Don't think I don't know every word you and Shakespeare have plotted together, pretty. Forget your scurvy witch. Have no doubt, I know who is responsible here."

"He's on his way already, Billy, and he's coming for you. And that's no frantic, hopeful curse thrown at you as I run away. Not this time. This time, it's real."

"*Chut! Je fais ce qui me plaît*, I'll do as I bloody well please. He does not frighten me. You cannot taunt me with his imaginary exploits and expect them to keep me from my own. An eye for an eye, *ma chérie*. I'll have my due."

"Did you think he would stop at Günter?" Maggie laughed, a cruel, hard laugh that spoke the truth. "He's only just begun and you're at the head of the list. The shining star in the cast of his revenge. He's closer by the moment--"

"Stop it, I said!"

"Why? Are you afraid? You should be. He's like a wolf, Billy. He'll track you to the ends of the earth. Are you so arrogant you believe you could hide from him?" she barked a disdainful laugh. "There's no trail he cannot follow. No obstacle he can't overcome. He'll never sleep. And he'll never stop. Not until he gets what he wants. Go on, kill me and be satisfied, but know this. He's not long behind and he's heading straight for you."

"Bitch!" In a fit of rage, Billy smashed her hard across the face again to stop the words that couldn't stop the future from unfolding. She sagged against the ropes.

"*Maggie*," Nigel called out to her weakly, but dazed, she didn't raise her head to respond. Shaking off the pain, he struggled to his feet and faced the captain of the ship of death. "There's no call for this. None at all. She's no sailor. Certainly no pirate. You cannot hold her to the code. It doesn't apply. *I* am responsible and it *does* apply to me. I demand my punishment. And as I'm taking responsibility for all actions, I demand you release her."

"Demand?" Billy's eyes blazed.

"That's right, demand. No wait, I'll go one better. As First Mate and Quartermaster, I put before your own crew your mismanagement of our resources for your personal vendetta. That *is* against the code. *Our* code. Let's put it to a vote, men. The evidence? Easy enough for all to see. Total lack of diligence in obtaining riches and not looking out for our interests in general. What do you say, lads? Does our captain need replacement? Give us a yea, all in favour then."

Billy snarled, "Anytime, Shakespeare. You are digging your own grave, *mon ami*."

As long as he kept talking, Maggie was safe, "Come on, lads. Let's put it to a vote as prescribed by our code. You have my word, and that's a solemn promise. You know I've not lied to you once and I won't now. I swear to you before God and witnesses, I'll make the future safer for us all." The rest of the crew stood frozen in place. He couldn't blame them.

"I can look after what needs doing and none of you will be responsible. What do you say, boys? A vote to change your futures. Right, let's see your hands then." They would never move against the captain no matter how much they might wish to or how much they respected their First Mate and Nigel knew it. Looking from one face to another, they turned their gazes away, justifiably terrified at the thought of defying their master. He couldn't ask it from them, "It's all right, lads. I understand." Nigel knew they were alone. He skewered Billy on a look, "I used to believe you found pleasure in death. Relished it even. But it's more than that, isn't it? Much more. Even since I've known you, a little worse each year. A little more… inhuman."

The captain snapped his fingers at Mr. Harris and a massive fist buried itself in Nigel's kidney. Knocking the wind out of him, it drove him back down to his knees and he sagged forward to rest his head on the wooden deck, gasping. Turning his back on him, Billy motioned for two of the men to untie Maggie from the mainmast and secure her wrists over her head to the rail of the poop deck. With an evil eye over his shoulder to Nigel, he sauntered over to her and tore the collar of her dress down, exposing her back.

He loosened the handle of a whip from the sash at his waist with deliberate concentration.

Wheezing, Nigel tried without success to get upright, "Bastard…"

Billy laughed. "By the code, *my* code, the two of you shall share equally. Both responsible. Both to suffer the same fate."

"I went there today," he had nothing to lose. Desperate, he added to Maggie's assurances to scare him into distraction. "Gave him directions to the ship…" Struggling for breath, Nigel was hard pressed to talk, but he kept at it. "I gave them to him… coming for you, Captain… coming…"

The lash whipped out and snapped Maggie across the back with explosive force, silencing Nigel faster than if he'd been hit. Three lashes later, she finally cried out and he laughed in satisfaction, "*Que oui, chéri,* yes, as it should be. *I* am master here and that's quite enough of your defiance. Time now to accept your due." The whip whistled out again and landed with a gratifying crack. Billy chuckled down low in his throat.

"Ship ahoy, Captain!"

"Ship?" Nonplussed, "What ship?" Billy struggled to pull his mind back from where he was already well lost. Blurry, he located the crewman up on the archer platform holding a spyglass. "Spit it out. *Report!*"

The sailor pointed down the coast, "Sloop, Cap'n. She's got wind, sir. Comin' with the devil on her 'eels."

Billy used his inhuman sight to see it for what it was and scowled. No navy vessel, it soared like a ghost in the night. Her square topsail hoisted on the extra-long bowsprit to make the most of the wind, he judged it doing a blistering eleven knots that would catch them up fast. And she was flying the Jolly Roger. A fight for territory with another pirate ship was not on his agenda for the evening. There was no way he was going broadsides with this stranger when he had better things to do.

He snarled and made a decision, "Weigh anchor, you Christ-cursed excuses for seamen. Get us the hell out of here. That's an order!" The crew scrambled and he turned his attention back to Maggie, "Such a short reprieve, pretty. Pity it's not your precious witch. Where could he have got to, do you suppose? *Est-il venu?* Has he come? *May non, ma chatounette.* Only you and I and everything you deserve." The lash whipped out again and caught her square across the back to steal any words she might have spoken.

Several satisfying snaps later, there was blood in the air and running down her back and full in the lust, he knew nothing else. Cackling with glee, the lash continued to whistle through the darkness without pause. Maggie hung from the ropes at her wrists without movement. Behind them, Nigel suffered through every lash along with her, making himself keep watch if only for the witness, so she wasn't alone. When her back was in ribbons and turned to pulp, he could no longer bear to look. Hoping she could forgive him, he turned his gaze off to the sea. The sloop still gave chase. Coming up fast, it would be on them before they knew it, but the captain was in a world of his own.

Nigel managed a grim smile and barked a laugh, "You'll be boarded before you know it, fool."

Billy's back stiffened with his arm frozen in the air and the whip fell to the deck short of its mark. "*De quoi parles-tu*? What are you talking about?" his voice rough with bloodlust and the desire it brought over him.

"The sloop, you stupid bastard. She'll be too close to use the cannon."

Standing stiff and alert with his arm in the air, Billy whirled on Nigel. The whip snaked out to twine around his throat, silencing him except for the sounds of his choking.

The captain's eyes were wild as he walked himself down the length of the whip. Pulling back enough to take up the slack with every step to keep it taut, he gave Nigel no reprieve. Both shoulders dislocated, he only managed to raise his arms at the elbows and graze the leather at his throat with his fingertips. But without any power, he continued to suffocate. At the end of the whip, Billy looked into his eyes and watched him choke a long moment, enjoying his pain. Turning his head one way and the other, he appeared to take him all in, gauging him, weighing him, studying his prey. A moment later, the heel of his boot smashed down on one of his legs, breaking the bone and making him gasp for air that wasn't there.

And then the captain dropped the whip. Hands hanging slack at his sides, his head came up, alert.

Nigel collapsed, gasping and choking. In that moment of reprieve, the Boatswain took it upon himself to yank him upright by one arm with an almighty crack that popped one shoulder back in. But before he could enjoy the use of it, the man used his own dagger on him to open a hole in his midriff exposed by his raised arm. Nigel continued to choke and when it turned to frothy blood on his lips, he dropped him back down again, snickering.

Maggie was still.

An eerie cry carried on the wind--anguished and enraged and screaming for blood--that raised the hackles of every crewman. Men crossed themselves and looked to each other with fear and then off the stern to the sloop that was almost on top of them.

"It be the devil hisself," crewmen nodded in agreement with the one who ventured an opinion.

"Quick lads, cut 'er down 'fore we're blamed for it!" Several crewmen ran to Maggie then and slashed through the ropes at her wrists. She fell into a boneless heap on the deck. They eyed her lifeless body and then turned away, cowering, "We'll burn for bein' a party to this business."

"It's our lot for taking on with this Christ-cursed ship."

"Aye, mates. God-forsaken we be, sure."

Crew bunched together to watch the progress of the ghostly pirate ship that continued to fly toward them. "Better make your peace, lads."

"Shut the fuck up, the lot of you," Billy snapped and raked them all with a disparaging look. "It's not the bloody devil, you imbeciles." Eyes narrowed, he scanned the smaller ship for a sign of Maggie's vampire-witch. He knew he was there, could feel him now, and willed him to board them. "*Il vient*," he whispered under his breath. "Let him come to me now."

"There be no escape, mates."

"God save us, there he be! 'Tis Ol' Nick hisself. Lord, his eyes does glow with the fires o' hell." A shaking finger pointed to the bow of the sloop. A dark figure stood poised in the wind with a cloak streaming out behind it. Full of the night and revenge, it was a dark reaper come to claim them all. "We're done for, lads. May we all burn in hell."

A splash interrupted their commiseration, "Man overboard!"

The smaller ship slowed and hove to near the two bodies left in the dark water of Pandora's wake. Nigel barely moved, but managed to keep Maggie from sinking. Pandora stayed her course and opened up distance between them while the sloop held position.

The cat-eyed reaper dove off the bow into the sea in the direction of the bodies.

9

(Canada – Present)

"**S**hit man," **Baby Bite leaned forward** in eagerness, caught up in the story, "she was still alive, right? He saved her, that Shakespeare guy. Man, anyone who could face off against Billy and get away has my total respect. Tell me you at least got to talk to her."

We were down in the labyrinth away from the rest of the bunch, myself and Alan and his six little mates I dubbed the Blood Runner Hunters. I felt ambushed, but they'd heard Billy's version of how he came to be marooned and wanted to know the real story. I wasn't keen on discussing it, but they were working hard to help me achieve my revenge. I suppose I felt I owed them.

Uncomfortable, I walked across the room away from them. I fiddled with the latches on some of the cases they used to transport their myriad computer paraphernalia. "No, I was too late," forcing the words out. "Maggie was gone before I pulled her and Nigel out of the water." Two-hundred-ninety-odd years had passed since that day. Turning my mind there for an instant dropped me right back on the deck of that sloop, dripping salt water and watching Billy's ship sail away while I held Maggie and Nigel. I didn't like it any better from the distance of time.

"You let him get away?"

"Yes." I made a disgruntled noise, "In that moment, I let him go." I glared over my shoulder at him, "What should I have done then? Drop them and swim after him?" Giving him my back again, I leaned my elbows on the cases and steepled my fingers while I spoke to the wall. "I had a fair idea who Nigel was from the note he left. I *had* gone back to the house after he'd been. I was commissioning a ship for myself, you see. I didn't miss him by much. Only just, it seems. If I'd only returned a bit sooner..," my voice gave out. Shaking it off a moment later, I made myself focus, "His note gave me enough to go on. He hung on long enough to tell me the rest."

Alan's friends murmured in sympathy. "So, he was the guy who helped her escape the first time. At least, you got some answers. Too bad the bad guy turned out to be who he is. Would have made your life a whole pile easier if he was just your regular garden-variety psycho. One of us should write this down and add it to the myth--"

I was horrified. "Don't even fucking think about it, arsewipe."

"Seriously, this is like some major history and--"

"Not a fucking word, mosquito," I was across the room before he blinked again.

"Whoa, man! Frankie say *relax*."

"Not so much as a syllable goes beyond this room," I drilled them all. "This is not some celebrity tabloid story here. This is my bloody life. I won't have it splashed about the goddamn world. Good lord, what the fuck is wrong with you?"

The seven members of the inner circle of the blood bank crew shook with satisfying alarm. Baby Bite put a tentative hand on the fingers that found their way around his throat, "Okay, Dad, let's not get ourselves excited here. Let's just put that hand down before you hurt someone. Namely me," trying without success to move the savage thing away.

"Say it," I got into his head.

Alan blinked hard and shook his head to get me out without success there, either. "Okay-okay! Shit, man. Anyone ever tell you you're a little too fucking intense for your own good? Jeez..." I drilled him some more and he screwed up his face against it, "All right, already, I give! No one's gonna write anything down, okay? Shit. Chillax, old man. Just mellow out. We didn't tell anyone who you are, did we? No one will find this out, either."

"Promise me," my voice was hard, but it was necessary. Life would be hard enough for them when I was gone. They didn't need anything more coming their way to blindside them without my protection.

Because I was quite certain tangling with Billy would make that situation reality sooner rather than later. I wanted assurance they would be as safe as I could make it for them in my own time. Planning would be pointless if their stupidity sent up a flag that tipped him off before I was ready.

"I promise."

"Like you mean it, little man. Swear me a vow that will attach itself to your honour. That you won't break."

"Don't trust me?" His thin attempt at humour went without laughter from his cohorts who were shitting their collective pants.

"Not even as far as I can throw you. Shall we see how far that might be, Alan?"

"No-no, I'm good, thanks. Okay, what was it you wanted? Swearing a vow? Not a problem. I swear, I'll never tell another living soul what you just told us."

"Nice try. How about the undead? Or any combination of any other form of life in this realm or any other? Say it like we mean it, class. All together now, little ones." When I was satisfied they were serious and I got a real vow out of them, only then did I take my hand off Baby Bite's throat and got out of his head.

He scraped his chair back in agitation and stomped around shaking his head to clear his brain from the extended invasion.

I hated to admit it, but I really was fond of the lot of them. And more concerned for their welfare than I was comfortable admitting outloud. Until they arrived, I never realised how much of an impression Myles had made on me. Myles had been so brief, though, and I already had them with me longer than I'd had him. Their time with me was doing something to me, filling a void. I'd fallen into the role of parent so easily, willingly even, despite all my grumbling about it. That lost opportunity with Maggie, the taking of our miraculous child along with her, was one wound that still wouldn't heal. Once I found out, I discovered a yearning inside me I was surprised to find had always been there. I never knew I could have a family and in all my time alone it never crossed my mind. Then I almost had one and Billy took that away from me, too. Now I had these little ones to worry over. I would never let Billy harm them. Never. He couldn't have them. Not while there was something I could do about it. I raked my fingers through my hair in distraction before I got all misty-eyed and blew my bad guy image.

"So," I shook it off myself and got them back on track, "you said you found some concrete information for me. This is a good thing, yes?"

Alan was rubbing his eyes with his palms and spoke from behind his hands, "Yeah. Very fucking specific, actually. Hey," he dropped his hands, "so when did you stick Billy on the island then?"

"Later," I grimaced. "This first."

"Yeah, but--"

"Not in the mood, Baby Bite. Leave it for later, all right?"

He gave me a long, hard look. "Okay, old man. Whatever you say." He was still looking at me funny. "You're the boss."

There was something going on with him lately, with all of them now that I thought about it. They were treating me like someone else and I didn't understand it. They were being respectful and concerned and it was just damned odd. "Fine, arsewipe. Can we get on with it? I'm not getting any younger, y'know." Well, it would never do to appear I liked it.

"Shit," that got a laugh out of him. "All right, Dad."

"I told you, I'm not your daddy, little man. Have a need for some de-craniating today?"

"*Eeek*, I'm scared."

"Get stuffed."

"Yes, sir."

"That's better." The little shit actually got me smiling. I couldn't decide whether I hated that about him or egged him on just to make him do it. Or maybe it was better not to analyse something like that.

Alan got down to business, "Okay, we can track him. Billy. Not too hard. We should be able to get a bead on him and already have a good idea. But you mentioned Mesopotamia, right?"

Distancing myself from them, I put myself on the other side of the room again. "I didn't think there would be anything for you to find in that direction. The reason I waved you off." They were all so nearly alive, sometimes it was quite distracting. Anything he had to tell me, I wanted to be sure I took in with a clear head.

"It was the exact right place to start, actually. We did a lot of research. Verification. Everything pointed the way. You're actually from Sumer, by the way. And that's not a guess. It places Billy, too."

"Sumer..?" I mulled it over. "No, that can't be right. Wait... Okay, I remember some before Babylon. Something... Could be Sumer, I suppose. Somewhere there about." I sorted through my own memories. "I don't recall a thing about any proto-vampires, though. That's a different sort of mythology. Then again, my memory's faulty. Perhaps, I've forgotten." I hadn't talked to them about anything important before. I mean, they hadn't been there that long, but they were comfortable to be around and it just came out of me.

"You know what it's like. The distance from real life. You have that same experience? The forgetting?" I inhaled deeply and looked up the wall at things they could never see, "I remember the area there, but was never certain how far back that was. Always wished I could. Mostly to recall which crypt-creeping, sanguineous corpse-waker did this to me, you know? To change it. Reverse it, perhaps," and lost my voice. I huffed a laugh, self-conscious, "Listen to me, eh?" They were all watching me. I could feel their eyes on my back and endeavoured to focus. "Sorry, I distracted you. You were saying?"

"Hey," behind me, Baby Bite's smile was genuine, "you don't need to apologise. We know what it's like. Things start getting hazy. It was so long ago for you. I can't even compute that." He became lost in thought and then shook himself out of it. "Well, the good news is, your memory *was* faulty. There was a lot of information, actually."

"You know," I said over my shoulder, "I could have never done that amount of investigation this fast." I thought back over uncounted years and the various things I used to occupy my time with. "I remember the medicine from that far back. Some of it. The way it was then, at least. Still have a few notes. Completely different point of view." I nodded again, "The flavour of the historical viewpoint behind it does lend some weight to being Sumer, I suppose." I waved them on, "Carry on then. Impress me."

He hesitated and then took a breath. "You were an important man then. Still are." He looked to his friends who all nodded in agreement, serious. "You were a priest-doctor. A big deal in your world," Alan leaned forward in earnest.

"Hold your horses," I held up a staying hand while his words settled into me. "*I* was in that information? *I'm* from Sumer...? Do you mean for me to understand that's *me*, specifically? You're speaking as though it's by name or something," I snorted in scepticism. "Well that would be an oracle-level feat since even I can't remember my own bloody name." They continued to look me head-on. I blinked, "Oh, right. Pull the other one. Clearly more of your Blood Runner shite, yeah? Not in the mood. Seriously." They were wasting my time, got my hopes up, and I didn't have time for fairy tales. "Erm, I was under the impression you were looking into curses and banishments? The way we were made, so I know how to unmake Billy. Specifics, remember? What the fuck does one have to do with the other?"

"I know how old you are give or take a couple decades for the length of your career. That specific enough?" One of the other 'Bites, Randy, found his voice and spoke up, looking hopeful.

My eyes narrowed without meaning to, "I know how old I am, little one."

Randy's eyes danced while he smiled, triumphant, "Doubt it. Not unless you've been studying antediluvian mythology for the last couple decades. Or suddenly got your memory back." He looked quite pleased with himself, "Facts parallel the mythology. We peg you alive about thirty-two-hundred BCE."

"The mythology? You peg me--" I snorted again and waved it away, "For fuck's sake... Stop. I've no time for any more of your Blood Runner nonsense. It's all bollocks. Okay, over here in the New World? Yes, I grew a bit careless and stayed in place too long and something could be going around. I'll cop to that. And yes, I'm painfully aware it's my own bloody fault. Ta for the reminder. But back then? Back when I had a life? Trust me littlies, no one wrote any badly rhyming psalms of my exploits for the simple reason there were none. Know how I know? I was there. I had a life, something happened, and then I was *this*. And so was Billy. Chase myths on your own time and give me something I can use to kill the fucker." I ticked the possibilities off on my fingers one by one, "Location, counterspell, banishing chant, preferred weapon..? Something. You've been doing research for weeks and you're telling me you couldn't come up with a simple counterspell?" I paced the other side of the room in frustration. "Brilliant. I thought you were supposed to be experts."

"We are," Baby Bite was still serious, "and you just have some of the facts wrong, old man. A couple. Listen, you were in Sumer, *alive* in Sumer. That part's important to know, so don't rip my head off yet, okay?"

I humphed grudging assent and clamped my jaws together while he went on.

"Sumerian is a dead language. And an anomaly. Meaning, not related to any others, dig? No one knows how to speak it. The ones who claim to? Some of those supposed devil-worshipping cults and your general, garden variety whack jobs on the Internet who think it's fun to cast curses? Nope, that's Akkadian. They should study their historical linguistics better.

"When the Akkads conquered the region, they kept the cuneiform writing from the Sumerian civilisation there. They didn't have their own writing system yet, so used it for commerce and things, okay? But the official spoken language under the Akkadian kings was, d'uh, Akkadian. For a thousand years. Spoken Sumerian died out. Funny related thing, though. They did this weird thing and adopted their god cults. And claimed all the technology that had evolved, so it was preserved. Myths and the stories, too. It's this freaky thing that never happened anywhere else. But anyway, as far as Sumerian writing goes? Representational only. Can't be pronounced since no one remembers how. Get me? You can read it and know what it means so you can understand the history, but there's no way to know how to say those words."

Informative, but since he wasn't telling me what I wanted to hear it only pissed me off more. "Good lord, make it stop," I massaged the bridge of my nose. "Unless Billy's address is preserved in there, seriously, what does this have to do with me?"

"What it means," another young blood, Suki, got out from behind her laptop to brave telling me to my face, "is when we were looking for what could do this to a person, to know how to reverse it to stop Billy? We found you in the history. In that older, preserved writing."

I looked her in the eye and could tell it was scaring her, but she was very compelled, "You found me? *Me?*" I wouldn't believe it from Alan even with his lack of pretence, but Suki was different. She wouldn't have said anything if she didn't believe it. I had to look away from her as I took it in.

I walked away and crossed my arms in contemplation. I couldn't recall anything more than ever being this thing that I was, not one fucking thing before, no matter how hard I tried. I spoke to the wall again, "Why would anyone write about me? Thirty-two-hundred BCE... Do you know how fucking long ago that was? You can't bloody well know it was about me. There's no way to verify that. There's simply no way."

Suki spoke to my back, "We know how you were made. Billy, too." When she paused, I knew I wasn't going to like it. "There's no counterspell. And even if there was one, we couldn't tell you how to speak it properly like Alan explained. But no, no counterspell."

Behind her, Natasha concurred her in her broken English, "*Da*, spell *net*. No spell."

An arrow through the back would have been less painful. I couldn't look at her, "Are you telling me you simply couldn't find it? Or it's been lost? Or are you telling me that in your concerted, *expert* opinions there really is no counter for this sodding nightmare? How can there be no counterspell? Everything is checks and balances. *Everything* old has an undoing, even *I* fucking know that."

Rage built up in me for the simple reason that revenge aside, underneath, I knew if there was a counterspell for Billy then there was one for me. I couldn't stop it, "You're fucking lying. This is more of your Blood Runner *shite*. Well, I'm not listening to it. Fat lot of good moving all this poxy crap in here did for me. You were meant to help me, but I know what's really going on here. You've got some cocked-up idea about trying to preserve me like some bloody national treasure or some other ridiculous nonsense. Well, fuck that!" I was so angry, the case I slammed my palm down on smashed and sent the 'Bites scurrying for cover. "What a pile of wank. I want all of you out of here. *Clear out.* And don't fucking come back!"

Suki's hand on my forearm stopped me dead. I was so wound-up I didn't even realise she was standing there. I blinked. She was still there. "What?" I snarled, but it was only because I was wounded. "Speak!"

I had dared to trust them when I trusted no one.

She didn't run and her voice was gentle, "There's no counterspell, because it's not a spell. Not a curse, definitely not a punishment. Not an anything like that. Not for you." She looked to her counterparts behind her for support. "You've been looking at it the wrong way."

They all came out, which I have to say, sort of threw me. They acted oddly subdued, not like their regular selves at all. I didn't like the look of this.

Baby Bite got back in charge, "Su's right. Short answer? Not a spell. There's a legend. And no," he held up his hand, "it has nothing to do with Blood Runner. That's a modern myth. Started by *you*, let's remember. This myth? It's old. Very, very old." He looked me hard in the eyes, so I would know he was serious. "You might want to sit down for this."

I looked from one to the other in confusion. No, I didn't like the look of this at all. "Why?"

Suki took my arm and led me to a seat, "Please. It'll be okay." She patted my hand as though I was her enfeebled grandfather. I would never admit I was glad for the reassurance just then.

"All right, already," I snapped without much vehemence. "Just spit it out. The suspense is fucking killing me."

Hamish and Dom dragged a table over to where Suki put me while Natasha and Michelangelo brought the chairs so we could all sit together. It was to be an official powwow of the 'Hunters and it only made me more nervous.

Baby Bite passed me some paper he printed off the computer, so I could see it firsthand. They were shots of clay tablets preserved through surviving a fire--instead of ruining them, all it did was bake them harder to withstand time. They didn't surprise me much, because that long ago they were commonplace. I'd used them myself.

I didn't want to look at them.

Now that I had some hard evidence in my hands, I was afraid I *would* remember. At least, I hadn't started out a killer. They said I'd been a priest-doctor, so I was right about the herbs in that I was a healer sometime before. Strange to go from one extreme to so far the other way. Preserving life, then taking it. I was afraid to find out how I got from one thing to the other, but there was no going back now. Maggie was waiting and I needed to know.

Alan skimmed another copy of the same papers while everyone settled and then threw them to the side. "So you hired a real pirate sloop? Bitchin'."

The words didn't register right off. "What the hell are you on about now?" He was back on the Billy story again. "No, it wasn't *bitchin'*, Baby Bite, it was practical," Alan's friends snickered around the table. They got an almighty kick out my calling him Baby Bite. I ignored it. "It was the fastest ship in the fucking harbour. Paid them well enough for their trouble. Easiest gold they made in years. They didn't even have to waste any cannon balls."

"Yeah, overtaking ships costs money and eats ammo. Learned that first-hand keeping the records for Billy."

"Wait." I blinked. "You were his Quartermaster?" I put my own papers down and clutched at the distraction, "I thought you said you set up computers for him."

Alan laughed, "No-no-no, old man. I told you, computer *databases*, accounting *programs*, expense charts. That kind of thing. Used them to keep track of everything for him. But I'm really just a hacker. That pirate shit is way cool, but it's not what I am."

"Alan, you eejit," I laughed without humour, "the master's accountant is the Quartermaster's job. Well, now I understand how you were so close to all his secrets there. That makes more sense."

"Quartermaster?" He looked perplexed, "Legit?"

"Yes, Quartermaster."

And then shrugged it off, "Whatev." He cocked his head to one side, considering, "So you know about boats, too, eh?"

I cringed, "Ships, you ignorant twit. They're ships. Good lord, how did you spend so long with that bastard and at least not pick up that part?"

The laughter was indulgent and confused me, "Okay-okay, ships. Don't hurt yourself, old man." He was nodding to himself and then looked at me sideways, "So, you did that a lot before then, I guess. Been around ships and sailing?"

"Well, of course." I had to think about that. "I mean, yes and no. I was no bloody pirate if that's what you're driving for. And what the hell does it matter? It was the fastest mode of transportation over long distances for the times. Will you ever mature out of this never-get-to-the-sodding-point thing? Bloody pain in my arse."

"Okay-okay," his head continued to bob while he considered, "then try this on for size. When Billy got in the middle of your life, you were up in the hills in the north of England. Okay Britain. As an herbalist. For a long time, right? How long were you there?"

"Who fucking cares?" I scrubbed a tired hand over my face. All his questions didn't seem to have any rhyme or reason, no connection. The whole thing was giving me a headache. It had been a while since I rested. Or fed for that matter. Maybe I was just tired. "What can that possibly have to do with anything?" My lip curled, the snarl right behind it, but I kept a lid on it.

"Indulge me. Answer the question. How long?" Suki nodded encouragement at my elbow, so for her I behaved. She was the quiet one of the bunch, polite and never spoke out of turn. I don't know. On the surface she seemed the complete opposite, but maybe she reminded me of Maggie some. A little. Surrounded by quiet dignity and authority even when she wasn't saying anything at all. She made me mind for no real reason beyond sitting there. I think they made her hang around to keep me in line, because I couldn't be impolite around her. Damn sneaky kids.

"I've no idea." I curbed my growling. "Hundred years maybe. Okay, less. A little less. Well," I huffed annoyance and crossed my arms over my chest, "about eighty. Eighty-three, I think, if you want to be technical about it. Why?"

"And before that?"

"Spain."

"Spanish Armada?"

"Certainly not," I snorted hauteur.

"How long?"

I gritted my teeth and cast my mind back, "About five hundred. Give or take a few. No one bothered me there for a long while. Though in the middle they lynched me and soaked my grave in holy water. Other than that, it was quite nice as I recall." I thought about it some more, "Right good weather there. Good place to grow my herbs." Didn't take me long to go there again in memory now that he was making me, "Fifteen-twenty... things you forget..."

"Like what?" Dom's eyes shone with curiosity.

"What went on then," I shrugged, noncommittal. "It was a whole new world and getting larger by the year, yeah? About that November Magellan's ships reached South America. We heard about it after the fact, of course, but big news then was all."

There was murmuring around the table. Baby Bite's eyes narrowed and caught my attention, "And before Spain, old man?"

"England again. I loved it there. The reason I went back. It had become home. Felt like it for a while, I suppose. Returned to the island several times over the years. Reclaimed the same land each time." I made a sour face, "Likely a car park or a shopping centre over it now, I'm sure."

"And when did you get there?" He was onto something and I wanted to know what. I caught him up with a little beguile and he shook his head, smiling, "No-no, that's cheating. Just answer the question."

I settled for a tethering stare that danced electric to the others watching us. "Well, it was about eleven-seventy, eleven-eighty when I left it for Spain. Don't even recall why I left, now that I think about it," curiosity caught me despite myself. I really couldn't remember a reason for leaving. "Packed up one day and buggered off to a place I'd never been. I'd been there for a bit, too. Settled in nicely. Couple hundred years."

"And before that, where were you? And when?"

"France. Well, Francia then. About four hundred and… thirty-odd years maybe? Left about, let me see... On the new calendar... Nine-seventy. Close to that. I'm sure the dates are in my journal if you want to be precise." The answers were becoming staccato to his questions. Locked together, he was pulling me backwards through the hazy place that kept the record of my travels while he jotted notes. In downward stair steps, we went further into the darker parts where I remembered less even though there was so much more. "There was a space in the middle that time. Took a battle axe to the back for trying to patch men up on a battlefield. Buried me with them."

He nodded encouragement, "Keep going. When did you get there? Why did you go there?"

"Five-forty-three. That one sticks in mind, because I went straight from Constantinople." My eyes swept their blank, young faces. "*Istanbul?* I needed a break. There'd been a plague."

"Uh… Justinian Plague? First outbreak of bubonic plague in Europe, right?"

"That's the one."

"Killed something like a quarter of the population of the eastern Mediterranean."

My lips twitched, "Closer to a third, actually. Quite nasty. Ran me ragged. Healers were few and far between there. Didn't know it at the time, but was glad for the practice about eight hundred years later."

Seven pairs of eyes were glued to me in rapt attention. Baby Bite was ravenous, "How long were you there? In Istanbul."

"Oh, not long." I shrugged, "A year, perhaps? Right during the fucking plague, actually. There was nothing else for me there. When it burned out where I was staying and I was no longer needed, I left."

"Funny how you just happened to go there then, wouldn't you say?"

That gave me pause, but I wasn't putting too much stock in it. "I suppose. But when you've been in the world as long as I have? You stop trying to analyse why you do anything anymore. Seriously, I don't look too hard."

"Fair." Alan turned over the papers he discarded and scribbled on the back. "All right. So you got there in five-forty-two. Where did you come from?"

"Egypt."

"Interesting."

"You keep saying that."

Baby Bite raised an eyebrow, "You don't think it's interesting you went all the way from Egypt to Istanbul for no particular reason and only stayed there to help a bunch of sick people before you left again for a different country altogether? You're kidding me right?" He continued scribbling. "Keep going."

Suki still by my elbow, I thought better of the cutting comment on the tip of my tongue. "Right, well, the Roman Empire was on its last legs. The Library at Alexandria burned sometime in there, too. Bloody waste that was. And these Arab traders..," I laughed in disdain. "When they passed through Thebes, they got hold of some opium. Traded it all the way to China. Good medicine, but, well... You know the later reputation."

"Wait," Dom looked confused. "I thought opium originated in

China?"

"No, little man. They grew poppies by the field full in Thebes."

"Shit, man..."

"*Udivitel'nyy*! It is wonderful..!"

"Shut up, guys. Shhh," Alan shot Dom a warning look. "Don't break his concentration." Alan waved a dismissive hand at Dom and then turned his whole attention back to me. "Look, forget about these morons over here. Go back further. Place by place. Just rhyme them off for as far back as you can go."

Huffing in annoyance, "Is this really necessary?" I raised my hands in futility. He made a face, so I settled into my chair and gave him back my attention. "There was Greece for a bit, but can't think of the year right off--"

"You were there for history in the making, man."

"Did you meet some of the greats? The philosophers? The kings?"

"--and Egypt before that with Greece again prior to. Went back and forth there, you see. Had motivation. Quite a lot of medical things going on at the time that interested me, so I lingered."

"Too bad you didn't have an autograph book."

"Can you imagine bringing that into Sotheby's or Christie's?"

"Would you guys shut the fuck up already?" Alan nailed them with a withering look.

"Sorry."

"Yeah, sorry, man."

"Okay, go on. Forget them. Keep going."

I looked from one to the other--they were hanging on my every word. I wasn't much impressed by the entire thing, but kept going if only to get my own answers. I cleared my throat, "I stuck mostly around the Mediterranean. At least, during that time. Well, I did nip over to India a couple of times. China. Japan, mysterious land of savages they called it then. So wrong... Britain, again, of course, prior to that. And Eire, *Ireland,* as well. What do you wanna hear, a play-by-play? Trust me, it would take too long." I started counting on my fingers, "Gaul, Turkey, out to the Steppes, Scandinavia, Israel, Judah, down into Kush, Persia, all around the Crescent, I suppose. Erm, Crete. When the hell was that now..? When did Plato open the Academy at Athens? Three-eighty-something BCE? I know it was before then, because when I left he wasn't born yet. Rome a time or three…"

It felt a pointless exercise. They were telling me nothing important while I did all the talking. Simply running through the short list I could remember off the top of my head took time. Events that later became notations of historical significance were tangled up with my travels. But only because they were part of the backdrop and none of it impacted my life. Not really.

Out of interest, I read Ptolemy's astronomical theories when he first published them. Saw the death of Marcus Aurelius and the birth of Christianity. Was there during Titus's destruction of Jerusalem and the burning of Herod's Temple. Saw the rise and fall of more kings and sovereigns than I cared to recall. Lived through cycles of plague and famine. I even visited the famous lighthouse at Alexandria before the fire. Saw the Colossus of Rhodes with my own eyes before the earthquake took it down. And the glory of the Sphinx when it was newer and yet already old.

I remembered when Michelangelo dreamed of flying and later witnessed the realisation of his dreams when humanity reached the moon. Watched from a distance while Caligula's opposition championed rumours of him as an insane tyrant. And Pompeii disappeared from the world. And America dropped hell in a canister on Hiroshima. Julius Caesar, Archimedes, Anne Boleyn, Confucius, Brian Boru, Nebuchadnezzar, Madame Curie, and Genghis Khan were people who passed through the world during unburied hours. Sometimes our steps happened in the same place at the same time as they did with Queen Victoria, Pierre Trudeau,

John F. Kennedy, Aerosmith, Professor Stephen Hawking and several incarnations of the Dali Lama and I told the 'Bites so, too.

"You know Aerosmith?"

I groaned. "That was hardly the point."

"They're way old school, anyway."

"Me, too, in case you hadn't noticed. And no, *of* them. Radio, remember?"

"Yeah," Hamish grimaced, "remind me to show you how to get more stations than CBC affiliates. Satellite radio. *Good* stations."

"Didn't I tell you guys to shut up already? *C'mon!*"

"Sorry, Alan."

"This is serious, you clowns. *Fuck.*" He gave them a blistering look and I watched his lip curl in a very good parody of my own snarl. I nearly laughed right outloud, but caught myself.

"Well, this has been fun kiddies, but I'm finished. This is such a--" Suki at my side reminded me to mind my manners. I rephrased. "You told me you had information for me. Specific information. Instead, I've been giving you my life story here. Did that serve a purpose or was that for your amusement?"

With a deliberate movement, Baby Bite laid his hands down on the papers he scribbled on. "Like we already told you, we found you in the old records. Look for yourself," he gestured to the papers I abandoned. "It's all there. How you were made. How Billy was made. When in history you come from. How you got in that place--"

"Cut the mystery, Baby Bite," I snapped.

Clamping his mouth shut, he watched me while his eyes narrowed in consideration. There was a long pause before he spoke again. "What are you afraid of, old man?" It was a hard question, but he wasn't accusing.

It wasn't something I wanted to admit, "Fuck right off."

"I see."

"You see jack shit, little man."

"Have it your way." He wasn't even pursuing it and that was worse.

Eyes on me in sympathy from all around the table were harder than Alan being a pain in my arse. I hated it. They didn't even squirm when I tried to stare them down. They all gave me a curt formal inclination of their heads and waited with eyes downcast for their spokesman to illuminate me. Oh, I really didn't like the look of this.

Alan gestured to the copied papers again. "Read them. All of them, okay? Then ask your questions," his voice sympathetic.

I didn't want to look at them. A quick glance and I tossed them aside again. "Well," I was being obtuse and knew it, "I don't know how you expect me to read that nonsense. It's pictographs for heaven's sake," I grumbled in annoyance at what didn't have anything to do with what bothered me.

"It's cuneiform, actually--"

"I know what motherfucking cuneiform is, little man."

"*And* you didn't even look."

After a strained moment, I picked up the papers and looked again, longer this time. And then slammed them back down making the 'Bites jump in their chairs. "I can't. A few symbols seem familiar. Nothing else. Not enough to understand. I can't fucking read it. Satisfied? If your goal was to make me look foolish, well you've accomplished it. Congratulations. I haven't a bloody clue what this says." I couldn't look him in the eye.

Baby Bite looked perplexed, "I don't get you. How many languages do you speak?"

"A handful," I huffed annoyance. "Fourteen," I threw out a random number.

"Seriously?" he gave me a pointed look. "Get real, dude."

When I turned my attention back in his direction with a scowl he didn't flinch. Somehow this was important no matter I didn't understand why. "Fine," the atmosphere over the table growing more charged by the moment, I gave in, "thirty-two or six. Maybe a dozen more I couldn't do more than order take-away in. Though could probably do you a decent translation on a newspaper article." I cleared my throat, "Just not this one."

He wouldn't let it go, "How's that possible? Cuneiform script was adopted as an international language by seventeen hundred BCE and I know you were here before that. You're probably just rusty. Give it a--"

"I'm telling you, I can't read this. I've not seen this before in my life. I don't know what the fuck language this is. It's nothing I know, all right?" The group of them stared at me, mystified. "*What*? Why do you all keep--"

"*Alan*." Suki broke in and came to my rescue. She patted my hand again, but I didn't mind so much. "He can't read it. Leave it alone." Silence descended over the meeting of the Blood Runner Hunters while I waited in trepidation. Michelangelo and Dom stared off into space and weren't about to get into it. In annoyance, Suki threw her hands up at the lot of them and then perched herself up on the table facing me. She gave Natasha a glance and got a nod in return. It appeared they were of like mind and she let Suki speak for both of them.

She took the papers from under my hands and threw them at Alan behind her, smiling at me in sympathy. "He's an idiot, but don't hold it against him. He was trying to prove a point. Make sure it was true. It's sometimes difficult to match up fact to the mythology attached to it, as you can imagine. Those really are the myths of Sumer, but a later version written in Akkadian cuneiform. Which was essentially gone by the time you were walking around again and have memory. That's why, if you are who you are, there's a high degree of probability you wouldn't understand them. This more or less confirms it. All be it, in a rather rude and uncalled for way," Suki glowered at him and that made me feel better.

His bravado left him and I watched over her shoulder as he slunk down in his chair to pout. And that made me feel even better. I looked to Suki with a million questions. "I don't understand. Can't you just tell me what the fu-- What's with all the mystery? I don't understand the melodrama here."

"Okay," Suki took a breath. "Until recently, for the most part, you've been shadowing Billy's movements around the world."

"Sor--" what she said made no sense. "*What*?"

"Not exactly, not step-by-step, but it's pretty close. From what you mentioned here, really close. He's obsessed with keeping lists of things he has and things he does, so it's all documented in his journals and logs. Alan's seen his records. Except," she held up a finger, "any time there was a medical need somewhere. You seemed to step out of the pattern to help and then caught up with him again later."

Dumbfounded, I ran my hands up under my hair in distraction to lace my fingers behind my head while I considered this.

"The thing with the ships might be coincidental, might be something. Sumerians are credited with creating the sail and moving trade goods by boat before anyone else so that's the world you came from. You wouldn't have been afraid to move around by ship, not feel yourself confined to one area like people from other cultures in antiquity, you know? Don't know if that's a contributing factor or just, like you said, the conveyance of the day. He sailed and so did you. But you're somehow connected. We don't know why."

"Connected..?" My voice was small and I didn't have a rebuttal. I didn't want to be connected to him. I wanted him dead. That we were both so old had meant nothing to me except we might have been made in the same way. But it appeared there was more going on. Much more.

I didn't know him. I'd never seen him until I caught sight of him from the deck of the sloop and then learned his face when I went back after him. But beyond that, we'd never met. And yet, I followed him around the world? I told Baby Bite I stopped trying to analyse why I was ever compelled into doing anything, but in view of this revelation, perhaps I should have.

"Bloody hell." I stared off into space, running backwards through time in my head, place-by-place, life-by-life. Flashing through every face I could remember. From my perspective, there was no proof, of course, but when I looked into Suki's eyes, I knew it was true. While I continued to hold her gaze for the company, I went back farther still. As far as I could go to where memory ran up against that brick wall of darkness I couldn't see beyond. I always assumed that was the point of my death.

But now I wondered.

It was darkness and blank, but when I applied thought to it could feel more on the other side. I rarely went there in memory, hadn't had much inclination to over the years, so never explored it. That was then, this was now, so what would have been the point? But I was trying like hell *now*.

Suki patted my hand again and smiled. It was becoming a habit. "It's okay. You can't remember him, can you? That's what you're doing. Thinking back to see if you know him and why you'd be following him around, right?"

I let out a nervous chuckle, "Was it that obvious?" There was an abrupt end to my laughter with a hitch in my chest I tried to hide.

"Don't worry, you don't know him, old man. Trust me, you weren't friends or anything."

"Shut up, Alan." Suki shot him a dark look, "You had your chance." She turned back to me and addressed me in a gentler voice, "You didn't know him. He didn't know you. It wasn't even about him until later. Over a thousand years later. Okay?" She raised her eyebrows, hopeful.

"All right," I liked it better when Suki did the talking. At least, she didn't make a career out of trying to piss me off. Maybe it was only because she actually told me things and wasn't playing twenty questions. Either way, I appreciated it.

"I want you to read something now. In *English*," she skewered Baby Bite with another dark look. "Hang on." She went to her laptop and printed off a few pages that she brought back to me. "I translated these myself. Here are the oldest ones in the original Sumerian cuneiform. This one's a myth. Couple more here, but this is the important one. These are some hard history facts. Lemme know when you're done."

Without asking me what I wanted, she made the mosquitoes leave the table and move to the other side of the room where they stood in conference. The distance was appreciated. It took me some time to read through the pages. Not because there were a lot of them, but because I took my time. It took several readings to make it sink in.

I didn't remember any of it. But knew it was the thing behind the wall. Felt it there.

"'A failing of the flesh without spirit'," desolate, I spoke to no one in particular and my voice sounded very loud in the silence. It didn't last, though, because right about then it gave out under the full weight of truth. "Forgotten..?" All I could do was whisper. It was too big and too awful. "Forgotten by time... I'm a forgotten accident of creation? An *accident*?"

It was pointless. I couldn't begin to articulate anything just then. I stood up without knowing I had and the papers slid to the floor unheeded. If it was true, if any of it were true, then I was alone. Truly alone in the entire world. It's what I'd always been compelled toward, of course, and explained quite a bit. But to be that alone? To have no brothers, no kin, no familiars beyond these little ones who weren't even created by the same forces? It was even more desolate than the life I lived. To know, to have the proof of it was worse. I wished I never encouraged them to look into it. I only wanted revenge for Maggie. Instead, I got my epitaph.

"There's more."

Baby Bite's voice cut off my introspection. Forlorn, all I could do was wait for whatever else they were going to drop on me. I couldn't even argue. At least, it explained why they'd been acting so oddly toward me. Alan looked contrite, as though he wanted to say something apologetic, but couldn't get it out. I was monumentally upset with him, because he was the one I trusted the most. He worked the hardest to bring all this shite to me and it was what it was instead of what I wanted it to be. He only did as I asked, of course. I had no right to be angry with him. But I had anger and didn't know where to put it.

The two girls had no qualms about expressing themselves to me. Unbidden, they came right over and tucked themselves one under each arm.

"You're not alone here," Suki pulled my hand around her shoulder.

Natasha's English was awful, but she was compelled, "See, *da*? *Uspokysya, vsyo harasho*. Easy, everything is okay." She put a hand to my face to make her point, "Self no. *Ti ne odna*, not alone. Family, *da*?"

The boys came over, too, then. Baby Bite hung back, scuffing his feet with his hands stuffed into his pockets and looking all the more the little boy he was. I knew it wasn't his fault and he was waiting for forgiveness he didn't even need. Being a big, giant arse was something I was admittedly good at, but I didn't need to play it for him. Not any of them. I knew they were mine, had known since the first day Alan came. So I suppose that truly did make them my family and kept me from being alone when I would have been. It was still huge, but made it bearable. I shrugged myself out of the group hug I'd got caught in and grabbed him up before he could move.

"Holy shit--"

"You may be right there, little man."

He was laughing before he got the rest of it out, "--you move fast for an old man."

"And don't you forget it."

"You never give me a chance." He held me hard about the neck and I didn't mind.

It was so easy with them compared with the living. They were as cold as I was. Their hearts stopped and started like mine. They craved what I craved. They *were* my family and I was suddenly very glad for them. With a jerk, I held him out at arm's length. "Forgive me, Alan." He squirmed, but I wouldn't let him go, "I was trying to shoot the messenger. It is what it is and I know you didn't do anything except find it. All right?"

He nodded, "Yeah, we're cool. But..." He looked around in uncertainty.

"But this isn't the whole story."

*****

Doing laps by myself in the pool later, I worked to burn the grief out of me. It could have all been bollocks or speculation, but it wasn't. Though a bit flowery, the myth was no myth. And every word of the verification they did struck me in a place I didn't have a name for. There were a lot of temple records. A *lot*. They tallied livestock, goods and wages, land sales, account records and names of staff in service to the gods. Mundane records in Sumerian cuneiform, those clay tablets were baked hard by the desert heat and preserved for all time.

Those I *could* read without remembering having ever studied it. And I was in them.

My temple in Nippur was the household of the goddess Ninlil. I loved her, so the story said. But I didn't need a story to tell me that. I knew. The memory of it was so large, it vibrated behind the blank wall in my memory. Something that heart-eclipsing could never be completely forgotten and struck a chord within me.

A very loud chord.

Time to the gods was moot. I was forgotten in the confusion of the temple destruction, of course. I was dead, so why would they spare me an extra thought when there was vengeance to be doled out to the desecrator? And rightly so. I couldn't blame them for that, either.

Billy was Naram-Sin, of course, and I knew it was true. There was no mistaking the same thieving pirate bastard who sailed his ships to the temple of the Most High to plunder its treasures while he set himself up in godhood. Well, he got his wish. He was immortal, though I doubted this was the life he'd had in mind. Looked good on him, too, disrespectful sod that he was.

That story was written in Akkadian, so there must have been witnesses from that newer culture to my rebirth. Billy's own men, perhaps, as they emptied the temple and killed the priests. No curse had been sworn on them for following his orders and that was only right. So they survived to tell the tale. They might have passed it on in oral tradition until the Akkadians developed their own writing to scratch it down sometime later.

Funny, I couldn't remember one thing about it. It was a void to me that far back. I have a few extremely old memories of waking in darkness with time having passed. Any of them might have been that day, though I'm quite certain that first was unique. Underground and buried below the connected storage rooms of other treasures worth plundering, it wouldn't have been a simple grave that held me. Buried by order of the great god? Likely a crypt room. If woken in unknowing as the story said, chances are I stayed inside in confusion and blankness.

The conscious memories I accrued in the modern world were gained through the time I'd been awake. I had no maker, no direction, no guidance, no instruction. All through the years, I evolved on my own while growing more aware. Much different now than I was in the past, I knew that even within myself. Woken like a slate wiped clean... Unconscious memories were in there, but beyond my ability to grasp except when they came out in response to circumstance. Like my ability to read Sumerian. Without much awareness at the beginning, I might have stayed there for centuries until something prompted me out. An earthquake that cracked the foundation and showed me a night sky. Who knows? Once loose, I was compelled to study. Manically so, to be honest. Travelling from place to place stuffing my head with new things to fill up the blank space.

Before that happened, though? For all I know, I might have fallen into that Land of Nod slumber through not knowing what I needed to live. I knew how long I could go without feeding. After three or four months, I'd have drifted off to the warm place and waited to be woken as my new self with nothing more than the instinct to eat upon waking to guide me. Could have been another thousand years gone by, though I doubted that long, because I remembered things from the still very old days.

Baby Bite got me to narrow down where my conscious memories began. About two thousand BCE, same as I always knew and what I had based my age on. Outside of myth, there were historical records with the dates of Naram-Sin's reign, which pinned it down further, almost to the year of my rebirth. Give or take a hundred or few years one way or the other of wandering in darkness, I'd been right, or close to it. If you discounted the millennium that passed in my initial burial.

I got to the end of the pool and dived under in a tumble turn to push off the wall and get going back the way I came, *Pretty good trick for an old man of five thousand.* I swam harder, faster, but couldn't go far enough now that I knew the truth. I worked to leave it behind. There was no way to feel better about what I did and I was in pain. No amount of mourning would be enough and I didn't know what to do about it.

Discovering Billy was Naram-Sin was nothing compared with realising who the goddess was. There was no proof of this, but I knew, because it rang true inside me. I always thought there was something otherworldly about her. Even wandering around in flesh without soul, I still felt the unconscious pull from the first day I saw her. While my spirit held her place in the Netherworld, she continued free to wander the world as she had, but I lost the ability to recognise her.

If I wasn't carrying on in half-awareness, I would have known and not cremated her. She could have come back to me in due course, in a god's time, which might have been anytime--days, centuries, lifetimes. I created my own hell by burning her body, her vehicle, leaving her nothing but spirit. No flesh and blood for her to entice me into closeness as she had before, it left her no possibility of making another attempt to bring me back into knowing.

She had tried so hard and I knew it. Thinking back on how she treated me, how she was never afraid. On random things she said that made no sense at the time. She knew who I was. Perhaps, she hadn't been quite certain at first since I wasn't exactly in the same state as she left me, but she discovered her own truths. No wonder she was so content to stay. Every day with me was spent putting me in touch with who I was, challenging me, helping me rediscover my humanity.

Billy was nothing more than an irritant and I couldn't muster up enough emotion to care about him anymore. The precious little I had I was using for myself. By my count, I was more guilty and I was the one who deserved death. I was once an honoured person, it seemed, but the gods had forgotten me now and just as well. In my ignorance, I destroyed the earthly vessel of a great goddess. And I was fairly certain there was no way to make reparations for something of that magnitude.

Likely, it had taken her that long to realise what happened and then find me. Just the blink of a goddess's eye. And Billy had got in the way, stupid bastard that he was. Of course, he wanted her. It was in his nature to be attracted to the divine both in the delusion of his own grandeur and for seeking a divinity who would trade for him. Both of which he could never have. It had been so brief while it lasted. When she died, I thought I was inconsolable. Now, for knowing the whole truth, I was gutted.

She was right there in the garden, sat in the sun where she belonged without the means to know it now. And it was my fault. I'd saved her before, more than once, and she lived. But there was no saving her this time.

Throwing myself out of the water in irritation, I stayed where I landed in a puddle on the deck. I wanted to go to her and didn't know how. I could always go outside and talk to her there, of course, right outside in the sun.

The 'Bites collective were in tentative agreement I might have never needed to stay out of the sun at all, but it was so far only a theory. I wasn't a vampire, after all, not in the sense they were. Soaked in divinity and by a complete accident of creation, there were no provisos on me that we knew. That was the sort of thing the gods would set down as imposed conditions as they had for Billy. No god had done so for me. They hadn't bothered with me at all.

The blood bank crew needed to sleep in the daytime and I never needed that with regularity. I could pick and choose to rest and always had. A reanimate body that needed the Water of Life I craved to stay vertical I might be, but a vampire I was not. I hadn't been made by another vampire. I only assumed I was when I finally met someone who seemed like me and told me the word. Of course, I grasped at it, so I wasn't alone. A vampire, not a vampire… It all amounted to the same sodding thing anyway, no matter the name except for Billy, perhaps. Probably closer to what people believed was a true incubus in that he preferred women, but it's all in the perspective, I suppose.

In the end, what did it matter?

The gods had made him Death and so that's what he was. The gods had made me nothing and so I was. Without purpose or even parameters to live by except those I placed on myself. I woke in darkness, so it's what I knew, but I didn't even know if I had to stay in it. If, in the end, it killed me to try, what did that matter, either? It's what I deserved.

In resolve, I got to my feet and looked for the kids. The sun hadn't been up long and I found them turning off their computers for the day before they went off to sleep.

Alan had a smart comment on the tip of his tongue while I stood there in my trunks, but caught the look on my face and changed gears. "What is it? What's wrong?"

"Your mobile on?"

"Always."

I nodded. "Good. Don't go off to bed just yet. I might need to ring you."

He cocked his head to one side. "You feeling okay?"

Suki glided over and laid a concerned hand on my bare arm, "Are you all right? Do you need anything?"

"I'm all right." I looked from one to the other, all seven of them in turn in case it was the last time. "Thought I'd nip out for a bit of air."

"Oh, is that all," Baby Bite dismissed it while he went on putting his computer things away until the significance hit him. "Oh, shit, you mean..?"

"Yeah," I gestured with my head topside over us, "*outside.*"

Everyone stopped what they were doing.

"Sonofabitch."

"Holy shit, man."

"What are you doing? *Net.*"

"Relax little ones. Not going far. It's only the garden."

"Yeah, the garden in the *sun.*"

"So, leave your mobile on like I asked."

He gave me a hard look, "You sure you wanna do this, old man?"

I appreciated the concern. After a moment's thought I nodded, "Yeah, only way I'm going to find out." The girls were very worried, but I wouldn't change my mind. "It's something I have to do. I have to know."

"*Vsego sekundu,*" Natasha came over and kissed me on both cheeks. "For luck, *da? Do skoroy vstrechi,* we see you soon."

"You be careful. Promise?" Suki had me by the hand and scolded me gently, "Don't run right out, okay? You'll still have a chance if... Well... You know? Don't be hasty."

It was so odd to have people in my orbit sincerely concerned about my welfare. So different from any other year I'd been in the world except for the ones with Maggie in them. It made me feel guilty, because I knew what I wanted to happen. I smiled at their worry, "I know. I'll telephone one way or the other. Well, one way, I suppose. If you don't hear from me all day? You should probably come looking after sundown with a whisk and a dustpan, eh?" It was supposed to be a joke, but somehow didn't come out as funny as it sounded in my head. They were horrified. "Sorry," I shrugged, still inept at witty conversation after all this time, "poor word choice. But still, don't panic. You all inherit everything, so you'll be set," I winked and left faster than anyone could say anything more.

I grabbed my mobile on the way through the labyrinth and back to the house. The cellar was dark and I wound through it without looking, eager for my punishment. I wanted to die and needed to know what could do it. My options had always been thin as it was. Sure, I wanted to see Maggie in the sunshine where she belonged. And I definitely wanted to find out if I hadn't had to spend several millennia hiding in the dark the way I had, but really? I wasn't even afraid as I went to it.

I didn't care anymore.

On the way up the stairs, I almost had second thoughts, but pushed them aside. At the top, I paused.

There were windows in my house now. Since Maggie, I put them in for myself despite the danger. I knew the sun was already up. The gifts I possessed--the sight, the sense of the world, the feeling of life outside myself--might have been nothing more than a condition of waking through the blood of meditative priests. Or simply that my lengthy presence in that place of the most divine meant reanimation would mimic the immortal and divine I'd dwelt near. Who knew? Whatever the reason, it let me know the sun was above the horizon on the other side of the door. That it waited for me. I went to such great lengths to avoid it for so long, it was hard to break the habit even when I wanted to.

I shook it off. With my hand flat on the door, in resolve, I pushed it open and walked out into the day praying for death.

*****

(A.D. 1729)

I watched Billy's square-rigger streak off into the night.

With my cold cheek pressed against hers, I cradled Maggie's lifeless body in one arm. Nigel hung over my other shoulder, moaning in pain.

I imprinted the bastard's face on my memory. It would never fade no matter how long it took me to find him. And I would find him. I swore it to Maggie, I swore it to the gods, and I swore it to myself.

All I did was nip out to hunt for a bit of supper that would please her and now she was dead. It was my fault. I left her alone again and something had happened to her, but this time I couldn't fix it. She was only human and only had one life to lose and I allowed it to be lost. Billy would pay. Beyond rational thought, I knew nothing else and wouldn't for a very long while.

Still breathing, Nigel needed tending to and though I didn't want to let go of her, I forced myself to put her down. Lowering Maggie to the deck with care, I eased Nigel off my shoulder onto the deck near her to assess his injuries. They were bad, *really* bad. How he ever managed to grab her up and get her off the ship was a miracle. But when I looked into his eyes, I saw the determination. And his heart. A man of honour, he'd done his best to look after her in the face of an enormous evil he wasn't equipped to fight.

"You have my sincerest thanks. There are no words…" I floundered, "If I'd only got here sooner. Only a little sooner." Of course, he failed, because it had been my duty to perform. But he gave his all in the effort and I would never forget that sacrifice.

He was spitting blood, but didn't notice. "I'm… so sorry… She asked me to keep a look out… that you would come for her..," he convulsed into coughing.

I waved it off, "Let's get you below decks and--"

"*No*," he grabbed at my shirt. "No time. I know I'm done for. It's all right, I know it. Need to tell you… so you know what… needs to be avenged…"

He wanted no comforts, only to accomplish what he set out to do. Something else I wouldn't soon forget. I was very glad he was there for her at the end when she might have been alone with the monster. No matter it should have been me, he was a worthy substitute. More worthy considering he knew he would be killed. Made me ashamed and feeling a coward. It only fuelled my bloodlust and determination to find Billy and make him pay.

I would never let it go.

Nigel thought I knew about the baby and with difficulty gave me his one good hand on it, "Make the bastard pay double, my friend. When you get your hands on that syphilitic, walking blasphemy… give him one for me, would you, old chap?" It wouldn't be a difficult promise to keep. Nigel died with his hand still clasped in mine, already colder than I was. When they brought the sloop back into port, I hired a carriage and took him home to bury next to Maggie and Myles in our little family plot that was growing with time.

As everyone connected with me died. As they always had and always would.

Out of my mind with grief, I turned straight around and went back out in search of Billy and didn't care who knew. I wasn't very subtle about it. I'd been in the world so long I had hordes of gold and silver myself and threw it everywhere to get what I wanted. Including the ship full of pirates who were more than happy to wait for me. They balked a bit once they realised who I was after hunting down for a second time, they knew his reputation, but I made it worth their efforts. We had the faster ship and Billy had no one but himself to plot course now thanks to Nigel's death. It didn't take many weeks to track him. He'd gone off to the east rather than his usual course westward and was making a run for the Pacific.

He never reached it.

Not long past the Cape of Good Hope, we slipped into the brisk

Antarctic current rounding the African horn and used it to our best advantage. Riding it into the Somali current going north that drew us along to India, it was there we caught up Pandora. East of Sumatra and Singapore and through to New Guinea are a million islands where men might become lost and where few ventured at that time. We forced him farther southeast in chase. Orchestrating his direction without having to, there was nowhere else for him to go with us snapping at his heels. I played with him. Let him run just for the pleasure of catching him up again, never knowing it was what he did to Maggie when she came to me, so the payback was in kind.

In some ways, we were much the same, he and I. Cruel and inhuman and unfeeling except for the borrowed bits that were always destined to die soon after we stole them. Already dead, nothing good within us could last no matter how much I might have wished it otherwise for myself.

With Maggie dead, I no longer had a reason to strive for the good.

Each sight of him fuelled my rage and I let it. It was all I had left that felt alive. When he ducked in and out of the islands hoping to lose us in the maze, we pulled closer still and there was no escape. Australia to the south and New Guinea to the east hemmed him in and he was caught.

Fourteen pieces of cannon to Billy's twenty, once broadsides with the larger vessel, the efficient sloop's crew soon overpowered his ill-trained and unmotivated gang of thugs and got us close enough to board her. Bent on revenge, I didn't even wait until the ships were quite lashed together before I let the night take me and leapt.

The usual defence during a boarding was to halve the crew up between the fore and aftercastles. Perched up high like castle turrets on either end of the ship, the crew would rain down a hail of gunfire and arrows at the centre deck where invaders were obliged to board. Only in this case it didn't work out that way.

Billy's men wouldn't fight for him.

At a distance, they lit the cannon but this close, they scurried for safety. When I leapt to the deck, they huddled up together on the 'castles in terror. Not a one drew a bow or pistol. I stood alone in the darkness with only a sickle moon for light and perhaps that's the only fitting companion for revenge. Full of the night and the darkness Billy had grown within me, revenge for Maggie was my only thought while the luckless crew of Pandora kept witness.

My eyes blazed over the forecastle above me, looking for the face I hunted. "Where is your master?" Not a word, not a breath nor a cough or fidget broke the flat silence that engulfed the ship. Only the sea lapping at the hull let us know there was anything outside that tense moment. I raked the aftercastle, too, "Don't believe for a moment I'll be put off. I can feel his black heart." No one would respond, but their eyes remained fixed down on me in prayerful disbelief. It only fuelled my anger, "Why do you protect him?!"

Almost a hundred crewmen were aboard. Though less than half they might have carried, the combined thudding of their terrified hearts broke against me so hard it took concentration not to sway back and forth with the force of that electrified current. It was difficult to think straight. Worse, I could feel Billy there. Felt him for what he was and had since I'd got close enough to fish Maggie and Nigel out of the drink. Easier to consider in the abstract while we chased the three-masted Pandora, now steeping in that vibrancy I craved with instinct urging me to fight him for defiling anything that was mine, all I knew was blind rage.

Turning in a circle, I gave them all a once over. "Pathetic band of wretched cringelings. Did you all stand in witness while he tortured her? Think to stop him while he murdered her? *Did you*?" I was screaming at them and didn't care. They'd all been there while Maggie suffered. "Where is he? Show yourself, coward!"

A truncated scream followed by a splash in the dark turned my focus. Wide-eyed, the crew clutched at each other for support as Billy the Black Death, master of the Pandora, appeared out of the darkness at the head of the stairs under the crewmen on the aftercastle.

"*Ici*. I am here!" his voice thundered in dark command.

Several crewmen ran to the rail to check for the deckhand Billy tossed overboard in callous disregard. They lowered ropes and went about retrieving the body with obvious efficiency gained through too much practice. It was only background noise to me while my prey presented itself.

"Where is your boarding party? After all that display, I should have thought you would bring more assistance to wrest a crew of this size and my lady from me." Glinting in the dark, his eyes spoke a volume more.

"It's not them I've come for, butcher."

"Mercy, sir!"

"Spare us our hides!" the men clamoured from the upper decks.

"*Chut*! Shut up, you gaggle of mewling infants!" Billy spat overhead at them before turning his attention back to me. "Our business is none of your pathetic concern."

Before the last word was out of his mouth I disappeared into the night to materialise at his throat, but he was already on the move. My equal in ability, exacting payment would be difficult to achieve, but I would not be denied.

Laughing over by the mizzenmast, Billy appeared unconcerned, "Oh, *mon Dieu*, such haste to bring our little meeting to an end when a rare pleasure to meet one of our own. Would you not care to stay for dinner?" With a snap of his fingers, his strong-arm, the giant Boatswain, Harris, appeared from below decks dragging a terrified slip of a girl into view. Congenial, Billy swept an inviting hand through the air in her direction, "Dinner is served, *mon ami*."

Grinning, Harris gathered her arms behind her in one massive paw and put the tip of a dagger to her collar bone. With a flick, he broke the skin in a shallow cut not meant to harm her. Despite myself, I watched in morbid fascination as her blood beaded up along the edge of the small wound. It had been a long while since I fed on a human being and the scent of it wafted in aching entreat across the space between us.

With great effort, I pulled myself together, "There's only one thing I want here. Leave the girl out of it."

"Tsk-tsk," Billy simpered in disappointment. "Have I been such an ungracious host? *Que non*! Please," he offered again, "I insist. *C'est à manger tout de suite*. There are some things that should be eaten straight away."

The girl's eyes were wide as she beseeched me in a voice ragged with terror, "Please, sir, for pity's sake. Help me!" Harris slapped a hard hand over her mouth and holding her face, pulled her head back for his master. She was breathing hard, a gazelle with a lion at her throat, and thrashed against the unyielding hold.

"Enough!" I demanded his attention, but Billy was already in front of her.

Coy, his innocent eyes over his shoulder at me were a sickening contrast to her impending demise, "If you'll excuse me, I shall be with you momentarily." Unlike myself, he did crave the suffering and was more satisfied without using the beguile to make his prey complacent. She would know every moment of the horror he was and he would revel in it until she knew no more.

This was all turning me from my task, but I wasn't about to allow him kill her for sport while I watched. The instant of his distraction as he lost himself in the momentary bliss to be had gave me time enough to act. In one of her rabbitting heartbeats, I was across the deck with my hands on Harris's oversized head. I snapped his neck before he got a word out and she fell with him, pulled down by the still-clenched hands that held her. She screamed as I dragged her up behind me and blocked Billy's attempts to snag her.

He snarled in feral wrath at the denial, "How dare you!"

I shoved her hard and sent her sprawling to safety in the direction of the crew cowering away from the drama. Hardened criminals all, she ran to them. They gathered her to them in a protective clutch away from their master who out-matched them all in devilish intent.

"No more games," I put myself in his path. "You know the reason I've come."

Rather than rush me, he appeared to recompose himself back into the semblance of a man and considered me with a critical eye. "What a strange sort of chivalrous devil you are. Coming to the aide of fair maidens in distress is a habit for you, it appears."

"A better habit than yours."

"*Touché*," he laughed and made a dismissive gesture, "yet inconsequential. They matter nothing to us, *mon ami*. We are gods dwelling among their lesser kind. They merely exist while we dispense life and death at our whim."

"Gods?" I choked on the word.

"Some of us apparently closer than others," he looked down his nose at me. "Your benevolence will be your downfall, *ne sais-tu pas*? Do you not know this? They are here for our glorious use and pleasure and that alone. A bountiful feast for our savour and nothing more. Surely, you've learned that in your time. We are kindred in exulted darkness, *mon frère*." And then sly look came over his face, "Join with me, brother god."

Staring hard into my eyes, he worked to get inside me. "Such wondrous sport might be had and shared by an association of our breed. Think on it. It could go on and on for eternity! Safety in numbers, brother. Protecting each other while we revel in bliss. Joined together, nothing might stop us. Think of the fortunes to plunder, the lands we might conquer as brothers-in-arms. We could claim dominion over this entire cursed world of short-lived chattel. With a dark army of our own making, we could establish a vast kingdom for ourselves. Be worshipped and revered in joint stewardship as the true deities we are!" caught up in his own wonder, his eyes gleamed at the vision of an entire world paying him homage.

All the while he spoke, he worked to find a chink in my armour, get past it and gain a toehold, but I was no pup. I ignored the attempt. "You're mad," I raked him with a disparaging look. "Kingdoms? What utter lunacy. Worshipped as gods--"

"We *are* gods," his voice harsh. "*I* am a god! And if you refuse to join me in the creation of my vision then there is no place for you in it." Too quick to see with a human eye, he reached out to grab me by the throat.

And I let him.

Raised voices rained down from the 'castles at either end of the ship, but I paid them no mind. I let him pull me closer in dead weight and he went over backwards in surprise for encountering no resistance, my own momentum throwing us both to the deck. With the effort, both of us appeared to wink in and out of view while we allowed the night to take us over and it fuelled what we were while we wrestled.

"Lord save us!"

"Didn't I place him lads? 'Tis Ol' Nick hisself come to claim his due!"

"The master's the Christ-cursed demon, me salties."

"Aye! 'Tis God's vengeance upon us all."

"You're wrong, boys. That be an archangel, by God. Sent to best the demon for us!"

"Oh, sweet Mother, give him strength for it."

"By all what's holy, if we pass this here night all of a piece, I'll change me thieving ways, I swears it!"

Billy was quick and matched me well, but had relied on others to do his hunting for so long, he was out of practice. His usual dandy appearance all-askew, I wouldn't let him up to engage in anything more gentlemanly than a down and dirty, full-out brawl to the death. Fuelled by horrendous grief for all he'd taken from me, I lost touch with any humanity Maggie might have instilled in me and soon gained the upper hand. I tore the cutlass from his hip and tossed it overboard and threw his dagger out after it while the crew roared.

Down on the deck and restrained, my only thought was to hurt him so he would suffer in payment for Maggie before I killed him. Pulling his heart from his chest wouldn't kill him, but it wouldn't be very fucking pleasant.

"Payment in kind, devil," I spat while I drew my hand back to punch through his ribcage.

Panting, he laughed, "An eye for an eye. I was not wrong after all, I see. Brothers! It is our way, *mon frère*. We are the same! *Quel animal!*"

My hand froze mid-air while the words sunk in. "I'm nothing like you. Nothing!" I snarled.

Even bested he was cocky, "*Seigneur!* You've only to look at you. Not even a life for a life. And what a delicious life she was…"

I saw red and roared.

"…not even satisfied with only my death in payment. You would prefer to tear me apart first only for the glory of it, no? I retract my earlier chivalrous assessment, *mon ami*. You *are* a beast. As much beast as I," his laughter was cruel and if I'd had a soul it would have stung me in it.

"Die!" I screamed while the crewmen surrounding us urged me to it. My fist was still in the air, but the moment had past and his words had got inside me.

I couldn't do it.

Howling with frustration, I couldn't force myself to be the thing that needed to exist to exact payment the way I wanted. Maybe more of Maggie had stayed inside me than I believed. Of course, it must have been her blood. The same thing that created my internal rift, split me in two and was still tearing me apart. It changed me from what I used to be and I could no longer be that beast in its entirety. Or, perhaps, she never really changed me at all and I was only what I was. I told her the truth when I said I never craved taking life, that it wasn't my need to make people suffer or kill for the sake of killing. Perhaps, it was neither, but in the end, I couldn't do it.

He saw the hesitation and laughed at me harder, "Ho! Behold that benevolence. Fool."

Choking on words that couldn't be spoken, I grabbed him up in a bear hug so he wouldn't get loose. Dragging him over to the side rail, I caught the dagger tucked into the back of my belt.

"And what do you propose now, *mon ami*?" he was still laughing, but his bravado wavered.

Using all my strength, I forced his head over the rail with the crew in frenzy around us. And slashed him across the throat without a word. He thrashed and bucked against me, but I held on in grim determination while his cursed blood spurted out into the sea.

"*Que fais-tu*? What do you think you are doing? You'll pay for this, *lâche*. Coward! Do you know who I am?" Ranting and roaring, he continued to threaten even as he weakened. "I will find you wherever you go, wherever you run to. You cannot do this to *me*! My revenge will rain down upon you for a thousand years... before I kill you... bastard brother..."

No shark fins broke the surface in answer to the blood. But dead fish rose to be tossed about by the waves.

Growing weaker by degrees, he finally stilled. I held him there long after he stopped moving to be certain. Not taking any chances, I let every drop that came run out of him before I was satisfied he wouldn't wake. Drained, he was off to the Land of Nod and it would give me time to plan my next steps.

The crew had gone silent as their master ceased his squirming. "Is there a brig?" my voice raw over my shoulder, it sounded very loud in the stillness. No one breathed. I narrowed my eyes and picked one crewman out of the darkness, "*You*."

His voice quavered, "Aye?"

"Brig?"

A shaky finger pointed, "In the master's cabin."

"Fetch me the key. Smartly now!" He nodded, dumbfounded. "We'll secure him there for now."

The sailor scrambled down from the aftercastle to get it. He gave us a wide berth while he gingerly picked through the Boatswain's pockets and eyed me with trepidation.

"You're safe now," I struggled to speak more softly in reassurance. "He won't wake." I hoisted Billy up and the crewman took a steadying breath before reaching out to help me. "No!" He yanked his hand back. "See the blood, there? And there?" I gestured to his neck and his shirt. I motioned over the side, "See the fish?"

He took a hesitant look into the water, "Lord 'a' mercy…"

"You mustn't let it touch you. Understood? I'll deal with this. Run ahead and open the door."

His face white, the sailor crossed himself and ran for the cell in the cabin.

I took Billy's keys and anything else he had in his pockets and we locked him inside. I gave the sailor the other key. "What's your name, crewman?"

"Palmer, sir."

"Pleased to make your acquaintance, Palmer. Pity it's not under better circumstances." I gestured at the cell, "Can I trust you not to open this door no matter what happens? Not even if he rises from the dead as a spectre and threatens to tear your head from your shoulders?"

"Aye, sir. You'll get narry a quarrel from me."

"Brilliant. Because you just never know," I nodded, satisfied. Making a conscious effort to avoid the body in the cage, I glance around the cabin, "Where are the charts?"

The locked safe occupied a spot behind Billy's desk. "You've the key there with the others, sir."

"Can anyone plot course?"

Palmer shook his head, "Mr. Shakespeare was Sailing Master. The cap'n was charting hisself lately. Harris, the Boatswain, has just been learnin'."

"Excellent. We can make do with that. Run fetch him."

He didn't move.

"What's wrong?"

"Mr. Harris is, uh, dead, sir," he pointed to the deck over our heads.

"Well, blast it."

Palmer considered for a moment and then looked afraid to speak.

I took a calming breath, "Go on, Palmer."

Uncomfortable, he shifted in agitation, "Well, if I might be so bold, sir." I waved him on. "Me an' a few of the lads who been with the master awhile was born to the sea. No fancy education, mind, but we know the water. Most all of 'em between us. If'n you let us put our heads together, we'd be pleased to give it our best."

"Good man." I unlocked the safe, "Gather them up and bring them down. We'll all have a go at it then, yeah?"

He cleared his throat.

"Now what?"

"Sir?" he eyed the cage and Billy's unconscious form. "Is he..?"

"No," I chose my words, "not dead. Not much could accomplish that, I'm afraid." The fear of their captain, even locked in a cage and appearing dead, was palpable and it caught my sympathy. "Unfortunate for us, he's the bloody devil, so we must take him to a place from where he'll be unable to return."

Pale with terror, his lips barely moved, "Aye, sir."

While I pulled out the charts, Palmer ran topside to fill-in the crew. In the end, I was forced to bring the charts up to them--they refused to stand in the same room as their demon captain who might wake despite his exsanguinous state. They weren't much keener on being close to me, but braved it as I bested the object of their mutual dissatisfaction.

After a great deal kibitzing and a course consult with my rented pirates, before night was over I released my hired sloop much to their relief and we were under way. The crew knew their duties and went to them with uncommon diligence with the promise of ridding themselves of the demon master spurring them on. We aimed for a blank spot on the charts, far from any islands known or even rumoured inhabited.

Much to my disgust, I found Billy's stash of beguiled women clutching each other in the darkness of the hold. It turned my stomach to discover first-hand the place Maggie had gained her fear of the dark. For all the things I couldn't do for her while she was in the same position, I took it upon myself to make it up to her through them in what way I could. I put them in the comfort of the vacant officers' quarters and promised to let them off at a suitable port of their choosing after we looked after the captain. They didn't mind the delay.

As Baby Bite would later question me over, I *had* been around ships and sailing a very long while. I could navigate by the stars myself, but didn't know these waters so deferred to those with greater experience. We sailed for a week before I was satisfied we were well into the uncharted water we aimed for and began scouting for a suitable island. There were several that looked promising and we finally settled on the smallest islet of the lot. It was a desolate place, nearly a sandbar, barren with no game or fresh water. Odds dictated an accidental waking wouldn't occur anytime soon with fewer things that might shed blood.

A party of six followed me ashore in the longboat when they refused to sit in the rowboat with Billy's lifeless body and I wouldn't make them do it. We buried him deep for extra safety, ten feet we dug down and then two more for good measure. We lined the crypt with hewn timbers across the bottom and around the walls and then sealed them with pitch to keep the insects out of the cracks. It still didn't seem enough to me, so I had the men bring me out an oak chest which we also sealed the inside of with pitch.

I regarded Billy's lifeless body where it lay in the sand, considering. It was only an illusion. One that no one but me truly understood. Right up next to the rage inside me burned a sudden, frantic need to ensure the safety of everyone else, anyone who might happen upon the monster. Using the rage to drive my actions to protect them, without hesitation I grabbed up one of the axes we used to split timbers. Raising it high over my head in the moonlight, with a snarl I drove it down hard in purpose. Harder than Günter had on Maggie.

And severed his head in one grief-driven blow.

The landing party gasped. I leaned on the axe handle a moment, panting, and worked to compose myself for their benefit.

I regarded them over my shoulder, "It needed to be done." My voice was tired and the words came out flat. Dumbfounded, they nodded in mute horror.

I let the axe drop into the sand and muscled the body into the oak chest. I hesitated with the head, though. It appeared he was looking up at me from between my feet, his eyes no more dead than they had been hours before. He was accusing, threatening, promising retribution still it seemed and I heard his voice ringing in my ears. "Brother-*god*," I sneered and spat on him. "Retribution? We'll see about that. Here's mine." I grabbed the head by his hair and without ceremony, tossed it into the chest on top of the body. We locked the unholy treasure he was up tight for safe-keeping before we lowered him into the pit and dumped a house full of earth over top of him.

I wasn't taking any chances.

We didn't give him a marker. I didn't want anyone to know he was there. We marked the spot on the chart as best we could, so they could avoid it in future and sailed away as the dawn came up out of the eastern sea.

Far from us, back at an English port and already spreading out into the countryside, rumours grew over my behaviour as I left. They would soon be fuelled by the eyewitness accounts from the hired sloop crew. I didn't realise how difficult it would be to stay there until I returned, but couldn't think that far ahead. All I knew was what I'd done and that it didn't satisfy me any more than the occasional rat I ate to stay awake. He wasn't dead and even if he had been, it couldn't bring Maggie and the baby back. It was what I hated him for the most.

For that morning, though, I had to be satisfied with going below decks to hide out in the master's cabin as the sun drew up over the tomb of Maggie's killer and former Captain of the Pandora, William, Billy the Black Death, Blackthorn.

10

(Canada – Present)

t was warm there in the Land of Nod as it always was. But there was no gentle surfacing from that comfort this time. I was thrown out of it with a snap.

The fire and thirst for revenge was in me so strong it pulled me forward out of the nothing. Something in the back of my mind screamed at me for wanting to die, because I still had a job to do.

I couldn't recall how I got there.

So strange. I didn't think it was that long since I ate anything. I'd been a bit tired, I remembered, but not *that* sort of tired. Last thing I recalled was swimming and then knew that was wrong.

Noise grabbed at my attention. I couldn't place it. Some incessant, fiendish racket that wound its way down into my brain and pissed me off for disturbing my tranquillity. There was warmth all over me rather than inside me the way it should have been. Odd. I felt strong, though. Strong and powerful and my brains sped up until thoughts raced faster than a mortal could sort through. But then, of course, I certainly wasn't that. I tallied every piece of detail that came to me in an instant while attempting to calculate how much time had past.

That noise had to go, though. I understood it was electronic in nature and that, of course, made it the enemy. When I experimented with moving, I found I wasn't buried. The air was fresh, too. And there was carpet under me.

My expensive, hand-woven Persian rug in the centre of the front foyer.

Sunlight undulated over me, warming my skin from the outside-in. My mobile buzzed around on the floor somewhere off past my head where it fell. I was almost blind.

Bent on self-destruction, I marched right out the cellar door into the full morning sun that hit me square-on for the first time in over five thousand years. It was bound to do something even if it didn't kill me. My eyes were pretty much seared useless for the moment and it had been painful enough to knock me flat on my arse. But I wasn't dead.

Well, I suppose that's a relative term.

I groaned, "Fuck me," and reached a hand out over my head to find the phone. Forced to locate it by the sound, I scrambled to make it stop before I resorted to smashing it. "Hello..?" My voice was rough and a little shaky, but it still worked.

"Holy shit. Yup, he's dead all right. He just said 'hello' on the phone."

"Fuck off, Baby Bite."

"Ah, so good to hear your voice, old man. Love you, too."

"*And* your horse."

Laughing in obvious relief, "So," Alan pressed me, "what happened? Where are you? On the stairs or..?"

"Not on the stairs. Not hiding behind the door. Not in the *dark*," incredulous, I struggled to make sense of it. "Knocked me right on my arse. Damned if I don't I feel I've a hangover the size of Alberta, but I'm still here, little man." Alan relayed information to the waiting 'Hunters who all stayed up to hear the outcome. I heard them cheer in the background. "Can't see a fucking thing, though. My own bloody fault. Marched right out the door and blinded myself. It'll right itself before long, I imagine. I'm on the floor here at the moment. Right on the rug in a lovely patch of sunshine roasting myself like a fucking cat."

"Hot damn."

I laughed without humour, "As good a description as any."

Currents of warmth crawled over my cold skin in little feather-weighted fingers that left a trail as they undulated and I grew lost in the luxury of it. It was hard to shake myself back to the moment. "I don't even know quite what to say. It's daytime and I'm in it. I can't believe I'm not... Can't believe..."

I lost my voice. I couldn't tell them it had been a suicide mission and no act of self-discovery. It would only frighten them. They couldn't survive alone yet and I resolved not to worry them over it. What they didn't know wouldn't hurt them. What I knew hurt me, but I was old enough to deal with it. Besides, it fuelled a goal. Then it occurred to me I now had an advantage. And could use it to achieve my own ends.

Baby Bite was still talking, "So are you coming back down? Need help? Want us to wait for you?" He yawned and I knew the day he couldn't see pulled him under a veil I had never understood. For all their similar strengths, they weren't quite as sturdy as me and needed rest.

I didn't need them for what I wanted to do just then, "No, you lot go on to sleep. I'll putter around up here for a bit, I think. Just because. Think I might like to see my garden in the daylight."

"Yeah," Alan paused, considering the luxury of it. "Yeah, jeez, take the opportunity, man. You waited long enough."

I huffed, "Understatement of the millennium."

"Hey, we want a full report when you get back down here later, though. Every detail, old man, y'hear me?"

He was being cocky and where normally I'd take the mickey out him for it, I couldn't do it now. I knew how they ached for the world they left behind and wouldn't deny them. "I promise. Every second."

"I'll hold you to that. Just watch yourself, okay? You're on your own out there."

"I've been out in the world all by my lonesome a long while, little boy. Don't worry yourselves into a lather. Quite certain I can manage."

I stayed there on the floor for a bit with the phone in my hand soaking it in. Knowing I was lying in the sun and doing it simply because I could.

"Happy fucking Christmas, old man."

When the new wore off that, I went to my room to change clothes. Also because I could. I hadn't bothered to dress after swimming--not like I was going to need fresh jeans before vaporisation. Used to walking around in the black, being almost blind was not the same thing. It became a more difficult navigation than at first thought, though I negotiated it without crashing into too many things. A lot of the younglings wore sunglasses and left them discarded all over the house, so when I found a pair made a prudent addition to my wardrobe. They were good and dark and blocked enough light that if I kept my eyes slit, I could see where I was going without too much discomfort.

Even behind the glasses, it was a whole new world to me. Or a very old one, but I couldn't remember the other anyway, so amounted to the same thing. Sun streamed in all over the house and changed the way everything appeared. Stumbling through my own home in wonder, a place of my own design and built by my own hands, it appeared I'd been transported to a whole different locale. Happy and bright, it shone in the daylight and it was amazing. It was what Maggie had done to my darkness. A reflection of her spirit, it truly honoured the way I had always felt her.

Being knocked unconscious had done more than struck me almost blind, though. It had taken me back, made me remember Maggie's death, and gave me fresh impetus. It hurt like hell again. And worse, the crushing guilt I had been deliberate in keeping from myself now sat heavy upon my heart. There was no more avoiding it--for failing to protect her, for failing to save her from the beast, for failing to come back to myself no matter how hard she tried to help me, for failing to recognise she would need her body so she come back to me. For a million other things that were my fault.

It was too much to make peace with. Only one thing would satisfy me now. It didn't matter Billy wasn't responsible for all of it. I made him responsible for his portion and the part that predicated my own guilty actions. I had no problem making myself pay for my own crimes and would as soon as I made certain Billy didn't get away with his.

Once I began, I wouldn't have time for much else so made a beeline for the garden while I still had the opportunity. To see it in daylight with my own eyes the way it was meant to. Worse than the 'Bites, I tore down the stairs and slid across the marble floor past the piano to throw the French doors wide open on the day. The whole room was alive with light and it infected me, too.

The light felt like music, so I did a mad thing and threw some on at full volume. The blood bank crew had made it their collective mission to bring me into the modern age by downloading me more music than I could listen to into the next millennia. I loved it all. I was fond of the blues and in another minute B. B. King tore through guitar riffs that matched the electricity in the air.

Bracing my hands against the doorjamb, I paused in savour, eyes closed. The morning breeze broke over me into the room while *The Thrill is Gone* wafted over my shoulders going the other way. And then I started to laugh there all by myself and couldn't stop. It poured out of me in ecstasy until I finally threw my head back and howled at my brother moon's brighter brother, Utu, whose company I'd not had the pleasure of in a very long while. I didn't stop until I was hoarse and didn't care.

Panting and still grinning like a fool, I forced my feet over the threshold into the naked day without benefit of the house for cover. It was terrifying and wonderful with every step across the porch closer to wonderful. Birds sang, all manner of birds from the forest surrounding me, filling up the yard as they followed along with the music.

Outside and not through the windows, light danced before my eyes. Even half-blind, my inhuman vision could see so much more detail in the air. The spectrum of light refracted all around in the glitter of coloured diamonds I was sure no eye before had the capacity to see. I had always felt life from the earth and saw the filmy evidence of it from anything alive, but in daylight, I discovered I could see so much more. Surrounding every living thing in a corona, each had its own unique aura and none of it was static.

Everything in movement, energy shifted and shimmered and shimmied backlit by sunshine and I tired out my eyes within moments taking it all in. It seemed a great privilege and I honoured it the best way I knew. I ran back inside and came out stuffing my pipe.

With the expensive tobacco.

I tipped the bowl heavenward, "Here you go, old friend. One from your reaper in the daytime for you. Did you ever think you'd see the like?"

Ignoring the swing in favour of wandering about my garden, I puffed in contemplation. Examining my herbs in the light of day, I could see the truth of their healing properties. As with everything that lived, each had its own energy, its own distinctive aura that was best-viewed backlit by the natural light of the sun. All different, all singular and remarkable. The reason they were each toward a specific purpose was obvious and it suddenly made sense to me. Most I used through experience and some by instinct, but here was the proof.

"Incredible," I puffed, lost in thought. If I could also see injuries or a body in illness in daylight, I would see with certainty how each cure would match up. I could likely write the definitive herbal remedy book.

Chuckling at my own ego, laughter that wasn't my own joined me and carried on the air over the garden. I pulled up short on the path. Midmorning, it couldn't be any of my little 'Bites and I grew wary in sudden concern.

No one came to my house. Ever. Not until Alan arrived and I knew how he discovered enough information to find me. I wondered who else had followed his lead, "Bloody hell. Not *now*." I crept down the path on my silent cat feet straining for signs of an intruder. And found none. There was no living person anywhere near me and no vampires, either. "Now you're hearing things?" I straightened up and swivelled my head around in confusion.

I was alone.

I stuck my pipe back in my mouth and sent some smoke up in question, but no answer came. "Shit," I scrubbed a self-conscious hand over the back of my neck. "You're losin' it, y'mangy, old sod." Laughing at myself, I started down the path aiming for the swing where I decided I should stay put and contemplate my sanity.

A presence popped up out of nowhere stopping me cold. No flesh and blood, simply concentrated living energy. Enough I could sense and nothing more.

Right next to me.

I jumped off the path in surprise, "What the fuck? Who's there? Make yourself known, dammit!" There was no one but the sundial doing its job in the morning sun. I'd never seen it at work before except in moonlight and then realised I couldn't see it now, either. There was something on top of it that wasn't there a moment before.

That sense of life was already gone, winked in and back out again and I had no idea where it went or where it had come from. And I didn't know what the things on the sundial were supposed to mean. Taking my time, I sidled up onto the path again alert for the mysterious life I couldn't see.

My brow furrowed, "What the bloody hell is this now?" There was a date soaked in honey and a heel of dark bread and a little satchel made of hide tied at the top with a piece of lacing. I swivelled my head in consternation to locate whoever put it there. But there was no one with me.

I didn't like this at *all*.

My brain told me it was a haunting, but mid-morning seemed an odd time for that sort of thing. And I didn't think spirits were in the habit of delivering snack food from the beyond. There had to be some other explanation. It was *food* for crying out loud. One morning out of a million and my first in the sunshine and I already had a mystery on my hands I couldn't consult anyone about.

Cautious, I crept up on the sundial. Nothing jumped out and grabbed me and that mysterious winking in-and-out life didn't make another appearance. The bread and the date looked innocuous enough, though they could have been poisoned for all I knew. But when I smelled them, my extra-sensitive senses detected no dark undercurrent threatening harm, "Strange..."

I turned the bread over in my hands, contemplating, as three sparrows rushed at me. Ducking over my shoulder, they landed on the face of the sundial to nibble the crumbs left behind. I looked at the bread in my hands and then back at the birds. They were so close to me, unafraid and not flying away the way most of nature did when I moved out among it in the dark. I'd never been this close to them before.

I could feel their little hearts a-flutter, but it wasn't in fear and something I'd never experienced. They were cheeping up a ruckus there on the sundial top, happy with the little slice of bliss the crumbs brought to them in that moment. It didn't appear to harm them any and they weren't afraid of it despite it appearing out of the nothing.

When all the crumbs were gone, they hopped about looking for more, chirping all the louder in plea. Tearing off pieces of the crust, hesitant, I put it among them, expecting them to become frightened by my hand so close to them and take off skyward. Instead, they chirped louder and more came to join in the sudden feast. Fascinated, I continued to examine them with great interest. Tearing off more bread, I spread it out among them when they needed more to keep them with me a few moments longer.

Whatever mysterious winds of fate guided the morning had cobbled together a pleasant little moment for me, so I refused poke at it too closely. Instead, I let it unfold and acted with what felt appropriate in each moment it continued there in the sunshine. The daylight was a whole new world, so there could be no second-guessing in it for me. I didn't fight it and went along in discovery with blues music pumping out through the open French doors now washing George Thorogood's *Bad to the Bone* over the garden.

Against feeding the innocent sparrows, the humour caught me, making laughter possible over top those hard feelings of grief and revenge that continued to percolate inside me.

Tranquillity from every corner, I could see I chose a perfect spot for my house, my retreat from the world. Though executed in darkness, I still chose it well for its daytime attributes. I could even admit I chose it more for Maggie than I had for myself. She would have loved it, after all. It was beautiful and full of life and nature and it made a nice view outside the windows that I never had the opportunity to appreciate until that morning. Now that I saw it, I was glad for the place I put her in the garden--her final resting spot was suitable enough for a goddess. She deserved nothing less.

When the bread ran out, the birds lingered around the sundial, picking this way and that looking for any leftover morsel they might have missed. I couldn't help but watch them. They didn't appear to want to leave me or seem bothered they sat atop a burial memorial. I would have thought they could sense the death under them the way they should have from me, but neither seemed to concern them.

And then snarling from the bushes shattered the serenity.

I knew the sound and grew apprehensive. I didn't understand how, but the wolf had crept up without my sensing it. Unlike myself, my little feathered visitors didn't seem troubled by its presence. I wasn't given any time to consider this phenomenon, though, when, without provocation, it leapt for my throat, "Fucking hell!" Ducking my head down, I threw my arms up to ward it off, but it was quick and hit me square in the chest with two big front paws. Now disturbed, the sparrows flew up as I crashed backwards over the sundial, knocking it from its mooring.

Before I knew what happened, I was on the ground with the wolf standing over me staring hard into my eyes. My last puff of tobacco smoke hung in the air over us a moment and then dispersed.

It must have been very hungry to brave coming out in daylight to hunt, but as it stood over me, it appeared more curious than threatening. On any normal day, wolves didn't cause me concern, but this one did. This shouldn't have happened in the daytime. Then again, perhaps I shouldn't have been out in the daytime, either, so the circumstance fit the occasion. Odd, though, I couldn't feel the life in it. One of my own blood brother hunters in darkness, while to the eye it appeared very much alive, it wasn't. Couldn't be. Despite weight pressing into my chest, it was at the same time somehow insubstantial, empty almost, or missing half of itself. Nothing natural could exist in that state.

The wolf's eyes were bright and shone with interest. It remained where it was and I didn't want to hurt it, but it kept me there, pinned. Nose-to-nose and lying on the ground, I ran through my options and discovered I had none. Chancing a look to the bushes to see if it was alone, while my gaze was off it, the weight disappeared off my chest. When I looked back, it was still standing on top of me, now more insubstantial and yet whole. That same disembodied laughter sweep across the garden again and gooseflesh walked across my skin. The wolf's head came up sniffing the air to track the voice.

There were mysterious goings-on in my garden my first day in the sun and I wondered if I had somehow disturbed the natural order by being out. Perhaps, it was a mistake. I was already a mistake, an accident in creation, and it might be I upset some delicate balance. I really didn't know what to make of it.

The laughter without source continued to waft over us until, as if in answer, the featherweight wolf jumped off my chest. Nosing around the fallen sundial, it snuffled the dirt in concentration. The honey date was on the ground, flung off the face of the memorial with the birds and the wolf sniffed its way over to it. And then snapped it up. Like the crust of bread, the date had appeared out of the nothing, but then again, so had the wolf, so seemed an appropriate snack for a make-believe canine.

I came up on one elbow, alert for any hint of danger in the mysterious goings-on, but there didn't seem to be any. It was all just weird and smacked of the Netherworld and I didn't want to have anything to do with it. My movement caught the wolf's attention and I cursed my own stupidity. Make-believe or not, its eyes trained on me and after a moment's hesitation, leapt right for me again.

"What the blue blazes..?" I thumped my chest checking for soundness. Though the wolf jumped at me straight-on, somehow it missed.

And then disappeared.

I felt odd. My head was heavy and my eyes tired from so much use in the bright. But it was more than that.

There was honey on my tongue.

I put my hand to my mouth in wonder. Like so many other things in the garden that morning, it wasn't possible, but it was there all the same. I hadn't tasted food on my tongue in so long I couldn't recall. I tried over the years, a time here and a time there, and always to the same result. None of it had any taste to me no matter I wished it could and it made me feel poorly. I always assumed that was some condition of becoming what I thought was a vampire, so no longer able to process it.

But I could taste it *now*.

The aftertaste of the date was there, also, and I liked it. More than that, I *remembered* I liked it. Remembered it from a very long while ago. The memory danced around on the edge of recollection. I knew the taste and that it had been my favourite. Dates in honey. Nothing special, simply a treat of which I was fond.

With a smile of discovery, I decided the morning was a gift--the sunshine, the birds, the taste, the true and clear memory of something in my own past. I had no idea what it meant, but appreciated it for all the things it was. I would have lifetimes to unravel it later. For the moment, I decided to savour it while it could last, because to be sure, it wouldn't.

While I considered the memory, my eye roved over the hide satchel. It had torn open near the sundial laying on the earth to scatter its contents across the dirt. Curious, I forced myself up with some difficulty. A devotee of alchemy, I tried to place its now-revealed contents, but couldn't. Coloured powder was what it amounted to. Ground fine as it was, it was impossible to tell what went into it. It had no smell. There was more than one element in it from the colour--obvious it was mixed with purpose, made-medicine. The birds returned and after a moment's examination, pecked at the powder on the ground.

I shooed them away, "Don't eat that you silly things. You don't even know what it is. What if it makes you ill? Go on now. Leave be." I waved my hands around, but they paid no attention.

They were as unafraid of the powder as they were of the bread. It made me wonder if they only acted on instinct that told them to eat anything in front of them or if they actually felt it was safe. Pointless to keep flapping my hands at them since they wouldn't be dissuaded, I dropped them and kept one eye on the little birds for adverse effects. I gave them their space and walked around them in a circle to get a better look at the powder. When I reached a hand out to take a small sample, before I touched it, one of the sparrows hopped onto my index finger.

"Good lord…" I blinked in surprise. It just sat there. Tiny and gentle, it had me at its mercy and I was afraid to move. It appeared unafraid for its current position. So small and yet so brave, I was wholly fascinated. Warmed by the sun, my skin was no longer cold to the touch. The little bird settled there in comfort, head cocked to one side examining me with interest through bright, dark eyes.

"What are you up to now, little one?"

Before I had much chance to think on it, a breeze came up. Stirring-up the scents of my medicinal plants, they mixed together over top the yard and the birds. Then the wind grew stronger still. Building in time with the music wafting out the French doors, it strengthened until every leaf shook. Roaring through the branches, it became the only thing left to hear as it soon overpowered the music.

It whipped the hair back from my face and ruffled-up the feathers on the birds that didn't seem to notice. Scents from the garden swirled together creating an aromatic balm. I could pick out each plant, aware it didn't include all that grew there. It seemed by design. Even in all my experience, I had no name for the combination or to what purpose it might serve. I looked around in expectation. No question the combination was intentional, had to be, because I knew what the garden smelled like all combined on the wind. This was something else. It was a healing spell. A medicine. An offering to the gods.

The little bird on my finger cheeped at me for attention. Looking back to my little visitor, with its gaze still on mine, it stiffened and fell to the earth. I gasped in concern, "No!" and then more as each sparrow fell after its brother.

All the mystery angered me. Especially, for who would do harm to something so innocent. But before I had a chance to consider it further, right before my eyes they all vanished into the ground under them. I leaned over the spot where the sundial had stood watching them disintegrate into the nothing and struggled to understand. And then jerked back to land on my arse when a feather tore out from the same spot and almost hit me in the face. A single feather, it shot straight up high before the harsh wind snatched it away. Then another pulled out of the ground. Not caught by the draft, instead it swirled around in a circle, winding up and down over top the sundial's impression in the earth.

Clearly magical business, it was unsettling. One moment to the next, I didn't know what was going to happen and wished I never went outdoors. "This is what you get for trying to commit suicide, y'stupid git," I grumbled to the lone feather as it swirled up and down in its own undulating draft separate from the wind.

The gods had forgotten me so long ago, but this had all the earmarks of supernal interference. They had given me a gift, though, and I couldn't quibble or dissect that part. After all, who knew the minds of the gods? Even five thousand years ago, something like this wouldn't have been fodder for interpretation. We had no first person perspective that would have allowed us to make that kind of call. There were only things that were and that happened and things we witnessed to be the effects of the actions of the gods. We saw no benefit from suspended judgement or in trying to puzzle these things out and I remembered all that very well.

"Damn..."

I remembered that.

I *remembered*.

Out of the vault of my memory, something else had slipped past the blank wall of obscurity. Something important was going on here, even if I didn't understand it yet. More came to me even as I sat there dumbfounded, the curtain pulling open before the stage of my real life. In expectation, I watched the lone feather ride its own draft, spiralling up and down while the wind continued to roar around me. Gasping in shock, my heart thumped up against the inside of my chest of its own accord. Not that it hadn't beat in the past five thousand years, but I hadn't fed on anything, so it shouldn't be.

But it did.

I remembered this feeling. This whole and total bliss of unstolen, brilliant and self-contained life. I wanted to sing with the joy of it, but it was too big and could only sit mute in wonder.

Disembodied laughter came again, changed now, higher and merrier.

It wound itself around my brain and my heart, warming me from the inside-out while the morning sun warmed me from the outside-in. It was glorious and so familiar.

"...*Kurshram... hear me...*" I fixed on the feather dancing in the light. "*Kur-Shram of Nippur, temple magus... healer of men...*" My eyes closed against the wonder of it. Afraid if I looked it would be stolen from me. "*Kur-Shram, High Priest of Ninlil... Consort of She-who-brings-life... Keeper of the Eki-ur for the Lady Air, sister of our Munificent Lord, Enlil...*" It was the voice I heard in my sleep, in my dreams, in my prayers. The formal calling of myself to the presence of the goddess heard so many times in those years long past. An announcement of my position among my contemporaries and the gods and what we were to each other, it welded the past to my present mind.

It was the end of my five-thousand-year-long dream.

Laughter teased me, "Open your eyes, you silly, old thing." The scolding familiarity brought tears to my eyes. "You waited all this time and now you ignore me? What am I to do with you?"

The words came without having to reach for them, "Holy Ninlil, Lady Air. She-who-gives-life," as I gave her the respect she would always deserve. I forced my eyes open again, so afraid I was imagining it, "Your servant is here." But the second I saw her, I knew it was real.

And remembered.

"My Kurshram," she smiled. Unbound by flesh, her elemental nature shone through brighter than the sun.

I savoured the shiver that ran down my spine when my name passed her lips. "Still the sunrise in my darkness, little bird..." Choking on emotion, I couldn't get any more words out, but ate up the sight of her for all I was worth. Standing in the place her memorial had been, she was whole again, without scar or the injuries she had never deserved. Perfect in spirit, Ninlil was not quite real, but more beautiful than I could ever remember seeing her.

She quirked an insubstantial eyebrow and it was so familiar I had to laugh. "Always a man of few words, you were. Is that the best you can do after all this time?"

"Apparently." A half-smile hung off the corner of my mouth, "I warned you long ago that wasn't likely to change." In her presence only a moment, joined together once more, time stood still. Any moment with my goddess drew us toward a different place not solely in the physical world, where a moment became a year. And I basked in each one, gathering them to me with gluttonous relish. I sighed contentment, "Gods, how I've missed you, woman."

"I've always been with you, my love. Never far away. You know I could never leave you. Not wholly."

"Spying on me? Not a very goddess-like activity," and she chuckled, but too soon any levity disappeared against my sudden seriousness. "Can you ever forgive me? Is it even possible to forgive what I did in my own ignorance?" For so much more than only my gracelessness, I ached for the absolution I didn't feel I deserved.

She waved it away, "What's done is done. No forgiveness necessary. You did nothing wrong, only what you felt in that moment. What you felt was right. Just as you do what you feel is right now." She paused in sadness, "I'm afraid I have little time here, my love." As if in evidence, the form of her shimmered and winked out and back in and I ached more for knowing she spoke the truth. Without followers as she was now, there was little to hold her essence to the mortal plane. Relegated to the god plane without her earthly body, it was a wonder she was able to manifest at all. A most stubborn entity, sheer will tethered her to me a little longer and I gave thanks for her endless tenacity. Forcing a smile, she held out her hand that wasn't there, "Now take yourself out of the dirt. Let's see each other while we can."

I picked myself up and faced her. A million memories came at me in an instant--all we experienced together and apart, life in the temple, everything I ever learned--until I was dizzy with it. "Why now? So much time's gone by without my remembering any of this."

She continued to smile at me, indulgent, "Circumstances have changed. Your time in the Netherworld stole so much from you, I know. But you have something to accomplish here still." And then narrowed her eyes and frowned in reprimand, "Don't think I don't know where your mind was earlier. What you were after coming out of that cellar into the daylight, you naughty thing."

I winced.

"Have no doubt, my love, you were sent back. So you could do what needs to be done."

I squinted up at her, ashamed, "You know about that?"

"Of course. And don't let me catch you at that again. I won't have it," she scolded. "You nearly got your wish. When the opportunity presented itself? You crossed, Kurshram. You crossed and touched the spirit plane. Luckily for you, there are other forces at work here and you were returned. But you best not try that again, do you hear me? The daylight is yours to savour and you're free in that. But no more praying for death, my love. Besides, it won't help your cause."

I pushed down the guilt and considered. "Billy?"

The form of the goddess nodded, "Yes, the Namtar. I realise you've been living in ignorance all this time, but it's been your duty to keep watch. Hold the balance. It's the way things are done and I know you understand this. The world hangs in poise between forces as it always has and you, my love, have been part of it."

From my new enlightened perspective, it made even more sense. Alan discovered my movements through the world had mirrored Billy's and now I understood why. Everything was checks and balances just as I told the mosquitoes. Even in punishment, a balance grew out of its own need. This part was slower coming to me, mostly because I was afraid to believe it. But Ninlil wouldn't let me wallow in timidity.

"Your awakening, that remaking of your flesh in the temple? It was no accident, my foolish man. Despite what you might believe. Or what you read. That myth is a human interpretation of events." She waved an insubstantial, dismissive hand, "Which of them could know the true heart of the gods or the earth, hm? No, my love, it was the world itself seeking to achieve balance. Our Great Mother Nammu acted on Ki and Enki's enlightened request as she has in the past. Your reawakening turned you into a being of similarity to the demon and yet so different. Such an important place you kept all this time. Humanity is well loved by them, as you know. You always wondered over the safe haven you provided to strangers and the healing you continued to perform despite yourself. Even soulless as you were, you were compelled. Part of what achieved balance."

"But so many years."

She shrugged her filmy shoulders. "Here, perhaps, yes. Not for the pantheon." Her eyes left my face and took in the surrounding garden. "You chose well," she said after a time.

"For you. Always."

Ninlil spied the memorial knocked to the ground. "Sundial?" she quirked an eyebrow.

"Seemed appropriate," and as the full scope of what she did for me sunk in, I frowned, serious. "You brought light to my darkness yet again. Despite how it frightened the life out of you to be in it with me. That did not go unnoticed, my little bird. Even in ignorance I recognised that." My brains swirled with memories far beyond my endless nights or Billy locking her in a dark box on his ship.

The Netherworld is an even darker place I couldn't leave her to those countless years before. Her temple was a place of light and celebration in reflection of her nature. And personal protection. It was to that secure place of brightness and hope I'd fought so hard to return her. "If I had only remembered how much..." Forced by duty to follow her brother into darkness after his sentence by the gods and later sentenced there by his hand, I knew exactly how much it affected her. And why she was frightened of it. The inverse of her nature, the darkness tore her apart and would destroy her. Her realm was the sun. She had braved her deepest fear to come after me and stay with me in the dark three hundred years before. It only made me love her more. "You never gave up on me. Not even then."

Her gaze was soft toward me, "No. And never." She looked away and studied the swing with the evidence of thoughts I could never hope to know flitting across her features. A moment later, she shook them off and gestured toward the swing, "You always knew what I liked."

"I couldn't leave it behind."

"I'm glad. Good memories…" And then focussed her attention back on me. "But there are more important things for you to remember now. Are you ready?"

"No," I laughed in futility.

"Silly man. No matter, it should keep you on your toes the way you need to be. Now take those wretched things off your face and let me see your eyes before I go."

I pulled the sunglasses off and winced as the sunlight hit me full on. "Better?"

"Hm…" She stared at me hard and then nodded. "Yes, better. I see you in there now. All right, you can keep them. No need to suffer. You've done quite enough sacrificing for me for one lifetime. That time is also done. As I said, circumstances have changed." With relief, I covered my eyes. "So, how do you feel?"

"I remember things now," I shrugged. "I feel--" I really had no answer and floundered for words.

She made an exasperated noise, "Your heart beats. You have memory. You feel the *life*, don't you?"

It was in me, but I was afraid to acknowledge it. "Yes. Definitely. But does it mean..?"

"You touched the spirit plane before you returned, my love. As it happened, what you meant as a way out was turned to another purpose. I'd like to tell you it's made you back into a man, I know how you've craved it. But that wouldn't be entirely accurate, I'm afraid."

My brow furrowed, "Almost a man, then?"

"More than a simple man, my love. *More*," she willed me to understand.

I put an uncertain hand to my chest, but I felt as real as I always had. Nothing seemed to have changed. "More?"

"Yes, more!" she threw up her hands in exasperation. "To keep balance against the demon, you couldn't be simply human. It would never be enough. And you've been traded for with Ereshkigal. The reason the unknowing has left you."

I'd been deliberate in ignoring the reason for the memories, because I knew what it meant. "But that was my sacrifice."

"Yes, it was. You set me free. The greatest gift you could have given and I know the cost. But your time of sacrificing for me is over. Your spirit is free again and yours to cherish. It's what you gained when you touched the spirit plane."

"Who would..? Not you, lamb." Concern thinned my voice out to a whisper, "Tell me you didn't."

"No, not me," her laughter rang out around the garden. "I wouldn't be here now if I had." She caught the stricken look on my face and continued with sincerity, "The Namtar escaped from where you imprisoned him. As often happens when the world seeks balance, the situation arose for a spirit to step forward. Another made the offer and struck the bargain of their own free will. The only way it could have come to pass. A substitute of equal character." She sobered and I knew it was out of respect. "Before he died, he was quite serious when he urged you to see justice done. You swore it to him on the deck of that ship."

I felt the cold of his palm against mine in memory. "Nigel."

"Yes, noble soul that he is. He sends his regards."

"Good lord…"

"He helped me then, and he offers his support now."

"Nigel took my place." Only a man, and yet far from ordinary. His uncommon valour in the face of events so much larger than himself would never be forgotten. "He doesn't even know me. I knew him a single moment in time."

"But he knows me and knows what it means for the world. Besides, it's already done and nothing you need to worry over. In all seriousness, he was happy to do it. Eager even. His contribution, he said."

The magnitude of retribution to come could border on galactic and it would never be enough. No doubt Nigel would agree if he were there to ask. His sacrifice would lend his arm to mine when the time came and I sent him up my silent thanks.

I had some doubts, though. Personal doubts in my ability to go beyond revenge and do the job Ninlil said I had ahead of me. Because this was about much more than only payback. I used to consider Billy my equal and never gave it a second thought. Now in full possession of the humanity I had craved forever, despite it being in addition to whatever else I was, I worried it would put me at a disadvantage.

"*Stop.*" Her voice cut into my self-doubt and swept it away with an exasperated snort. "Five seconds of humanity and I see a thousand brands of uncertainty behind your eyes. Who are you?"

I looked at my feet and scratched the back of my head in discomfort, "Sorry."

"Knock it off, Kurshram."

I smiled at the unconscious shiver creeping over the back of my neck, "Yes, lamb." Damn, but I loved when she said my name, my *real* name. It was heaven.

"Were you listening at all?" She sighed and her voice softened, "Not only human, my love. More. More than enough to perform your duty. A gift from my Lord Brother himself. You quite impressed him, you know. And you know he's not easily impressed."

I was gobsmacked. And then instantly suspicious. Our last interaction ended a universe away from doing favours for one another.

"For your heart and care, he's raised you to the pantheon," there was joy in her voice. "Low in the household, mind you, but still. Enough to equal the Namtar's creation. Somewhat as you were, but done with purpose. To achieve the balance. Do you understand what I'm telling you? Rarely does he intercede this way. My love, he's made you one of the lesser gods now. When this business is done, you have Enlil's blessing to join us in the palace of Father An. The Bull of Heaven, remember? We can be together there." She gave me a demure look, "If I still please you, of course. What you do is by your own choice. As it always was."

My mouth opened, but no words came out and it only made her laugh.

"Still so eloquent after all these years. Must be why I fell hopelessly in love with you." She reached out an insubstantial hand toward my mouth in that same curious way she did for as long as I'd known her. But not in defiance of my perceived curse as I believed in unknowing. Instead, long years in the past it was brought on by my usual lack of verbal expression. A joke, to verify I still had a mouth. It meant nothing and everything, because it was something she always did. She couldn't touch me now, though, and her spirit hand grazed my mouth with no more weight than the feather she arrived on. It was the hardest moment.

The wind in the yard stopped with such sudden decision the silence deafened. She dropped her arm and looked away, appearing to listen. The presence of the Lord Air grew all around us, "My Lord Brother calls."

Being his sister's consort meant nothing to him and had never afforded me special consideration. Usually, the opposite. Master of us all, though, I dropped to a knee and bowed respect as I was required to, still contemplating my brother-in-law's sudden change of heart.

Ninlil inclined her head. "Yes, brother. As you wish."

I never heard Enlil speak myself and likely never would. Impressed he may be, but I would always be too far beneath him for direct address. Still, I was more than grateful for my gift. His presence was gone in a blink for which I was even more grateful. I loved his sister, but when your intended's sibling has no conscience and the power of all heaven and earth and time and space at his disposal, it makes a man nervous.

She sighed, "My time is done, Kurshram, so listen to me. Of all the pantheon, you and the Namtar are all that remain in flesh. It's your duty to curb him. You're his watchman and the only one left able to put him in his place. He would make himself a god and it can't be allowed. That darkness should never overshadow the light in the world. Unchecked, he would destroy the earth."

"He already believes himself a god." I thought back. "We had a rather revealing chat when I last caught up to him. Even if I didn't seek to see justice done for myself, I know what he's after and know it can't be allowed. He's even more powerful now. And building an army. An army like himself. He told me, bragged about it. He's not right, little bird. A demon in a man's form in the modern world? People have no protection from these things. No understanding of what it means."

"A mistake, I'm afraid," she sighed. "In a moment of anger, my brother didn't give much thought to the continuing consequences of that action. Only the swift and exacting punishment. But it's time to rectify that. In this, he gives you leave to attend to it alone. May seem like a punishment, I know, but it's meant in gift. An honour. You were the sacrifice for my return, after all. And then the demon later took it upon himself to anger my brother further with my murder. It's your duty to avenge it for him on behalf of the entire pantheon." She lowered her eyes and her voice, "My heart belongs to you, Kurshram. Your duty, should you wish so, I would ask you make also for me."

"I accept." I nodded with confidence while I ate up the look of her one last time. "But you've never had to ask me for that. My duty has always been for you. The same as my heart."

"Live, my love. I would hate to be without you again."

"You can't be rid of me so easily."

"I know… too crabby to die..," laughter followed her as she faded from sight. Too soon, but I had a lot of work to do.

"I've missed you, little bird." It was a trite thing to call after her, but there was really nothing beyond it.

"Do well and you won't have to any longer…" She winked right out and the little sparrow feather fluttered to the earth and lay still.

I picked it up and held it tight in my closed fist, allowing her fading essence to seep into my palm.

*****

I sprawled in my wing chair facing the back garden with Mozart filling up the air as the sun went down. In no way was I ready to go back underground. Not yet. Sundown was a pleasure I certainly wasn't about to deny myself. My head was so full, I didn't think I was capable of conversation with the 'Bites, anyway. They wanted a full report, of course, and I wouldn't deny them. There was time for it, not a lot, but enough, and I would fulfill that promise to them in addition to my others.

Sunset was brilliant and even where the trees obscured it, it lost nothing in its splendour. Everything shimmered with refracted light. Everything became its own unique *objet d'art* to consider for the fullness of itself. Hypnotic, I let myself grow lost in it. Especially, in the sacred transformation, the changing of the guard. When Nanna set out in his reed gufa boat across the heavens to bring light to the pitch-dark lapis lazuli sky and allowed Utu the evening's respite.

It was magic, the oldest magic of all. Gods working in tandem. And I gave it the full benefit of my witness for the singular wonder it was.

In this gift of my newest rebirth, everything became new to me again. So much of it was good and wondrous and celebratory. And then some darker than anyone alive could know while it cut me deep in its deliberate hurts. That I laid eyes on my Ninlil again and knew her was the most exquisite agony of all. I knew my purpose now, but couldn't help I wished it all away for a single moment more in her presence. It had been so brief, too brief, but then it always was with her.

I loved her madly, wholly, right down to the soul and the only way fitting to love a goddess of her stature, I suppose. I always had. If she still pleased me..? Even in unknowing it was the same. Yes, she still pleased me. Bloody right she did. Five thousand years later was the same as the first day and the distance of time dulled nothing. Whatever needed doing would be accomplished if only for one second of her back again.

Not long after the sun slid down past the trees, the blood bank crew tramped out of the cellar for the night. They came at a run. In concern I knew, because I turned off my mobile when I was in the garden. I didn't want anything breaking the spell that still held me until the last possible second. Lost in the gathering darkness, *Don Giovanni* thundered around me while they piled into the room. And then pulled up short inside the entryway. I felt their eyes on the high back of my chair and their sudden hesitation.

The music crashed so loudly it made conversation impossible. I let it buy me an extra moment of solitude before I stuck my hand over my head and shut it off with the remote.

"I turned off my mobile." No one said a word, so I spoke to the open door in front of me, instead, "The sunlight was... exquisite. And extraordinary. I don't have words to describe it, I'm afraid. Nothing could do it justice. The garden, the forest, the air... all so alive in daylight. I'd quite forgotten. I danced to music. Fed sparrows. Oh yes, and played with some manner of ghostly wolf or other, if you can imagine that. Quite an interesting day all tolled."

Fear eclipsed their curiosity. I could feel it, but they had no reason to be afraid of me. I didn't want that, not from them. I peeked around the side of the chair, "What? No twenty questions? Who the hell are you and what have you done with those myth-hunting little bloods who make a career out of annoying the holy piss out of me?" Awe on their faces, they wouldn't come any farther into the room. After a strained minute, I hauled myself out of my chair and put an end to it.

"All right, that's it. Get your arses in here." Used to my ordering them about, they responded without wanting to and piled in, pushing Alan ahead of them. I huffed, "That's more like it."

The girls had made a habit of hovering over me, but even they didn't brave approaching me yet. Suki broke the silence, "How is this possible?"

Of course, they could feel the difference in me. The life and more. I regarded her from under my eyebrows, "You could say I was given the, ah, official, stamped approval to kick Billy's arse."

The most knowledgeable in it and closer to me and what I was about, "Holy shit," Baby Bite caught on it straight away.

I quirked a smile, "Yes, that would be the official title," and wandered out the French doors to stand on the porch with my hands hooked into my back pockets. I spoke over my shoulder, "What a difference a day makes."

Curiosity now caught, Alan was right behind me, "Nice shades, old man."

I forgot I still had them on and laughed, "What are you? My fashion consultant?" And pulled them off. "Told you I was about blind there. They did the job."

"Whoa, man, check it out. Well, shit, now you have to tell us what happened."

"Come again?"

"Your eyes."

"What are you talking about?"

He stared at me hard. "They used to be dark, almost black."

I darted a look from one face to the other. "*Used* to?"

They all nodded their heads at me.

"Freaky," Baby Bite chuckled, shooting me one more peculiar glance and then let it go. Curious, I made a mental note to check on that myself when time allowed. But in the face of so many more immediate things, I also let it go.

Hamish pointed to the overturned sundial, "Can we ask?" I hadn't set it back upright. It would erase the space where she stood and I wasn't ready to do without that yet. Not just yet. It reminded me it hadn't been all in my head.

I leaned against the railing to face them and crossed my arms, "Go on."

"Was it her?" Suki's voice was gentle.

Despite myself, my smile was self-conscious, "Yes, she was here."

"*Zamechatel'no!*" Natasha clasped her hands over her heart, "Oh, how wonderful!"

"You remember now, don't you." It was a statement.

Uncrossing my arms, I stuck out my hand and spoke to Alan, "I don't think we've been properly introduced. Kurshram. High priest and consort of the Lady Air, Ninlil. Out of Nippur, Sumer. Now-extinct. Pleasure to make your acquaintance."

The hand he took was warm. "Bitchin'," Baby Bite stared at it in examination. And then frowned, but didn't look up. "You're going after Billy now, aren't you?"

"Yes. My job."

"Then I better tell you."

I took my hand back and recrossed my arms, "I don't like the sound of this already." No one was talking. "Okay, kids, tell Dad what's wrong."

"It's Billy. We were tracking him."

"And?"

"He's here."

"Details, please, Alan. In the house?"

"Ontario." He hesitated. "About five hundred kilometres from here."

The growl was involuntary and he took a step back, "Look, I only just found out when I got up. I swear. I loaded everything we found into the computer and went to sleep while it ran some probable triangulations. I found it when I woke up. There was only one. He's already here."

"Bloody hell."

"Near as I can figure, he set up shop last year."

"Fabulous."

Alan stared at his shoes. "I don't know how he got here ahead of us. I mean, we were all working on it. We should have figured that out right away."

"Fuck." I scrubbed my hands over my face and then dropped them and took a breath. "I have to ask. Do you think you were followed?"

"No!" the answer shot out of him. "No, never. We were careful. I promise."

My back stiffened. Arms akimbo, the potential danger to all of them made my voice harsher than it needed to be, "That doesn't mean anything and you know it, Alan. Not where he's concerned. Good lord, he might have been creeping around here already. Shit!"

"But--"

"I'm not ready yet. Not yet." I barked a hard laugh, "Likely also holding him up. Well, if it's revenge he's after, and that's got to be obvious even to you, he'll want to make it permanent. He's out for blood, little man. Fucking hell."

I turned away from them and lost myself in the garden as I gathered resolve. "Well, so am I."

*****

Hours later, I sat alone on the swing in the garden. It seemed empty now without Ninlil's laughter, so I was glad for the distraction of work with purpose. I was remembering the old days, working to recall old things that would help me. A few of the medicinal journals I kept were open on my lap and spread about next to me. Sadly, they were woefully thin in demon-banishing spells. Too many years playing medic left me out of practice in most anything more elevated than lancing boils or curing fevers.

"Bugger."

Ever try to remember something you trained for, could do without even thinking, and then find it gone the next time you needed it? Yeah. I was giving myself a headache fighting to pull it out of the back of my brain.

In my temple days, I wasn't only a healer--Alan only scratched the surface and there was much more to it than that. During that time, we approached medicine from a very practical and whole person perspective. Holistically, body and soul. And due to that particular view of health, two specialised varieties of doctor evolved.

In the day-to-day, there were *asuu*, physicians who mixed pharmaceuticals. The poultices they created were still surprisingly valid and effective in the modern world. And then there were the sorcerer-priests who worked in concert with them. Similar to Brahmins who appeared later or ancient Druids who developed far from us during the same time, it was a specialised, honoured position of the highest status. Called on to determine correct diagnoses, they did so through consideration of the spirit and outside influences or energies on it that might affect the flesh. For something with a physical cause and curable by an *asuu*, they would then often hand off the case when appropriate.

More toward the mystic, like all shaman, the sorcerer-priests would preside over circumstances beyond the physical. Imbalance or spells or even the displeasure of the gods could cause illness so as those closest to the gods and the balance of energy, it was up to them to determine which of these causes affected someone and then right it. They could heal, as well, of course, and crossed disciplines, as did the *asuu* who occasionally cast their own spells. The many years of study required to learn the scientific magic of that complex discipline, however, to grow in tune with the energy of the god plane to determine accurate diagnoses made them revered in their communities and a position difficult to attain.

This was what I had been. An *aszipu*, a sorcerer-priest.

We took an objective worldview, dealing in the tangible and the cause-and-effect of things. Though a modern person might consider it hocus-pocus, the alchemy and pharmacology we practised worked and we didn't subject it to interpretation. That it worked was all that mattered and it was a serious business. Accomplished through a combination of resonating chants, spoken spells, simple antiseptics, and by mixing various elements together in harmony to align the spirit--aroma therapy for the soul, you could say--we could right any imbalance.

Including demons.

From my now-modern perspective, I could analyse it for what it had been and found much of it still valid. If I could remember it all and combine it with my other knowledge learned over time.

Another hour went by while I struggled with combinations of spells before I closed my books. The more I worked at it, the more came back to me and I had some idea what I was doing now. In the abstract, at least. For something this persistent and complex, back in the day I would have consulted another priest to check my thinking. Still out of practice, I didn't yet trust myself for something simple let alone this. But I had no one to ask. And then I had an idea and pulled out my mobile.

"Hel--?"

"I need a medical consult."

"What..? *Hello*? Shit, man, it's a simple thing, y'know. I answer the phone and you say h-e-l-l-o."

"Fine," I growled. "Good day. Hullo. *Salut*! *Hôla*! Kiss my arse. Now *damare*! Shut the fuck up and listen."

"Nice to see godhood hasn't adversely affected your personality any."

"Baby Bite--"

"Okay-okay. Whaddaya need? Talk to me."

"I need to talk this out with someone who understands this sort of thing. Another perspective. I've been working on spell combinations, but I'm not kidding myself, I'm rusty. I need someone to bounce ideas off."

"Well, what kind of person we talkin' about here, old man? Like a witch or a Wiccan or something? Dunno anyone like that. Not my area."

"No, not some fucking kitchen-witch, you twit. Not curing a sore throat here. An alchemist. A sacred spell caster. A Druid would be good. Someone along those lines."

"Man," Alan laughed, "you check the year you woke up in this morning? I dunno any potion mixing wizards and if you want a real live practising Druid who still knows the stuff you need? You're gonna hafta time-travel back about three thousand years."

"Shit."

"Why don't you tell me what you need from them and I'll see if I can think of a modern equivalent. There's gotta be someone around."

"Well, what I really need is someone like me, what I consider a priest, you know? Not the kind with a collar. I need to discuss balancing energy, so someone who's in tune with the spirit world. Knows the interaction between body and soul and the outside forces affecting it. How to manipulate it to some degree with mixed medicine, meditations, combinations of phrasing. What we called spells. Get what I mean?"

"Maybe. Sounds like a voodoo witch doctor. Hey, what about a Chinese apothecary?"

"Hmmm... possibly. Know any close by?"

"Sorry, Kurshram."

There was a foul word on the tip of my tongue and then I tripped over it. It was odd hearing him say my name and I wasn't used to it. I laughed at myself and tried not to let it distract me. "Anyone else come to mind?"

"Thinking." I heard the blood bank crew babbling in the background.

"Hang tight one. Lemme ask my posse."

I ground my teeth and waited through the bull session. Keyboard clatter erupted in fits and starts and then Alan came back on the line.

"Well?"

"A medicine man."

"Alan, I don't need a medic with a bag of herbs here. This is a bit more complex."

"No, not *that* kind. The other kind. A native holy man. Deals in medicine *and* mysticism. Gods and energies just part of the fabric of life, right? Would probably be your best bet."

"Hmmm, sounds about right. So, do we know any?"

"No."

"Well, hell's bloody bells, why the fuck did you--"

"*Wait* before you get your panties in a bunch. No, we don't know one personally, but I know *of* one around here."

"Fine."

"There's this legend."

"For the love of-- Do you deal in anything concrete?"

"I found *you*, Mister Blood Runner, didn't I? Gimme some credit, will ya?"

"Fair play. Just give me the Reader's Digest Condensed version."

"Not much to tell. Actually, it's more of a rumour circulating through the local bloods. Considering you're 'just a guy', there could be something to this one, too, right?"

"I suppose."

"I heard an Algonquin shaman was turned to the dark side by someone who thought they had a sense of humour. Very uncool."

"Who the hell would..? Oh, never mind. Can you find them?"

"You doubt me?"

I growled.

"All right, all right. At least, they wouldn't be afraid to talk to us, right? Would def be easier to explain the situation."

"Well, that would certainly be convenient *if* you could track them down or *if* they even really exist. You'll have to excuse me if I don't hold my breath just yet."

"I know, I hear ya. I'll get to work on it and call you back."

It was almost dawn before I heard from him again. Baby Bite sounded tired, "Sorry, old man. Just spent the past few hours messaging an army of blood geeks. Turns out the shaman thing was a joke. Totally bogus. Dunno what else to tell ya." The disappointment was evident in his voice and while a setback, I still appreciated the effort.

"Right, well, that would've been too perfect, yeah? I'm not fussed about it. I'll manage." He didn't respond and I could feel his sense of failure through the open line. "Alan, it's all right. Not all the myths can be real or as exciting as me, eh? And besides, I'm a bloody god now. Perhaps, I've some superpowers I don't know about yet." I tried to lighten him up, but he wouldn't go for it. "I really should be putting it together on my own anyway, so no harm done. Honestly."

His mood was dark and I knew it was only because he hated to disappoint me. But I wasn't disappointed in him, not in the least, and as we spoke, my thinking already changed gears. "Alan?" It was almost morning and I knew he needed to rest. He felt compelled to stay up with me, though, and I could feel him there underground struggling against the invisible hand that drew him into sleep. "Quit obsessing. It's not your job to sort me out. Truly. It's my fight, yeah? You're not responsible, little man."

"Yes, I am," his voice was small. "I led him right to you. I know I did. We were major careful, but you and I both know that's how he got here. Why he came. We left ahead of him and, you know, kept coming back here searching for you. I showed him the way and I can't even give you anything to help you." He gave a deprecatory laugh, "Shit, I just didn't think. You weren't supposed to be real. Didn't know you'd be so--" he caught himself and didn't finish the thought.

"Come on, Baby Bite. Leave off."

"No, it's my fault. And even worse? I fucked myself. I fucked us all. Royally. When he comes and finds me here? He's gonna know you know everything I know about him. And then he's gonna take me out."

A long silence spun out between us. I started back into the house with the mobile at my ear, "Where are you?"

"Why? You gonna kill me first? Guess I wouldn't mind that so much. Better by a friend."

I was already on my way down the stairs, "Oh, for heaven's sake, would you quit." I slipped through the panel behind the shelves. "Possibly for being a giant pain in my arse, but not for not being able to produce someone who doesn't exist. Answer the fucking question."

"I'm downstairs. What does it matter?"

"In your computer room?" Phasing out as I went for speed, I let go of the here enough to move with the gloom, half off the earth plane. One of my new old god tricks, I no longer needed to connect with Ninlil to accomplish it as I had in the old days.

"Just do what you need to do, Kurshram, okay? You don't have to come down here. I'll just--" his words dried up when I appeared in the doorway with the phone still at my ear. I put it away and looked him in the eye.

"I won't let him kill you."

I let Myles go and he lost his life when I wouldn't do anything to prevent it. Billy took my child when I failed to protect Maggie. I wasn't about to lose another one. Alan was mine to protect. They all were.

He opened his mouth to say something and then snapped it shut again. The rest of the Blood Runner Hunters looked on in concern, not sure what was going on.

"Don't you think you might have found me for another reason, little man? Maybe this was the time for this to happen. You're part of it, yes. To set the stage for me, let's say. Give me a proper kick in the complacent arse even. No," I pointed a warning finger at the parry he didn't get out, "*no*, don't bother trying to analyse it. Sometimes? Things simply are. Everything happens for a reason. Now is the time and it was always my job. Always. You didn't do anything wrong, Alan. You're only along for the ride."

"You can't know that. I made him come here. How can you let me off the hook for that?"

"I just did, so shut the fuck up about it. C'mere, shit-for-brains." Alan didn't move. I growled and caught him before he could blink again and spoke right in his ear while he tried to get loose, "I won't let him kill you, Alan. That I promise you." Billy terrified him on a good day and I knew it. He felt responsible for bringing that same threat to us all and the guilt was a heavy burden on his too young conscience. I wouldn't let him claim that responsibility.

Because it was mine.

"Don't you know you're important to me? Family, remember? Bloody hell, don't make me get all sappy on you and say it, you little shit." I cuffed him up the back of his head with an arm still clamped around his back and laughing, he sagged against me in relief and acceptance. He was sniffling, but I didn't bust his chops over it, "Yeah, what you said."

"I'm sorry, Kurshram. I really am."

"Stop. No more, okay? It's done. Time for me to get to work. You lot already did your part. Understood?" He didn't respond, so I poked him hard in the ribs, "You hearin' me, boy?"

"*Ow*! Yes, sir, Mister Blood Runner, sir." He pounded me on the back with affection. "Okay, Dad."

For once, I let it pass, because I suppose I was. I set him out away from me and barked at the rest of them, but it was with warmth. "What are you gawking at? Get to sleep. Trust me, you'll need the rest. We've a trap to set."

*****

During the day, I busied myself with the things they couldn't do. Alan had given me an idea. The Blood Runner turned out to be 'just a guy', so I decided it was time for that mythical character to make an appearance. When Billy called me out, he was only playing his own part in it even if he didn't realise. And when the mosquito crew showed up it was a message to me. So now?

I would send one of my own.

If we did it right, the rumour would spread that Maggie's witch had engaged the services of the Blood Runner to seek his revenge. With any luck, the Blood Runner-made-flesh would rattle him some and whatever kept him off-balance was worth the effort.

Billy, the Namtar, Ninlil called him, was close-by already. A home court advantage didn't seem a bad idea to me, either, so if this was where it had to happen then so be it. If he hadn't already been casing the place, I would bring him to me and then I would make it be over.

With my bag heavy against my hip, I walked my land in the rising sun and surveyed what I had to work with. It was a big area, but would give me room to manoeuvre and maybe the house wouldn't be destroyed.

"What's one more, eh, old sod?" I laughed into the forest without regret. Wouldn't be the first house I lost, of course, although it would be the last and that only made it memorable. If it didn't survive, the 'Bites would have all of the underground to occupy later and that's all that mattered. It was a good place for them, separated from the modern world, and would keep them isolated from the fight. Better for safety all around.

Up on the high ridge, I went up past the windmills and hunkered down right on the crest. Perched on the backbone of the land, the sun warmed my shoulders as I grew still. There were sunglasses over my eyes now, but I'd done the same thing a thousand times in the past, put myself up high and close to the gods to meditate.

When I lured Billy here and he set his first step on the land, I wanted the resonance to scare the piss right out of him. He was still in unknowing, but the result would reach him. Since I had the surprise of radiating life now rather than death, I would use it all to my advantage.

He wouldn't even know it was me until the last moment.

I slung the medicine bag off from around my neck. Pulling out a handful of pure Frankincense ground down to fine powder, I spun on my heel to trickle it around me in a wide arch right on the rock. This one was for the gods and would begin to clear the land in preparation for what I was about to do.

Back home on a different continent, my technique would be different, but here, I drew it out anti-clockwise to work with the energy of this land. There were no absolutes in what I knew. Everything was dependent on the circumstance and the area, which was why it was so difficult to learn. And why, I suppose, mine along with other disciplines of similar varieties died out. No one would spend the time required in the study of it. But it was here I had a definite advantage. Studying every discipline during the long years I was awake, I discovered their common elements. Melding them together into a wide-sweeping, combined discipline, I could make medicine from a variety of perspectives and a good thing, too.

Because it would take them all to disperse a demon created by the Most High.

I looked heavenward, toward my Ninlil. "Is this why this couldn't happen until now, lamb? Not until I gained the knowledge. Because that's what it would take?" suddenly quite certain this was a large part of it. As I said, everything happens for a reason even if this wasn't the original one.

I built a little pile of tinder outside the circle and lit it off a wooden match. The sulphur from the match head would foul the spell if I lit the incense with it, so I caught a taper and touched it with that instead, and then let it smoke. Resting in the centre with my eyes closed in reverence, its haunting fragrance washed over me and the land in smoke cleaning consecration. I didn't rush it. Woody, spicy and with a hint of lemon over top, I inhaled it deep and let it calm me on the innermost level as it worked the same magic on the land. Bringing stillness and inviting the goodwill of the gods.

Once the smoke dispersed in the wind, I made another circle over top the first. This one to keep negative forces out of the same area. I laid down small, dried twists of white sage from my garden. One large bundle tied with cotton string would have done the trick, but I was going for a specific purpose here at the top of the ridge. Along with cleansing and setting up charms to disperse all things demon dark, I was making myself a conduit to the other plane. In the absence of a temple, this prayer circle was a temporary holy place that could have several uses. I could step into it for protection and sanctuary or to cleanse myself if Billy tried to take a bite out of me. None of which I hoped to need. But there could be other uses I flirted with, though didn't have quite worked out yet. I wasn't concerned. They would come to me if it were correct for the circumstance.

Once I smoked the sage out over top the lingering Frankincense to create the second layer of the charm, I held my now-meditative state and went on a hike. Mentally feeling for the edges of the underground labyrinth, a braid of Sweetgrass tied to a tree trunk at each of the four corners marked a secure perimeter. Inviting good energy while clearing the negative, it offered spiritual protection and made certain no outside influences were trapped inside. Plus, it gave me a sight line to work with in mind, so I could build a Ward spell to keep all the little 'Bites safe inside it. Walking the border let me see the lines. Then I stood in the trees outside it to follow it in mind while I built up the spell.

It was a simple spell, simple and ancient magic, and always effective. Using the balance of light and dark energy allowed me to create a keep-safe box around whatever needed to be kept safe. Starting at one corner, I called it Black and allowed the polarity of blackness to build up there with strong intent. As it grew, I assigned it to ward off anything unwanted in that corner. Then turning my mind toward the next corner, I declared it White. Moving my intention of protection in that direction, I dragged it around that corner while directing its polarity. Naming the third corner Black and the fourth White, I continued drawing my protective intentions along the perimeter and then closed the box in my mind's eye back at the point I began. Not good enough to leave it lay only on the ground, in my light trance, I envisioned the walls of the box descending into the earth to protect everything below ground where the labyrinth sat.

When I was satisfied it went deep enough, I crumbled some dried Mandrake root on a half shell and burned it. Offering the smoke to the four corners to honour the spirits of that place, at the same time it added more protection and enhanced the protective spell. And then I waited for the sign. In this type of spell, it wasn't only the skill of the spell-caster but the co-operation of the earth that made it work and that took listening and trust. A conduit for whatever existing spirit there would manifest, I waited in patience to receive the image of the volunteer guardian. It could be anything and whatever came to mind was always correct. It wasn't long before I saw the owl in mind and knew it was a right and fitting guardian over my family of night dwellers. With my thanks to Mother Earth and my volunteer guardian, I allowed the spirit image to cover the entire area. Trusting it would keep them safe, I walked away and moved my concentration on to my next task.

Climbing back up the ridge, I continued building my prayer circle. Since I did most of my meditating for a couple of centuries where the herbs grew, the garden would have been a stronger position to work from, but it wasn't high or remote enough for my purposes. It had to be somewhere less obvious. And then I knew why.

To trap him inside.

Working toward that end, I marked the rock with sacred signs in charcoal on my way up and infused them with my intention. When I reached the crest, for a third time I turned myself anti-clockwise to trickle an incense circle. This time, a blend of Frankincense, Sandalwood and Myrrh for further blessing and consecration of the ground. I added some crushed charcoal for more purity and cleansing for good measure. Good for wisdom and knowledge and touching the spirit plane not to mention increasing the strength of spells, I figured none of that could be a bad thing.

If it helped me remember more, that could only be to my benefit. If it built a prison with a direct line to the ethereal and dispersion, so much the better. The spot already well-sanctified, this time, I knelt with my forehead touching the rock in reverence. Smoke wafted over me and I breathed it while the rest rose as an offering to the gods. As I dedicated the space to my purpose, the charged energy around me resonated soundly in accord.

By the time the breeze carried off the smoke, day was nearly over, but I was satisfied. It was a good beginning. I only wished I knew how much time I had left to prepare. I could work on the fly, of course, but whatever I could do ahead of Billy's arrival would be to my advantage. For the moment, though, the Blood Runner Hunters would soon be awake, so I packed it in. With a final prayer to the patron god of sorcerer-priests, Enki, and one more for my Ninlil, I brought myself back out of extended focus. Leaving my new holy place, I aligned myself with the world again as I wandered down the slope in the slant of the setting sun.

Along the way back to the house, I deposited several muslin packets of various healing herbs for further protection around the general area. While they wouldn't cover every inch in an actual spell, they would help attract positive energy. Like attracts like, so with the newly cleansed and consecrated holy place up on the ridge powering them, it would change the atmosphere of the land. When Billy arrived, he would feel it and he would hate it, because it would resist the demon of him. Knowing it would rein-in what he could do gave me impetus. I would add more varieties to shackle him from other angles if I was allowed the time.

Before the young bloods invaded my peace, I hurried to replenish my bag. I ran my hands over the herbs hanging to dry above the fresh potted plants growing in the solarium attached to the back porch. At least, that's what I called it, but it wasn't as grand as all that. Just a glassed-in part of the porch where I grew warm climate plants for medicines and where I hung my herbs to dry in the daytime sun. It was a good system. The room warmed well and had served me many decades. While I debated over what other charms to use, I ground up some High John. This first charm was for me.

High John has a lot of uses, but I would take advantage of its ability to promote success and conquer any situation since that's exactly what I needed. Because I *would* conquer this one. I tipped it into a white flannel drawstring bag and then some cut Mandrake root after it. Used in exorcisms to drive out demons, it would also enhance my ability to make magic. A wise precaution given the uncertainty of what I would encounter. I hoped it would loosen the Namtar's grip on the world every time he came near me. After a moment's consideration, a little Devil's Shoestring and Dragon's Blood rounded out the protective charm. Satisfied the white pouch wrapped it up in my positive intention to ward off evil and harm, I tied the bag shut and shoved it in my pocket. When it all hit the fan, there would be no time to find it later. Some smaller pouch charms of only Mandrake root to scatter about later would work at sapping Billy's hold on the earth. And hopefully weaken him.

Everything I wove into coordination around the property would help pry him out of the world, but the plan was fluid and grew as I worked at it. Weaken him, frighten him, make him doubt himself… Cleanse the demon by sending him into the beyond from where he wouldn't hurt anyone ever again. Seemed simple enough, though these things rarely are.

With the holy circle built and waiting, while I didn't know if it would hold him as he was, by the end of the day I was leaning in that direction. Strengthening it during as many days as I was allowed was probably the best use of my energy. Perhaps, something more would come to me later, but I needed a break. The sun disappeared long before I finished with the charms and I forced myself to stop and check on the little bloods.

The 'Hunters were subdued when I found them swimming rather than at their computers. Tied to their electronic gadgets, the first thing they did every day was check social media, play a game and then go hunting in varying order depending on their mood. This was certainly different. They seemed fine, felt fine, but it made me wonder.

"I had no idea they waterproofed World of Warcraft."

"*Privet*! Hello, Kurshram," Natasha waved from the deep end as I raised my hand to all of them.

"Hey, Dad," Baby Bite sat on the edge of the pool, grinning.

"Watch it, little man."

"You love it."

"Sod off," it was good to play with him again for as long as that could last. "So? What's this? Did all your computers crash or has the Internet become obsolete?" Michelangelo slapped a handful of water in my direction, but I was too quick for him. "Keep practising, little boy."

"Yeah-yeah."

They were in good spirits and it made me happy to see them that way. I was used to the way they were, on the surface carefree, but thrumming underneath with anxious intensity. I felt none of that from them this evening. Over the hours since Ninlil manifested, I continued to change and grow more aware and could now see them in a different light. A condition, I assumed, of my newly bestowed godhood.

In the same way I saw everything outside, a visible aura surrounded each of them. They weren't alive, not like the things in the garden, but they were animate with their own version of life. Something I hadn't had the ability to know until now. More than only surrounded by serenity, they projected it into a tangible radiance. It appeared as a blue-white mist that crept about and between them and I knew it was a good thing.

"Mind letting us in on it?"

I blinked and focussed on Hamish, "Sorry?" It crept all over him and I was amazed he didn't seem to notice.

"What are you smiling at?" All aglow, Suki pulled herself up out of the water near my feet. "You were going to say something and then stopped."

"Did I?"

"*Da*," Natasha giggled. "*Chto ty delayesh*? What do you?"

Suki was also laughing at me with indulgence, "Kurshram, you've been standing there five minutes grinning to yourself. What's going on?"

I lost time and didn't know it. The blink of an eye or a thousand years, I was in touch with the gods' time now. I'd have to make a conscious effort to stay in touch with the Now. I waved their laughter away, "Sorry. I'm just glad to see everyone so happy." But I was thinking about their energy. "Do you lot feel all right tonight?"

"Are *you* all right, old man?" Baby Bite dived in and surfaced alongside Suki. "You're not having some weird Netherworldly breakdown we should be worried about, are you?"

"Smartyarse."

"Always."

"Too bad I don't have a spell for *that*," I glowered at him in fun.

"Is that what you did today? Worked on spells?" He pulled himself out and grabbed a towel. "You said something about setting a trap."

In a blink, my evening plan changed and I knew what I needed them to do. Without considering it further, I knew it would work. Ignoring the glow, I put my head back in the game, "That's right. I laid the groundwork for it already."

"A little more complicated than shaking a rattle at him, I take it?"

"Just a tad. But you needn't worry yourselves over that bit. That's my job. I have one for you, though." I glanced at them one-by-one. "You're going to bait him for me."

Dom cleared his throat, "Um, did you say *bait*?" He looked concerned, "Not to sound like we don't want to help or anything, but I really don't wanna be anywhere near that fucker."

"No, no need to see him. What I'm really after is for you to start a rumour. You know," I wiggled my fingers in the air, "with that messaging malarkey you were on about the other night."

"Phew!"

Alan perked up, "How do you want it to play?"

My smile was wicked, "Blood Runner lives."

"Hot damn," he pulled on clothes fast.

"I assume Billy knows your hobby, yeah? So announce you found him. Tell everyone you can get a hold of. Everyone. I want it to reach him quickly."

"Done."

"*And*," I continued to explain on the way to their computer room, "Maggie's vampire-witch, the sadistic bastard who buried him on the island? He found out Billy's loose and has connected with the infamous Blood Runner to seek his revenge."

"Whoa," Alan was impressed, "I like it. And I can take credit for this?"

"A dream come true, I know. Try not to hurt yourself patting your own back."

"No worries."

"Okay, get busy doing whatever it is you do on those glorified typewriters."

Baby Bite was at my elbow, "Location? You want that let out right off?"

"No," I was serious. "Only after you let the rumour circulate. Billy's close already, so let's wait until he's caught on. No doubt, he'll send out his own feelers to verify. When you've got one asking, put them off and come fetch me. I'll tell you how I want it done. We don't want the entire universe here in the middle of this. Only him."

"Makes sense."

I made to leave and then appeared to have an afterthought, "Oh, one more thing." I considered that blue-white energy shimmering around him one more time. "Don't start it here. Chat with someone in Britain first and get it going from that direction. You have contacts there?"

"D'uh."

"Okay, then do this… Start there, all of you working on the same city. Then together, the Caribbean next. This is important, so mark this down."

He started scribbling, but looked puzzled, "You have a particular order?"

I gave him a hard look, "Unh-huh," and didn't expound.

"Like to share with the class?"

"You have a world map?"

"Hunh?"

"Humour me." From the look on his face he had no idea. He passed me an atlas. "Can I write in this?"

"Go for it."

I took a marker and circled the vicinity of several cities around the world and numbered them. "Follow this order exactly, yeah? Has to be exact, no skipping about. Clear?"

"Sure. Follow the numbers. You gonna let us in on why?"

I held out the marker without saying anything. Stubborn, he wasn't about to move on it without clarification and wouldn't take it. I growled, but he wouldn't go for it. "Fine," I snatched back the hand with the marker in it. "It's a spell."

"Say again?"

"*Spell*. To follow the order makes a banishing sign. Look," I traced the order with my finger. "A backwards drawn pentagram. The perfect math of it tapping into the energy of the earth to use for a specific purpose. We want him out of the whole world, yeah? It'll draw him here where he needs to go and away from everyone else."

"Seriously?"

"Don't get excited. It won't make him vanish, that's not what it's meant for. But it *will* draw him if you believe it will, little man. If you keep that as your intention while you do this."

Baby Bite traced it with his own finger, "That'll really work? I mean, that we can make that happen. Seems like something you should have to do to make it come out right."

"Look, Alan," I sighed and motioned the rest of them over. "Listen, all of you. I don't have time to educate you in this, because it would take a couple hundred years, but trust me. It will work. It will *because* of you." Their new blue-white auras continued to undulate around them. "I made a lot of medicine while you slept. I cleansed, changed the nature of energies out in the forest, and made them white to control him when he comes. You can't see it, but yours are changed, too."

A murmur ran through them and they examined each other for differences.

"You feel different, yes? Calm, centred. Free even, maybe? I can see it." I held up a staying hand before they pelted me with questions, "Trust me, it's visible. Darkness is being deflected away from you. This area, the underground here, is wholly under the protection of the Wards. It's a white spell, made out of a positive intention. Positive energy, understand? Nothing negative can come to you here. Your own energy is clean now, as well, and that's why this will work."

They were quiet but accepting though they had a thousand questions they never spoke. So did I. As a consequence of working on the land over and around them, I had somehow cleansed them and none woke compelled to hunt. I didn't know if I broke their own particular curse, though I could see they still weren't alive in the regular sense. I had affected them somehow, though. In a positive way and toward light.

I didn't know if it could last. Didn't quite know what to make of it to be honest, because it was outside the realm of my experience. I never heard of a vampire in the ancient world. Not their type, at any rate. I knew no spells against them beyond cleansing and balancing. Whatever the cause and whatever had happened, at the very least, they were purified and able to assist me in this one thing. And, perhaps, that's what it was meant for. I didn't have time to study it, though, so like them, I accepted it and used it for what it could do for us.

"All together, start at the first point. All of you concentrate on one area at a time with your rumour-spreading. After the fifth city, then go back to Britain and do it a second time. Seven of you, working six points plus the sign itself. A little seven numerology on top of the sacred geometry can't hurt. And keep your intentions to draw him out of the world top of mind while you do it. Clear?"

Suki broke away and came over to put her arms around me tight. "You made it so he can't get in here, didn't you?"

She was always so sweet. But this time it made me uncomfortable, because I didn't want to talk about it. My voice was gruff, "That's right."

"To keep us safe when he comes."

"Yes."

"And after you're gone."

I hung my head. I should have known one of them would catch on. I didn't want to answer, but I'm a shitty liar and a lie of omission is still a lie, "Well, yes." Awkward, I held her closer and tried to avoid all their eyes.

"Kurshram?"

After a pause, I nodded over the top of Suki's head and watched Alan's back stiffen. Instead of following Suki's example, he squared his shoulders and grew still. "C'mon guys, we have work to do. Let's get busy," his voice was firm, but his eyes told me what he wanted to say.

Damn, I was going to miss that little boy.

I lost an hour sucking on a mint leaf contemplating what was to come.

Finished running the property to deposit more charms, I took some quiet time for myself in the prayer circle. In touch with my newer self, it took work to keep focussed on what happened around me on the physical plane. That newer self was peculiar. On one hand, a modicum of humanity in all its sizzling brilliance. It still dazzled me with unexpected nostalgia and a wanton wish to dance to the song that no longer ended. But on the other? Far outside humanity. A steely overview of the world and everything in it--hard, impassive and with a vision so long it took in the past and future and the connective tissue between everything subject to the forces of heaven and earth. It gave me calm assurance in my ability to succeed. Even while my human heart tripped at the thought of what my other half told me I was required to do.

"You could have rung my mobile."

A week since we decided to set our trap, for this evening, mint was the most wondrous thing in the known universe. Something to taste and something to savour and another very old favourite.

Four days before, I found a spare moment to satisfy my curiosity over Alan's comment about my eyes and dug out the hand mirror I almost took to the Caribbean. A very long while since I bothered to check my own reflection, I almost failed to recognise myself. And he was right about my eyes. They were no longer dark. A luminous green flecked through with amber made them difficult to look at head on for no other reason than they didn't seem natural. Of course, with centuries of practice being anything but, I could deal with it. I wouldn't have to for very long, anyway.

"Yeah, but then you woulda missed the pleasure of my utter fabulousness. Didn't want you to suffer."

I snorted so hard it set the swing in motion, "Like I keep saying, if I only had a spell."

The backswing caught him up and he settled in beside me, "You wish, old man." The tip of his toe scuffed the dirt beneath us as he crossed his arms and stared off into the night sky, "Won't be long now, I figure. Been a couple days since that guy of Billy's was asking questions."

"I expect so." I offered him a mint leaf.

"Thanks." I watched him from the corner of my eye as he put it in his mouth without a second thought.

We ruminated in comfortable quiet while I thought ahead to prepare for what I would do, the plan now more concrete than a few days before. There had been a lot to prepare, but I managed to turn the bones of an idea into something complete. It would be difficult, but it was doable and I would see it through to the end. There wouldn't be much longer to wait now and I soaked in the comfort of my garden while I had the opportunity. My bag packed with the supplies I would need had been within arm's reach since I decided how the game would play. It sat next to me in the dirt beside the swing.

"What are the girls up to?" Curious, I eyed him across the top of my shoulder, checking for signs the cleansing was beginning to wane. But it still held. Watching him suck on the leaf, it was easy to see he was changed on a fundamental level. All of them were. Perhaps, I'd changed the course of their collective existence, but I couldn't be sure. More than anything, I worried over the continuation of it. Okay, and the girls I worried over a little more. Of course, I was responsible for them all, but five thousand years later? The influence of the patriarchal society I'd been born into still coloured my perception of gender roles.

"They're fine, Dad. Don't worry, all us *boys* are making sure they're looked after," chuckling, he understood.

When I was gone, Alan would be in charge and he was already taking responsibility for them. He led them here to relative safety and a place they could survive, after all. Hell, he was in charge long before they came to me, but didn't know it yet. I already took time to leave him a few things to find later that might help him as their leader. Not so much a boy as when he came despite his seeming frivolity and lack of concern, he was thoughtful and careful and would always take time to do things for the benefit of the rest.

In another life, I would have been pleased to take him for a student and protégé. But all we had was this one, so I was glad I had the opportunity to call him friend. I hadn't had one in a very long while. Quiet spun out between us, but we didn't fill it, because there was nothing else to say.

"Alan," in seeming nonchalance, I pulled the leaf from my mouth and took a final unhurried look around my garden, "time for you to go back in, little man."

Still swinging, he didn't feel it yet. But my tone was explanation enough, "Ah, *shit.*" He shot a furtive glance back toward the house and over his shoulders at what he knew, but couldn't yet detect. "You sure?"

"Unh-huh. Quick now." I unfurled myself from my resting place and slung the strap of my packed medicine bag over my head. "This is it."

"Kurshram…" If he hadn't been a vampire, the colour would have drained from his face. Hesitating and frustrated when no words came, he stuck out an awkward hand.

I clamped a determined hand over his, "I know," and pulled him to me. "No time, little man. *Run* and don't come out no matter what happens. You'll know when it's safe again."

"But--"

"*Now*, Baby Bite," I spoke in his ear. "You'll be safe. I promise." I pushed him in the direction of the porch. "Hurry."

Scrambling up the stairs, he knew it was necessary, but this was the end of the way things were and it kept him outside another moment more. He turned around when he reached the French doors.

"Boy," I hissed, "get your arse in that house before I come over there and kick it for you. Go!"

His smile pained, I watched him turn away with effort and run for the labyrinth. When I was sure he was really going, I stopped wasting time and ducked into the forest to greet my guest.

Letting go of the here and my concern that tied me to them, I let the wolf take over. Head up and attuned, there couldn't be room for compassion any longer and I needed the savage even in sacred duty. The Namtar's presence became a weighty thing the closer I came until I saw the snaking black evil intent drift out ahead of him announcing his arrival.

The forest air vibrated with a sudden inhuman roar as the charms touched him. The air grew frozen with the combined fear of every living thing that hunkered down to hide from the impending battle. When the roaring grew pained, I'd be lying if I said it didn't bring me pleasure to know I caused it. Righteous vengeance gave me permission to enjoy it for every hurt he inflicted on my Ninlil. Righteous or not, though, I made myself find the strength to put it aside. I calculated the first step in breaking the animate shackle tying him to the world.

Sudden warmth in my pocket told me my protective charm was still there, but I wouldn't need it. Because this wasn't about me. Only my sacred duty to the world crying out for balance mattered. In a moment of clarity, I understood the world had evolved. The days of manifesting gods wielding the energy of creation and destruction while holding the balance of life and death between them were over. Now was the time of mortals.

Immortal beings, myself included, no longer belonged on this plane. We upset the balance of the new natural order.

"Well, fuck me…"

He appeared just ahead of me through the trees. My human soul convulsed against the sight of him stripped of the veneer that had allowed him to wander unrecognised. Dark and ancient, he was a curse set in motion. Pinned in place by the charmed ground, he thrashed against the cobweb of combined spells enveloping him. And then he saw me.

"You..," he snarled. "*Mêle-toi de tes affaires*! You never could keep to yourself. Bastard, what have you done to me?" His head whipped from side to side in frantic search, "Well? Where is the other? *Ton ami*, Blood Runner. *Laissez-le venir ici*! This changes nothing, do you hear me? Nothing. Call him, let him come. Do it!" He stared into my impassive expression for a full beat and then barred his teeth against the truth, "*Et alors*? I might have known. This changes nothing. You will die. An eye for an eye, *mon frère*."

Refusing to be drawn into conversation, I ignored the viper teeth he barred from his lion's mouth. I pondered the horns that resembled bony, folded wings curving back behind his upright ears. A projection of what he believed himself to be, they showed how deep it ran. Back in our ancient world, we depicted our higher gods with three sets of horns to indicate their place in the pantheon, lower gods with two. That even he would never have the nerve to believe himself on par with the great Enlil didn't diminish that at his core, at the moment of his sentence, he believed in his own lesser divinity so much it reflected in form. Now I knew why I'd been elevated.

It barely made us even.

Scaly armour covering the stout and sturdy body of a war horse below the shaggy lion's head reflected his power as did the many muscular arms flailing against the white magic that ensnared him.

"*Tu es complètement fou*! Are you mad? This is unconscionable, brother. If you seek to fight me, then do so if you must. But this..? You cannot believe *this* is some fitting retribution for that little, human tart." That one touched a nerve and he knew it, too, but I said nothing. His voice turned slippery in enmity, "Not even worth her weight in service, *mon ami*, and not worthy all this carry-on. Why, the entire Pandora had at her and to a man found her a distasteful little waif. And before *I* grew tired of her--" his taunting dissolved into screams as I threw a handful of black salt over him.

I could feel him working to get in my head, but concentrated on my work and ignored it. And made sure to keep distance from those arms. In reality, there was nothing holding him but surprise and not understanding the white magic. He would recover and retaliate. That part I wasn't quite as concerned over, because I meant to lead him into the circle at the top of the ridge. All I had to do was not get myself caught in the process. I worked quickly at doing what I could to erode his strength while I had the opportunity.

Taking a stand, I swallowed down the fear from my human spirit and drew strength from the earth. Extending my right hand to invoke a resonance spell, I envisioned the blue-white energy of it building up under my palm while directing it outward. "Run out, thou who comest in darkness, who enterest in stealth. See the shadow of every god and every goddess surround thee. Let thine eyes be opened to the light and darkness no more. The world cries out, seeking light, remove this darkness from my sight!"

Cleansing the area left nothing but white energy, so I gathered it fast and concentrated it on the demon. It poured from my fingertips in a sizzling blue-white stream that hit him hard and set him screeching for blood. The stench of singed demon hide hung in the air and made my eyes water. The large, incongruous and flat, dead eyes in his pseudo-cat's head burned red and murderous.

I ran for the ridge.

Almost insubstantial for speed, he paced me step for furious step. Bestowed with godhood or not, sweat trickled down my neck while I ran flat-out to keep ahead of the grasping fingertips grazing my back. The ridge within sight, I felt a momentary triumph in my so-far success. That then instantly dissolved when he leapt for me and those multiple arms caught me up.

Before I registered what happened, I was off-balance and flung hard. Amid a great cracking and the scream of splintering wood, a maple broke against my back and crashed over. Tearing down the smaller limbs of neighbouring trees, they rained down over me where I came to rest in the leaf litter.

I groaned, "Fuck me," a very ungodly pain jarring my spine.

The strap of my medicine bag pulled tight across my throat as the Namtar twisted it with savage glee and dragged me up out of the pile of broken wood.

"*Pourquoi diable as-tu fait ça, mon ami?* Why on earth did you do that? That you could despise me so when we are the same? We are the only equals in this accursed place. All there are, brother. More's the pity to know you refuse to band together with me. We could be like the sun. Instead? We are here. What, exactly, is it you believe you will accomplish?" His mood grew darker and he gave me a shake, "There are no witches, you bitch's whelp. *None.* We are gods and you should learn to conduct yourself as one," he was ranting, but I knew what the real problem was.

The leather strap cut into my neck and I didn't try to loosen it. This close, the stench of his charred skin made me wrinkle my nose, but I tamped down revulsion and let him feel the life of me. Let the blood I could feel oozing down my neck confound him. He was only what he was and without soul. His instinct, murderous as it was, would help me bring about his downfall.

Easier said than done, however. He'd had four thousand years of practice controlling himself when the occasion called for it. For the moment, he was still too strong.

Suspended by the thin leather, half off the ground I hung still while he sampled the air surrounding me, "How is this possible?" he spat. "There is no unmaking for our kind. What trick of magic is this? You will tell me!" The hands holding the strap vibrated with his fury, but didn't relent. The human body I still possessed was running out of air and made me panic, lessening the strength of the surrounding web of charms. Fear was my greater enemy here and I knew it, but it was involuntary and he gained back strength before I could control myself.

"Ahhh..," he inhaled with abandon, feeling the slip of the charms. "And now here we are again. Except this is rather more to my liking," and gave the strap a vicious yank that opened the cut in my neck.

The ridge wasn't far. I could almost see the prayer circle out of the corner of my eye. But my human body faded. I couldn't allow that or I'd never get him there. We were all that remained in flesh, Ninlil said, and had considered that I needed it to defeat him. I asked Baby Bite to bait him for me, but now I knew the only bait I needed was myself.

Both the bait and the sentence, I truly was his judge, jury and executioner.

Clamping off fear for my human life, I reached my left hand out under his arms. Drawing out a banishing sign on the leathery hide, I sacrificed my remaining air to resonate a determined spell. "Walking darkness, be filled with light, remove this demon from my sight!"

The sign became visible and glowed white-hot. Burning into his skin, he gasped in pained surprise, releasing his hold on the strap at my throat. A little oxygen was all I needed to scramble away. With each spell I cast his power lessened by degrees. Still, he was tough and old. And mad with revenge and the scent of my blood that hung on the wind. Determined to have his day, he was right behind me again and gaining.

"Why do you hurt me, brother?" he snarled in hot pursuit, crashing through thicket and trees to reach me while everything around us kept hidden. There was no finesse in his chase, just an all-out race to get his hands around my throat. And then for no reason everything stopped.

For the briefest of moments, dead silence descended and I chanced a look over my shoulder to see what he was up to. And found him gone. Gone from my sight, but I felt him there still. Enlil had made him Death and the black fog of his erosive energy continued to ooze around the trees, dragging life off them enough the leaves hung limp. Everything else remained still and I froze, scouring the dark for a sign. It came too late to react as a large rock sailed out of the mist. Whistling with inhuman speed, it caught my temple, dropping me where I stood.

"Bugger," I spat out a mouthful of dirt and worked to keep my bearings. Snaking a hand into my bag for something to buy me time, my fingers grazed a small bottle of exorcism oil before the bag was torn off me and flung into the brush. "That won't help you now, demon," I spoke to the ground with the Namtar at my back.

"Demon am I?" He stomped a heavy, clawed foot into my back to hold me in place, "Brave words, but pointless, witch. Vampire. Or whatever you now believe yourself to be." He inhaled with relish and chuckled down low in his throat, "Whatever you believe, you smell like a man to me." More blood ran from my temple and added to the copper in the air. "What did you hope to accomplish with this necromancy, fool? Look at me," he gestured behind me, unseen. "Seems you've done nothing more than given me more means to achieve your death."

The foot in my back grew heavy as he held me fast and despite my abilities, my head spun from the rock. My mind raced. I still had the charm in my pocket to strengthen any spoken magic, but all my herbs and oils were beyond my reach. At the bottom of the ridge where we now were, the prayer circle wasn't far above us. The strong, white energy that would trap him was so close I could see where it cast a visible glow against the night sky. One way or another, I had to get him there. A large branch pressed against my face, but from my position, I'd never build up enough momentum to hit him with it and knock him off. And to speak to him, engage him in conversation, would only validate his existence and fuel his tie to the world. I had to go another route.

I pressed my lips to the earth and whispered a sincere prayer for assistance.

Despite instruction to remove him from the world at any cost, there were some resources I couldn't tap. Though it might help me, to call upon an energy, any spirit if you will, to inflict harm or to wish harm in spell was off limits. I knew better. The momentary gain through the harm would ultimately turn that same negativity back on me. Balance must be kept, favours paid for, lessons learned. There's always a price and I wasn't willing to pay it with Ninlil waiting for me.

The job of dispersing him was mine alone. I simply needed a small favour. I prayed harder and waited for the small boon that would allow me escape under my own power. I felt the energy around me shift and smiled to myself. I promised when the time for retribution came, his arm would be together with mine. A vow sworn before the gods, nothing could obstruct its execution.

Not even a Netherworld sentence.

The foot in my back grew heavier as the Namtar pressed his weight into it, "Nothing to say in your own defence, *mon frère*? Pity you didn't bury that box more deeply. A good effort, if I may say. Yet pointless in the end. Your shovels were no match for the modern back hoe digging the foundation bed for the structure over me." His laugh was harsh, "The crushed bodies of the insects that fed me as they dug were not much to my liking. Though I found the construction crew infinitely satisfying." His weight shifted in sudden disorientation, "*Connard!*"

It was quick, so quick. Too quick to avoid, the essence of Nigel Shakespeare whipped past the demon. Winked in and back out again while passing close enough to upset his balance.

The foot came off my back as the demon staggered. I thanked Nigel and especially Ereshkigal for allowing it and legged it, vaulting a fallen log to catch up my bag as I went. The Namtar crashed up the way behind me, spitting curses and roaring his rage at my escape. It wouldn't be pretty if he caught me again. I had a crazy flash of telling Baby Bite I would de-craniate him and didn't find it so amusing from my current perspective.

"*Lâche!* Coward! Face me!"

The sacred signs were all around on the rock. As we neared the crest of the ridge, the air was of a different quality than the air below. Changed by cleansing and purification, it reached him through his rage.

Not far from the circle, he stopped in his tracks, the changed air taking his attention from me. He surveyed his surroundings in careful confusion. Examining the signs and then the circle, he shook his shaggy head, "More necromancy?" Laughing, he breathed in the scent of my blood that now stained the side of my face and neck, perfuming the wind. "These games you play." And then paused while he examined the signs and the circle again. "Is this how? Is this how you accomplished it? Unmade yourself?"

Continuing to ignore his attempts at conversation, I grabbed another handful of black salt from my bag. Holding it out on my open palm, I gave him all my attention from across the circle. "Darkness exist in harmony with light. Ye great gods who shine with the sun, let this one's eyes be opened to the light. Remove this darkness for himself and for the protection of the world." Rather than throw the salt at him, I blew it off my left hand while holding out my right to direct the energy. Picked up on the light breeze, it drifted across the cleansed circle, purifying it, and dusted him on the other side. Gentle compared with how I delivered it earlier, the effect was instantaneous and much more powerful. His scream echoed through the trees.

"You will die, witch!" he stumbled in place. Still outside the circle. Still more dangerous than anything alive no matter he was weakening.

He was right, though--I would die and I accepted that. We didn't belong in the world, neither one of us. If my only reason for coming into being was to achieve balance, then I had no reason to continue later. And I was okay with that. I was tired and missed my Ninlil and four thousand years of wandering in confusion was bloody well long enough. Blood Runner would go down in legend. I was sure Baby Bite and the 'Hunters would complete his story now that the whole world knew. And maybe that was only fitting. Every story needs an ending, even mine. The last of our kind still walking in flesh--it was only right we went out together.

I put a hand to the cut on my throat and then held out the blood, offering it to the Namtar. Only what he was, even in confusion he could never resist. I took a step closer and entered the holy circle with my hand extended.

His eyes widened in surprise and his nostrils flared at the scent and he licked his lips despite himself. Wary still, I felt him work to get into my head and I let him, allowing the momentary triumph to confound him.

Faster than any human eye could see, the Namtar leapt for me, his many arms gathering me in Death's embrace. Once across the threshold, the light inside the confines of the circle captured the darkness around him. And secured everything he was for the safety of the world outside. To my relief, it held fast.

The feel of him even in thought was beyond repugnant, but it wouldn't be for long. A clawed hand grabbed the side of my head and forced it back with voracious abandon even while my own hand clamped around a bottle of exorcism oil. Lost in the bliss of taking my human life, he was too preoccupied to notice.

Of course, human wasn't the only thing I was. More than a man, Ninlil said. I continued to function even when the human part of me ranted against the darkness. Calm and centred and ready for it, I waited until he bent his head and began to feed. Let my heartbeat invade him, tying us together tight so he wouldn't let go. The outline of the sacred circle glowed in resonance, light against darkness, while I prayed in corresponding resonance to strengthen the conduit to the beyond.

With his mouth on my throat, I clamped a hard arm across the back of his neck to hold him there and sprinkled the oil over his scaly back.

"To the gods, do I pray,

Pay witness now,

To my strength to flay,

This curse held in darkness,

Death without death

No more will he pay,

With my words and my will do I hold this at bay."

The bright of the circle grew up from the earth creating a wall of light around us while the Namtar thrashed under my arm. Now in pain, he was without the strength to break his own feeding hold. My blood continued to get inside him and help unmake him.

"I call upon the gods of light…

I call upon the energies of universal balance…

I call upon Mother Ki and Father An in perfect harmony…

As beneficent Devi tempers Shiva

I bind us and banish you forever!

I make this protection against thee,

For all mortalkind,

By my will and my words,

Upon you and your own self to be burned,

Vesta and Bast, goddesses of fire,

Cleanse the darkness from this circle…"

The walled circle of light grew brighter and became a wall of flame and under my arm, he shook hard up against me. His teeth in my throat were razors that continued to cut into me as he gritted them even while he fed and distracted me. But there was no going back now. It hurt like hell and made it difficult to speak, but I continued to force the words out.

"By order of the gods and by my will,

By the Lord Air, Enlil, master of all,

Enki, keeper of the sacred law,

Amon-Ra in your sun fire brilliance,

In the name of Anu and Zeus

By the Great Spirit and of Thor

You who are all and yet nothing,

I invoke all great gods who shine with the sun,

Stand in witness and agreement

Of the end of what was never meant to be and so to be no more..."

Sweat ran down my face while I continued the many-parted spell with the struggling demon locked against me. Each part of his sentence had to be broken, each thing he was unmade, and each way of return taken away. It was complex and lengthy, but there could be no shortcuts here. Not of the upper pantheon like the one who made him, what the Great One could do in the blink of an eye would take everything I had. Stifling, the heat inside the circle worked on my body. Taking a strengthening breath, I ignored the pain in my neck and the feel of my human life draining and concentrated on the greater good.

"By air and earth, by water and fire,

So are you bound with this rite entire,

Time to leave, time to end,

Time for rest, no more to rend.

Away and farewell,

With Ereshkigal shall you lie,

Not united in spirit, but only to die,

Flesh to disperse and then to be gone,

Farewell and away, no more, but beyond..."

The Namtar screamed as smoke poured from his hide. His power was broken, but it wasn't enough. There had to be nothing left to return to and I knew what it would take.

And what it meant.

The surrounding purifying fire turned in on itself and needed to consume everything within. Including me. Watchman of the Namtar, I had to follow him to the end. Damn, but I hated fire. My skin hurt as it roasted along with the demon and made it even harder to speak. I gritted my teeth and kept at it, forcing the final words through my scorching throat.

"With this fire burning, out, out, *out*...

Spirit of evil be gone and to ashes returned,

Bound and by my will are we both burned...

Here makes your peace and are carried to rest,

My own will grants you blessed…

By the sacred power of Mother Earth, Ki

And Father Enki, Alchemist of the Gods,

I make this shield for all of the earth,

For all of heaven and all of worth…

I cut the cord and unlock the chains,

I sever all ties by which we were bound,

With impenetrable walls, the world I surround,

My will forever locks the door…

Be bound and be clear,

Naram-Sin, from Enlil's curse… your delivery… here!"

The heat scorched my throat shut, but it was done and locked together with what was left of the demon, the fire took us over.

For one long moment of still-human consciousness, I knew the agony of burning alive. Watched my own skin blister and blacken and smoke until I was burned blind. Then all I knew was the same darkness I'd been reborn into and this roasting agony of my final death. Forever in an instant, everything I hated about fire--its cruel, indiscriminate consumption, its mindless snaking destruction--performed its work on me and the Namtar that was now welded to my body by the savage heat.

Ash swirled in the up-draught of the fire stream. Taking us away to be dispersed on the cooling wind above that might one day fall harmlessly to the earth again, brought by rain. No more to hunt. No more the wolf. No more stalking death. No more tied together in unknowing.

My thoughts drifted up with the ash until in relief, the pain fell away. Light and purified by flame and all I had left, they were worthy enough to approach the Palace of the Bull of Heaven. Someone waited for me there. Someone I remembered. Someone I loved.

Someone I discovered I was denied.

I did my job well and fulfilled my purpose. And there was the cruel irony.

I was never meant to succeed.

Still jealous as he ever was, Enlil had hoped to be rid of me. But I won. And now, Ninlil was kept from me. Or rather I from her. She was allowed to see me knowing full well I'd kill myself to get near her again. And so while I destroyed myself in the process, the essence of what I was held onto her as I had from the first day. In part, I survived. All to be near her once more. But it wasn't happening.

In five thousand years, Enlil never deemed me worthy enough to speak to. But now I heard his laughter filling up the heavens and the Netherworld before all of our equals in eternity. And knew it was the laughter from the garden.

Over the ages, they had often referred to him as Munificent Lord, but I knew better. He was cruel and petty and jealous. With my god's eye view, that wasn't a mistaken perception of a human mind struggling to interpret the actions of a god that would make more sense in the long view.

We were adversaries in eternity with a mutual prize. We were opposing forces in the myriad minutia of the universe. I don't know how it happened, but we were.

Locked together for all time with opposite long views of the whole entire thing, the enormity of it went so far beyond only his most recent jealous betrayal. My understanding of the fabric of the universe expanded exponentially to know it.

No, he was far from munificent and in my new understanding saw he didn't deserve his place at the head of the pantheon. He never had. Perhaps, he only achieved it because he was the first one there. Or tricked the rest into giving him that honour. Or, perhaps, frightened them into never questioning it. I don't know. What I do know is that if the pantheon were a ship, the rest would have already mutinied against a leader who didn't see to their welfare and interests. But it wasn't and there was no place to jump ship and turn landlubber, so we were stuck with him.

On my way back to Ereshkigal and the Netherworld, I wondered what I might have changed and knew there was nothing. I would do it the same way again. All for the love of a goddess, a legend was born out of a misconception and a misspoken word. And I'd rid the world of a nasty demon while I was at it, so I suppose it was worth it.

Nigel Shakespeare chuckled from his place hanging on the wall behind the seventh gate in the Palace of Ereshkigal. "Yes, I should say it was worth it. Quite so, my friend. Good show! What could you have changed, after all?" He smiled in humility, "Yes, quite good show. I wished to have provided more assistance, but no one else might have accomplished this. It had to be you. Now the past has been avenged. And more importantly, balance achieved. If only humanity knew what you've done for them."

Unconnected with the demon, the spirit of Naram-Sin kept a much more rational place near us than he had under his curse. He nodded to himself, "My most worthy adversary. You, Kurshram, have my respect. Your enemies will know of your qualities before they would ever meet you." He was still a power-hungry megalomaniac from the old world, but only a man again, he was no longer a threat. Didn't mean I had to like the guy.

Eternity wouldn't be so bad. At least, I had company this time. And besides, you never know... Someone, somewhere, sometime, might trade to get us out again. True, the only one of us with an earthly body that wasn't destroyed was Nigel, but really, what did that matter? I was an *aszipu*, a sorcerer-priest. And let's face it, now I was a god for heaven's sake and in full consciousness of everything that went along with that. So assured of his own success, Enlil never thought I'd survive, so didn't only grant me a boon or award me with a special gift. There were no provisos on me. He bestowed my godhood in a broad, undefined manner without considering any continued consequences of that action.

He was always a bit short-sighted.

Four thousand years of study only made me more knowledgeable. And now my god-view let me see the connection to everything--life, death, past, future, space, time… A lesser god, I suppose, but a god is a god is a god, yeah? Ninlil couldn't escape Ereshkigal's Palace unaided, because she'd been sentenced for a crime and ordered there. But I committed no crime. No judgement was pronounced over me. As a matter of fact, I did the world a favour and somebody owed me one by my count. Ninlil wasn't much of a rule breaker, either. Despite her unjust sentence, she'd played by the old rules no matter her brother didn't have much respect for them.

But I didn't play that way.

My Ninlil… It didn't seem to matter what her brother did to her, she gave him her undying loyalty and continued to defend him. If I didn't know better, I'd say she was bewitched. Or suffering from Stockholm syndrome. Or perhaps closer to the truth, only terrified and waiting on me to give her sanctuary once more.

My job as watchman of the Namtar was done. But now I saw Enlil for what he was. And the world still cried out for balance while he continued to exert influence. I couldn't ignore it, but I languished in the Netherworld while he was free. Perhaps, Nigel and I could stage a mutiny and turn the Netherworld on its complacent head. Or I could use my new god powers to unravel the fabric of the universe and rethread the loom. Or my ego could become so unbelievably huge I'd trip over my own self-importance and fall and flatten the earth.

We had a good chuckle over it hanging on our respective walls. But when I looked into Nigel's eyes, behind the laughter was the same understanding and I knew one thing above all.

Enlil better watch his arse.

Author's Note

For the sake of accuracy... Anal-retentiveness..? Potato-potahto...

The building of Enlil's temple Ekur didn't occur until about 2700 BCE. That means it would have been impossible for Kurshram to be buried there if he'd really been creeping about in 3200 BCE. I was most distressed history wouldn't co-operate with my nefarious purposes, so I made it fit, okay?

There are multiple versions of every myth about the ancient Sumerian gods such as Enlil. Depending on the era they were written, stories evolved through those successive more modern cultures or at least appear to in my limited understanding. Ninlil is sometimes described as the sister of Enlil, father of the gods, and sometimes she's his intended. The later versions, into the Akkadian era, moved her into the role of his sister. For my own quirky reasons, I stuck with the oldest versions of the myths for background, but used the later roles assigned these two gods, because the brother-sister, incestuous juxtaposition was more interesting not to mention the side order of "ick" that upped the creep factor.

After much often-conflicting study of antediluvian history, the prehistory of Iraq and Sumerian mythology, it was with moderate confidence I stitched together elements from several ancient myths into one for this story and added my own twists. Their mythology's got it all, I tell ya--jealousy, sacrifice, betrayal, love, abuses of power... Fabulous.

The fantastical recounting of a human storming the palace of Ereshkigal to save his beloved was probably the one that started it for me. And the demon that brings death, Namtar, really is a mythological character as is the imperfect man who could not eat or drink, though not one in the same and not the punishment of Naram-Sin except in my universe. Naram-Sin, grandson of Sargon the Great, was actually not a bad guy in history. As part of the invading culture, though, in later myth they painted him as a devil. So much the better for me--I didn't have to fudge that part.

The reign of Naram-Sin ended in 2218 BCE and he really is attributed with the downfall of the paradise city Agade. Myth dictates he sailed his ships to the steps of the temple Ekur to raid it of its treasures and Enlil called upon the Gutians as his divine avengers to smite the new capital city, Agade, from the face of the earth. He also pronounced a rather lengthy and foul curse over it and for no explainable reason, no one has so far found any tangible evidence of this city. It's believed to have existed right under Babylon or there around. However, not a single piece of pottery, brick, tablet, *nothing* has ever been found and the only witness to it comes from neighbouring trading cities.

Myself? I hope they never find it. To me, that lends the wrath of Enlil all the more credibility and I'd hate to find out the truth was anything less exciting than godly vengeance.

~ JDS ~

Bibliography

I read a lot of books before coming up with background for this story. This is what I referenced most:

Kramer, Samuel Noah. Sumerian Mythology (A Study of Spiritual and Literary Achievement in the Third Millennium B.C.). 1944, rev. 1961 and Forgotten Books, 2007.

Kramer, Samuel Noah. History Begins at Sumer - Thirty Nine Firsts in Recorded History. Philadelphia: University of Pennsylvania Press, 1956, 1981.

Roux, Georges. Ancient Iraq (Third Edition). England: Penguin Books, 1992

Kramer, Samuel Noah. Sumerian Mythology - A Study of Spiritual and Literary Achievement in the Third Millennium B.C., Revised Edition. Philadelphia: University of Pennsylvania Press, 1961, 1972

Oates, John. Babylon. London: Thames and Hudson Ltd., 1979 and 1986.

I also made use of some historical background fill from one website section in particular that's now closed, unfortunately (the author, former journalist/sub-editor and historian, Dan Byrnes, has since retired). Byrnes, Dan. "Lost Worlds Page 11 - From 500AD to 1000AD". LOST WORLDS - The Website. www.danbyrnes.com.au/lostworlds/timeline/lwstory11.htm, (2006, 2008, 2011).

About the Author

JD Stanley is an award winning historical speculative fantasy author and solitary Bardic Druid following the OBOD teaching path. JD honed voice and audio editing chops in the 80s as a radio announcer and studio engineer before embracing a lifelong guy-behind-the-curtain freelance career as a commercial and content copywriter, voiceover artist, proofreader, ghostwriter and script doctor. Landed Entertainment director Junga Song once called JD "the greatest writer nobody's ever heard of".

The fictional worlds of Mary Stewart, Colleen McCullough, Tolkien, Heinlein, Cervantes and Shakespeare bent JD's world perception into a magical place of unlikely heroes, quests, the interconnectedness of past and future and that though bad things happen to regular folks, a dollop of wit can make it bearable. Unapologising mythology and ancient history junkie, sorcery of science lover and student of human interaction, JD's combined passions weave rich speculative explorations into traditional concepts of good and evil where flawed heroes most often struggle to get out of their own way to do the right thing.

JD enjoys long, meditative walks through graveyards, reading encyclopaedias, and accepts that guinea pigs do, in fact, take over your entire life. JD's spirit animal is a cranky unicorn.

JDStanley.com

What's Next?

Sons of Enki
Blood Runner - Book 2

After a mortal decade in the flaming palace of the Netherworld, destiny throws Kurshram and his protégé, Alan, back into the thick of the pantheon's dysfunctional family drama as She-who-had-no-maker orders Kurshram back to defend humanity from an earth tearing itself apart.